Second Chances

K.J. McClelland

TATE PUBLISHING
AND ENTERPRISES, LLC

Second Chances

Published by Tate Publishing & Enterprises, LLC
127 E. Trade Center Terrace | Mustang, Oklahoma 73064 USA
1.888.361.9473 | www.tatepublishing.com

Tate Publishing is committed to excellence in the publishing industry. The company reflects the philosophy established by the founders, based on Psalm 68:11,
"The Lord gave the word and great was the company of those who published it."

Published in the United States of America

ISBN: 978-1-62994-590-3

1.Fiction / Romance / General
2. Fiction / Romance / Contemporary
13.09.25

Chapter 1

As the car jerked, sputtered, and knocked, Grace Summers found herself praying for the first time in years. Just two more miles and then it could die. She promised god and her car that she would not drive anymore today if she could just get to the next town. One more town wasn't too much to ask. Was it?

She patted the steering wheel and tried to talk the car along the last two miles but the car was as stubborn as she was. It rolled to the side of the road and gave one last desperate chug and with one last convulsing sputter it died.

Pleading with the car to start she tried the engine only to have at it laugh in her face, literally. It gave a gritty couple of cranks and finally would not turn at all. The tears had started but she would not let them fall.

Placing her head against the steering wheel she gave her head one good bang against it. Maybe it would clear the fog that she seemed to have been living in for the last few days, or maybe it would jar something loose in there. Either way she was not going to get the stupid car to budge.

With the final croak of the car she let the tears fall. It wasn't like anything else was going right on this crazy trip. Maybe it could make her feel better. Besides there was no one around now to witness her disgrace. With one final sniff, she gave into the tears that had been threatening to fall since Idaho.

Why she diluted herself into thinking that she could do this was beyond her. Her mother had certainly made herself known that Grace would never accomplish what she had set out to do. It wasn't like she was wishing for the moon or world peace. She only required her car to get her to her new life. It wasn't so very much to ask for, or so she had thought.

Now sitting on the side of the road with a dead car and no cell phone service did she finally realize just how wrong she had been. It was too much to ask and she should have just stayed home but she didn't want to be a robot anymore.

She didn't want to live her life how others instructed her to do. She wanted to start over and run. Run from the past and the shame that she had been feeling for so long now.

Two years ago she had been happy, or so she had thought. She had the career she had always wanted. The man she had always wanted and a perfect life, but she soon learned that nothing that is perfect can last forever.

It has started with Kurt. Even thinking of the man made her stomach hurt. He had been a prince. He had always said the right things and had been charming. She should have seen the signs then but nope, not her. Grace always did what she had thought was the best, only what she thought was the best was never the best for her.

At the age of ten she had been in the top of her dancing class and been recruited to dance in a private school. It had been everything that she had thought that she had wanted, just like Kurt.

While Grace loved dancing she had never thought about the type of lives dancers actually led. They were disciplined, steeled to a nearly impossible schedule and never allowed to have any fun. For the first couple of years that had been fine with her, it wasn't like she had friends anyway. She had stuck to the diet and never allowed herself to do anything other than concentrate on dancing, but by the age of sixteen it had started to take its toll.

She had been tired to the core of her being. The daily workouts, the hours of instruction and the constant dieting had been maddening. Dancing at that time had been her job not her passion and she had been done then, but her mother true to her form refused to let her quit.

She couldn't really blame her mother. She had just been trying to do what was best for her as usual, but her mother's best was wearing on her nerves. At one point she got so desperate to quit she had considered breaking her own leg just so she would be able to be done, but like every good solider she had pressed on.

It helped that she had been accepted to Julliard to dance. At least there she had been able to meet other people experiencing the same things she was. Grace had made friends and found herself picked to be the headliner in the American Ballet Company.

It had been everything that she had been working for her whole life. The first couple of years with the company was a dream but with perfection comes a price. Grace soon found it hard to date, or to have a life of her own. Her demanding schedule had left her traveling constantly, never being in the same place for too long.

That is when she had met Kurt. Seven years into the company she had met the bane of her existence. He had been smart, charming, and funny. It had seemed like he knew just what to say to make her laugh and could make her feel good about herself for the first time in years.

The two had met after a performance of the nutcracker that she had been doing in New York. He had come backstage after the show with a dozen of red roses telling her that it was the first time he hadn't fallen asleep at the ballet and he thanked her.

It had been easy to like Kurt. He was laid back and didn't seem to count calories like others in her life had. He seemed to take such joy in the little things in life.

Two years after they had met he had purposed. She had found that dating Kurt had been easy. Even though she had to travel a lot Kurt always seemed to be coming in the same direction she was heading. He had arranged for them to meet up often and she had fallen in love.

She shook her head against the steering wheel. No it wasn't love because there had been no love in that relationship. Grace had always wondered about Kurt. When they had first started dating he had told her that he wanted to get to know her before taking her to bed, and that he wasn't trying to rush into anything too quickly. For Grace that had been nice but if she was being truthful, kind of weird to her. In her experience little that she had, she had found that with most men that was the only thing they seemed to want, but not Kurt.

After eight months of no sex she had broached the topic with him carefully. He had smiled and told her that he would much rather wait until after they were married. While Grace really wanted to respect his wishes she found herself curious about the physical parts of relationships. With such a rigid lifestyle Grace had never got to experience the act of physical love herself, there simply wasn't time.

As the months wore on Grace found herself getting frustrated. She wasn't a sex addict and she didn't want to push but she didn't want to wait until they were married either. What if she didn't like it? What if Kurt did nothing for her? Then they would be stuck in a miserable marriage and she couldn't let that happen.

One night three months before the wedding Grace was to meet Kurt in a hotel just outside of Denver, Colorado. She was certain she was going to make it happen whether he wanted it too or not.

Snorting at the memory she shook her head. How naive she had been she thought to herself. She had taken the time to really doll herself up, something that she never really cared to do. With the makeup that she had to wear on stage and the tight outfits, Grace found that when she was off stage she didn't want to be dressed up, but for that evening she had made an acceptation.

She had taken the time to go and get waxed. She had even summoned up the courage to go into Victoria Secrets and purchase lingerie for the first time in her life. It had been embarrassing considering she didn't know the first thing about trying to be sexy but she had done it.

Purchases in hand she had headed back to the hotel room to get ready. She had taken the time to do her makeup and make her eyes really pop. Praying for courage, she had slipped into the skimpy little outfit she had bought and waited for Kurt to come.

Lying on the bed, robe partially open, she breathed through her mouth trying to calm her racing heart. When the door handle turned she could have sworn her stomach was in her throat. It had become hard to breathe but she was not going to let that stop her.

As the door pushed open she gave her long hair one final toss and waited for the man of her dreams, but the man that had shown up that night was not the man of her dreams. Instead it had been Kurt's best friend David.

Embarrassed down to her core she had straightened when she saw him enter. Jumping up from the bed she did the best to conceal herself only to have David laugh at her. The tears had started then.

She had wanted to have the perfect night and it had turned out to be the night from hell.

After David finally reigned himself in from his laughter, he had looked straight at Grace and said, “You’ll never be able to tempt him like that.” He said gesturing to her all of her.

Grace had always been the perfect solider. The disciplined one and she would not give into the tears that had threatened to spill then.

As David laughed at her and gestured to all of her a little piece of herself broke in that moment. Grace had never considered herself beautiful but she had never really been normal either.

For starters because she was dancer she was required to be rail thin. Her flame red hair and large green eyes had always been frowned upon but she had refused to dye it. That was one part of herself that she was not willing to give up.

She found that she didn’t have normal curves like most women had. She was tall and elegant but curvy did not apply to her. Because of her tall thin frame her breasts were barely the size of apples but she thanked god that she had at least had those; most dancers she found were flat chested.

As she felt his laughter and her shame roll over her she started to shake. She would never give him the satisfaction of seeing her tears but the shaking had been involuntary. With a shaking hand she walked over to him and slapped him, hard.

She was almost as appalled by her conduct as he had been. He stared at her a moment before straightening. With one last chuckle he sneered, "Kurt would never go for someone like you. I came here to tell you that he has decided that he would rather be with his wife tonight. He doesn't want you and never will. She is everything that you're not. She has curves and a killer body and she doesn't need lingerie to entice him. She's the twice the woman you'll ever be."

The words cut like a knife to her soul. A deep intense burn came with the cut and a calming numb that she had let herself drift into.

After that night she hadn't even tried to call Kurt and he had not tried to contact her. That was fine by her; she didn't want a married man anyway. Grace had thought about being petty and calling the misses, just to tell her of her husband but decided against it.

That night had broken something inside of her that she couldn't seem to fix. Dancing was no longer her main priority, running had filled that slot and that was why she was here. Wherever here was. She wasn't even sure which state she was in now. The only thing that had been important to her had been to get away.

Her mother had called her numerous times wondering where she was. Her company had called wondering the same thing and as she looked around she was finally starting to wonder where she was herself.

Running had seemed like a good option at the time. She had been a little responsible and at least given her company a fair warning that she was leaving. Well, she had called them before curtain call and told them that she quit but that was as far as she had been willing to go.

Being on the road two weeks now she wasn't sure what she was doing anymore. It was obvious to her that she had gone off the deep end but she was entitled to that. She found out that her fiancé was married and didn't want her. She had been living her whole life to please her mother but now she could be free.

Freedom sounded like such an ease thing for everyone else. For Grace she found that there was not a lot of freedom in her life anymore. Constricted by schedules and traveling, diet and exercise she was done. Done living the life that was never designed for her.

While driving she had come to reevaluate her life. She wanted something for herself. She couldn't name it yet but it was coming and maybe she could find it here, or at least that was what she had talked herself into along the way. She never had a true destination in mind. She just knew when the time and the place felt right she would know.

Still crying she heard a knock at the window. Debating with herself if she really wanted to wind it down the knocking increased. She didn't bother to wipe the tears away or lift her head. If it was a serial killer at least she wouldn't see it coming.

"If you're here to rob me the purse is on the seat. If you don't have a ride then you're shit out of luck here because this piece of crap isn't moving from this spot." She said winding down the car window slowly.

She could hear the deep rumbling laugh of a man next to her. She sighed to herself. Great it really was a serial killer and she had lost her mind. She banged her head a few more times and finally lifted it to look at the man. What did it matter if she saw it coming?

She was pretty sure that she stopped breathing when she looked. The man standing next to her car was a god. It was the only way to describe the Adonis. Perfect jet black hair, slightly feathered and damp on the ends framed the most perfect face she had ever seen. His chiseled good looks and strong jaw only confirmed the god like status. Piercing blue eyes as clear as the sky above looked down at her probing her, looking for answers that she didn't have but his body. Now his body was really a work of art.

If he was a serial killer then she wouldn't mind dying by his hand. Any woman with common sense and half a brain wouldn't mind dying by his hand. Hell they would probably welcome death if he was the one delivering it.

She couldn't form a thought at the moment but she was pretty sure her mouth was open. Closing it quickly she shook her head and rubbed her eyes a few times just to make sure he was real. When she opened them he had a perfectly arched brow raised in an unasked question. Finally realizing that she was staring long enough she cleared her throat.

"Can I help you with something?" She asked embarrassed to be caught staring.

The man smiled and god lord he had a dimple. It was such a perfect dimple she wondered how he had one. His chiseled face and body suggested that he would never be able to have such a mark but it too was perfection. She forgot to breathe again. Looking away from the man for a moment to get control of her brain and her hormones she took a deep breath.

"Well are you going to stare all day?" She snapped.

He laughed and she was drawn to it again. His laugh was such a deep timber that she could sit here all day just too listen to it.

"It's your mouth that was open with drool, not mine sweetheart." He said grinning.

"Look," she started, trying to slow her racing heartbeat at the endearment. "As you can see I'm having a private break down here. I'm sorry to be rude but do you mind. I was finally going to get it all out, alone with no one watching and then form a game plan. If you want the car or my wallet take whatever, just please leave me in peace."

Cole looked at the beauty before him. He wanted to laugh but he could see the frustration behind the tears in her eyes. He had stopped mainly because he had heard her crying. It just wasn't possible for him to leave a woman crying by herself on the side of the road with a broken down car.

While he had been running he had saw her coming toward him car chugging along. He knew that the car was going to die but rather hoped that she would at least make town. As he ran down the road he heard it cough then die and he knew that she had not.

His mother god rest her soul would have yelled at him something fierce if he hadn't been the gentlemen and turned around to help her. Turning back toward her he walked instead of running hoping that she would get all the tears out before he got to her.

He knew women, when their cars died they cried. When the broke a finger nail they cried. They tended to cry about any old thing. At least his mother and his sister had. Over the years Cole had become oblivious to tears. Maybe that was the reason why he was such a stern bastard but her tears. He couldn't name why her tears were affecting him so much.

Maybe because when she had started to cry it sounded as though it was coming from her soul. It sounded like she had just lost the love of her life or her longtime friend and there was pain there. He hated the tears but the pain had been like a knife to his heart. He couldn't name the reasons but it was there and for the first time in a long time he wanted to cry himself from hearing her.

Walking up to the car he could still hear her but she had been banging her head off the steering wheel. His first thought had been that she was drunk. His second thought had been what was hiding behind the mass of flame red curls.

Approaching the car slowly as to not frighten her, he could see the hair and little else. It was a hard thing to miss. It was flame red with wild fat curls curling well past that seat. The hair was so full and thick he couldn't imagine how she could hold it all up.

When he had finally gotten up to the window he had glanced down at the silky strands wanting to run his hands through it. It was like a beacon of red flame curls calling to him to touch them.

He knocked on the window curious about the rest of her but as she looked up with tears streaming down her face he couldn't help but notice the eyes. She had wide set almond shaped eyes that were a dark emerald green. Her small pert nose and high cheek bones were covered in the smoothest porcelain white skin he had ever seen.

The slight blush that she was wearing now only enhanced her beauty and her slender frame and long neck had him gripping the door hoping that he would not tear it off it touch her. He had never been this affected by a woman and when she spoke, it was like a fist of lust so strong and forceful hitting his balls like an iron fist that he was sure that he stopped breathing.

As she rambled about her stealing the car or robbing her, he wasn't sure which, he knew that speech was not an option to him. He simply could not form the words. Only god knew what would fly out of his mouth if he actually tried to open it.

Her low pouty voice made him think of a phone sex operator. Not that he had ever to call one but being a late night person himself he had seen plenty commercials for them. There was an almost whisper of a voice filled with such sexual appeal he could stand here and let her talk to him all night.

All the thoughts that he had been having flew from his mind and all he could think about was getting her out of the car and up against it. He shook his head trying to concentrate. She was speaking to him again but he only caught the last of it. His mind registered something about staring. Hell he knew that he was staring. How could he not? But he guessed that she would require an answer, “It’s your mouth that was open with drool, not mine sweetheart.”

Liar his mind screamed. If she would have been paying more attention to him she would have found him drooling as well.

He caught the comment about him taking the car and her wallet again and he smiled. She was a wildfire alright but he wanted to know more about her but to get that accomplished he would need to speak to her again.

“Look,” he said leaning against the door frame. “I’m not a thief the last time I checked and I don’t do the whole grand theft auto thing anymore. I’m the sheriff here. I was running on the trail when I heard your car die. I just wanted to come and check on you. I haven’t seen you around these parts before and we take care of our own here, so with that being said are you alright ma’am?”

Grace blushed all the way to her toes. She had insulted him and she felt low but she was having a hard time around him. He was just too good looking for his own good and it threw her off kilter. Figuring that she had already stuck her foot in her mouth she tried again.

"I'm sorry sheriff it has been one of those weeks. I'm fine, really. I just need a moment then I'll be on my way. Thank you for checking on me but I am fine, really."

She tried winding the window back up but his hand stopped her.

"And just where are you heading ma'am?" He asked casually.

"Please call me Grace and I'm not sure. Where is here exactly?"

"Are you sure that you're not drunk?" He asked laughing.

She smiled and laughed and Cole found himself drawn to her laugh. It was just as husky and sexual as her voice.

"No sheriff I'm not. I actually wish that I was but I don't drink and drive. Now could you please tell me which state this is and where I am?" She asked still shaking her head.

He wasn't about to argue with her. If his guess was right he wouldn't get anywhere with her anyway. She didn't smell like she had been drinking but she didn't even know where she was. He shrugged, not his problem he told himself.

"Well you're in New Hampshire and this town is Jackson that you're coming up on. Where are you heading?"

"That's the problem. I'm not sure exactly. I just started driving and figured I would find the place for me soon enough. I guess this is as far as I go for today though. My car is broke and I'm pretty sure that it's not going to get fixed any time soon."

He didn't want to do it but he knew that he was going to get himself into trouble. Instead of staying out of it as he should have. He found himself saying, "Well now. Your car is going to need to a tow and you're going to need a place to stay for a few days. You're in luck because I have both. My brother Ross has his own garage and we have a fully furnished house not far from where we're staying. Why don't you let me help you out? I hate to see a woman in distress and you have distress written all over your face sweetheart. What do you say?"

Grace bit her bottom lip. She didn't know this man from Adam and here he was offering her a place to stay and to get her car fixed. It wasn't like she had many options she told herself. It was already getting late and she didn't even know if this town had a hotel available.

"All right sheriff, I'll let you help me only because I have no other options but I insist that I pay you something for your house and time. I won't take no for an answer."

He smiled at the proud beauty before him. When she got her grit back it was with a vengeance. He watched as the tears dried and the perfect posture came to her aid. She wore a mask of indifference but he had seen that he had affected her. For now he would leave it alone, until he could learn more about her, but if she wasn't going to be here long as he suspected then he was going to know her and very well if he had his say in it.

Chapter 2

Grace opened the door and stepped out with the sheriff. She grabbed a few things that she could carry with her along the way but the rest would have to wait until it was towed.

"Which way sheriff?" She asked facing him.

"Please call me Cole. As I said before I'm a sheriff here but I don't start until Monday. I have just been elected here. Now Grace, why don't you tell me a little about yourself."

Grace debated how much to tell the good looking sheriff. When she had gotten out of the car she noticed that he was taller that she originally thought. At five foot nine, Grace was considered tall for a woman but he was at least a good six inches taller than she was.

"Well to tell you the truth there is not much to tell actually. I am Grace Summers. I don't suppose you watch much ballet?" She asked laughing as they walked along.

"Not really. I think I was made to endure part of one in New York. It was the nutcracker I think but I fell asleep in the middle of it."

"Well then, you would have seen me if you hadn't." She said snorting. "Don't worry sheriff I don't hold that against you. Most men I know tend to fall asleep. I personally think that it's the music."

"Wait I do remember you. It's the hair. I remember seeing that hair before, only it was up in a tight bun but I remember. You were the headliner in it right?" He asked as he stopped and really looked at her.

"That was me. Now I'm not sure what I want. I thought that I could run from my past," she said laughing. "As though such a thing is possible. I got into the car a few weeks ago with no true destination in mind. I thought that I would travel for a while. Stay in a few places. Get a feel for what I really wanted to do with my life, and then I would decide for sure. I'm not sure if I was kidding myself or what my problem was but I found myself here. Broke down in the middle of the road crying my eyes out and I am still not sure where here really is. I understand that I'm in Jackson, New Hampshire but to tell you the truth I didn't even realize I was this far east. I thought I was somewhere in Ohio. Insane right?"

"You can't run. Running never solves anything trust me. I ran at one time too. I ran from here. I ran from my family, my responsibilities but I found I had just as many of them waiting for me when I came back." He said shaking his head.

"How long did you run?"

“Since I was eighteen and that was well over twelve years ago. What about you? How long have you been running?”

What a tough complicated answer Grace thought to herself. She wasn’t sure how to answer that but she was going to try.

“Well I think I started running at ten. My mother always wanted me to be a dancer. It was her dream that she never got to fulfill and I think that she was trying to live it through me. At the time I thought that it was what I wanted to do with my life. It was a rigid schedule but I didn’t seem to mind, until I started to mind. I think that I was about sixteen at the time. You know teenagers, they want to run and have friends, and be free, something I’m sorry to say I didn’t have time for. It was a tradeoff, I got the dancing but I gave everything else up for it. I didn’t have friends. I didn’t date and I didn’t have a life. I was a robot, a perfect tool shaped into being the perfect dancer. As I said for a while I wanted that but then, I don’t know. I felt like I wanted something more, something that was my own. I wanted to break my own leg just so I wouldn’t be able to dance anymore. My father god love him is a military man and told me soldiers never quit. I was my mother’s solider and bailing on her was a big no, no to my father, so I “soldiered up,” as he like to call it and kept dancing. College was a little better; at least there

I got to meet people that were made just like me. After a few years I went to the American Ballet Company. I was with them for a little while before quitting. Now I'm not sure what my next move is. How about you, now that you are done running are you settled?"

"Settled is the last thing I'd call myself. I had a sister. She was everything a baby bother could ever ask for in a sister but she was taken too early from us. I was on my fourth tour of duty when I was told that she had passed. My sister and I have always been close but I feel as though I never really knew her. She had a daughter named Emma. She is such a sweet child but she won't speak. When my sister died, she gave custody of Emma to me. I couldn't believe it but I wouldn't turn my back on it. I decided to come home and take care of her, so here I am taking care of a kid that doesn't talk and being a sheriff living the American dream."

He didn't know why he was telling her all of this. For him he never talked to women like this. It was easy to love them and leave them but with becoming a sheriff that would have to end. He couldn't risk people talking about him like that especially with Emma around. She didn't need to hear her uncle was screwing half the female population in the town where they lived.

In fact, night after night for the past three months he had been reminding himself of that fact. He would sneak over to the neighboring towns when it got really bad but with Grace it would be easy to do. He knew that he was attracted to her. He knew that she was not sticking around and he could satisfy his lust for her. Maybe then he wouldn't be so confused by her.

When she had been describing her life to him, it was like he couldn't form a thought. He had been hearing all the words but it was her body that was the problem. Her small round tits were driving him to distraction and he could feel the weight of them in his mouth.

When she had starting talking, he had stopped his lustful thoughts to listen to her and that had been a first for him. Usually he would act like he was paying attention to what a woman was saying. He would answer at all the appropriate times but with Grace it was her voice that was just so appealing, that he had no choice but to listen.

Her very voice could make him come if only she would moan a little. He shook his head at his thoughts. He didn't know the first thing about the woman and already he was groaning because of the way she made him feel.

He was used to lust. He knew that emotion well enough but this was something different. Her slender thin frame had him wanting to protect her, to take care of her and cherish her body as he slowly loved on it.

He knew that she would leave and he was fine with that but he wanted her lovingly which was a big no, no for him. His rules were simple, give them the greatest pleasure they had ever known taking a little for himself and walk away. It was the best for everyone involved.

Cole wasn't delusional; he knew that he was a mess. The things that he had seen and had to do had made him that way. It was part of the military but more than that was Emma. He wouldn't subject her to an endless parade of women coming in and out of her life. It wasn't fair to her that she had lost her mother but he would make sure that she knew that he wasn't going anywhere, even if that meant living like a damned monk.

"Oh my," Grace said interrupting his thoughts. "This is the most beautiful waterfall I think that I've ever seen."

He noticed that when she smiled her whole face lit up. He wondered if she had anyone waiting back home for her to see that smile.

"Is there anyone back home waiting to hear from you?" He found himself asking.

"Well there is my mother and Tom. I'm sure that he is worried sick about me but other than that no. Why do you ask?" She asked looking at him confused.

"Well I know that there is no cell phone service here. I just wanted to make sure that we move along before it gets to dark out here."

He wanted to curse, of course she had someone back home waiting for her. She was just too damn beautiful for her own good. Wanting to kick his own ass for sticking his foot in his mouth he grabbed her by the arm and pulled her along instead.

"Are you alright? You seem a little different now." She asked pulling away from his hold.

He could see the fear in her eyes. She just didn't understand how close he was to howling in frustration. He was rock hard and calling himself ten types of stupid for thinking that he could have her.

What had he been thinking? She was a world famous ballet dancer with a killer body and flame red hair. What man wouldn't want her? Hell she probably beat them off with a stick most days. He silently cursed himself for scaring her.

"Listen I'm sorry. I didn't mean to frighten you but I don't think that you get it. You're in bear country now and if that sun dips before we get to the house than we are dealing with them out here. I for one don't want to meet up with a bear if you get me and I'm sure that you don't either. I need us to move now."

"Yes of course." She said nodding in agreement. "I'm sorry I didn't realize there are bears here. In California there are only bears in the zoos but if you want we can always make a run for it. I'm at least pretty good at that."

He groaned to himself, pleading for mercy. He could imagine those strong long legs gripping him around the hips, thrusting herself up towards him, wrapping around him and pulling him closer to her heat.

He tried to shake away the erotic fantasy but he couldn't do it. It was there right before his eyes as she strained to get to closer to him, to bring more of him inside her liquid heat, hearing her moan his name with a sexy desire to have more. Pleading, begging him for his touch alone to cool her heated flesh.

God he was going down tonight. He would need to get her settled in before he would have to make a drive. He didn't want to drive into the city tonight but he had no choice now. He was just so damned horny that he couldn't think straight. Maybe if they would run like she had suggested then he could forget about her for a while.

"I think that running is the best option. Are you up to it? The house is a little over two miles from here."

"I run every day. Well until recently but I shouldn't have a problem keeping up. Lead the way sheriff." She said gesturing him ahead of her.

As Cole began to run she smiled, from back here she would be able to watch that perfectly formed ass of his run in front of her. She sighed and tried to mentally check herself. She knew that she should stop these thoughts about him now.

He was a sheriff here for god's sake and she didn't even know if this was the place for her. Until she could figure that all out for herself she would just need to keep her hands to herself, but she really didn't have to keep her eyes to herself. At least not right now.

She smiled as he raced along and she found that she followed with ease. Having the world's greatest view of the hardest ass she had ever seen hadn't been bad either. Knowing that a man like him would never be single she tried to reign herself in.

As they ran she couldn't help but think what he would feel like inside of her. She had never known a man's touch but she didn't mind fantasizing about it. As they raced along the dirt path her heart beat quickened. She was pretty sure that it was not caused from the running either.

There was just something about Cole that drew her to him. Maybe it was the pain that she saw behind his eyes, or maybe it was the way that he tried to hide the cocky male attitude that he seemed to have.

No he hadn't come right out and showed her of that attitude but she could sense it. It was the very thing that made her flesh heat and her heart quicken. It was the thing that made her see them together in a roll of tangled sheets, arms and legs every which way. It was the thing that lived between them when he would step just close enough to smell the clean male scent of him. It was the burning lust she had seen in his eyes, if only for a brief moment.

She sighed slightly. Maybe she was reading too much into everything but she couldn't help but feel like he had been disappointed when he asked if she had someone waiting to hear from her at home. Maybe it was the mention of Tom's name. She wasn't sure but he hadn't bothered to ask and she was not a one night stand type of girl anyway.

Grace had dreamed of being loved and cherished. Of course it came hand in hand with the pleasure that she would share with another but it was not going to come at a cost of her self-respect.

In her years at Julliard she had learned all about one night stands from some of her friends and the shame that it could bring. It had brought pleasure and broke hearts in one punch. Her roommate Sara Long had been one of those cases.

Like Grace, Sara had been made to live a sheltered life, which meant no boys. Sara had been rebelling from her parents one night. Looking back Grace knew that was the reason Sara had acted so carelessly. Grace herself had wanted to do the same but she knew the consequences of being careless, it would mean not only giving something of herself up to a person that she barely knew but living with the shame and heart break that would come with it.

Sara and Grace had snuck out well after lights out to hang out at a little club down the street. At first the thrill of breaking the rules had been enough for Sara but soon she wanted more. She had started drinking. Grace also knew the effects of drinking and she didn't want any part of it.

She could never see herself losing that much control for a drink that didn't taste good anyway but she had let Sara have her fun. Grace had tried to slow her down when she realized that Sara was getting to drunk. That was when disaster had struck, he had come.

He was the most popular, best looking, and most talented guy in their class. The man was practically a living legend in the dancing industry but he was also their instructor. When he had found them Grace had thought that he would reprimand them and send them home but he had not. Instead he had set out to seduce

Sara. Of course he had tried with Grace as well but she had not been drinking and not been dumb enough to make that mistake, instead he had focused on poor Sara. Grace had tried to be the standup friend and take her back but she had refused. Sara had made Grace promise that she would not utter a word to anyone about it and if anyone came looking for her to cover her.

With no friends Grace did what she was asked. It wasn't like she liked the situation but she didn't want to lose Sara either, so trying to be a good friend she had done as she had been asked. Later that night Grace had made her way back to campus and snuck back in. She mound up Sara's pillows to make sure that it would like she was still sleeping just in case someone would come and check on her.

Sliding in her own bed Grace stayed up all night waiting for Sara to come back but she never had. She didn't know what to do. She had been concerned about her friend but she didn't want to break her promise to Sara either.

Grace had attended morning classes thinking of Sara the whole time. During those few hours she found out how much worrying about even a friend could affect her dancing. She had been so worried about Sara that she had danced poorly. It really hadn't been a big deal for a day but it had made her realize that if she let anyone close to her in that time she would suffer for it. The only thing she could do was to keep people and men at bay. It wasn't like she didn't have much time to date anyway but that morning had only instilled that dating would be a bad thing for the rest of her years at college.

When it came time for the class that Sara and Grace would see that particular instructor, Sara had been back. She had looked drained but somewhat happy, at least she kept smiling at the instructor like he was the greatest thing she had ever beheld but for Grace she watched as Sara mooned over the man and he completely ignored her.

She wondered what had happened between the two of them but she had let it go until she had talked to Sara later that day. Sara had explained that she had gone home with the instructor and had the perfect night together and that had been Sara's turning point.

Grace knew that Sara was in love with her instructor but he was not seeing any of it, or he just didn't care. Either way Grace was forced to follow Sara to every event the man had attended. They would wait outside of the ballets when he would come out with another woman each time.

Each time he had come she had watched a piece of her friend's heart break. It had been close to three weeks with Sara constantly crying when Grace had told her to snap out of it. Sara that day had looked at Grace with such a tortured expression on her face that her own heart nearly broke.

Sara confessed that she was late. Doing the only thing she could do for her friend she had taken her to a doctor to get her checked out. It was normal for a dancer to skip a period every now and again when the body would change. Grace had even missed a few herself and she prayed that was the answer but they soon learned the truth. Sara was pregnant with her instructor's child.

The pain and loss had almost drowned her friend in a well of sorrow so deep that Grace wasn't sure if she would be able to find her way out. She had suggested starting with the professor first, explain to him what was going on. He was after all the father and should want to help Sara out but he had done the opposite. Instead of supporting her, he had thrown her under the bus.

He went to the board of directors personally and told them that he had learned one of his students had gotten pregnant. He told them that he had overheard other girls in the class talking about it. When Sara had been presented to the board for her trail, she had told them that it was him that was the father.

They had all laughed in her face. They had told her that it was not possible for Professor Tyler to be the father when he was engaged to another professor and was constantly with her. There was also the fact that he was a teacher and would never cross that line.

As everything unfolded Grace didn't know what to do. She could go to the board and tell them the truth about the professor. She could tell them of her friend leaving with the professor but to what avail. It would get her into trouble for breaking curfew and he could just lie and say that he had been taken Sara home when he had found out that she had been drinking too much.

With no other options she went to Sara to discuss everything with her but when she found her she was already packing. The sobs that tore from her chest made Grace's own eyes water in pain and heartbreak.

The two had discussed everything but Sara told her that it was no use, not only was she not allowed to dance at Julliard for the rest of the year but her mother and father were sending her away until she had the baby.

Sara had grown up in a rich home where getting pregnant before marriage was a taboo. Her parents had given her an ultimatum, either go away and have the baby quietly putting it up for adoption, or Sara would be on her own.

Sara didn't know how to survive on her own so she had chosen to go away. Grace didn't like the choice her friend had made but it was not up to her to say. She had asked Sara if she wanted her to testify for her. Her friend shook her head telling her that she would only be next if she did.

Sara told Grace that she appreciated her caring but she couldn't bear the thought of Grace getting kicked out as well. Grace knew the risks, if she went up against a teacher he would be able to destroy her hopes of a career but also graduating, so Grace had kept her mouth shut.

That decision had always haunted her. Even to this day she still wrestled with the thought that if only she had spoken up, it maybe not have changed Sara's fate and she probably would have gotten kicked out herself but she would have been doing the right thing. Now she had live with the fact that she had helped a monster. He had preyed upon an innocent girl and gotten her pregnant but worse. He then made sure that she was never able to dance again. It wasn't fair. He had been the golden one. The one that should have been a man and taken the responsibility for his actions. Instead he had gotten Sara thrown out of school and made Grace's life a living hell.

After the trails were over and Sara had gone he had been on Grace. It had started out with him telling her that she wasn't dancing right, and then it got to the threats. He told her that if she spoke about the truth to anyone he would make sure that he would end her career for good.

She never paid him any attention. After the first semester in school she never really saw him anyway but when she did, when she looked into the eyes of that cold heartless bastard she wanted to spit on him. That day had been Grace's changing point.

She knew that she wanted to experience love and sex but she would never give herself to someone like Sara had given herself to the professor. Grace swore that she would never do a one night stand with a man that she didn't know and suffer the consequences for it.

Reaching the house she noticed the tears that lined her eyes. She tried several times to get them to go away but the pain of losing Sara never would. The day Sara had left Julliard had been the last day that she had ever talked to her. She had tried to look her up online but there was nothing. It was as though she never existed. She wiped the tears away as Cole swung to face her.

"What's the matter? Did we go to fast? Did you hurt yourself?" He asked with pure concern lining his face.

"No I'm fine really." She said shaking her head interrupting him. "I was just thinking about something. Don't worry, I usually cry when I run."

"Why?" He asked cocking his head to the side.

"Why do I cry when I run?" She repeated laughing. "Well I tend to be thinking when I run and it makes me remember things that I would just as soon forget. Don't worry, I'm sure that if you run into me when I'm out on another run you will see them again."

Cole didn't know why he liked her crying, it wasn't like he liked seeing her in pain. It was more along the lines of it was something that only she did. The act of crying while running was something only a female would do. When he ran there was nothing, it was him alone inside his head listening to his heartbeat and nothing else. It was the only time he could seem to get away from thinking too much and she was the opposite.

Obviously she had been thinking of something sad to make her cry but it was very feminine and he found that he liked that flaw in her. Hell he was just starting to like her period. The sooner that he got away from her the better to his way of thinking.

"Come on I have to get the keys to the house and then I'll take you over to get settled in while I have Ross go and tow your car."

"Thank you," she said smiling at him. "I really appreciate that but as I told you before I want to pay you something."

He nodded but mashed his teeth together. If only she knew the dark thoughts that were now running lose inside his head. She wouldn't even think about owing him a favor in return. He smiled at the thought, and then shook his head. He may be low in some ways but he would never do that to her because even though he just met her, he found that he liked her already.

He ran his hands through his hair in frustration and turned for the house. The sooner that he got her away the sooner he could take that drive and right now he needed it, almost as much as he needed her. He groaned to himself and stomped in the house. She was off limits. She was another man's woman and it grated on his nerves. Cursing himself yet again he walked into the house as he called for Ross. Maybe it would get better when she left in a few days. He could only hope.

Chapter 3

Ross appeared at the door the moment Cole had called his name. His brother with the goofy perpetual grin and warm heart was always waiting for Cole when he came home. It had never changed but he watched Ross as Grace came through the door. He wanted to see his brother's reaction to the beauty.

True to his brothers form he came smiling. When he spotted Grace he drop the wrench that he had been holding and stumbled over his words.

"W-where have you b-been?" He stuttered out looking at Grace.

Just as he suspected, it was not just him that was affected by her beauty. Ross would stutter each time he was nervous or ran into a really beautiful woman. Ross had always been the funny one in the family.

He was the one with the big heart and even bigger personality. He could charm the pants off anyone, unless they happened to be a good looking woman and then he couldn't seem to form a thought. Looking at his brother now fidgeting with the wrench he had his answer.

"This is Grace Summers," Cole started clearing his throat to gain his brothers attention. "She's new in town and her car broke down about mile up the road from the falls. She didn't know that she was in even in New Hampshire, so she didn't make reservations for the hotel here. I told her that she could stay at the other house for a few days while you fix her car. She insists on paying for everything though." He finished snorting.

"No ma'am, we can't take money from you. Here everyone helps everyone else, it's what we do. Taking money from you wouldn't be right." Ross said shaking his head.

"But I insist," she said cutting him off. "To tell you the truth I don't even know if my car is capable of being fixed and I'm sure that the parts are going to be expensive if it can be. I tell you what, you can take a look at it for me but we will decide if it is even worth fixing first. If we decide that it's going to cost too much to fix then I'll pay you for your time. How's that sound?"

"It sounds like you are talking around me taking from money from you. All the words sound great but guess what; it still leaves you paying me which isn't going to happen." Ross said crossing his arms over his chest.

Grace laughed, when she had first met Ross she had thought that she had thrown him off. He had been stumbling over his words and he had dropped his wrench. He probably wasn't used to his brother picking up strangers on the side of the road. That had been the reason he had been stumbling she told herself. She had thought then that she could talk around the situation about money but he had been quicker then she had first thought, but her mind was made up and she would not take no for an answer.

"But I don't feel right not paying you. Do you think that you could allow it this one time? I know that I would feel better and I'm sure you understand why. Don't you?" She said lowering her eye lashes at him.

"Well, all right. I don't want to make you uncomfortable or anything." Ross blushed shuffling his feet.

Her head snapped up and she laughed kissing him on the cheek.

"I just knew that you would see it my way."

"I have been suckered. Haven't I?" He asked smiling.

Cole watched the exchange between Grace and his brother. As soon as she lowered those lashes of hers and spoke in a very low voice he knew that his brother was a goner. He would never tell her no when she would look at him like that and Cole knew it. Ross was as big of a push over as they came.

He smiled when Ross had agreed and Grace's face lit up. Confusion had lined his brother's face and Ross realized that he had been played.

"Hey that's not fair." He said pouting.

"I always win. Just remember that and we will get along together fine." She said laughing.

"Would you like to call the people back home waiting for you? I doubt that you have cell service yet but you could always use our phone out in the kitchen. No one will bother you there," Cole said smiling at her cunning.

"I guess if I must. I know that they worry but I'm a big girl. I feel as though I'm still answering to all of them." She pouted.

"It's called being responsible. All of us have someone to answer too." He shrugged.

"All right, I get it but I don't have to like it. I insist that you send me the charges for the calls though."

"Not going to happen." Ross said growling. "Go on now and call them before they come looking for you. I'm sure that they are worried by now."

Grace nodded and said nothing more. Now wasn't the time to argue. Now was the time to think about what she was going to tell her mother.

As she walked into the kitchen Grace couldn't help but smile. This place was definitely lived in by bachelors, or at the very least men with no live in girlfriends. There were dishes everywhere and there was food still left on the stove, from what appeared to be last night's dinner.

As she reached for the phone she could be nice and do dishes. It was the least that she could do considering they didn't know her and were willing to help her out. As she started the dish water she decided that Tom would be the better person to call first. At least with Tom it could be short and to the point.

As the line rang she prayed that he was not home. Looking at the clock it was already 7:00 here. What time would be in California? As she thought about the question a familiar voice answered the phone and she wanted to cry, just hearing Tom's voice sometimes did that to her.

"Hey Tom it's me I just wanted to let you know that I'm alright."

"Man are you in trouble. Where are you and when are you coming home? Janet has been blowing up my line looking for you. The company called her and told her that you just quit and that you didn't give any type of notice and that you called off the wedding. Don't ask me how she knows that one but she is out for blood and I think that you're the target." He said laughing.

Grace winched. She really didn't need to explain to her mother why the wedding was off, but she would deal with that later. Right now she had bigger problems.

"Listen, don't worry about me and I'll deal with her. Right now I don't want her to know where I am. I don't need momzilla coming to look for me. I'm almost thirty for god's sake; you would have thought that she would have learned that I can be flighty by now."

"When have you ever been flighty? You're the most grounded person that I have ever known but don't worry I'll let you handle her on your own. I know that she can be difficult but where are you? I promise that I won't tell her but I'm worried about you. You up and left. The only time I got to hear from you was when you called the machine and told me that you're moving away. I haven't had the chance to talk to you. Tell me what's going on."

Grace sighed loudly. She knew that this was coming but she wasn't ready to deal with any of it. She had been getting good at running and she didn't want to give it up now but she also knew that lying to Tom was not an option. He would find her whether or not she wanted to be found or not.

That was the beauty of Tom. He was gentle and caring but loyal to fault. Knowing that he would never break a promise she needed to soothe him.

"Well right now I'm in New Hampshire, a little place called Jackson and don't worry I'm fine. Well sort of. My car broke down and I'll be here for a few days but when it gets fixed I'll set out again. I haven't picked the place where I want to settle but for now I'm going to kick back for a while and think. I need to do something. I'm not sure what yet but I'll get there. I'll call you soon and let you know what I have decided."

"I knew that car was a piece of shit." Tom said sighing. "You should have let me buy you a new one like I wanted but no, not miss stubborn to her bone Gracie. Maybe that car breaking down was a good thing, it's part of the past that you're running from and maybe it's time to let it go now. Look I'll give you the time that you seem to need but if I don't hear from you in a few days I am coming for you whether you like it or not. Do you understand me Grace Marie?"

Grace cringed at the threat. She hated it when Tom used her full name. She knew that if she didn't keep her word that he would come and it would mean trouble for everyone.

"Look, stop trying to be macho with me because we both know that it won't work on me. You have bullied me before and it got you nowhere fast. Why would you think that it would work now?"

"Because if I don't hear from you then I will assume the worst," he started. "If I assume the worst then I'll bring the Sarge with me. Do you really want the Sarge to come with me Gracie?"

"No I don't want Sarge coming and don't threaten me. I know your secrets to Tom. I could turn him on you instead." She snapped out.

"Yeah but you, you're the one that he is having issues with at the moment. I'm a small fish compared to you. Just promise me that you will call me because I don't like worrying about you."

"Alright Tom I promise. Now back off. I'll call you in a few days. There are you happy now?"

"Very and remember Gracie, block the number when you call Janet or there will be no where you can hide to get her off your tail."

Grace pulled the phone away from her ear and cussed. She had forgotten about caller ID.

"Son of a bitch alright, alright you got me but I'm not staying here anyway so good luck finding me. I'll call you soon," and she disconnected the call before he could argue.

While she loved Tom she secretly hated the man at the same time. He knew things about her that no one should know but she never had anyone like she had Tom. She loved his caring nature and his fun attitude. If only he wasn't a pain in the ass all the time.

Scrubbing the dishes she wondered what she would tell her mother when she called her. She knew that it was going to be a fight but she couldn't put it off any longer. Drying her hands on the dish towel Grace picked up the phone again and blocked the number. She then dialed her mother and prayed that everything went well.

She would just call to tell her that she was fine and she would call in a few days. Knowing that it would be a fight if she stayed on the phone for any longer she spilled it out and disconnected the call before her mother could say a word.

Pushing her hands through her hair she knew that this was the best. Giving Janet no time to talk was always best but she knew that she couldn't run from her mother forever. Eventually if she didn't come out and talk about it Janet would use other means to get what she wanted, and if Janet did there was no hiding for anyone. Her mother would bring in Sarge and she couldn't let that happen because there was no hiding from that man.

Her father John "Sarge" Summers was the best at what he did and the only thing he did was track. He had been the top tracker in his platoon. There was no hiding from the man. He was the dog on the trail and she was the trail. He would find her if he wanted it bad enough and she knew it.

Grace secretly wondered why her father had not already come. Snorting she pushed aside her thoughts, her father would give her some time but he would not want to put up with Janet long and he would come if her mother wished it. Janet Summers was ruthless when it came to Grace. Oh it wasn't for her safety or wellbeing no she had learned that lesson long ago.

Janet Summers would come because Grace had just given up the one thing that Janet had never been able to do herself, dancing. There would be no way to walk away from that without the consequences and right now she didn't have the strength to pay for them. The fact that her mother loved Kurt only made it worse and she had walked away from him also.

One time she just wished her mother would listen to what she wanted, to what really mattered to Grace instead of always pushing her but in pushing her so hard she had also pushed her away. Most times Grace didn't even call Janet mother, she plainly called her Janet which her mother had hated.

Getting up from the table to finish the dishes she knew that she had been over this again and again. It wasn't simply going to be easy to walk away from the life that she had always lived that much was for sure.

As she turned she ran right into a little girl with big wide eyes. Thinking that she frightened the child she walked closer to her until she started screaming. She took a step back and covered her ears as the child screamed the most tortured scream she could ever remember hearing. As the world spun and turned to black she wondered what she had done.

Ross and Cole had been standing just outside the kitchen door. From this point in the house you could hear everything that was going on inside the kitchen. Cole didn't know why he was so curious about whom she was going to call but he found that he had been.

Thinking of picking up the other line he shook his head. He wouldn't betray that type of privacy but he had been damned tempted.

"Why are we standing here?" Ross asked.

Cole shushed him and listened to the conversation coming from the kitchen. He could hear Grace's soft sexy voice talking to what he could only assume was Tom. When the words "don't threaten me" came, he was half temped to pick up the other end.

He wondered exactly what she had been running from. From the sounds of things she had not been answering to anyone in a while and she would need too. He knew that running never solved anything, running only caused more problems but apparently she had yet to learn that lesson.

"Why is she here and why is she staying at the other house? You don't even know what it will do to Emma." Ross whispered to him as he listened to the conversation.

"Listen to me," Cole whispered facing his brother. "She's in some type of trouble. I found her broke down on the side of the road cry her eyes out. What would you have me do, leave her there? No both you and I know that I would never be able to do that and she isn't going to be able to get a room this late at night. I wanted to make sure that she was alright. Now will please shut up so I can hear."

"You like her." Ross said snorting. "I can see it. I'm just wondering why her? There are so many other's in your life that have been waiting for you to commit. Why would you take on a virtual stranger that we know nothing about? Have you ever thought about the fact that she has problems? You have enough going on without adding her stuff on top. Plus what if she decided that this is the place for her and stays? You know that you'll never commit to her, so why chose her? You don't know anything about the woman Cole. Think with your brain man and not with your penis for once."

"Listen carefully because I'm not going to talk about this ever again." Cole snapped out slamming his brother against the wall. "If you ever bring this up I will deny it but there is something about her. I'm not sure what that something is but today when I found her crying…." He let his brother slide to the floor and pushed his hands threw his hair. "I don't know how to describe it. You know that I don't open up to people, that in some ways I've been closed off for years but with her. I don't know. When I heard her crying it made me want to cry with her. I don't know how to describe it. I haven't let myself cry for anything. Not for what I had to go through. Not for losing Vikki and not for my own loses but today. Today I almost lost that battle and cried for all I was worth hearing her. There was such pain behind her cries that it made me feel as though her pain was my own. I know that I lust after her. I know that I like her but I also know that I talked to her. Not about anything in particular but I talked and actually listened to what she had to say and that has never happened to me before. We all know how I am but with her." He sighed, "I don't know, with her it's different. Now don't ask me why or what because I don't know but for now I want to protect her. Keeping her close even for a few days will help, now leave the rest alone. If she decides to stay then

I'll deal with it like I deal with the rest of them. Now shut up and let me listen."

Ross stepped back holding up his hands. He had never seen Cole like this. Most times Cole was closed off and stand offish but his stone cold brother was opening up to him. He would have to admit that this would be the very first time Cole had ever opened up about anything. Usually he kept everything so bottled Ross didn't understand how he could survive. He knew that his brother had seen things that no man should have too. He had seen his fellow soldiers die right beside him. He had seen his sister die leaving him his only niece to take care of.

Ross knew that someone his age should never have to see half of what Cole had seen. At thirty one Cole was the baby by all accounts. Ross was only a year older but it always seemed that Cole was the more mature one.

Seeing his brother acting like a school boy was actually entertaining. It had been the first time he had seen Cole smile so much since he had been home. Ross knew that his brother had flaws, what man didn't? But he also knew that he deserved some happiness for once in his life.

When Cole had been eighteen he had run off to join the Marines. He had wanted to step into their fathers shoes. The oldest Bret had done the same and he was still trying to fill them, but Cole had been in for twelve years. Four years was too long in Ross's mind but twelve that was just insane.

Cole had wanted to retire a military man and in a way he had but he had been made to leave before his twenty years were up. Victoria's death had done that.

Ross had never understood his sister even though they had been twins. He just didn't feel connected to her the way that he had seen between Cole and her. It almost seemed that Cole should have been Vikki's twin instead of him. The two of them shared a bond most people didn't understand. He had even seen it for himself and never understood it.

Anytime that Vikki had been hurt or in pain Cole had been there. It was a sixth sense. He could remember when Vikki had found out that she was pregnant with Emma, everyone including himself had been floored.

It wasn't like his sister to do something so careless but she had and when the father left, she had been broken. Cole had instantly known that something was wrong with her. He had called home insisting on talking to her.

Still to this day he never knew what they had talked about but Vikki had changed after that. She seemed to have perked up and became more her old self after talking with Cole. No one, not even their mother had been able to console her the way that Cole had and it had been something to see alright.

He could remember getting the call from Cole to talk to Vikki. She had tried to refuse but Cole had been persistent as he usually was. When she had gotten on the phone they had talked for about an hour while Ross had been sitting right next to her.

She had not said much as the conversation flowed but he had been watching Vikki's face. She would nod every now and again then she started to smile. After she started to smile she had started to laugh and at one point she had sucked in a breath and told Cole why she was crying.

Ross never knew what Cole had said but he saw Vikki rub her stomach and smile. The smile that she had smiled was one that he had never seen her smile before. Her whole face seemed to glow and she was blushing. She never said much just listened.

After that night Vikki had changed. She had become intent on being the best single mother ever. She had moved out of the house and had the brothers build her a large house next door. She had even asked if they could build her a larger building next to the house with hard wood floors and mirrors.

Ross had never been one to question his twin but he had. She smiled at him and told him that the space would be used for a dancing studio one day. While

Vikki had danced in her youth she had never become a great dancer. He had never known that his twin had wanted to open a dance studio on their property so that she could make a school.

She explained to him one time that those who can't do teach. While it was a simple enough motto he never understood dancing. Vikki had called it walking art but he could never see the art in it.

Since moving Emma in, they had been made to watch more ballet then he cared too but he would not disappoint his niece. Lord knew the girl had gone through enough. She was just eight years old and lost her father, mother and grandmother in her short life.

Dancing was the only thing that seemed to bring any light to her eyes anymore. He didn't understand it but he had done what his sister had asked of him. She had opened the school before she died but he had been the one to keep it going. He had found a wonderful dance teacher and even named the school after his sister. It didn't seem enough to him but he watched as Emma walked over to the school every day.

She would sit and watch all the students but when asked if she wanted to join she would simply shake her head. She had been intent to watch, just never participate.

He wanted his niece back. It was bad enough losing a sister but losing his niece was not something Ross had been prepared to deal with.

The day that his sister had died had been the last day Emma had talked. She had become withdrawn and almost scared looking. She seemed to be jumping at shadows. She never cried, never asked for anything and never made any trouble but then again she never participated either.

She seemed to be just drifting through her life and no one, not even Cole himself could bring her back. They had taken her to doctors. They had taken her to psychologist but nothing had come of it.

They all had said the same thing. When she is ready to talk she will. Until then there was nothing anyone of them could do. The only thing they could do was move her out of the house that she had shared with her mother and in with them.

The brothers now all lived together with their niece. Since none of them seemed to know what to do with her, they decided that it would be best if they all tried together.

When Cole had come home for Vikki's funeral he had moved her in then. Ross didn't mind sharing his space with his brothers or Emma for that matter. He was just at a loss on what to do with her. What did he know about raising children?

Like his brother Cole, Ross found that he didn't have trouble getting dates. That was never the problem. The problem was finding one that interested him enough to stay. He had yet to meet that special someone but watching his brother he knew that Cole had.

Ross had seen the countless women in Cole's life. He had been trying to hide it because of Emma but there were constantly women calling for his brother. He knew all too well his brother's ways.

Like himself, Cole didn't know how to stay. It was easier to find fun and then leave. That had been the brother's motto ever since they had been old enough to understand what sex was.

Their mother had been a good mother. She had told her sons that she didn't mind the countless women in their lives but cautioned them that if they would ever get one pregnant, they would answer to her.

They all knew the rules. It was alright to sleep around but never get them pregnant and always make sure that they protected themselves. It had been an easy thing to do and over the years they had stayed the same.

Even Bret at his age of thirty five had no intentions of settling down. It was known to everyone in town that the Baker boys didn't do commitment. If you were looking for fun or great sex they were your men. If you were looking for a husband, better look somewhere else.

Looking at his brother Cole, he wondered just how much he liked this Grace. Ross had been watching his brother since they had come in the door. He understood the attraction to her, after all she was a very beautiful woman but he could see the possessiveness there already. He was going to question him more when they heard it. If he lived another hundred years he would never forget the sound of that scream. It seemed to tear straight from the chest of his niece and into his own. The sound cut straight to his soul and his feet seemed to fly into the kitchen to watch Emma scream and Grace fall.

Chapter 4

Grace was slow to come too. She wondered why the little girl had screamed and why she had fainted. Fainting was not something that she was prone to do, so why would she start now?

Pushing herself up on the couch she found Cole hovering close by. The little girl she noticed was now standing beside her uncle with a nervous look on her face. Trying to shake the cobwebs that now surrounded her brain she asked. "What happened?"

"I think that you were scared by our Emma. I'm so sorry that she screamed but you see she has been waiting to meet you. Is that the reason that you screamed Emma?" Cole said looking down at his niece.

The little girl Grace noticed was no longer looking at her, or anyone else for that matter. In fact she was now looking at the ground as though she was embarrassed by something. She didn't look up but she gave a timid nod.

Grace smiled at the little girl sitting all the way up. She already knew that she had scared the little girl more than she should have. She didn't know the first thing to say to reassure the girl that she would not hurt her.

Grace pushed her legs over the side of the couch and smiled at her even though she was not looking straight at her.

"You must be the famous Emma. As you have already guessed I'm Grace Summers and I assume that you know who I am."

The little looked up at her and the pain in her tiny eyes was like a knife to her heart. It should not be so apparent the pain that she held but it was there and it was heavy. Looking up at her uncle she nodded in Grace's direction.

"It's alright Em. She's real, go on now, she won't hurt you." Cole said smiling.

Emma rolled her eyes and then smiled at Grace. The way her eyes transformed while she was smiling was something to see. She nodded indicating that she knew her.

Grace wondered how to have a conversation with a girl that didn't talk. She smiled back at her.

"Sorry for giving you a scare but I can't decide if it was you or me that was more frightened. My you got a set of lungs on you girl."

Emma blushed then giggled still nodding her head. Grace patted the seat next to her on the couch. Emma took a timid step forwards then almost looked back to her uncle. Instead she shook her head and quickly walked forward taking a seat next to Grace.

Grace desperately wanted to look to Cole for answers but she would not. She couldn't imagine the pain that this little one was going through right now. Emma would know that people would think her odd and she would not show her that she was one of those people. Turning to Emma she smiled.

"So Emma tell me. Do you want to be a ballerina as well?" Emma started to nod then shook her head. Grace nodded, "ah I see. I understand that completely. When I was about your age I thought that I wanted it. I wanted it so badly I went to every class I could. I always thought that ballerina's were the most graceful people in the world. I thought they were…" Grace leaned in close to her ear and whispered the rest. "Fairies." Grace laughed when Emma nodded.

"So you see it's not just you. I wanted to be graceful like they were. I watched them whenever I could but I learned something along the way Emma. Would you like to know what that is?" Grace asked still smiling at the little girl.

Emma nodded quickly. Grace leaned in again and whispered.

"You have to want it. It's a lot of hard work but if you're willing to do that you too can become a fairy. Would you like me to show you what I'm talking about Emma?" The little girl grinned and nodded pulling on her hand. Grace laughed, "Now if you want to see we need a little more room. I'm sure that your uncle likes his furniture. How about outside on the porch? There seems to be enough room out there but first you must go and get your shoes and a coat. I don't want you getting sick." Emma nodded and raced off before Cole could even catch her.

"What did you say to her?" Cole asked facing her.

"Nothing that was important. Girl things, but she is getting her coat and I told I would meet her outside. If you'll excuse me," and she walked off leaving a very confused Cole standing in the room.

Grace walked out onto the porch and stretched. It had been almost three months since she had danced. Putting her leg up on the railing she heard the screen door open. A very excited Emma stood on the porch looking at her expectantly.

"Now then should we start with the basics?" Graced asked stretching.

Emma nodded again and Grace noticed that Cole and Ross had followed their niece out. Great what she needed after being so bad was an audience. What did it matter what they thought of her? It wasn't like she would be terrible or they would know the difference for that matter but something about Cole watching her made her blood boil. Pushing the thoughts aside she focused on Emma.

She turned to face Emma and placed her feet in opposite directions toes pointing away from each other. It was the way a dancer usually stood.

"Now then Emma, a dancer must always be limber and graceful, or so that is what they tell you. For me I found that it was always much easier to focus on how I was feeling for the day and let it show in my dancing. Here I'll show you."

Grace straightened and started to rise up on her feet. The last part was always the most difficult. Standing on straight tip toes was never an easy thing for any dancer to do. It was strenuous and thoroughly painful. She rose even higher up watching Emma's eyes widen looking at her until she was standing straight on her tip toes.

"Now Emma comes the hard part, moving." She took the baby steps across the porch getting closer to Emma as she moved.

Never taking her eyes away from the child she drew Emma towards herself with the movements. Emma walked forward with wide eyes and a hesitant step but Grace would not let her. She danced all the way up to her and grabbed her hands and set off across the porch in the opposite direction.

She held her hands and motioned for her to move her feet. When Emma got the hang of what Grace wanted her to do she started twirling into her and releasing. While she was dancing she was laughing so loud that it had drawn the other brother out of wherever he had been hiding. Grace sparred him no attention now. She was too busy concentrating on Emma's laughter. There was pure joy in the laughter and she found for the first time in a long time she was laughing as well.

Cole and his brother's all stood dumb founded as Emma danced across the porch laughing. It had been so long since they had heard her laughter that none of them could possibly move.

It was already dark but they had always made sure that the yard and front of the house was well lit in case of animals. Now dancing in the moonlight were the two most perfect people in the world. They created a happy chaos with their dancing and Cole secretly wondered if Grace was magic.

Being close to Vikki, Cole always considered himself closer to Emma in a way also. She was so much like her mother in appearance that it sometimes hurt to look at her. Seeing her now happy and laughing had opened something up inside of him. He wanted to hear the laughter again. He wanted to surround himself in the happy chaos that only Emma could bring.

He shook his head trying to clear his thoughts. He missed this but it had come not from him and his brothers as it should have. It came from a stranger, that same stranger that would soon be leaving in a few short days. Swallowing past the lump in his throat he called out to them.

"Sorry to interrupt girls but I need to get Grace settled into the house and Emma you have a bath to take young lady."

The two of them looked at him and Emma frowned. Grace laughed and clucked the little girl under her chin.

"You can always come and see me while I'm here. Your uncle Cole will know where to find me."

Emma nodded and hugged Grace close. She then turned and ran back into the house leaving her standing alone. The three brothers just stood there staring at her that she was unsure if what she had done was wrong.

"Please say something. I can't stand all of you standing there staring."

"Come on let's get you settled in for the night." Cole said taking a step forward. "Ross will bring your car along shortly just in case you need anything from it."

Grace nodded but could not help like feeling as though she had done something wrong because if she had she would need to talk to Cole about it. She didn't want to hurt this family any more than they already had been. Lord knew they had already lost so much in such a short amount of time.

Following Cole in silence she was really starting to wonder. Normally she would never ask but she couldn't help herself.

"I can't help but feel like I did something wrong back there."

"You did nothing wrong Grace. Don't worry about it. Listen it just took all of us by surprise that you of all people could make her laugh."

Grace stepped back as though he had struck her, as though she was some type of person that was incapable of making people laugh or feel joy. At one point she had thought that it was what she did for many people every day and now he was attacking that.

She shook her head as they started for the truck again. She would not let another man get to her like again, even if he was an extremely good looking well-muscled man.

Getting in the truck she had appreciated everything that he had done for her but from now on she would have to make her own way. That was the thing that she had instilled in herself before she had begun this crazy trip and no man would take that from her again.

More positive with her decision she relaxed into the silence that now seemed to surround them. She would not make him any more uncomfortable then he already seemed to be and she would just learn to ignore him while she was here.

Reaching the house she noticed that they would be really close by. In one hand that could be a good thing. She was in a new state, in a new town and she didn't know a soul save for him. At least if she was getting mauled he would probably be close enough to hear her.

She snorted at her thoughts; the way that he was watching made her think that he might just help the bear. She couldn't figure him out. At first he had seemed nice, playful and almost flirtatious. After the mention of Tom he became almost agitated, although she didn't understand why and after dancing with Emma. Well now he looked like he wanted her gone from here and the faster the better.

As they exited the truck her stomach rumbled. Crap it had been how long since she had eaten? She shook her head. She couldn't even remember the last time she had taken a meal but she would die before she asked him.

Cole looked over at the proud beauty before him. Since his comment back at the house she seemed to withdrawal from him. He knew that it was for the best but he didn't like seeing that look in her eyes. It almost looked like she was hurt by what he had said.

He really hadn't meant to hurt her. He just couldn't wrap his head around the fact that she had gotten Emma to laugh. Emma was always quiet. She never laughed, never giggled and certainly hadn't blushed like that before.

He liked the change in his niece when Grace was around but he was thinking of the future. What would happen to Emma once Grace left again? Would she not laugh anymore? Would she think that someone else in her life had left her? Would she hate him because he had not convinced Grace to stay?

The more he thought about all the questions with no answers. The more his stomach started hurting. He never wanted Emma hurt again and he would do anything to ensure that. Even trying to convince Grace to stay.

As he thought about it the more it sounded like a good idea. What if he could convince Grace to stay? Then Emma would laugh again and maybe just maybe start talking again. He prayed that it would happen but the real question was. How to make her stay?

He thought about the possibilities for a minute. He would need to make her stay that was for sure but he would need a good way to convince her. As they got out of the truck he heard Grace's stomach rumble.

That would be one of his in's. Clearing his throat as they reached the door he tried talking to her.

"Grace I completely forgot about you not eating all day. You know that there's this really great take out place. How about some pizza, since I'm sorry to say that there is nothing in the house."

Grace wondered what was coming over him now. He almost seemed to be a different person now. It was confusing her and she was wondering if he wasn't one of those multi-personality people. He certain seemed to have more than enough for any one person.

As they walked in house she sucked in a breath. The house was simply beautiful. There were no other words to describe it. Since it was night time and dark in the forest it had been hard to see the outside but now being inside she didn't care how it looked because the insides beauty certainly would make up for the outside imperfections if there were any.

She ignored Cole and walked around the house slowly. It was the most gorgeous home she had ever seen. Hard wood floors were as far as the eye could see. The couches were newer and were done in neutral tones that highlighted the floors.

As she walked she could tell that this house was owned by a woman. The living room had been sunken in and made to be in a circle. The one wall was done in all windows that stretched high above the first floor. It was so open and light she found herself looking forward to the morning just to watch the sun rise.

High ceilings and an open kitchen only enhanced the house. Walking back the hallway Grace found the laundry room. The study that had been well stocked with books and a half bath. She made her way up the stairs and found the bedroom on the second floor. There was a walk along balcony so that a person could see the whole living room from up here.

She knew that Victoria had probably done the design of the house. With someone with a small child it was ideal. If she was upstairs and Emma was in the living room she could easily see her from up here.

Walking into the master bedroom had been magic. The double French doors had given the house the elegant feel but still went with the hard wood throughout the house. The bed was a King sized and still made as though it was only slept in yesterday.

She pushed the second set of French doors open to reveal the master bathroom complete with garden tub and double sink. Walking back into the bedroom she pushed open another set of doors that led to another balcony on the outside. As she walked out and breathed in the air she could see the other building from here.

She wondered what that building would be but didn't bother to ask. Cole was watching her intently but she paid him no mind. Walking back into the hallway she pushed open the other door to the other bedroom and sucked in a breath. Everything was covered in pink.

The walls were pink, the bed was pink and even the hardwoods had been covered over with pink rugs. Grace smiled as she looked at Emma's old room. It kind of reminded her of her own room when she had been a girl.

Closing the door because she felt as though she was interrupting something private, she faced Cole.

"It's perfect. Thank you so much."

"You're welcome." He said wondering why he liked her smile so much. "Sorry we weren't expecting someone to be using it or we would have cleaned it but it will do right?"

"Of course Cole. Come on now, I have some questions for you before I ask you about the take out."

Cole nodded but inwardly flinched. He wondered what these questions would be. He didn't want to disappoint her or offend her again but he was having a hard time reading her now.

When he had first met her she had been in a vulnerable position. She had been crying for god knows what and she had a broken car. He should have count his blessings that he had found her then because he knew women like her. Catch them off guard and they couldn't react as quickly but catch them on their game, he wouldn't stand a chance.

Since he had made those comments in the car he knew that he had caused her to change. He could see it in her eyes. They were guarded now and closed off from him. Now he had no clue what she was thinking or feeling and he couldn't help but swallow. He only hoped that he would be able to live through it. Walking back into the kitchen Cole decided that food would be the best course of action first.

"How about that pizza? I haven't got to eat yet either and it seems that someone cleaned our kitchen. I wouldn't want to mess it all up again."

Grace debated with herself, since meeting Cole she had thought that she had a pretty good idea of his personality but now she wasn't so sure. Her stomach rumbled again and she knew that she would have no choice. It wasn't like she knew who to call for a pizza and her cell phone was still not working.

"Alright, that's fine with me and I like everything except anchovies." She answered carefully.

"Good, just give me a moment to order it and we can talk."

Grace nodded and looked around the kitchen again, everything was so new. She could easily like this house. There was just something about it that made her feel as though she was at home. Maybe it was all the feminine furniture but she found that she liked it.

She took a seat at the island in the kitchen as she heard Cole ordering them food. She wondered how she was going to start this conversation. Hello are you a mentally insane person? She shook her head and snorted at her thoughts.

"Pizza will be here in thirty minutes." Cole said walking into the kitchen and taking a seat next to her.

"Thanks, listen I usually don't do this with people I just meet but I was wondering. Are you insane or something? Am I not getting it here because I'll be honest, I can't figure you out at all. When I first met you, you seemed…flirtatious maybe. I don't know but you weren't this." She said gesturing at him. "Then at the house you seem agitated, then you said something that really hurt me and now you're being nice again. I will tell you, if you have issues, I'm not prepared to deal with them. I can't even deal with my own and besides I've had enough of men with issues for a while. Tell me, did I do something to cause the changes in you? Did I offend you in some way? Tell me because I would really like to understand instead of coming to the wrong conclusions about you."

Cole sat back and ran his hands through his hair. She thought that he was mentally unstable. Hell maybe he was. He couldn't even tell anymore. She had provoked feelings in him that he wasn't even sure if he had anymore. He liked her, not something that usually happened for him. Yes he liked women but spending time with them not so much but with her that was different.

Usually women were coy and shy but that was different with her also. She was the type of woman that said whatever was on her mind apparently and he never had that before either.

It was like being on a boat with her. She was calm one minute. Strong and almost violent the next. Then she had the ability to make you want to embrace her and protect her. It was damn confusing and the more her moods changed so did his. That was the only explanation he could give but how to give it to her.

He looked at her face that was looking at him for answers. He couldn't come up with the answers. He didn't have them so he just grabbed her and kissed her. Maybe he could get her to feel what he was experiencing within himself. It felt like he was a dying man and she was the salvation. He didn't know how else to describe it.

He thought that it would be a brief kiss but it turned into something that even he had not been prepared for. Her arms came up around his neck and she was kissing him back. Her soft moan of surrender didn't help him clear his mind. It only made it worse.

The burning ache that he had been feeling since he had met her intensified and he was going down in a ball of flame. Fire filled his veins and he pulled her closer. He tried to slow it down to pull back from the heat of it but he couldn't. It was in the way that she pushed herself closer to him. It was in the way that she was playing with the back of his head with those small soft fingers of hers. It was in the broken moan that tore from his own chest.

Usually he could separate himself from this part but with her there was no running and no separation. If she didn't stop soon he wasn't sure if he would be able to. He pushed himself closer to her and she turned placing himself between her legs on the chair. He groaned when he could feel the heat of her beckoning him.

Grace didn't understand what was happening to her. She had believed that she was going to have a conversation with the man and here she was straddling his lap and pulling him closer to her. She didn't seem to mind that she didn't know a thing about him. She didn't even seem to mind that she didn't know much about this stuff. The only thing that she did mind right this second was getting closer to him.

Pushing herself closer to him she felt it. It was hard proof of his arousal for her. In one hand her heart soared that she had this much effect on him with only a kiss but the other part of her made her pull back for a moment.

She knew that she didn't have the first clue about any of this and it felt as though she was rushing into something that she wasn't ready for with him. Hell she didn't even know the man and here she was on his lap with his tongue in her mouth.

As the fog lifted she seemed to be thinking clearly. She pulled back from him and watched as his clear blue eyes glazed with sexual hunger. She wondered if she could ever recall seeing that look in another man's eyes and the answer was no. No one ever looked at her the way that Cole was looking at her now.

She could feel the liquid heat starting to spread just watching him but she would not rush this. She had never done this before and if she was being truthful with herself she was scared. She didn't understand the feelings that he was provoking in her and until she could sort it all out she would have to stop this. Sucking in a breath of air she slowly got up from his lap.

"I'm sorry I usually don't do things like this. I know that I'm throwing you all sort of mixed signals here but I can't do this Cole. I don't know the first thing about you other then I'm attracted to you. While I'm familiar with attraction and all that it can do, I'm not ready for this. Not yet. I would like to know you better but I leave the decision up to you. I'm not built for one night stands despite what I've just shown you. If you walk away from this I'll understand but I just wanted to be up front and honest with you. I don't know the coy games that other women seem to know and I will not act like I do. This is me and this is what you get but a one night stand is not one of them." She said blushing as she looked at the floor.

Cole was trying to get his own head on straight. He understood the attraction to her. That he could handle but he had been pulling himself back from her not wanting to rush her the moment their lips met and that was not something that he was familiar with.

Usually it was easy to stroke their lust, to know just where to touch and push so that the other person would respond to him willingly but he didn't do that with her. With her he had been content just to hold her in his arms and slowly kiss her. He didn't push and he didn't touch. Hell he hadn't done a damn thing other than kiss her and he was still panting with need.

He stood and paced the floor. He didn't understand his own mind with her around. Maybe getting involved with her wasn't such a good thing after all. All he knew at the moment that she thought that he was mentally unstable and she didn't do one night stands.

He knew that he should say something, anything but there was nothing there. He wanted to convince her that he was not mental but he wanted to convince her of something else but he had no idea what. That he was the man for her. He shook his head at his thoughts. He never got involved, never cared. It was easier that way.

He turned and faced her as he paced. The words were there but they wouldn't come. He started pacing again. Fuck, what was wrong with him? He needed time away from her. Maybe then he could figure it all out. Maybe then he would be able to sort out all that he was feeling but he couldn't do it here. Not with her staring at him waiting for an answer. Not in his sister's house and certainly not with this mind a mess the way that it was.

His head snapped up when he heard Ross pulling up with her car. He had forgot that he had told him to come here first so that she could get her things for the car before it was towed back to his house.

He looked at the beauty before with her swollen lips and wanted to kiss her again. He was a man in pain and on the edge and he needed time but he couldn't get the words out so instead he turned and walked for the door. Air was what he needed and the sooner the better to his way of thinking.

Grace stood in the kitchen as she heard the door shut behind Cole. Since she had heard Ross pulling into the driveway with her car she figured that Cole had went outside. As she walked to the door she heard the tires peel out of driveway. Opening the door Grace stood there watching as Cole raced out of the driveway. Maybe this was for the best. They didn't know a thing about each other and already they seemed to be totally wrong for each other.

She sighed as she walked down the steps that led to the driveway. Maybe him leaving now was a good thing. It would give her time to think about everything that had just gone on. She hadn't even known herself back there. She never kissed strange men. She never opened up to them either but it was apparent that he was affecting her differently.

Even with Kurt it had been a few months before Grace had been able to open up to him and they had known each other for a while before she had. She didn't understand her own mind when she was around Cole. He made her want to scream in frustration when he would get quiet on her. He made her want to laugh when he was being charming and he had made her lose all of her common sense with one kiss.

Those types of things never happened for her. She had always been in control of her thoughts and feelings but with him that was different. Around Cole it seemed that she was saying everything that was in her mind without so much as a thought about it. She had laughed more than she had in the last month and she had also cried more than she had in a month.

If she was being fair it wasn't really Cole that had made her cry but she could feel the sting of tears in her eyes but she would not let them fall. That had been the second man that seemed to have run away from her when she had been like that. Kurt had been the first.

She remembered the first time that they had ever seriously kissed like that. Cole's reaction had been the same as Kurt's. Kurt had gotten agitated, then he had turned and walked away from her as well.

He had at least had tried to explain to her that it wasn't because of her that he had walked away. He had told her that he just wasn't ready for that type of relationship with her. That was the reason that he had walked away but Cole. He didn't say a word except fuck. She had heard that one plain as day and couldn't figure it out. He then stomped away from her and drove away as fast as he could.

She shook her head and stepped up to Ross, for tonight she would not think about it. Maybe after some dinner and a nice bath things would come more clearly, or at least she could hope.

Chapter 5

After eating her dinner in silence Grace thought about a bath. It was the only thing she could think of to get her head on straight. She took her cell phone with her so that she may call Tom if she could get any type of service.

If she was going to be here for a few days the least she would need is a rental car. It wouldn't be fair to ask Ross or Cole to drive her around. The only problem was she didn't know a thing about this town or what it had to offer.

As she ran the water she undressed and thanked god that she had at least two bars to call Tom. She had no clue what she was going to tell him but hearing his voice might help. As the line rang she prayed that he was not asleep or out for the evening. She needed a friend now or at the very least a friendly voice.

"Yeah kid, what is it now?" Tom said in a way of greeting.

"Hey I called but I need a favor also. You know that my car died and I'll need a rental. I don't know a thing about this town or where to find one. I was wondering…"

"Don't worry about it." Tom laughed cutting her off. "I'm all over it. I couldn't stand the thought of you out in the middle of the woods with no ride. I called the only car rental place in town and rented you a nice sturdy ride. I also took the liberty of looking up the town and its history on the internet. You will be happy to know that you are sitting in one of the most heavily trafficked tourist attractions around. Did you happen to see a bunch of water falls on your way in?"

"Yes I did. They are gorgeous Tom. I have never seen anything like them."

"And I doubt you ever will again. They are known as the Wildcat Falls. I don't know why they were named that but I found numerous pictures of the falls and you're right, they're beautiful. Also you are now in bear, and bob cat country. Maybe that's why they are named Wildcat Falls but I want you to be careful. From what I've seen of the pictures of the place most of it is woods. There are a few family homes but nothing like you are used to. These are the real woods where actual living things seemed to live there. Oh and I also found something else there, it took me by surprise because it's so backwoods but there is also a ballet school there. It is called Baker Ballet Company. Have you ever heard of it?"

Grace sucked in a breath. That was Cole's last name. Could the ballet school be owned by him? She shook her head. No he couldn't possibly own the ballet school. He had even admitted that he had fallen asleep at her ballet. Why would he open up a school?

"Grace are you there?" Tom asked.

"Yeah I'm still here. Listen I do know some Baker's here. Actually that's where I'm staying. Cole Baker is going to become the Sheriff here in a few days and he's the one that found me on the side of the road crying when my car broke down. I have heard of them and they are a really great school. I think a Miss. Honey is the instructor. She used to work for the American Ballet Company but quit before I started. I wonder if it's the same family."

"Good possibility considering they are the only Baker's in town."

"And just how did you know that?" Grace asked laughing.

"Well you know me, when I saw the name on the caller ID I had to make sure that you were alright so I got on the internet and traced the number back to a Ross Baker. I then goggled him and the rest of the family. Ah the miracles of modern technology. I found out about the whole family. The father was military along with the son Bret and the other one Cole. Cole has an extensive military record along with his brother. Bret is currently on active duty. I had someone pull some strings and look in some files. He is a good guy, a commander in fact and highly recommended. The other one Cole, well he had a record as well. It's long that's for sure and he was a lieutenant but had some issues with attitude it appears. It was locked up tight but he lost a rank because of it, whatever it was, and retired when his sister died. Her name was Victoria and she is the one that started the school. From what I have been able to piece together she was the one to start it but its Ross that keeps it going, at least his name appears on the deeds. I'll find out more if you want."

"How do you do that? And no I don't want to know anymore. I don't even know if I'm going to be staying here yet. I don't want to spy on people for god's sake."

"Listen it's not called spying. It's called personal information that's given on the internet for everyone to see but that is not the worst of it. The family is a good one from what I've been able to gather. They are all really close and respected in the community but Cole he's a loose cannon. He has been mentioned on Facebook quite a few times by different women and he's a lady's man. I don't know all the specifics but I want you to steer clear of him Grace. He's not like other men you have come up against. I want you to protect yourself from him because he's a heart breaker and I don't want to see you hurting anymore."

"I'm a big girl that can take care of herself Tom."

"Who are you trying to lie too Gracie? I was there when you came home remember. I was the one that you cried on when you found out the truth about Kurt. Do you really think that I want to go back through that again? I saw what he did to you and when I find him he's going to wish that I hadn't but men like Cole, they are different Gracie. They are used to taking what they want and turning away from it. Are you really ready to do that to yourself? To open yourself up to someone that could really end up hurting you. Trust me he's not the one for you."

"I never said that he was." Grace said sighing.

"You didn't have to Grace but I know you. You're the type of person that loves someone that is broken. You think that you can save them all. It's in your heart Grace but we both know that not all people want to be saved Grace and that sometimes you need to be saved yourself. You need to work on yourself and find the happiness in your life before you can even think about trying to save someone else."

Grace didn't like what was telling her but she knew that he was right. Right now she had enough problems on her own shoulders without having to worry about anyone else's right now. She needed to find the direction in her life and take care of herself for once. Cole Baker would just have to figure out his own problems without her.

"I get it Tom and thank you for everything. I understand what you are saying and I have every intention of working on me first. You know you are kind of creepy when you get all philosophical on me."

"Yeah well one of us has to be the grown up for now and I guess that is me for once. Hey Janet called and screamed at me for about an hour after you called her. She is really pissed and I think kind of worried. Lord knows the woman doesn't have a soft bone in her body when it comes to you but hand her something or I'm going to change my number. She's like a dog with a bone. She keeps questioning me. At least tell her the truth about Kurt. Maybe then she will understand a little and back off. The woman is giving me a headache and the Sarge isn't helping matters. He said and I quote "you tell Grace the next time she calls you that if I have to live with the bitching then by god so is she." I think that you're running out of time with them. Give them something more or they will be coming for you."

"Yeah all right. I will tomorrow, right now I'm trying to relax. It's so quiet here and I'm not used to it."

"I remember hating all the noise but when I used to travel to remote parts I found that I couldn't sleep without the noise. It helps if you put on the radio really low. Listen Janet is calling again and if I don't answer then it will give her a reason to come here. Take care of yourself kid and call me soon. I love you," and he disconnected the call.

Grace leaned back in the tub and thought about everything that had just been told to her. It really shouldn't surprise her that Cole was a heart breaker. How could the man not be? He was gorgeous and like Tom said it was remote here. It wasn't like there were a whole lot of options for women if the town was that small.

Shaking her head she sighed. It wasn't her business and besides, she had told him that if he couldn't handle her conditions then he was free to leave. He had only been too happy to take that option and she would not convince him otherwise.

Other than having to see him when she went to check on her car she would just avoid him. After all with having to settle in for at least a few days she would have more than enough to do then see him.

As she thought about everything she started to relax. Having a mission to complete would keep her thoughts busy long enough to keep her mind off him and the kiss that they had shared.

The more she thought about it the more the heat started to spread. Frustrated with herself she rose from the water only to have Cole standing there watching her. She gave a startled scream and reached for her bathrobe in time to watch the world go black.

Cole had cussed himself for coming back here but he couldn't leave her like that. He had just walked out on her and he was no coward. Running from women was something that he never really did until tonight.

When he had driven out of the driveway he knew that he was doing the wrong thing. What would it hurt to just go and talk to her? Tell her what he was really thinking. Maybe then she would turn away from him and he could get her out of his head.

As he drove he thought about everything that she had said. She had told him that she couldn't do issues. That was fine by him. He didn't need her to deal with his issues. He was dealing with them all by himself like he had always done but there was something else. Something that he had heard but not really listened for. She had told him that she had; had enough of men and their issues. He was never one to read between the lines but to him it had meant that she was single.

He didn't know why he didn't see the signs earlier. She had been flirting with him. She had even kissed him and he knew women like her. She would be one of those women that were loyal to fault. She would never knowingly hurt someone; it just wasn't in her nature.

He had seen enough proof of that when she had been with Emma. Dealing with a child that didn't talk was hard but he had watched her closely with Emma. When other people would talk to Emma they would always look to him as though to ask. What do I say to her since she won't answer me? But Grace hadn't. She had not looked away from Emma from the moment she had spotted her. It hadn't mattered to Grace that Emma hadn't said a word to her. Grace seemed to understand Emma with just a shake of her head at her and to him that had meant the world. Grace may not understand Emma and the pain that she had carried but she had known enough to not look away from her and make Emma feel uncomfortable.

That one little knowing sign had been the conformation that Grace was a caring person. Caring people didn't set out to hurt people on purpose and Grace would never hurt someone that she had tied herself to. This to him meant that she was single.

He didn't know why he had breathed easier when he had figured that all out. Cole had every intention of driving to the city tonight to take care of his lust but he couldn't bring himself to do it. There was something about Grace that made him want to turn taking a peek. There was something about her other than looks but right now he wanted to look at all of her.

Her long generous legs were every man's dream. He could picture them so clearly in his mind wrapping around him and pulling him toward her lust burning in her eyes. Erotic thoughts filled his mind and he found himself reacting to them. Normally he was a man that was much in control of himself. He didn't need to fantasize when there were so many willing, except her. It seemed that she would be the one that would resist him at every turn which only added to her mystery. What was it about her that drew him to her?

As he studied her he thought about the question. There was no doubt that she was a beautiful woman but he had seen other women that were just as beautiful if not more so. So why her? He thought maybe it was because he had found her broken and crying. He hated women's tears but hers had been gut wrenching, torn straight from her soul.

Her silky flame red hair was spread out behind her like a halo surrounding her head and he wanted to touch it. Lips the color of coral were parted and he wanted to taste them again. Disgusted with himself for looking at her in such a vulnerable position he wrapped her in a robe and stepped away from her.

around and try to talk it out and he found himself doing just that.

He had just made the U- turn back towards the house when he had seen Ross coming from her house. Judging by how long Ross had been there he could only assume that they had talked.

He stopped in the road to tell his brother that he would be home in time to put Emma to bed tonight.

"Well this will be a first. Usually you set off right after Em goes to bed. Not going tonight brother?" Ross asked shouting with laughter.

"Not tonight." He snapped out. "Tonight I need to make a quick trip to talk to Grace then I'll be staying home tonight. Maybe I can finally get through that manual I've been trying to read for the past two months."

"Nice to see you settling down finally." Ross said and smacking the side of truck.

"I'm not saying all of that. I don't even know if she's staying but I said something stupid and I need to go and apologize. I'll be home soon."

"And if you need to talk you know where to find me. Happy hunting little brother" and he set off before Cole could respond.

As he pulled into the driveway he wondered what he was going to tell her. It wasn't like he had many excuses for what he had just done. She had been right, since meeting her he had been acting strange. He had flirted with her. He had gotten agitated and he had even convinced himself that he needed to be nice again so that she would stay.

He wasn't acting at all like himself but more important was that she had been able to see it. Not many people were able to read Cole, something that he had always prided himself on. He didn't like to show people his emotions. That was all thanks to the military but she had. She had seen right through him and he didn't know what to make of that.

He knocked on the door and waited for her to answer but she never came. Maybe she went to bed he thought. He looked at his watch and saw that it was only 8:30. He shook his head. No she didn't go to bed this early. Did she?

He knocked louder and when no response came he started to get worried. Using his spare key he let himself in and listened for her. If she was sleeping he didn't want to wake her but as he walked up the stairs he could hear her voice. She was talking to someone.

He called out to her but she kept talking. He didn't want to startle her so he knocked on the bedroom door but he couldn't hear her talking anymore. Maybe she fell asleep. Knowing that it was a bad idea to walk into the bedroom after their last encounter he debated

with himself. He just wanted to make sure that s was alright. Then he would be able to leave in peace.

He pushed open the door and walked in to th bedroom. She wasn't in there but he wanted to make sure that she didn't fall asleep in the bathtub. As the dark thought ran through his mind he tapped lightly on the bathroom door.

Again there was no answer. He pushed it open in time to watch her rise from the tub completely naked. The sight before him would ruin him for other women that much was for sure. He had never seen someone as beautiful to him as she was.

She looked like a sea nymph rising from the water beaconing him to her. He couldn't seem to find words or a thought. Screaming in his mind that he should stop staring and turn around to give her privacy, he saw her eyes roll into the back of her head. She swayed for a minute and he lunged forward just in time to catch her before she hit her head off the sink.

Wrapping her in his embrace he walked back in the bedroom and laid her on the bed. That was the second time that she had fainted dead at his feet and he wondered what was wrong with her. He shook his head at his thoughts but remembered that she was not wearing anything.

As he watched her perfect skin rise and fall he knew that he should cover her but he couldn't help but

He ran his hands through his hair as she slept on. He couldn't leave her here like this but he didn't have the first clue what to do either. If she didn't wake up soon he would never make back in time to put Emma to bed.

Reaching for his phone he knew what he needed to do but he didn't want to hear his brother's mouth. He knew exactly what Ross would say when Cole would call him and tell him that he couldn't leave just yet. It would be an "I told you so" moment. While he was admitting to himself that he liked Grace he was not willing to admit that he was ready to settle down with any woman.

For now he had too many loose strings to deal with. He was going to be starting a job on Monday and he had Emma. Plus there was the fact that he had his issues to deal with, as Grace liked to put it, before he could take hers on too. He didn't know what Grace had been running from but she had been right when she said that starting something between them would be no good.

She was due to leave any day now and he would have to be here. She would move on and if he let her close enough she would wear him down. He knew that. It had already started. He cared about her thoughts and feelings already and if she stayed he knew that it would only get worse.

The best course of action would be to avoid her while she was here. Time and distance would be the thing that he would have to give her. Then she would be free to leave and he would be able to move on and focus on what he really wanted. This was for Emma to talk again.

As she started to stir he thought about everything that he had talked himself into. It was a good plan but looking into her emerald eyes he thought that decision just may be the death of him.

"What happened?" Grace asked sitting up slowly wrapping herself more securely in the robe.

"Well it seems that it was me that scared you this time. Sorry but I did knock. I didn't want to startle you but I wanted to make sure that you didn't fall asleep in the bathtub. I knocked on the outside door but you didn't answer. I used my key to let myself in and I could hear you talking then it went silent. I usually don't come in unannounced but as I said I was worried." He finished shrugging.

Grace shook her head trying to clear it. Why was she fainting all the time? That had never happened to her before and she couldn't understand why she would start now. It wasn't like her. She had never been sick a day in her life and now she was dropping all the time.

Whatever it had been seemed to have passed now. That left the question of why Cole was here to begin with. He had made it perfectly clear that he didn't want the same things that she wanted and she was not willing to bend to him. At least on the one night stand issue.

"What are you doing here Cole?" She asked standing.

"Well I just thought that I shouldn't have left it at that. I wanted to come back here and try and talk to you but well you know what happened. About earlier I am sorry. I really didn't mean to hurt your feelings with my comments and you're right starting something between us really isn't a good idea. I know that you are going to be here for a few days but from now on I think that it would be best if we go our separate ways. You were right when you said I have issues but I sense that you do too. I know that you aren't prepared to deal with mine and I'm sure not prepared to deal with yours. I have enough on my plate. I have a new job. I still need to get Emma settled into a routine and I have to be focused here. If you want to stay in town that's fine but I can't be who you need me to be and I just thought that I should be fair to you and tell you up front."

Grace sat back down on the bed. It wasn't like she didn't appreciate his honesty, in fact she could never remember anyone being that open and honest with her before and she found that she respected him for that.

He was actually trying to be a gentleman and tell her what he wanted and what he was willing to give. It was the first time that any man had been that honest with her and she liked him all the more for it.

"Alright, I just want to say that I appreciate your honesty Cole. I understand that we are attracted to each other but like you said we don't need to see each other. For the next few days while I'm here we will just avoid each other. Believe me when I say I don't want to interrupt your life here and I don't even know what I want to do with my life yet. You're right I can't deal with your issues because I've yet to deal with mine. It's not fair to either one of us but thank you for helping me. Lords knows I could use all the friends I can get now."

Cole replayed the conversation in his head. All the words sounded right but why was he feeling so miserable about it. He shook his head. It didn't matter what he had thought of it there was no other way. He cared about her already and he didn't want to hurt her anymore then she already was.

"Alright, then we will try and avoid each other. I don't know how possible that's going to be here since it's such a small town but we can try. I'm sorry that it has to be this way but it's the only way I can keep myself straight inside my mind. I wish you luck Grace."

"You too and just so you know you're one of the good ones Cole. Someday you are going to make some woman really happy because you are such a great dad. I can see the way that you care about Emma and she's going to be very lucky. Good bye Sheriff and have a good life." She said turning to go back into the bathroom.

Grace knew that if she said everything that she really wanted to say she would start to cry. It had been apparent to her that Cole was a good guy. He had open and honest with her about everything. He had not tried to hide one part of his life so far and she had to let him go. She needed to focus on her life and he needed to focus on his and Emma's.

Sitting on the rim of the tub she gave herself over to the tears that had been plaguing her since she had left Denver. It was finally time to come to terms with her own demons. As the door closed she gave herself over to the pain and let herself cry from the loss that she had been made to endure.

Chapter 6

Early the next morning after a long night of tears and no sleep Grace got up from the bed. Once the tears had started it was as though they wouldn't stop. Even though she didn't get any sleep last night Grace had felt much better in the morning. It was as though she could finally move forward with her life. Crying had helped get rid of the pain and now it was time to move on and it started with going to get her rental car.

Getting up and dressing in her running clothes, she decided that she would run to the car rental place. It wasn't like she couldn't use the exercise after last night's pig out. Pizza always had that effect on her. She loved it but it didn't like her in the least. Anytime that she would eat it, it seemed that it went straight to her ass.

She needed a car, and then it would be to the grocery store. She would need food if she was going to be here for a few days at least. When she had talked with Ross last night he had assured that he would do everything he could to fix the car fast. It wasn't like she had anywhere to go but she had decided that it couldn't be here.

While the town was beautiful it could not be the town for her. She would need to move on so that Cole could also. He had been right last night. They weren't made for each other. The attraction was there but he wasn't ready for commitment and she found that she was.

She had wanted to start a marriage and have children. At the age of twenty eight it was well past time that she finally met someone that she could settle down and start a life with. It didn't mean that she was willing to do one night stands but she was willing to date and see where it would lead.

Walking outside she got to see the house for the first time. It had been so dark last night that she could not see the house at all. Now looking at it in the morning sun did she realize just how beautiful it truly was.

The house was made completely out of wood. A large deck sat in front of the living room windows with patio furniture that seemed to go with the house. It too was made of wood complete with wooden swing.

There was something almost magical about the place. It was surrounded in woods and as Grace stood back to appreciate the house she heard it. It was small footsteps within the woods. There was a slight panting as well.

The hair on Grace's arms started to rise. Thinking that it was a bear or some other type of animal that she did not want to encounter she started back to the house not wanting to look behind her. A twig broke right behind her and as she started to build up a good scream, she heard a voice.

"It's only me."

The voice was whisper light but human. Grace turned to face Emma. She was dressed in tennis shoes and jeans. Her shirt was put on backwards and her hair didn't look to be brushed.

"Emma what are you doing here? Do your uncles know that you're here? And you talked." Grace stated bending to the little one.

"I've always been able to talk. I just haven't talked to them yet. Can we keep it a secret for now? I'm not ready to talk to them just yet. Please?"

"I won't tell but why. They have all been so worried about you Emma."

"Could we go and sit on the swing for a little while. I promise that I'll tell you but I miss my swing." She said pointing.

Grace debated with herself. She knew that the men would be worried sick about Emma and she wanted to hear what the little girl had to say for herself but she couldn't deny her the swing either.

"Alright, come on but just for a few minutes. Your uncles are probably worried sick about you by now."

"No they're all still in bed. I made sure before I left." Emma said shaking her head and Grace smiled at the girl's cunning.

"Come on jail bird. You can come up and sit for a little while and then I'll take you back home."

"What's a jail bird?" Emma asked giggling.

"Someone that was caged but broke free, just like you did this morning. Come and tell me some things about yourself Emma and I'll tell you about me."

Emma held out her tiny hand and Grace latched on. What would it be like to be Emma? She found herself wondering. This little one had seen so much and dealt with so much in such a short amount of time. Grace could only imagine and shuttered with the thought. She would never let Emma see the tears that threatened to spill just thinking about it.

Cole woke with a start. Something was off and he knew it. Looking at the clock it was only a little after seven in the morning. Had it only been two hours that he had been sleeping?

After his conversation with Grace last night Cole found that he couldn't sleep. He had thought about making the drive to town but he had found that he didn't have the heart too. The only thing he had wanted to do was go home and sleep it off. The problem was however that he couldn't sleep.

The look on Grace's face when she had been telling him good bye had haunted him. It was as though he couldn't get her out of his head. He knew that he was doing the rational thing but it was bugging him.

He found himself wondering if he wasn't making a mistake. He knew that they were wrong for each other. He knew that he wasn't ready to settle down yet but there was something else bothering him. For the first time in his life he wanted to be there for someone else other than family.

Being with his family was a responsibility, one that he gladly embraced but with Grace he wanted to be there for her. He wanted to hear her story. He wanted to help solve her problems and fix them. Hell he just wanted to be a part of her life and that was scarier than anything.

He had never found himself wanting to be a part of someone's life. Sharing a brief moment in time yes but actually staying was considered a commitment, one that he was not prepared to give.

Sighed at his thoughts as he got out of bed the feeling that something was wrong intensified. Reaching for the door he jerked it open and went running for Emma's room. As the door flung open his stomach dropped and his heart raced. She was not there. Where the hell was she?

Taking a calming breath before he totally lost it, he went in search for his brothers. Bret was gone and Ross was still sleeping. He had gone charging in screaming. Ross was the first to shoot up out of bed.

"What in the hell are you doing man? It's seven in the morning."

"She's not here. She's not here man. Where the hell is she?" Cole shouted looking around frantically.

"Where is who?" Ross asked shaking his head trying to clear his thoughts.

"Emma dumbass. Who else did you think I was talking about?" Cole snapped and Ross jumped up from the bed when the words started to register.

"Well where would she go? She couldn't have gotten far from here. She usually isn't up until eight and I didn't hear her door open like I normally do." Ross said pulling on pants in the process.

"Hell if I know. Bret is not in his room. Where the hell is he?" Cole asked pushing his hands through his hair in complete agitation.

"I sent him to Wolfeboro to get parts last night. He was staying there over night before heading back. Come on, I'll help you find her. She couldn't have gone all that far by now."

A million thoughts all went racing at once. What if she fell? What if she was to run into a wild animal? What if she was hurt? All the possibilities were swirling and none of them were good.

He needed to get a handle on himself if he was going to get through this. As he raced to get dressed he heard it. At first it was very faint but it started to grow louder and he was running before he could even put on his shirt.

As the door crashed open both brothers stood on the porch watching Emma and Grace holding hands walking up to them. They were both laughing and Emma had flowers in her hair. The first thing he wanted to do was shake Emma for running away. The second thing he wanted to do was hug her because he had never been so scared in his life.

Dealing with the enemy in Iraq had been nothing compared to the true terror he had felt when Emma had gone missing. Even though it had only been a brief moment in time, it was the most horrific he had ever experienced. If he lived another fifty years he didn't ever want to feel that again. Grace walked up onto the porch and smiled.

"Someone came and paid me a visit this morning. I figured that you all would be worried so I brought her back. She of course had to show me the way. Didn't you Emma?"

Emma nodded and looked at the ground. Grace motioned for Cole and Ross to hold a moment. She knew that they wanted to scream right now but she could feel Emma's fear. Emma had known that she had scared her uncle's. It was written all over their faces but Grace couldn't let them rant at her. She would need to give everyone a moment to calm down. Grace crouched down in front of Emma and whispered to her.

"You need to let them in honey. Sometimes we have to open ourselves up to feel the love. They love you Emma and always will. Learn to trust them just a little and you'll see that not everyone has to go away. I know the hurt that you are feeling. I know the pain that you've had to endure little one but only the love can heal you and guess what? They have the love you need to heal. Can you do that for me? Just give them something to hold onto Emma. Just give a little and see what you get in return. You know my story now it's time to let them hear yours little one. They need to understand so they can help you. You only have to look at them to see their love for you. Look up and see."

Emma raised her head with tears in her eyes. She seemed to study each uncle for a set amount of time before turning back to Grace willing her to understand.

"See it's there." Grace said smiling. "Just trust them honey. In life we all need someone and they can be it for you."

Cole didn't understand what was happening but as he looked at his niece he could see the change in her. Her eyes were teary which was tearing at his heart but he could see the light again. Grace was starting the healing and he didn't even understand how.

"I'm sorry that I worried all of you. I just needed to be with Grace for a while because she understands me. I'm sorry. Can you forgive me?" Emma asked in a whisper wringing her hands together.

Ross who was never known to show much emotion crouched down and opened his arms. Cole was too stunned to do anything but stare at Grace. She had looked beautiful and she had gotten his niece to talk to him. It had been so long since he had heard her voice he barely recognized it.

"Grace explained that now you're my daddy and that I needed to learn to trust you. Is that true Uncle Cole? Are you now my daddy?" Emma asked looking up at him.

Cole could only stand there looking into those brown eyes and nod. He didn't know what else to do. Emotions came flooding and his eyes started to tear. He couldn't wipe them away as he scooped up his daughter.

This tiny thing that had brought such light into his dark life would be his forever. It was a heavy burden that he wasn't sure about carrying but as long as she always looked at him like he wasn't the monster he thought he was, he would be whatever she needed. If Emma wanted to call him dad instead of uncle, than he would be more than happy to have that. Grace smiled and patted her back as she embraced her uncle.

"See Emma I told you. You just need to be a little open honey and they'll know what you need. If you would like to come and visit me again please make sure that your dad knows first. I think that you have frightened him more than enough this morning."

"Thanks Grace and I'm sorry that I frightened you again this morning as well. I thought you were going to scream again when you heard me." Emma said giggling.

"I thought you were a bear. I think I would have screamed down the forest if it had been."

Emma giggled and squired away from her uncle. She walked over to Grace and held open her arms. Grace smiled and hugged the little girl tight.

"You behave from now on. You got yourself a good thing here munchkin and keep practicing. It will get easier."

"Do you really have to go? Can you stay here?" Emma asked still nodding. Grace knew this question was coming. She just didn't know how to answer it.

"I'll be here for a while as I explained before but I need to deal with a few things myself. I haven't picked a place to live or what to do but for now I have to go. I need to straighten out my own life but who knows, one of these days you may see me again and it's not good bye yet. I still have to fix my car before I can go, so you see we still have a little time left before I leave."

"Then how about breakfast? I love my dad and uncles but they can't cook." She whispered loudly and Grace laughed as she looked up at a stunned Cole. He was not quite over his shook yet.

"I have to go but how about I cook for you, just this once. I can't see a growing girl go without breakfast but you have to help. That way your uncle and dad can get their bearings back together."

Emma nodded and smiled. She grabbed Grace's hand again and led her into the kitchen before Ross or Cole could move. She knew that she needed to give them time to get over their shock but she also needed to make sure that they would be good with Emma.

Grace had learned this morning that Emma was way beyond where she should be in years. She had been forced to grow up in such a short amount of time that it had aged her. She was far more perceptive then others her age. For such a short little thing she had such a maturity about her. It was in her air, in the way that she would talk and move. There was such grace there.

This morning on the swing Grace had opened herself up to the little one. She had told her of her life growing up and she had listened to Emma's life for herself. It was one thing to be told of a person's past but hearing from that person was so much better.

Emma had told her things that she was pretty sure no one else got to hear. It was the inner most thoughts and feelings of the eight year old mind. Emma was far beyond her years but so very lost in her life. She didn't understand why people always had to leave her.

Emma had explained her life to Grace. It started with her father leaving. Even though she had never met the man Emma felt as though it was her fault that her father had left. Maybe if she had been a better daughter then he would have stayed.

The problem was Grace didn't know her story or why the man had left. She had broached the topic very carefully. She explained that sometimes people didn't know how to stay. That sometimes they feel as though they are not right with being parents. That had been the easiest and the hardest thing of their conversation.

Once Emma had started everything had come out and like every child she seemed to switch topics often. She talked of her mother and grandmother. She had talked of her uncles and her dad. She had been the one to call him dad not Grace.

Grace she could already see that Cole was more than willing to take on the role but Emma needed to tell him what she wanted out of him. If she wanted her uncle to be her dad it was up to her to tell him so.

The two of them had talked for over a half an hour before Grace had called a halt to the conversation. She knew that the child needed to unburden herself but they also needed to get back. The men were bound to be worried sick about her.

Now standing in the kitchen making pancakes she could see the changes. They were small but they were there. Yesterday she had seen a broken and caged child with her feelings and pain. Today she saw the little bird starting to learn how to fly and Grace smiled. She had helped this little one. She had told her that she would need to open up and let people in and that not all the time were people bad. Great words if she could only follow her own advice.

This morning telling Emma these things had made Grace see that she was not doing that in her own life. She had been so closed off emotionally for so long now that she had never really opened up to anyone.

Yes she had given them glimpses of herself but never the true her and she was about to change that. It would have to start with her mother. For the first time in her life Grace wanted to tell her mother everything. What she really thought of dancing, everything about Kurt and about what she wanted for her own life. She was going to tell all and if her mother couldn't handle that then she would just have to be in the dark again.

Grace had been silent for far too long. While she loved dancing she was done being the ballerina. She wanted to be a teacher of dance. Like Miss. Honey. She wanted to find a school that could really use her and teach children like Emma how to dance and interrupt dance.

It would be the perfect solution for her. She knew the dancers life. A person could only dance on stage so long before they were done. It would either start with getting hurt or it would be age that would end it. She would rather give up the stage on her own terms and with her body still intact.

Feeling better about some of her decisions she turned her focus back to Emma. She was now smiling and stirring the batter. She was chatting away and Grace smiled at her.

"Wow now that you have started talking again you seem to have a lot to say."

"I haven't talked in three months. That's a lot of words I missed out on." Emma answered giggling.

"You're right about that. How about I finish up for you here and you go and wash up."

Emma jumped down from the chair after handing her the bowl and turned to Grace.

"Will you still be here when I get back?"

"Yes now go on. Wash up and I'll stay just until breakfast is served, then I have to go. I need a car." Emma nodded and smiled running off. Cole was coming into the kitchen and yelled out. "Slow down Em. You're going to trip."

He laughed shaking his head as he walked into the kitchen. Grace knew that her face was red. She really couldn't help it. Cole was still without a shirt and it looked as though he had no intention of putting one on. Well if he wasn't going to mind then neither would she.

Grace turned to the skillet and started to pour the batter. Cole walked up to her and she could swear that she could feel the heat coming from his body. Carefully flipping the pancakes she tried concentrating instead of looking at him and risk burning herself.

"Are you going to tell me what happened this morning, or are you going to stand there and ignore me?" He asked propping himself up against the counter next to her.

"I'm going to ignore you. That's what I'm choosing to do. Can't you just say thanks and you're the greatest and leave it at that?" She said looking up at him.

"Just when I think I know what is going inside of your head you say something to throw me. Alright for now I'll leave it alone and tell you thank you. Oh and you are the greatest. You gave me back my daughter." Cole sighed and ran his hands through his hair. He placed his hands against the counter and looked over at her. "Daughter, wow. I have to say I didn't see that one coming. I always thought that she would see me as just another uncle not a dad but I got to say I like it. I have to ask, was that her idea or yours? Last night you called me her dad and I just realized it now."

Grace grinned over at him and gave the pan a little flip. Setting it back down she faced him.

"First off it was hers and you know it. How could you think that you would step into the uncle role? You and your brothers are all she has left. You do everything for her and she understands that. She also understands that you care for her the same way her mother did. It only makes sense that she sees you as the father figure. Come on Cole I was there. I saw your face when she called you daddy and you loved every moment of it. You may not be ready for it but it's here. Now you get to be the big bad dad. Not such a bad role if you ask me because you have one hell of a great kid."

She turned back to the pancakes as Emma came rushing into the room. Emma stopped and looked at Cole frowning.

"Dad aren't you going to get dressed? You can't be half naked in front of Grace. She's a woman and you need a shirt." She said as she threw a shirt at him.

"You're something else kid. Come on, let's get you settled in with some pancakes and then I have got to run, literally. I have to be there by nine to pick up the car." Grace laughed and hugged Emma close.

Emma sat at the table and pilled the pancakes high on her plate. Grace motioned for Cole to join his daughter and filled his plate as well. She even yelled for Ross as she sat an extra place for him as well. When everyone was settled in Ross asked.

"Why don't you stay for breakfast and I can take you over to the rental place after?"

"Thanks but no I can't." Grace smiled and looped her ear piece around her ear. "I have to run. It seems that Tom has arranged for me to do a few things this morning and I have to go now. I like running, it helps me think and right now I need that. You all go on and eat. You have my number so just give me a call when you know anything and Emma." Grace was making her way out of the kitchen when the little girl looked up at her. "You behave yourself and mind your manners. Let someone know where you are going, after all we all have to answer to someone." She said looking at Cole. She winked and walked out. That was all she was going to give herself.

It wasn't like she knew the first thing about flirting anyway. Through Emma this morning she had learned all about Cole and the more she learned the more she liked him. She knew that a relationship was a big no, no but maybe he would be willing to teach her a few things.

She knew that she was not ready for a one night stand but maybe something else. She didn't have the first clue on what it would be but she knew that he would know. Besides what harm could it do if she was leaving and he didn't want anything serious anyway.

It could be a give and take kind of relationship. She could take his knowledge and apply it to future relationships and she would give him his daughter back a little at a time. Knowing that it was not right was not about to stop her. It wasn't like she would be using Emma as a tool to get to Cole but she needed someone to teach her. It could be a trade. She would teach him to be the father that he needed to be and he could teach her things that she did not know.

It was a good play but how to ask. As she set off down the road she thought about that. How to ask someone to show you the art of seduction without giving away her heart? She would just have to learn to open up a little like she had told Emma. She would have to tell Cole what she needed and see if he would be willing to take her up on her offer.

She would never lie to him. She would tell him her whole plan and see if he was willing. If he wasn't than she would need someone else to teach her because if she was being honest. She was starting to get restless. It was like a slow dull ache that would not go away and it only got worse when Cole was around. It was like an itch she couldn't seem to scratch and she wanted to learn. Praying that he did not laugh in her face she stuck the note in his truck handle before she started to run.

Chapter 7

After a very filling breakfast and a long talk with his daughter about not wondering off Cole decided that he would head into town to look over his new office. He had been a deputy on the Jackson police force but he had never really taken the time to look over his new office.

He had taken some time off after the election so that he could get settled into his new role. It had been days since he had been in the office and he was itching to get back into the routine of things.

There were so many things that he would need to learn about the job before he could assume the position but that meant spending time there. While he was itching to get back he also found that he wanted to stay home and hear Emma talk.

Since it was summer she would not be going to back to school for a while and he wanted to spend some time with her but duty called. As he reached the truck he found the note.

It read: *Dear Cole,*

There's something that I want your help with. If you don't want to I will understand but it would be better if I explain in person. Know up front that I don't like asking favors but I am going to ask this one.

Please meet me at the house at 6:oo if you are free. Love Grace.

Cole shook his head. He couldn't even imagine what the woman would want now but he smiled. If Grace was going to ask a favor than he was willing to bet anything that it was going to be a big one.

He had thought that he knew her. How wrong he had been. He didn't understand the first thing about this woman. When he had first met her he had thought that she was drunk or insane. When he had been able to see her face and figure he had thought that she would be elegant and quiet just like her build would suggest. When he had gotten to know her better she had been louder and more vocal then he had first thought and when she kissed him. My god she was built for passion.

She was a bundle of energy and light, of fire and a promise of mystery. She was everything that he had never found in any other woman. She was unique. Most women that he knew wore their emotions on their sleeves but not Grace. It seemed that she was constantly changing and just when you would think that you have a handle on her she would change again.

It was confusing that was for sure but damn entertaining to watch. As he slipped the note into his pocket he smiled. Yep it was going to be one hell of a favor and he couldn't wait to see what it would be about.

Reaching the office the first person to greet him was his partner Jeff. Jeff Gray had been his partner for the past three months. It was only by chance that he had been voted into office. The Sheriff that Cole had been working for had been ready to retire and so they had a town vote on who would be the next sheriff.

Usually with electing the Sheriff the elections would be held in November on the tickets but Sheriff Burns had been sick and had no choice but to retire early. His second in command hadn't wanted the job and it fell to a vote.

Cole had only been working on the force since he had arrived back in town but that didn't seem to stop everyone from writing him in on the ticket. Since he had only been serving on the force for under a year he had not been allowed to run for the office officially but the town voted otherwise.

He understood their reasoning he thought. They wanted him because he was retired military. Their family had been a part of Jackson as long as anyone could remember and his brother Ross had been willing to help anyone out that needed it.

Their family had tried to be good neighbors and support the town with the ballet school. It would be for the best if one of the Baker boys was watching out for it, or so he had heard but to him he just wanted something permanent. He liked the responsibility and he found that he had liked working for the old sheriff. Sure he was a pain in the ass most days but he had strict values that Cole always found admirable.

The sheriff's first rule had always been. You work all homicide cases yourself. Make sure that if there are important calls coming in, your face was the first they would see on the scene and last but not least. Make sure the people know you care but to Burns it didn't matter how small the case was, if the people demanded the sheriff then he was to go no questions asked. Cole could live with that. He didn't mind if he was ordered to every little thing because he knew everyone here anyway.

There were perks to small town life and also draw backs. It seemed that everyone else knew everyone else's business no matter how small. It was a blessing and a curse. If someone was getting mistreated everyone would know by night fall. If someone starting seeing someone else they would know by night fall. It was a constant rumor mill but Cole had never minded. Sometimes it seemed to help.

When word got out that Emma was not speaking the town had made it a point to help him. People would constantly come up to him and Emma in the street and talk to the little girl. They would hug her and tell her how big she was getting. They made her and him both feel loved and like they belonged.

“Hey man you here?” Jeff asked waving his hand in front of his face.

“Yeah just thinking. Why what’s up?”

“Can’t blame you. I got to meet the lovely Grace Summers that’s now staying at your sister’s house. Man you should have called me I would have helped you out.” Jeff said laughing.

“Helped with what exactly?” Cole asked confused.

“Grace told me that her car broke down. I don’t know the first thing about cars but for her I would be willing to learn. Man that woman is a piece of work. Nice as pie too. Everyone is starting to ask about her. What should I tell all of them?”

“What on earth are you talking about?” Cole asked still trying to figure out what was going on.

“You forget where you live. Everyone already knows where she’s staying. They’re all asking if she’s single, if she’s the same Grace Summers that’s the famous ballet dancer. How long she’s staying? Things like that; you know how it is here.” He said playfully tapping Cole on the arm.

Cole didn’t want people talking about Grace. While it was perfectly fine to assume things about him he didn’t want people assuming anything about her.

She was from California. What did she know about small town living?"

"Look tell them nothing," he said running his hands threw his hair in agitation. "I don't know if she's single because I haven't asked her. I do know that she was a ballet dancer but she didn't want to talk about it and I wasn't going to push. I don't know how long she'll be in town because her car is broke and she doesn't know how long it is going to take to fix. Ross is already working on it but who knows and for the rest of it they will just have to ask her if they want answers because I don't have any for them. Why would I? I saw a woman on the side of the road and offered to help her out. There is nothing more."

"Yeah I would believe that coming from anyone but you. That's alright I get it, I understand. She's a beautiful woman and a mystery. She's intriguing everyone but all I'm saying is, be prepared. Already this morning she has been asked out by three different people. I walked with her to the car rental place because she was getting hounded by everyone. You would think that they had never seen a beautiful woman before."

"And you did this out of the kindness of your heart?"

"Hell no," Jeff said snorting at the thought. "I asked her out myself but she turned me down.

Although she did say that if I were to ask another time if she was still here she would consider it. Didn't have a clue about that answer but I figured I'll give her a week. If she's still here then I'll ask again."

Cole wanted to slam his fist in his friends face. A week and he was going to ask again. What if she said yes? What if she was still here and decided to stay?

Last night he had convinced himself that she needed to stay so that she could help with Emma. Later that night he had convinced himself that she needed to go. Now standing here he didn't know what he wanted anymore. The little minx hadn't been in town five minutes and was already stirring up trouble. He wanted to go home and talk with her but he needed to be here and for the rest of the day he would need to focus.

"Well good luck. I can't seem to figure her out at all and I'm not sure if any person can. She seems to have a lot of issues going on at the moment but if she says yes why not?"

He wanted to mash his teeth. He knew that he was encouraging Jeff and he wanted to kick his own ass but he couldn't seem like he cared either way. Too much caring and people would see right through him, so instead he had encouraged him and discouraged him all in one punch. Let Jeff be confused about her, it wasn't like he understood her any better himself.

"Ah thanks I think." Jeff said looking confused.

"Come on," Cole laughed smacking him on the back. "We have work to do and not much time. Besides since Jacobs didn't want the job then I guess I'll be making you my new second in command. I need to talk to the sheriff and get his ok first but I don't see a problem with it."

"Alright, if you're sure that's what you want. I know that we have been partners for as long as you have been here but don't you think that you should let Jacobs keep his position?"

"Listen I like Jacobs," Cole looked around shaking his head. "Don't get me wrong but there is something about him that I don't trust. I've always learned to trust my gut and I'm following it now. He is a good guy but not the one I want watching my back. I want my partner as long as he's willing to put up with my shit."

"You know me, I'm always willing. How about after we finish up here for the day we go out and have a few? It's been a while since you and I have done that. I mean I understand that you have Emma now but Ross and Bret are home, couldn't they watch her for an hour?"

"As much as I would love too and we will soon I have something that I need to do tonight. Maybe after I am not sure, I'll let you know but if you don't hear from me by eight go on without me and I'll catch up with you another day. I promise."

"Yeah you keep saying that but you haven't been doing that. Man I need a date at least then I wouldn't get stood up all the time. I wonder what Shelly is doing tonight?"

"You are barking up the wrong tree there buddy, that's all I'm going to say." Cole laughed as he held up his hands.

"I forgot she was one among the many on your list. Tell me something; is there anyone here that's over the age of twenty that you haven't had?"

"Yeah all of them except Shelly. She was the only one from this town, now other towns like Wolfeboro not so much."

"You dog. Gesh man I need to catch up with you soon. I think you need to tell all and I can live vicariously through you. It's not like I can't find dates, that's not the problem at all. It's getting them to stay that is the problem. They all want the Baker boys and I find that I don't have the stamina that you do. Sorry pal not happening here."

"Well now, we can't all be me now can we? Besides Jeff you were built to be a one woman type of guy. I on the other hand haven't found that special someone. I'm sure that she's out there but it may take me some more time and energy before I find one." Cole said wiggling his eye brows.

Liar his mind was screaming. He had found her and he couldn't even bring himself to ask her to stay. What a liar he was but he was not going to let it get to him now. Later he could deal with Grace and his feelings but right now he had a job to do.

"Come on lover boy. Let's go and talk with the sheriff and then I can learn what I'm supposed to be doing here."

"You mean other than charming the pants off the women and looking pretty. I would say not much. You leave the police work to us and we can make you look better. Hum just like being partners again." Jeff said still laughing.

Cole laughed and punched him in the arm. Jeff was a great partner and the only one to drag him out the hell that his life had become. When Cole had come home it was Jeff that had been there when he needed someone to talk to.

If Cole felt like going out to get hammered for a night, Jeff was there to drive him home. And when he had been having problems with Emma Jeff had tried lending his hand. He had been a great friend and even better partner but he had better not touch Grace or it would be over. He sighed at his thoughts again and walked along with Jeff looking for the sheriff. The sooner that he got this day over with the sooner he could see the about the favor Grace was going to ask.

Pacing the floor for the tenth time Grace looked up at the clock. It was almost six and she was not even sure if Cole was going to come. What had she gotten herself into? It wasn't like she knew what she was going to say to the man. This whole plan didn't seem like such a good idea anymore but she needed to learn and he would be the best teacher.

While out and about today she had gotten to learn all about the Baker boys. Sitting in the local diner had been ruff. She wasn't used to all the attention she seemed to be getting here. She was used to California where it was not unusual to see a celebrity walking down the street.

There she had been a small fish in a big pond. Here not so much. Everyone was curious about her. Of course they had all been polite but it was kind of strange to her. At home no one seemed to know who she was or what she did.

When everyone here had learned who she was they had all flocked to her it seemed. This morning just running to the car rental company she had been stopped three times. All of them had been men and all of them had asked her on a date.

She had found that she wasn't used to it. Everyone in California seemed to want the pretty blond girls with the fake breasts. Here not so much. Everyone so was normal looking and beautiful in their own ways but Grace had stood out.

She should blame it on her hair. It was like a beacon that screamed look at me. She shook her head and laughed. This town was getting to her. She didn't understand how they had known that she was staying at the Baker house but they had. Most of them were nice with the questions though.

The same who are you? How long are you staying? Are you the famous ballet dancer? What are you doing here? And the famous, would you like to go out sometime?

Sitting in that diner she had learned all about small town life and the Baker boys from Doris. She was the owner of the town diner that didn't have a name. She had told Grace all about the family and how long they had lived here.

She even told her that the Baker boys couldn't seem to help themselves when it came to women. For some reason according Doris women seemed to flock to all them. Of course Doris was older and didn't see the Baker boys the way she and every other female seemed to.

Women both old and young alike had offered their opinions of the Baker boys. Everyone said how good they all looked. All of them had talked about their reputations but none of them had said that any of them had done a serious relationship and now standing here waiting for Cole to come did she wonder why.

He was a nice man. He was good looking and he was going to become a sheriff. Why didn't he do serious relationships? Every female it seemed was lined up waiting for the opportunity, so why not? Had they just not met the right woman, or was it because they liked all the different women. Someday she would have to ask but not tonight. Tonight she had other things on her mind.

As she heard the knock she knew that it was not her business. It was time to do this and get it over with. With a thousand butterflies she opened the door to a gorgeous Cole. The man simply couldn't help himself she thought.

He always seemed to look good even in the mornings with his hair completely tousled. As she thought about him this morning, shirtless and looking good her cheeks started to heat and the fire seemed to spread.

"Grace are you alright?" Cole asked.

Biting her lower lip so she wouldn't jump him she pulled the door open.

"Come on in. I didn't know if you had already eaten so I made a little something. You don't have to eat if you don't want to. This is not a date or anything like that. I just…"

"Are you that nervous about this favor?" Cole laughed interrupting her. "I've never seen you so rattled before. Come on and you can tell me about it." He said walking in.

Grace shut the door behind him and took a breath. She needed to get a hold of herself and she wasn't even sure if she could. Being around Cole had that effect on her. For some reason the man set her off kilter and made her ramble when she didn't want to. Grabbing the wine she looked at him.

"Would you like some?"

"Should I be scared that you're trying to get me drunk to ask this favor?" He asked raising his eye brows in surprise.

"Why you have nothing to worry about, it's not like you don't know what you're doing." She smiled pouring them wine.

Cole took the glass and sipped. He waited for Grace to sit before he started.

"Alright I'll bite. What is it that I know how to do so well?"

Grace bit her lip trying not to laugh. If he only knew how much hearing the words "I'll bite" affected her. Her cheeks grew warmer and it felt as though she was burning alive. If she didn't spit it out soon then there was no way that she was going to.

"Will you seduce me?" She rambled out.

Cole was watching Grace fidget. She was so adorable when she was irked about something. Watching her bite her lower lip was going to be the death of him. It made him think of really bad thoughts and he had already established that it would be a bad idea.

He knew that if he ever started to touch her he just may not stop. With that goal in mind he tried to relax but he liked her blush. It was so warm and red that it made her even sexier than she already was.

She was wearing a tight red tee-shirt and snug fitting jeans that screamed come and tear me off. He tried to concentrate on her words but he was looking at her lips. They were so full and lush that he wanted to reach across the table and take them.

The words "will you seduce me" finally registered in his mind and he spit his drink. He couldn't have heard her right, could he? He looked up at her. She was now looking down at the table and pulling on her napkin.

"It was a stupid thing for me to say. Just forget this night ever happened. Please?" She said as she got up from the table.

Cole jumped up and grabbed her arm pulling her back down into her chair. He walked back around the table and sat with a heavy thud.

"Would you please explain? I didn't say no Grace but I'm a little confused here. I thought we agreed no starting anything."

"But I don't want just anything," she said rushing out to answer. "I mean I want something but how to explain. Oh I got it. You're going to be my teacher. You'll instruct me in the ways of passion and I'll help you with Emma."

"A trade, is that right? I'm still wanting to know why me?"

"Well for a few reasons actually. I know that we said nothing more than friends and I'm still willing to let it be that way. I don't want a relationship with you but you need to understand something about me Cole. I didn't have time to learn about this stuff."

Of all the things that she could have said this was nothing something he was prepared to hear. He would have thought with all of her looks that she would be having a problem with all of them trying to touch her. As she talked he became more intrigued to listen. Another first for him he thought to himself.

"As you know I've had to travel a lot. In college I had a friend that had a one night stand. I saw the devastation that it brought to her life Cole. That's the reason I won't do one and I have no intention of changing my rules but I've always been curious. I never really got the chance to date much. I don't know the first thing about being sexy, or how to give myself to someone when that time comes. I want to know what I'm doing without actually having to do it."

"You mean to tell me that you're a virgin?" Cole asked holding up a hand. "Do I have this right and you want me to teach you about passion just not actually take your virginity?"

"I know that it's not the common notation these days but yes, I am a virgin. As I said before Cole I never dated much and I couldn't see myself giving that part of myself away to just anyone. I know that I don't want to wait until marriage but I don't want to lose it to the wrong person either. Oh I am making a muck of this. The point is I want to know what I'm going to be doing when the time comes without actually giving that part of myself to you. You do know how I would presume, no offense but I heard enough about your charms today to last a life time. I figured that you would know all about it and we are attracted to each other. I know that you make me feel things in body that no one else really has and after we can always stay friends, or if I leave then we won't have to worry about it. I know that it's a lot to ask but I am asking as a friend. I don't have anyone else to teach me and I want a husband and children. I don't understand how to be a girlfriend or be sexy. I don't know what men like and do like. I want to understand Cole. Please?"

Cole sat back in the chair and drained his wine. When he had come here tonight he would have thought that she was going to ask him to help her find a permanent place, or if he could go with her to buy her a new car. He was really not expecting this. This is so out of his league. Yes he knew how to seduce a woman but this was Grace and she was a virgin for god's sake. What did he know about seducing virgins?

He sighed to himself. Well if he was being honest a lot actually. He had his fair share of them but he found that he was unsure of how to proceed with this. Yes he was attracted to Grace. What man wouldn't be? But she was asking him to teach her how to be with another man and it wasn't going to be him.

Great just what he needed, to teach the one person that could destroy him how to destroy him but for someone else. He wanted to groan, to get up from the table and walk out the door but he couldn't do that to her.

As she had been explaining he had been watching her face. It was apparent that she was innocent while he was the experienced one. He could teach her things that she would never dream of but to what extent. She had told him that she would help him with Emma while he would teach her this. The only problem was he didn't know if he was going to be able to stop. That was the problem with Grace. She affected him differently than the others had. She was so light while he was so dark. She was the innocent and he hadn't been innocent since he had been fifteen.

"Alright Grace. I'll help you with this if you're sure that it's what you want. I'm agreeing to help you with this but I still would like to be your friend after, even if you do move away. You helped me get my daughter talking again and for that I can never repay you so count me in. Whatever you are willing to do we will figure out but I want your promise. If I do something that you are not comfortable with, or if I go to fast you'll tell me and along the way you'll let me in. I want to know you better Grace. I want to know the woman behind the mask and in exchange you'll help me with Emma and I'll let you in. For some reason I'm able to talk to you and that has never happened to me before. Deal?"

"And I want to add that during the time that you're teaching me please feel free to do whatever you normally do. I may not understand about all of this Cole but I do understand that you'll be seeing other people on the side. I just don't want you to think that you need to change because of me. I may not want details but I won't stop you from being you."

"All right, as long as you are willing to date as well, I wouldn't have it just one way Grace."

"I can try but like I said I may not be ready for that just yet. I'm one of those people who like to concentrate on one thing at a time Cole but I'll try." She shrugged, draining the rest of her wine in record time.

Cole reached out his hand. He knew he had just made the devils bargain but he got the best of it all. Grace was giving him a golden opportunity and he wouldn't pass it up. Even if he did feel like the world's biggest asshole as he shook her hand.

He would just have to remember this was a teaching thing and at the end she would be leaving, or giving herself to someone else. For the time being he would let things go where they were heading. He couldn't say no but wanted to kick and scream for saying yes. Iraq may not have killed him but Grace Summers and her innocence just might.

Chapter 8

After shaking Cole's hand Grace wondered what it was going to be like. She had heard enough talks and read enough books on the subject but actually experiencing was something different.

"Ah so when does this start?" Grace asked.

God she wanted to curl up and die when he raised that eye brow again. She sounded almost desperate to herself. She didn't want to rush him but she wanted to find out soon. The low dull ache that he had made her feel since the first day that she had met him wouldn't go away. And if he started it then by damn he was going to take care of it.

"Are you in that much of a rush?" Cole asked.

"I feel as though I just made a big decision in my life. For me I just want to start it as soon as possible." Grace shrugged trying to not as embarrassed as she felt.

"I understand that but for tonight we're not going to start. Tonight I want you to tell me something about yourself. Come on let's move into the living room and you can tell me something no one else knows and in return I'll do the same." Cole said getting up from the table.

He smiled at her. He knew exactly how he was going to handle this. It may have taken him a moment to sort it out in his mind but he had finally figured it out. He was going to teach her about passion alright but he was also going to date her. She just didn't know it.

Doing it this way was going to take the pressure off of him. He would go through all the motions of dating her and she would never have a clue. She didn't understand him yet. She didn't understand that things like commitment were hard for him. It wasn't like he didn't have women willing. He had plenty of them in fact. It was just hard to stay with them when all they wanted from him was the sex.

The women in Cole's life he found were shallow. He was great to look at, great in bed but they never let him close to them. In doing so they had all hardened him. He no longer looked for relationships and when one would get interested in him, he would be the one to break things off.

Doing this with Grace would be better. He could get as close as he wanted to her and she would think that they were still doing their deal, that way if he found he couldn't handle things with her then there would be no hard feelings.

It was the best of everything. He would learn about her. She would teach him to open up and handle his new role as father and he would get to teach her about passion. Being a military man he had been made to weigh the pros and cons for everything.

Before he had even agreed to Grace's request his mind had been racing with all the possibilities. He would get to see her date which could tell him how he was really feeling without getting to serious. Yes this was the best plan for everyone, even Grace herself.

She didn't even understand what she wanted in her own life yet. He could tell with little certain things that she would say. They would be able to be close to each other without trying to hurt each other. He would learn about commitment and she would learn about passion. If he couldn't handle just her then he always had her permission to go out and be with someone else.

They walked into the living room and he opened the doors to the balcony. When he had been helping to build this house for his sister, while he was on leave, he had always loved it. The design that she had come up with had been amazing and Cole found that when he retired he wanted a house just like this one.

In fact his brother Bret had the same plan. When you would walk on the path through the woods to his house from here there was another open clearing. That land was going to Bret's when he retired.

The whole family owned more than twenty acres of land here. They all decided a long time ago that they would always live very near each other. It was the way that they were raised. Sunday dinners had been a common thing in his house. Anytime he had been on leave he had been ordered to come home for dinner. In fact he had wanted to continue that tradition but after his mother died that had stopped.

They all had different lives and different things to do now. With the loss of Vikki it only seemed to get worse. Ross was at the garage constantly and since Cole had to work all night shifts because of Emma he was usually sleeping during the days. Now that too would change. As he thought of this another problem arose. What would he do with Emma during the days while he was at work?

He couldn't leave her at home alone. She was too young yet. She couldn't go with Ross out into the garage. Yes it was out on the property but she could hurt herself. He had asked Doris before Grace had come to town and she had suggested hiring a nanny.

That had been the plan but maybe he could ask Grace to take Emma. He was willing to do almost anything to make everything work but he hated the fact that Emma would be going to a person she didn't know.

Cole sat on the couch and ran his hands threw his hair. It wasn't fair to ask to do this when she had her own problems to deal with but he was going to ask anyway. Besides the worst thing she could say was no.

Grace saw the change coming over Cole. At first he had seemed almost amused by her request. Then he had been thinking something over and then he started to smile. She wondered what was going on inside that mind of his. It seemed as though it was always changing and thinking of something else.

She walked with him to the living room. He walked over to the doors and opened them. When he had first faced her he had been smiling. Now he seemed to be thinking of something different.

Now he seemed almost agitated with something again. Since meeting Cole she had come to understand him a little more clearly. Yes his moods always changed but that was because he had so many things on his mind. She sat on the couch and laughed.

"All right Cole what is it now? I know that your mind is somewhere else. Would you like to clue me in?"

"See already you are starting to understand me. Yes I was thinking of something else but it can wait."

"Oh no," she said shaking her head. "I want to hear this. What has your mind all worked up? If you are interested in mine, it's only right that I get to see inside yours as well."

Cole wanted to applaud her cunning. Already she was beginning to understand him better. It wasn't always one thing that went through his mind. In fact he found more and more his mind would circle five or six issues within minutes. It was like he couldn't concentrate on any one set thing.

"Stop trying to figure it out and just say it. Maybe if you get it out, it will all make sense and you can focus on one thing at a time."

"All right I'll try. I find that I need a sitter for Emma. I had asked Doris if she knew anyone and she suggested a nanny but I don't like the fact that Emma will be going to a stranger. She has had enough problems without her thinking that I'm dumping her off on someone. I can't send her with Ross all the time because he's in the garage most of the time and she could get hurt. I used to works nights so I could be with her during the days but my new position is all day light. I don't know why I didn't think of it before but I feel like I'm cheating her again. She just started talking and I have to work all the time."

"Well what about Bret? Couldn't he watch her for you during the day time?"

"Bret is only on leave for another few days. He goes back when I start the job. Damn I should have thought about this beforehand. Sorry I'll deal with it later; right now it's about you."

"Nice try, but if I didn't know any better I would think that you were going to ask me to take her during the days."

"Well you did say that you wanted to pay us for the house. How about another trade? You take care of Emma for me during the days and I don't charge you anything. How about it? Emma loves you and this way you can help her understand me and me understand her better. I would beg if it would help."

"I would love to help you out but what about me leaving. I haven't even figured out if this is the place for me yet. I need to get my own life in order. What about a job? I have to think of these things too you know." She said trying to frown at him but failing miserably.

"Fair enough, but how about this? You help me with Emma for the summer. That's three months. She will be going to back to school then and it wouldn't be such a big deal by then and you can work for the ballet school here. You did want to be a teacher at a school that could use you didn't you?"

"You were spying on me the night I was in the tub?" She asked trying to hide her shock.

"Maybe just a little bit. You can't blame me can you sweetheart. You were naked in the bathtub. I may be a lot of things but a man is one of them. Besides I waited until it got silent and then I really did start to worry about you being in there alone after you just fainted." Cole chuckled holding up his fingers pinching them together. Grace punched him lightly in the arm.

"You pig. I should have known. Men, what should I expect? Alright I will admit that I do want to become a teacher and I need a job but how am I going to do the job and take Emma everyday as well. Huh Mr. spy. I would really like to know how I'm supposed to do it all."

"You are amazing and besides you can teach at night. Miss. Honey just put out an ad for evening classes. They start at four and end at eight. You would fit the bill and besides if you needed to go in during the day Emma always wants to be at the studio anyway. You can do it all."

"Are you trying to butter me up?" She asked raising an eye brow.

"Yes and is it working?" He asked innocently.

"Yes damn it. I love Emma and I can't see her doing well with a stranger either. Fine I'll take her but what about my stuff. I wanted to find somewhere permanent and move my things. I can't leave them in California forever."

"Well who is this Tom person you keep talking about?" Cole asked.

"Why are you switching subjects?" She asked instead of answering.

"Because I am a multi-tasker, I find I like to work on a whole bunch of problems at once."

"Tom is my half-brother. He was born from my father's first marriage but we are closer than any real brother and sister. I love him dearly. Why do you ask?"

Cole's chest eased a little. He didn't know why the mysterious Tom was bugging him but he had been. Now that he knew the man was no threat he could breathe easier.

"Because I have another plan."

"The man with the plan. All right, what now?" She laughed.

"Just move here, at least for the summer. At the end if you decide that you want to move from here then I'll be more than willing to pay for the expenses. You can stay here move all your things in and teach me as I will teach you."

Grace considered it a moment. Live here in Jackson. In Cole's sisters home. It wasn't a bad idea but she didn't understand what she was going to do with all of Vikki's things.

"What about Vikki's things. I have my own house back in California Cole. What am I going to do with all of it?"

Cole considered the question a moment. He knew that he didn't want to get rid of sisters things but he couldn't ask Grace to give up hers either. She laughed cutting him off from his thoughts.

"All right Einstein I will handle this one. How about I sell the house and everything in it? Right now Tom and I are living together. I know a brother and sister living together but that was only because we both travel and it just seemed easier to do it that way. I'll have Tom pack up all of my stuff and ship it here and I'll just sell him my half of the house. I'm sure that you don't want to get rid of your sister's things and I know my furniture will not go with this house. Besides when I moved I was going to buy new things anyway. I like my California stuff but it's too modern for me. Tom picked it out while I was away. Does that solve all the problems so far?"

Cole wanted to kiss her. She didn't understand the burden she had just eased from his shoulders. Dealing with Emma was hard enough. Taking a job that was going to make him be away from her even more and now Grace was easing that burden. She really was a wonderful woman. He didn't know how to express it to her though. He cleared his throat.

"I want to thank you Grace, that was a lot to ask of you and you and I don't know each other that well but you did it anyway. Would you mind telling me why?"

"Well for a number of different reasons. I'll tell you something only Tom knows about me and then we are going to get into your life. Tom knows everything about me so there are no secrets there but what I'm about to tell you I have told no one. It's one the many issues on my list. About three months ago I was at the height of my career. I had it all. I had the perfect job that allowed me to travel extensively. I had the fiancé. I had the perfect life but I realized something then that I never really paid attention too before. There is no such thing as perfection. It can be perfect one moment and turn the next. My mother always pushed me into this life. I loved it for a time. I even loved it for the most part after college. I thought that I was bringing joy to people's lives for a moment in time and in a way I was. You see I love ballet but I love other types of dance as well. My mother thought that since I was so good at ballet that it was the one thing that I should stick with. In a way I suppose she was right. It's all I have ever known but I wanted a change, something for myself. I wanted a life, a normal one. One where I could see my fiancé other than meeting him once or twice a month for a brief few days while I was in that town. I wanted, I don't know, something different maybe but it wasn't meant to be until it all came crashing down around me."

She sucked in a breath. "It didn't even seem to happen a little a time. You know the ones that sneak up on you. Well mine just punched me in the face, hard. I was in Denver when it started. We were starting a new ballet and I was the headliner as usual. You have to understand in the dancing world its cut throat. There is always someone younger, better and more hungry then you are. I went to rehearsal that morning and met her. Her name was Jennifer Sides. She's smart, beautiful and very talented. Because I was a headliner for so long my company didn't want to not give me the position but she was better. Even I'm willing to admit that. Somewhere along the way I lost my drive, my passion for dancing and everyone knew it, even Jennifer. She told our boss that she would like the shot at the headliner position. I watched as she took my place on that stage and danced the way that I used to. I had a decision to make. I could be selfish and demand the role or take her position in the back. I watched her Cole. I saw me in her. I used to be young, eager, passionate, everything that she is now and I'm not. I couldn't mess up her dreams. I had those same dreams so long ago, so I told my boss to let her have it. I called my mother and told her of my decision. She didn't listen as usual. She told me that I was throwing the only years that I had left in me to a younger version of a talentless hack. What kind of person says that? I mean she is my mother. She should have listened to me when I was telling her but as usual she didn't. She never really listens to what I want with my life. She just always assumes that I am grounded Grace."

Grace smiled, "Well that's what she used to call me. I was grounded, set in a rigid routine with no way out. My mother pushed and pushed and my dad just went along with her. I think that I ran away to make a statement. I wanted her to see that I'm no longer grounded Grace. I wanted to be free. I want to be able to go out and make mistakes in my life, so I quit my job and ran. The problem is I am not a runner. I like having the routine. It's all I have ever known but now. Now I'm not sure what I really want. I know what I am good at. I know what I can do to make money but I had to get away to think and this place gives me that. It's so back woods that no one can reach me by cell phone. There is no number to call me on here so Janet can't reach me and then I get to help Emma too. So you see Cole it all works out. It gives me the time and distance I need. Plus it gives me a routine that I'm used to with Emma. That's the reason that I agreed so quickly."

Cole sat absorbing all that he could. Her story was an interesting as well but a fiancé. He never knew about a fiancé. He wondered what happened to him.

"What about the fiancé? What happened to him?" Cole asked.

"No way, now it's your turn. I told you enough for now. I will say that he's no longer in the picture but that is all for now. Now it's your turn to tell me something about yourself that no one else knows."

Cole nodded because for now he wouldn't push but he would find out. Why would a man ever give her up? What had happened between them? And how could she be a virgin with a fiancé? The questions are what he wanted answered but he had agreed to this. This is what he wanted. Now having to tell her he wondered what he really had gotten himself into.

Cole was a private person all that he had seen and felt in his life made him that way. He felt that if he were to open to someone it would only hurt again but he had promised. Now it was time to pay up. He would feed her a little at first like she had done with and see how she would react. Maybe if she didn't go running scared then he would open a little more and finally get it all out.

"All right, here it goes but if you go running scared don't say I didn't warn you sweetheart."

"I'm right here. I'm not going anywhere, at least for the summer. Come on I already know some things. Like the fact that you're Lieutenant Cole Baker. Tell me something more."

"You spied on me?" He asked looking at her stunned that she already knew.

"All is fair, now it's time to spill it. Tell me why you lost a rank. That's a story I would like to here."

"How did you find out about that?" He growled.

"I have my ways. Now come on. You can tell me. I promise I won't tell anyone." She said as she laid her head against his shoulder.

"Ok I will but this isn't pretty." He said as he wrapped an arm around her shoulders. "I wanted to be like my dad. I wanted to be a Marine so I enlisted at eighteen. I thought that I was big shit. I trained with him and made sure I knew what to expect but I didn't have a clue. Basic training sucked but after it was over I was shipped out to Iraq. The war had just started and there was chaos. It wasn't like it is now twelve years later. This was the very beginning and I was trying to work my way up through the ranks. We were ordered to set up a camp outside the city of Baba. It's a little town on the edge of the Zagros Mountains. It's also a heavily watched area because of the drugs that come out of it. My commander thought that they were moving heavy shipments of drugs out of the area trying to pay for their own weapons. I did as I was ordered and I was put into charge. About four months of constantly monitoring their movements we were ready to move in when we got word that they had an American hostage, a news reporter of some sort and three others including his translator. The United States has strict policies in place about hostage situations on foreign soil but we all understood the silent orders. Go and get them out but no one would give the order. You have to understand they may not deal with the terrorists with hostage situations but they'll make damn sure that someone handles it and that lucky someone was me. I tracked them to a little village not far from Baba. The prisoners were held in a clay looking house with bars on it. The only time they were allowed out was to use the bathroom and they were escorted by an armed guard. I watched for forty five days waiting to get my chance. One of the men had managed to escape but he had been so sick from malnutrition he didn't get very far. I had to stand by and watch as they stripped him bare and beat him with whips. They couldn't kill him since he would mean money for them but what they did to him was worse. The compound was so heavily guarded that there was no way to get to them without risking everyone in all the neighboring camps. It meant risking everyone's life if we screwed something up or went in to early but

I had seen enough. I didn't tell anyone where I was going because I didn't want to risk them."

He swallowed tightly remembering that night. "I went in alone. I didn't tell anyone, that way if I was caught it would be me that would be punished for it alone. I walked right into that camp and let them take me. It was the only way. I wasn't going to get past their guards and I knew it. I dressed as a commoner so they wouldn't know that I was military and walked right in as though I was a tourist that was lost in the mountains. I got down on my hands and knees and thanked them for helping me. I looked into my enemies eyes and thanked him Grace. The same people that I had watched kill the man beside me. The same people that took my best friend. The same people that beat a man because he had enough courage to run. I looked into their evil eyes and thanked him for finding me and do you know what I got?"

"No Cole what did you get?" Grace asked shaking her head with tears in her eyes.

"I got a god damn butt of a riffle smashed in my face. I still carry the scare of that gun right here above my eye." He said pointing. "I didn't even know these people and just because I was American I got hit. I also got beat from them so that I couldn't run and placed into the little house with the others. I thought that I was going to be a damn hero. What a crock.

When I was thrown in all the others ran to me but I was so badly beaten that I couldn't even stand. They ended up having to patch me up so that I could find a way to get them all out. I stayed in that prison for thirty days. Thirty days of watching and waiting for my opportunity. It came late one night while a guard was asleep. I was being walked to the bathroom when I flipped the tables on him. I got the one guard by himself and killed him. Gutted him with a knife that I had made out of the coils on the springs of the bed I was made to sleep on. I watched as I took another person's life. I watched the light die in his eyes and do you know what I felt?"

Grace shook her head crying. She couldn't answer him but she knew that he needed to tell it, so she did the only thing she could do, she let him continue.

"I didn't feel a damn thing. I didn't feel pity or remorse. I felt nothing. I couldn't even rationalize it. I thought that I would have felt something, anything. Anger for them taking me and beating me every day. Pity because I had taken my first life. Remorse for taking that life but there was nothing. It was as though my brain had shut down and there was no one. I couldn't see myself anymore but I couldn't see anything anymore. I was made to be a killer. I wasn't serving my country. I was killing people and calling it honor. Where was the honor? Where was the duty in that act? Where was I? They were soldiers just like we were. They were made to follow their orders just like we were. The only difference between them and us is if they don't carry out their orders to the letter they get killed. They didn't have a choice it was death either way for them but I was the one to take it." He asked breaking on a sob.

Grace had never dealt with this before but she knew that if she didn't do something or say something soon then he was going to break. She knew that he needed to get it out but not like this. Cole was a strong man and he would view this as a weakness and she would not let him do that to himself. He had made to endure more than even she could imagine and she would not fail him.

"Did you get them out?" She asked touching the side of his face.

"Yeah I got them all out." He said looking at her.

"I never doubted it for a minute." She said nodding her head and smiling.

Cole smiled and wiped at the tears. He knew what she was doing and he appreciated it. He was losing it and she was trying to make him smile and pull back from the pain for a moment.

"Yeah well I did and I got promoted to Lieutenant for my act."

She looked at him confused and asked, “Then how did you lose it again?”

“That is for another time. When you tell me about the lost fiancé, I will tell you that story. For now that’s enough.” He said placing a soft kiss on her forehead.

She nodded because she knew that it was what he needed. He needed to pull back from the pain for a minute, to regroup and pull himself back together. She had seen her dad do that often enough when she had been little.

Grace had never asked about the stories of her father but sometimes late at night she would hear him crying and praying. Her mother would come and put her arm around him. She would never say anything to him but she would comfort him. Maybe that was what Cole needed for her to do now.

She sat up and pulled him toward her and hugged him. She didn’t say anything but she didn’t need too. Cole stiffened for a moment and hugged her back. It was a moment that she would never forget as long as she lived.

Even if this was all she could give him then she was more than happy too because Cole was a good person. He just needed someone to unburden too and it seemed it was her that was going to be the lucky one.

Cole didn't understand what was happening to him. He never told anyone that story. Hell even his family had never known what happened to him over there and he here he sat spilling all of it to her. The question was why? Why could he open up to Grace and not anyone else? Was it because she was full of light and love while he was still filled the darkness of his past? Was it because he was so haunted by his actions that he needed to justify it to someone other than his brothers, or was it because she was just a stranger that didn't know him and wouldn't judge him?

After the thirty days he had spent in that prison his commander had told him to take some time off to get his head on straight. By that time he had already lost Brian and made to endure more than he should have. War was never pretty but there was so much all at once.

He had even earned a metal for that act but he could never find the act courageous. He had taken a life, an evil one but a life none the less.

He pulled back from her for a minute and looked into her eyes. There was not pity there but understanding instead. That was the emotion he had been hoping to see. He couldn't take the pity that he saw when he had been ordered to a psychologist. It was part of the healing his psychiatrist had told him but she had looked at him with pity in her eyes. With Grace that was different as well. There was no pity there, only the understanding and in that moment he broke. Cole Baker never broke down and cried but for the first time for as long as he could remember he did.

He pulled her close and cried like a baby for the first time in his life and she just held him. She didn't say anything. She just held him in her arms and let him get all the pain out. He tried to rein it in but there was no use. There was no holding it back any longer. If someone would tell him that men don't cry he dared them to see the things that he had and not cry. If it made him less of a man damned if he would care tonight.

For tonight only he would get it all out and then forget it ever happened. Tomorrow he would be better, he could only hope as he hugged the life out of her and slept peacefully for the first time in years.

Chapter 9

The next morning Cole was slow to wake to the sounds and smells around him. He had slept peacefully with no nightmares for the first time in his life. The darkness that had plagued his thoughts and dreams seemed to just drift away.

He cracked open an eye and could hear people talking softly in the background. The smell of fresh blueberry muffins taunted him and his stomach growled in protest. He didn't want to get up and face the people in his life after his big break down. What if Grace told them everything? Would they look at him differently now? Would they think that he was a monster? Did she think that he was a monster?

The sun was bright in the morning sky and he found himself squinting his eyes from the brightness of it. How long had it been since he had not woken up in a cold sweat of terror? Years at least he thought to himself.

Wanting to put the people off as long as possible, Cole stretched on the couch. He noticed that his head was on a pillow and his shoes had been removed and there was a blanket covering him and everything was staked in a neat pile in front of him on the floor.

He smiled thinking of Grace taking care of him last night. His head had been a mess but how long had she stayed with him? As he looked around he could hear Emma's bell voice in the background asking Grace how to make pancakes and he smiled.

When the male voices in the room hit him he tensed. He knew those voices and he wondered why his brothers were here. Knowing that he couldn't put it off any longer he slowly sat up trying to get his bearings.

"Daddy you're up. Grace called us last night and said that you were sick and she was going to take care of you. We came over this morning to make you breakfast. Are you feeling better daddy?" Emma said as she walked toward him.

"Yeah munchkin I am and what are we having for breakfast? I'm starved." He said running his hands over his face.

"Grace made just about everything. There are eggs, blueberry muffins and pancakes; there is also bacon and sausage. She said that if all the men were going to be here for breakfast then she would need to cook a lot to feed you all. Isn't that right Grace?" Emma asked looking back at Grace.

Cole looked over at Grace that was now standing beside the table where his brothers had already made themselves comfortable from the looks of things.

They were both seated with coffee and orange juice in front of them.

Bret was reading the morning paper and Ross was grinning at him like a fool. He shook his head at all of them and got up. From the couch Cole had not been able to Grace fully but when he stood he got the full picture.

She was dressed in black lounge pants and a tank top. Her mass of red curly hair was pulled up on her head in a sloppy bun and she was gorgeous. She was smiling at him slightly.

"Come on you two, you both need to eat and we have a big day ahead of us. If you both want to join us you need to hurry up."

"What are you talking about?" Cole asked looking at her completely confused.

She smiled as Emma sat at the table and began to pile things on her plate. Grace smiled while she walked around the kitchen.

"Well we all decided that since it's going to be a nice day out and Bret is going back soon that we should spend the last weekend before you start work, doing something fun outdoors. I love to fish and so does Bret. Don't you big guy? And he is sorely missing out, so we are going to go and get me a license to fish here and then we are going to spend the day lounging in the sun fishing."

Cole noticed that Bret put down the paper when Grace said his name and smiled at her. What was going on here? Did he wake up in some alternative universe? His brother Bret never smiled at anyone. In fact he couldn't remember the last time that he had seen his brother laugh or smile. He also couldn't remember the last time they had all spent the day fishing together either.

"Come on daddy, Grace said that she'll teach me how to catch frogs and other things. I want to go fishing. Grace even said that she would teach me how to bait my own hook. She said that I would have to touch the worms but she doesn't mind touching them and neither am I." Emma said pulling on Cole's hand bringing him to the table.

Cole looked down at his daughter and smiled. This was the first time that she had called him daddy without asking his permission first and it was a good change but he couldn't help but wonder why Grace was doing all of this. This was not a part of the agreement.

"Grace called us last night and told us that you were staying here, she also invited us all to breakfast this morning. Sorry to crash on you all but I haven't had good home cooked food in a while." Ross said smiling like an idiot.

"I hate to agree with the man but I wouldn't miss Grace's cooking for the world." Bret said as he looped an arm around her middle and pulled her down onto his lap. He even gave her a quick peck on the cheek before standing her up again.

Cole noticed that she was blushing again and his teeth ground together, seeing his brother touch Grace was not something that he was prepared to deal with this morning after last night.

"Thanks doll this is a great spread." Bret said winking at her.

"Behave yourself and thank you, it's not often I get to use the kitchen when it's just me." She then turned to Cole saying, "Well come on don't just stand there staring, sit down and eat. I made enough to feed an army of men. I figured with all of you here that I would need that amount."

"Can I talk to you for a moment?" Cole asked gently pulling on her arm.

Ross looked at Bret with his eyebrows raised and then turned his attention to his own meal.

"Yes, of course. How about the balcony?"

Cole nodded and followed her out. He didn't bother looking back at his brothers. They were acting to strange to tell him anything anyway. Once outside he breathed in the air there was something about the fresh morning air that always seemed to calm him.

This was the time of day that he was normally getting off of his shift and went for a run. It always seemed to take the stress away from that day.

"Just so you know I didn't tell them anything." Before he could say a word Grace started. "I told your brothers that you came here last night and fell asleep. I think that they think you and I…well you know what they think but I didn't want to tell them anything, on the other hand I didn't want them worried when you didn't come for Emma. I told them to tell her that you were sick and I was taking care of you. I am sorry but it was the only thing I could think of. Also I'm sorry if I pushed with the fishing thing. I know that you guys used to be close and I just thought that it would be a nice thing to do with Emma. You go back to work in a few days and aren't going to see her much so I thought a picnic would be nice. Just so you know up front she also asked if we could all have Sunday dinner together tomorrow. I told her that she would need to ask you because I don't want to over step any boundaries or anything but I couldn't say no to her. It seems it is a common affliction with your family I'm afraid and last but not least I haven't told them about me taking Emma for the summer. I thought that it should come from you." She finished taking a deep breath and blushing.

Cole chuckled, "and you thought what? That I would be mad about this?"

"Yes actually, I'm afraid I have never been in a relationship that is as unique as this one is. I don't know what is appropriate for me to do and not to do. I feel like I'm the one on unfamiliar territory. I don't want to push you or make any demands but could you tell me what I'm supposed to be doing. I get how to be the girlfriend I think, but I don't have a clue on this." She said as she gestured between them. "I'm afraid that I don't even know what this is. Could you please tell what I'm supposed to tell people when or if they ask and how I'm supposed to be acting because I have no clue."

"Alright sweetheart breathe, this is just two friends helping each other out. If someone asks you tell them that you're single, that was the agreement. If people start to ask, you're helping me with Emma and you and I are just friends and as for everything else you are doing fine Grace, there are no demands here. You just need to be yourself. It's not a bad thing from what I can tell. You care about people rather they want you to or not because it's in your nature. Everything else we can figure out along the way. How does that sound?" Cole said hugging her close.

"Good because this morning when everyone was questioning me I freaked. I just told them to come over for breakfast and we would talk about it. I didn't know what else to say to them. They were kind of worried when you didn't come home last night and I figured that it wasn't their business why you were really here. I didn't want to be rude but I just figured you could handle it from here. I mean telling them about me taking Emma for the summer."

"You are something else, and thanks by the way for taking care of me last night."

She looked up at him and he knew that he was going to kiss her if she didn't look away soon. Her big green eyes were sparkling in the sun. Just then Emma tapped on the glass.

"Come on dad. I want to eat and Uncle Bret said that we had to wait for you too."

Cole pulled back from her and took a step back. What was the matter with him? He didn't want to put any labels on what they were but he didn't want to stop touching her either. He needed to get his head on straight. He didn't have time to get fully involved right now.

"Come on we're being summoned."

She walked away from him as though their brief encounter meant nothing to her. He needed a moment to calm himself before his brothers caught the proof of his arousal for her. He had barely hugged the woman and he was as hard as a rock.

"You go on. I will be in, in just a minute. I need the air." He said waving her inside.

Grace nodded and tried not to race back to him. She knew that this was what she had asked for. There were no demands and she would not demand a thing from him. When he was ready he would tell her but she would not be the first to crack in this thing they had going on, it was bad enough last night that she had sounded so desperate. She had been the same way with Kurt and where had it gotten her, nowhere fast but with a broken heart and the cruel laughter from an evil man still ringing in her ears. She would never be desperate again. She would not beg or plead for him to touch her but when he pulled back she didn't want to say how affected she had been. She had pulled back still tingling from the brief touch and so the only thing she could do was walk away and back into the house as he had asked.

That was the bargain. That was the deal. There were going to be no demands from either of them and she would not break that. If he felt that he should then she would let him but she would not lead him to that. She had tried to demand and push with Kurt and it never worked so for now she would just have to be grounded Grace for a little while longer until he knew what he wanted for sure.

She knew exactly what she wanted from him. She wanted his heart but she knew that it would be a tall order. Cole Baker wasn't going to be one to give it away easily but she knew that when he did he would do it with everything in him.

In hearing his story last night she had gotten a better picture of the man that he truly was. He had been asked to sit by and watch while others were hurt. She also knew that it had broken something in him from seeing that. Cole would always be the man with the plan. That was the reason that his mind tried to do so many things at once. He was constantly thinking of everyone else and how to help them but he never worried about himself.

He had been made to endure true horror and pain and he had come out a better person for it. She never knew Cole before he went to war but the man that had come back had not been the same. She could tell just by the way that he would talk and act.

When he would look at Emma there was light in his eyes. When he was thinking too much that light faded and he grew solemn. It was as though he was trying to solve the world's problems all at one time. It was a heavy burden he carried all the time. He had Emma and his sister's death in one punch.

He had been made to go to war and endure. He had lost his mother and now he was trying to pick up the pieces of not only his life but of Emma's as well. The other brothers were there yes in a way but it was Cole that had been forced into the father role.

She couldn't even imagine half of what running through his mind any one given day but she would help where she could. It started with Emma. She would help him find the old Emma and help him in learning to deal with her. What would a man like Cole know about raising a little girl?

He knew about guns and killing but he didn't have the first clue on how to truly love. Yes he had the love of his family but it was a different type of love. Emma's love would be that of a child and a father and she knew that he knew nothing about it.

She snorted as she filled her plate. Really what did she know about that type of love? It wasn't like her own mother or father showed much of it but she was determined. She was not going to give up on him or make any demands on him. She would lead him a little and let him make his own way. She only prayed that he would come to his own conclusions and make the right choices.

"Did you ask daddy about tomorrow?" Emma asked pulling on her sleeve, breaking her thoughts.

"I mentioned it but you're the one that has to ask." She said smiling fondly at the little one.

"All right but I don't think that he is going to like it."

"Why not?" Ross asked Emma.

"Because it's hard for him. He remembers Sunday dinners like I do. Mommy and grandma used to be there but they aren't anymore and I know that it makes him sad." She said frowning. Grace was stunned that she was perceptive for one so young.

"Listen sometimes it takes a new tradition to get rid of the feelings of the old but it's not all bad. You get to have the memories of the old and add new ones on top of it. Maybe you and I can come up with something new to add to it that way you still remember the old fondly but it's something new different and maybe not so painful."

"I think that may work."

Ross and Bret were both smiling at her at her and she felt like being childish for a moment. She stuck out her tongue and grinned at them turning to her own food. Bret was staring at her and she couldn't take it anymore.

"What are you staring at?" She demanded as Cole walked in to join them.

"I love your smile and I was staring because I wanted to. Does that bother you Grace?" Bret asked chewing his food slowly.

"You confuse me." She said shaking her head.

"Same to you honey." He said laughing at her face.

She shook her head and lowered her eyes. She didn't know what it was about the silent brother that confused her. Last night after Cole had finally fallen asleep Grace had called the house to tell them that he wouldn't be coming home.

She had thought that Ross would pick up instead it was the oldest brother Bret that had answered. Since being here Grace had never talked to the older brother much. She told him the situation and he had immediately started to laugh.

She couldn't figure out why he would laugh, it wasn't like she had said anything funny. In fact she had been so nervous that she had been fairly tripping over her words. She asked what was so funny and Bret had replied. "My brother is a dumb ass."

When asked to elaborate he had simply said, "He fell asleep. "Hah" and he disconnected the call. She didn't understand what he had been talking about. In fact even now he was talking way more than he normally did and she couldn't seem to get a handle on this at all.

Ross was easy he was the funny, charming one. Cole was the dark brooding one but what was Bret. Bret was like a mystery. She didn't know a thing about the man other than he was in the military and a commander.

There was just something about all of them that drew women to them. All of them had the same dark hair and blue eyes but Cole's were the bluest of them all.

Ross and Bret's were beautiful as well but none could compare to Cole's. His was the bluest of blues even the clear sky would be in envy of them. Bret and Ross had a mix of blue, green and gray mixed. Bret's were the grayest of the two but he was more built then Cole.

She sighed again. Why did she care anyway? It wasn't like he was hitting on her. She needed a date and bad from the looks of things. She was starting to lose her own mind. She couldn't tell if Cole liked her or if she was just one among the many.

Now even Bret was acting different around her. She shook her head. Maybe going out on a date wouldn't be a bad thing, it's not like she couldn't use the practice. As she put the muffin into her mouth Bret cleared his throat.

"Grace?" Bret asked breaking her from the thoughts now running through her mind.

"Yeah Bret?" She asked taking a drink of orange juice.

"Would you like to go out with me tonight?"

Grace's cup crashed to the table with the orange juice going everywhere. She jumped up from the table and grabbed a towel while everyone was picking up plates from the table. As she was wiping everything she looked at him. Had she really heard him right? Had he just asked her out on a date?

She looked over at Cole that wore a perfect mask of indifference. What would he have to say about this? As she watched him he gave her nothing. What did it matter if she did go out with him? Like Cole had told her, they were making no demands on each other but this was his brother. She looked at Bret who was grinning like a fool, God she just wanted to smack the man.

"What did you say?" She asked still trying to figure out his game.

"I think that you heard me but I asked if you would like to go out with me tonight. I know that I'm not in town for long but I have some PTO time coming to me. I may decide to stay for the summer and who knows what could happen. I'd just like to get to know you better."

Cole was sitting across the table when Bret asked Grace out. He wanted to scream and rage but to what end. He had just told Grace that there were no demands here. He had just encouraged her to go out and date. He just didn't think that his brother would be the one asking.

Now sitting here hearing her fluster and ask what he had said did he realize that he didn't want anyone to touch her but that would mean that he would need to stake a claim and he wasn't willing to go that far just yet.

He watched as Grace faced him blushing. He could see the question in her eyes but he would not give it. He would let her decide what she wanted. Who was he to say who she could or could not date?

His brother on the other hand was a dead man later. He would make sure of that but he would not do this in front of Emma. Later after she went to bed would he make sure his brother knew not to touch Grace.

Grace looked to him again but he would not budge. It was up to her, if she wanted to date his brother then he was in no position to stop her. Fire licked his veins making him ball his fist beneath the table but he wouldn't let it show on his face. He worked to control his temper while he waited for her answer.

Grace didn't have the first clue on what was going on here. Cole was not saying a word; in fact it didn't even seem that he had heard the question. Ross on the other hand was looking back and forth between the two brothers as though something was about to happen. Emma was happily chewing away and nodding her head.

Grace sat heavily on the chair. What was she supposed to do here? It wasn't like Cole and her were an item or anything. It wasn't even like they had talked about a future beyond their deal.

Bret was waiting for an answer and she felt as though she was falling. Was it right to date one brother while secretly crushing on another? Oh she didn't have the damn answers and she was getting more worked up by the moment. Unfortunately in doing so she also blurted out the first thing in her mouth. "Sure why not."

Grace sat back. Had she really meant to say that? She ran over the conversation inside her head again just to make sure. She looked at Bret how was now grinning a wolfish smile and she shuttered in response. What was really going on here?

She looked over at Cole who was now eating. He didn't look at anyone he just kept shoveling more food into his mouth. Ross however was smiling like a fool again and she just wanted to throw something at him.

It was as though Ross had ring side seats to a fight. She looked between the two brothers again that were now silently frowning at each other. She got up from the table and walked outside. She needed a moment of fresh air to think straight.

She didn't understand what had just happened to her back there. She was pretty sure that she liked Cole so then why did she agree to go out with Bret? Maybe she really was starting to lose it she thought to herself.

As the door opened behind her she thought that maybe it was Cole coming out to check on her instead it was Bret. He was walking right toward her with a big smile on his face. He braced a hip against the railing beside her.

"I know that you like my brother." He said matter of factly. Grace faced him and waited for him to continue. Bret turned and looked at her saying, "I know that you like him and he likes you. I know that but he's a stupid proud man that will never admit it. I get why you agreed to this Grace. You don't understand the depth of your feelings for him and it's the same for him. He doesn't know how to open up to people because he never has. The only one that he did open up to was my sister and she's gone now. It wasn't only Emma that was scared by her passing, Cole was as well. He just doesn't understand but I do. I watched him this morning with you. I see the light coming back into his eyes for the first time in years and I miss that. I miss my brother that has been lost to me for so long now. Something in him broke over there and he has never recovered. He has been asked to take on too much for age and he has had to endure things I could never dream. I saw him this morning wake as though he had rested. I saw him wake with light in his eyes and I'll push him if that's what it takes. You can heal him just like you healed our Emma and I know that you can. He is just too stupid to know it but not me. I have had to do and see things like he has, not to the same degree mind you but I know what he feels. I know what is like to wake up each morning empty and hollow. I know the faces that haunt his dreams and I know why he doesn't open up to people but you changed that. Since the day that he drug you back with him I watched him. He woke with tears still in his eyes but the light was there. He opened up to you Grace and only you can heal him. Give me back my brother. Do this for me and I'll give you anything. Anything that you could ever want, just heal him again. I'm a proud man as well but I am begging you to heal him Grace. That's the reason that I asked you out. Don't get me wrong you're beautiful but you belong to him as he belongs to you but I wanted to push him. He will never come to terms with his feelings unless he feels as though he's being threatened and it has to be me because when he breaks again there is going to be no stopping him."

"I don't know if I can." Grace looked at him with tears in her eyes. "You must understand something Bret, it wasn't only him that has been broken. I too have a past and a bad one. I don't know if I can open myself up to that again."

"He is worth it I know that he is. Just don't give up on him because he needs you Grace just as you seem to need him." Bret said hugging her close. Grace pulled back tears streaming down her face. "It's not that easy. He knows some things Bret but not all. I don't know what to say about it. How do I make someone understand something that I didn't understand myself?"

"Then make me understand Grace. Tell me and I will help you if I can." Bret pulled her over to the swing and sat her on his lap.

"It's so shameful." She whispered.

Bret pulled up her chin, "Did you do something wrong?"

"I don't think but I don't know." She said trying to pull herself away.

"Come on Grace I just poured out my heart to you. Which by the way I make it a point never to do, now it's your turn to return the favor."

"Alright," she said sighing. "I had a fiancé. His name was Kurt and we dated for about two years before he proposed. He told me at first that he wouldn't sleep with me because he wanted to wait until marriage. At first I respected that but as the months wore on I couldn't help but wonder about it. What if I didn't like it? What if I couldn't...you know please him or something? Oh I don't know but I worried about entering a marriage without doing that part first. I tried to broach the subject with him a few times and he would get all moody and change the subject. One night I decided that I wouldn't take no for an answer. I got all dolled up and waited for him. I thought that it was him coming in the room but it was his friend David. He told me that Kurt was married and I wouldn't be able to entice him because his wife was more curvy then I was. I was mortified because I never even knew that he was married. Honest god I wanted to kill him, or at the very least call his wife and tell her but I couldn't. I'm just not made that way so instead I ran and have been running ever since. I am a virgin and I talked Cole into helping me explore that part of myself without giving that part of myself up. I told him that I don't do one night stands and I won't change that rule but I don't know what he wants. I thought that we had an agreement but he keeps changing the rules on me and I'm confused. I know that I like him but I don't know how to give myself to someone like that." She finished blushing playing with his shirt.

She didn't understand what had made her open up to Bret, it wasn't like she went around telling everyone this embarrassing tale but he had opened up to her first. He had been honest and truthful about what he wanted and she had appreciated that.

She knew the older brother didn't open up to people. She could tell by the way he would stumble over his explanation and give her worried glances. She had always been a firm believer that honesty was best policy and she found it only fair to do that with Bret.

Bret laughed a great booming laugh that almost made her fall off of his lap. He was laughing so hard that he had tears falling down his face and she wanted to crawl into a whole and die. She had just told him something private and he was laughing at her, just like David had done.

She tried to ease from his lap but he held her still until he could rein himself in. He wiped the back of his eyes and grinned. "What a dumbass, he had a beautiful woman waiting in his bed and he turned her away. Oh the man is gay alright."

"What do you mean?" Grace asked looking up at him.

"Come on Grace even you can't be that naïve. The man is gay. Can't you tell? I mean think about it for a minute, he has another man come and tell you that he's married. He won't sleep with you and you met him at the ballet and he didn't fall asleep. Think about this logically, I fall asleep at the ballet and Cole and Ross are the same way. Every straight man I know falls asleep and he doesn't. You practically throw yourself at him and he turns you down flat. He would have to be dead to turn you down, dead or really gay and trying to hide it."

"It's not funny it was embarrassing." Grace said punching him lightly in the arm.

"For who honey? Certainly not you for because you're a knockout Grace. Trust me the man was gay. I don't know him but I would lay money on it."

Grace thought about it for a moment and it kind of made sense in one way. Kurt was always a nice dresser, he constantly would tell her what shoes to wear with what outfit since she couldn't figure it out. He was always buying her makeup and he knew just what to buy. When they would meet up he would always want to go shopping and for manicures and pedicures. The man was a fem and she had never seen it.

As she went over everything inside her mind she started to relax, it was as though a great burden had been lifted from her shoulders and she started to laugh. She started to laugh so hard that she started to cry and as she started to cry she hugged Bret closer and cried all over him.

"So see Grace it wasn't you, it was him." He whispered patting her back.

She nodded but continued to cry. How could she have been so blind? She had been dating a gay man and the tears turn from tears of sadness to ones of amusement. She laughed so hard she doubled over from the pain of laughing so hard. She could finally breathe again and it felt so good. When she had finally reined herself in long enough she looked at Bret. “Thank you,” she said kissing him softly on the lips.

“You’re welcome, now you can let it go and help my brother. He needs you. Just take a look and see what I am talking about.”

Grace looked up and found Cole not far from the windows with a murderous look on his face. She swallowed tightly, “I don’t know Bret he doesn’t look to happy right now.”

“But he is mad at me,” he said grinning. “Right now that rage is directed at me. This is where I want it to be because I need to crack him. Are you in?”

Grace looked up at the pain in Cole’s eyes. Yes she was in because whether she wanted to admit it or not she was starting to love Cole Baker just a little and he should return that favor. She nodded, “I’m in, just tell me what to do.”

Chapter 10

Cole stood just inside the doorway ready to scream. He couldn't hear what Grace and his brother were talking about but he could see them clearly through the windows. When Grace had walked out he had been ready to get up to follow her when Bret motioned for them to sit.

He watched as his brother went outside and talking to Grace grinning like a fool the entire time. He watched as Bret had a really long conversation with Grace. Then he watched as he took Grace and settled her in on his lap.

He had thrown his napkin down on the table intent to go out there and see what the problem was but Ross stopped him. He shook his head at Cole and motioned over to Emma who was looking outside nervously.

He sat back down and called for Emma to eat. He didn't know what was going on outside but he was damned irritated by it. Even Emma kept looking outside as though she was nervous about something.

He didn't want to add to her distress so he had sat back down. As he sat he watched the food in front of him went untouched. It wasn't like he had an appetite now anyway. He watched Grace cry and then start to laugh. She was laughing so hard that she was doubled over. What were they talking about out there?

Bret was also laughing and wiping tears away from his eyes. Oh his brother was a dead man alright. He just didn't know it yet but he would soon, that is if he could finish concentrating on the meal.

Emma was asking him if he was feeling sick again. She even looked outside and asked. "Should I go and get Grace daddy? She knows how to take care of you. Are you feeling sick again?"

He knew that he would need to ease her but his mind was a mess again. How could she do this to him? How could she console him last night and be on his brother's lap in the morning? He shook his head as the thoughts ran darker.

Would she give herself to his brother? Would he be the first to take that sweet perfect body of hers? Would he be the one to make her scream with pleasure and beg for more?

He couldn't take it. He was like a caged man but Emma required an answer. He sucked in a breath and answered his daughter.

"I'm fine little one. Just give Grace and Uncle Bret a moment and they will be back. Go ahead and eat, I'm fine but my stomach is a little upset right now."

Ross snorted and Cole cut him a look that said. Don't even think about it. Ross held up his hands and went back to eating. Cole faced the windows again as Bret and Grace walked back in smiling at each other.

God why did his brother have to look so smug and why couldn't he stop touching Grace? Could he just leave her alone for a moment?

He pushed back the chair from the table and stalked out the front door. He couldn't sit here another minute. As he paced the driveway he cussed himself for being so stupid. Why couldn't he just tell her how he really felt about her? Why couldn't he just tell her that he didn't want her dating other people because he had no intention of doing it himself? Why couldn't he just be a man and come to terms with his feelings?

He paced and snorted. Because people like Cole Baker didn't know how to care. He was trained not to care. He was trained to bury that pain deep down and not let anyone see it. He was taught to mask his fears and his feelings.

The only person that had ever really understood him was Vikki. She had been one of the last bright spots in his life. She had been easy to talk to. She always made him better and she always had a kind word no matter what he told her.

She had been able to drag him out of the hell he had created for himself. She had been able to talk him down from the ledge that he felt he had been standing on and in return he had done the same for her.

He had called home anytime he could feel her pain. It was like a knife to his heart and he knew that she needed him. It was getting the same way with Grace. When she had been crying out on the balcony this morning he wanted to go to her. He wanted to comfort her just as she had done with him only last night.

These types of feelings didn't happen for him but he was drowning in them. He didn't know Grace. He didn't know what made her tick, or what made her laugh. He had only known her a few days but it had felt like a lifetime.

He looked forward to what she had to say. He looked forward to her smiles and now she was giving them to his brother. What in the hell was the matter with him? This is what he had agreed too. This was what the deal had been about.

He shook his head and kicked the dirt as the door opened. Grace stood there looking at him with a worried look on her face. God he just wanted to take her into his arms and kiss her but he wouldn't. He couldn't all because of his brother. When he looked at her all he could see was her in his brother's arms laughing.

"Are you alright Cole? Does it bother you that I'm going out with Bret tonight?" She asked.

He wanted to scream hell yes it bothers me, break the date or I am going to break my brother's neck but he couldn't do that. He had asked for this and he would not tell her what he was really feeling.

Instead he shook his head, "No why would it? I have a date tonight myself. I just needed to talk to Ross about baby-sitting tonight. Since Bret and I are both going to be out someone will have to watch Emma." He could swear he saw a hurt look on her face but it passed to quickly to tell.

"Do you want me to ask Ross to come out and talk with you? I'm sure that he wouldn't mind and I know that Bret and I aren't going to be all that late. I'm sure Bret could take over after our date."

He shook his head. He was being a bastard on purpose and he knew it but he couldn't stop it.

"Yeah ask Ross to come here for a moment. I need to make sure that he's going to be there because I won't be there tonight. I think that I'll be staying out all night again and I want to make sure that he's good with it before I go."

Grace wanted to cry. Couldn't he see how much he was hurting her? But she would not let him see. If he wanted to act like a jerk then it would be on him. She was done taking the blame for men and their stupid ideas.

"Of course," she smiled. "It's no problem. I need to go and get dressed for fishing. I'll tell him on the way back in. Are you sure that you're alright Cole? You seem a little different this morning."

Hell yes he was different. He had just poured out his heart and soul to her and she was going out with his brother instead of asking him. He wanted to grab her and shake her but he wouldn't. He couldn't so he dug himself deeper.

"Nope I'm fine. Hey maybe you should practice a little with Bret tonight. You know open up to him. I know he's good with women. Maybe he wouldn't mind teaching you some things that you'd be comfortable with."

Grace wanted to step back from that blow. He acted like she was some desperate virgin looking to throw herself on the next man available. How could she ever think that Cole was different? He was just like every other man on the planet. He only had sex on his mind.

"You know that's a great idea. You know while I'm at it, why don't I just place my virginity up on the internet for the highest bidder? You know I think that I read about someone else doing that so I won't be the only desperate virgin looking for a quick fix. That's a great idea I don't know why I didn't think of it sooner. You asshole," and she turned slamming the door behind her.

What the fuck was wrong with him? He hadn't meant to say that. Had he? He didn't know his own mind anymore. She was turning him upside down and inside out. The problem was he didn't know how to stop it. Ross came out a few moments later.

"Grace said that you wanted to talk me. What did you say to her? She was really upset when she came back in."

"I am a bastard. Just give me one good hit to my jaw. One quick blow right here," he said pointing to his jaw, "just to know that I'm still here and not dreaming that my world is turning upside down."

Ross looked at his brother's tortured face. He wanted to laugh but kept it contained. Cole was going down in a ball of flames for the fiery red head and he didn't have a damn clue. It was about time Ross thought to himself. High time indeed that his brother came back to the living.

Since Vikki's death Cole had been walking around in a fog. It was like he wasn't the same man anymore. Every time that he had come home from the war he had gotten a little more distant. a little harder to reach and Ross didn't know how to help. Now with Grace here that was changing. She was changing everyone around her without even realizing it.

She was making them closer. She was bringing back Emma a little at a time and Cole as well. She was stepping in and helping the only way she knew how. That was by loving all of them.

This morning when she had called to invite all of them to breakfast he knew that something was different with her. She seemed somehow cheerier then her normal self. Watching Cole this morning had been a change as well. There was light in his brother's eyes. There were also tears and he couldn't be more pleased.

He knew Bret's game. He would never hurt Cole with Grace and Ross knew it but apparently his younger brother did have a clue. He thought that Bret and Grace were really dating but he knew the truth. Bret was trying to bring Cole back just like he had been doing himself all these months. The only one that would be able to bring him back was Grace and they all knew it. Even Emma had asked him last night if her daddy and Grace were going to start dating.

It was apparent that Grace had won Emma over whole heartedly. Now it was time for Cole to admit the same. The problem was Cole was a proud man. He had been hardened. He didn't understand how to open up to anyone. It was in his nature to suppress that part of him but it was already starting from the looks of him.

Even now his brother was pacing and pulling out his hair. He was cussing under his breath and he wanted Ross to hit him. He smiled at his brothers back. He would never let him see the joy that he was feeling now because Cole would pull back. If he felt like he was being played it would be all over, for everyone and he would lose his brother forever. Losing his twin had been hard. Losing his niece for a brief time had been hard but losing Cole to the darkness would destroy them all.

Cole was the glue that held the family together. He was the one that knew everyone else enough to open them all up and make them a stronger family. He was the one that tied them together and always would be. His destruction would mean the destruction of the family and Ross couldn't allow that. He only prayed that Bret knew what he was doing because he was playing with fire.

The front door banged open and Bret filling it. Ross side stepped his brother. He knew that look. Bret was about to kill someone and he thought that it maybe Cole himself. He didn't understand what Cole had said to Grace but she had come in with tears in her eyes.

She had tried to hide it for Emma's sake but she was losing. She had squeaked out her request to Ross and told them that she needed a moment. Even Emma had called out to her but she had just told her that she would be right back.

He knew that Bret would go after Grace but Ross knew that Emma would be alone. He stepped back into the house and closed the door behind him. He knew that they would need a few moments alone and he was more than willing to give it to them.

He may not understand what his brothers had went through with the war but he did understand enough to stay out the way when they were pissed. Right now Bret and Cole both looked pissed off enough to kill each other. He only prayed that Emma wouldn't see because she would never understand and there was no way to explain it.

Crossing his fingers that neither one of them broke anything he motioned for Emma to come and join him on the couch. He flipped the television on and turned it up. Maybe she wouldn't hear the screaming that was about to start.

Bret knew that he was going to have to hurt his brother. While he didn't relish the idea he was warming to it considerably. Since Grace had walked back into the house he had known that Cole had gone and said something stupid again. The problem was he couldn't let Cole know his plans or he would lash out. In hiding his plan from his brother he was also opening up Grace to a world of hurt until Cole could figure it all out.

He just didn't understand that Bret was done watching his brother die right in front of him. Oh he hid it quite well lately, especially from Emma but Bret could see it. The light had died and Cole was drifting through his life. He wasn't living it and he was damn tired of not being able to reach out to his brother like he used to.

Cole used to be the fun one. He was always one for a good time and trouble. Now all he was good for was taking care of others. He never considered his wants or needs. Yes he had women but they were a release. They would never be able to bring him joy or laughter the way only Grace could.

In the few days that she had been here Bret could see the change. Cole was acting like a caged animal now but that would change. Soon he would break and when he did Bret would have his old brother back. That was if he didn't kill him first.

When Grace had come in crying he knew that Cole was being mean again. She refused to tell him what Cole had said but he could only guess. He knew that Grace was a tough one. From what he had been able to find out about her life he knew that she was tough.

She had been forced into a private dance school by the age of ten. He may not know about dancers but he damn sure knew about the training. He knew about the schedules and special diets. He knew the routine and the toll that it could take on someone both mentally and physically and she had done it.

She had then attended Julliard and that was one of the hardest dancing schools around. He knew that she was required to be perfect. She had been required to have training and discipline, just like Cole. She had been made to not have a life or freedom like Cole. The two couldn't be more suited for each other but there was one difference between them.

Grace hadn't been beaten down by it. She was light and love and Cole was full of hate and darkness. They just didn't understand that they needed each other in different ways. Cole needed her to open him up and heal the damage done inside and she needed him to show her how to love and be loved.

While listening to her this morning he knew it. Grace had never been loved. She had never had someone that loved her just for her. She had people love her for what she could give them but never for herself. She needed to be healed in a different way and Cole would be the only one to do it. That was if his stubborn-to-the-bone brother didn't fuck it up first.

"What did you say to her?" Bret roared.

"Nothing that concerns you." He spat.

Bret wanted to smile but kept it contained. His brother was itching for a fight and he just may be accommodating.

"I mean it Cole. What did you say to her? She was crying for god sake's."

"You two are so buddy, buddy. Why not go and ask her?"

"I did and she wouldn't tell me. She is protecting you. God knows why but she is. Now I want to know what you said to her Cole."

"Nothing that didn't need to be said," he said shrugging.

"Is this because I asked her out?" Bret asked slowly advancing down the steps. "Is that the reason you are trying to hurt her? Because you think that she's betraying you with me? You are the one that told her to date other people Cole. You can't have your cake and eat it too."

"She told you about that?"

"Of course. We are going out tonight and she felt that it was only fair to me to tell me everything."

Cole ran his hands through his hair. So now his brother knew everything. Now he was more curious about the conversation that they had. He wanted to know it all. He wanted to know why Grace had opened up to his brother. He wanted to know why she had been crying and he wanted to know why she didn't come to him instead.

"What did she tell you?"

"Everything," he said shrugging. "She told me about the agreement. She even told me about the fiancé. Stupid man if I do say so myself. Why do you ask?"

Cole couldn't keep it contained any longer. She had told him about the fiancé that he had specifically asked about. She had told his brother but she hadn't told him. The question was why but right now he wouldn't ask it. Right now the only thing he saw was the red.

Cole walked right up to his brother and fisted him in the face, hard. He had never hit his brother before and it caught him off guard when Bret grabbed him around the middle and hauled him down to the ground in a cloud of dust.

From there everything got worse. He could remember being hit and hitting back but it was as though someone else was in his body. He couldn't remember kicking his brother in the knee or the pop that had come from it but he did remember the scream.

If he lived another fifty years he would never forget the scream that tore from his brother's chest. He didn't just scream he roared and came head first right for him. Cole didn't even try to block the blows anymore.

He had simply lost his mind in a matter of days. Grace had changed everything. She had given Emma back to him. She had made him crazy and now he was fighting with his brother because of her.

Cole let Bret get it out and gave a couple of quick jabs but he was done fighting with everyone. He was captured by her and he couldn't understand how or why it had happened so fast.

Grace looked out the window when the scream came. It made chills race up and down her spine and her feet flew once she knew where it was coming from. Before she could even make the door she heard it. It was a familiar voice and she didn't understand why she would be hearing it here. She stopped right at the door with her hand still on the knob praying that she was wrong.

She turned it to face the man that she didn't really want to see hauling a screaming Bret off of his brother. The other man picking Cole up made her heart race and she stumbled out the door wondering what they were doing here.

"Gracelyn Marie Summers I would venture to guess that you have something to do with this young lady." The stern voice said.

Grace cringed at the anger and mild amusement in that voice. She knew that voice. She had heard for as long as she could remember and when she looked up into the familiar eyes of her father she wanted to weep. Why couldn't he be like normal father's and butt out of her life? Instead John "Sarge" Summers was the most devoted father a girl didn't want.

Most times he was embarrassing and thoroughly frustrating but he was her father. She next looked at her brother that now was a dead man. He had that stupid lopsided grin on his face that said, I know that you are going to kick my ass but just try. She knew that grin and she was going to wipe it off of his face but first she needed to distract her father for a moment.

"Daddy," she said as she ran for him.

As he usually did when she ran for him he opened his arms dropping Bret to the ground in the process.

"Hey pumpkin, why have you been hiding from us young lady?"

"Dad when you say us. Do you mean you and Tommy?" Grace asked swallowing hard.

"Not a chance pumpkin." He laughed a great booming laugh. "Your mother made me track you. She has been bitching at me ever since you left and I couldn't put up with it for another moment but I did you give you the advantage. I left her back at the hotel first so that I could come and assess the situation."

"There is no situation dad." Grace said rolling her eyes.

"Could have fooled me kid," he said grinning back. "Look here, you got two men and military men to boot fighting over you in the driveway. You run off after you find out Mr. Patsy Ass is a jerk and I haven't heard from you in well over two weeks. I'm willing to protect you girl but you're asking me too much when you disappear on her without a trace and no explanation." Grace looked at Tommy that was now helping Bret to stand again. "This was all you wasn't it? You had better run Tommy because you are a dead man. I can't believe you lead them here. Are you insane? I can't put up with her now. How could you do this to me?"

"Now don't you go blaming your brother. He didn't tell me anything but I thought I had been damn specific when I said no credit cards Grace. You used your card to rent a car. You didn't think that I of all people would be able to track it."

"But dad I didn't use the credit card." Her sight cut to Tommy, "You, you used my credit card. You used it because you knew that he would be looking for me." Tommy took a nervous step back when Grace approached him.

"Grace now let me explain. It wasn't easy for me either. Janet kept blowing up my phone and dad wasn't helping either. You know how she gets. In all fairness I told you what would happen if you didn't call her and you didn't, so you can't blame me totally."

Cole was watching the mysterious Tommy who was rather large for a man step back from Grace as though she was a threat. He could see the murderous look in her eye but this was Grace. She was one hundred pounds soaking wet maybe and he was acting like he was scared of her. Cole snorted and Tommy cut him a look.

"If I were you I wouldn't think that you know everything. You maybe military trained but guess what, so is my sister and when she's pissed she gets mean. Come on man help me out here before she kills me. I covered your ass enough."

Cole shook his head. He couldn't figure out what the man was talking about. He had never met him before but he had other things on his mind. He knew the man standing in front of him and he was wondering how he couldn't have guessed it before.

John Summers, Cole's personal drill instructor from hell was her father. He would have never in a million years dreamed that they could be related but it made sense now. Watching father and daughter together had been proof enough for him.

Grace was tall and built of a slender frame, just like her father. The emerald greens eyes were also his. Although he would say that Sergeant Summers were darker. He even still had the flame red hair that he had learned to hate.

The man had made his life hell during basic training and now he was standing before him studying him with those piercing eyes like he had all those years ago. He had learned to channel the anger he felt for John Summers and put it to better use. Like getting through training. The man was a nightmare and a mean son of bitch when riled. Another family trait it seemed.

Cole watched as Grace walked slowly toward her brother. Sarge stepped in front of her saying, "Let me straighten this man's knee before you kill your brother. I'm sure that he doesn't want to be dropped again."

Grace shook her head and stepped forward again causing Tommy to take another step back with Bret going with him. Bret winched and Grace stopped. She nodded once and John stepped up to Bret.

"Let me have a look son." He urged.

Bret didn't argue because really he couldn't figure out anything at the moment. One moment he had been fighting his brother and getting his knee blown and in the next moment there were other men. Military men from the looks of things picking him up off the ground.

He watched Cole as the men approached. He knew on instinct that his brother knew the older of the two men but couldn't understand how. For now the man was probing his knee and Bret wondered if he was going to be able to go back.

A jammed or blown mean meant early retirement. Maybe not such a bad thing after all. He had been in too long now. It was going on eighteen years and he was about done with all of it anyway. He really could retire anytime he had felt like it but there was nothing for him here.

Ross had his garage and Cole was a sheriff. If he retired he wondered what he might do with his life. The military was all he had ever known. It was what he was good at. What would happen to him when it was all over? Would he be the same man? What would he do with all that free time? Would he miss the military life?"

Hell he didn't have answers but then again he hadn't been asking them until now. Why was now so different that he would even think about retiring? He loved his job most days and screamed for mercy the others. It was always changing and he never did the same thing twice. It was nice considering he tended to get bored easily. As he thought he felt the snap of his knee getting put back into place and he sucked in a breath. He really hadn't been expecting that. The man that had been holding him up stepped away from him and he tested it.

He bent it a few times just to make sure that it was working right. It wasn't like he had never had his knee give out before. He had just never had his brother on the giving side. He looked at Cole that was now watching Grace with a smile on his face. What could the bastard be staring at now? He thought as he too looked at the man beside him back away and Grace stepped forward.

Bret had seen that look on enough men's faces to know that something bad was about to happen. He couldn't figure out why the man was backing slowly away from her but her eyes. He knew that look and she was not happy right now. He wondered what she really was capable of herself. He had heard Tommy tell his brother that Grace was military trained and couldn't figure out how.

As he watched her movements he knew that the man hadn't been lying. It was in the way that she was walking toward him. They were slow exact steps meant to put the fear of god into the person that she was stepping to. If his face was any indicator then this

Tommy really was in fear and lots of it. He smiled in anticipation.

Chapter 11

Tom Summers knew he was a dead man the moment his sister caught sight of their father. It was right there in her eyes but he also knew that he had done it for her own good. Grace had been running for too long now. She just didn't understand that she needed to get rid of the poison of the past and let it go so that she could move on.

She may not understand it but he did. He knew his sister better than anyone. She was scared of nothing or no one. She was as tuff as steel but she had been acting like an injured pup ever since that asshole broke her heart.

Tom was willing to admit that she would need time and distance but she had enough. And he had enough of his father and Janet constantly questioning him. He wanted his old sister back. The one that would rant and rave when she wasn't getting her way. He wanted to hear her laughter again. Hell he just wanted to see the light come back into her eyes.

Grace was a loving caring person. She would give you the shirt off her back if she thought that it would help but there was the other side of her as well. She didn't show it often and certainly not to the men in her life.

He knew that Kurt had never known the real Grace. If she had shown him, he would have been running for the hills a long time ago. Grace was deadly when she was riled. Oh she never showed it. She never even admitted that she had the skills but it was there, like a constant low bubbling stew just waiting to spill everywhere and right now it was directed at him.

He had trained with Grace enough to know what her true talents were. She was made to be military but she never got the chance. Instead she had been forced into a life that was chalk full of discipline, just not the kind that she had wanted, or needed.

Grace needed someone strong. Someone that she could spar with and he wouldn't fall apart. She needed someone like Cole Baker. The first night that she had called him he had done his homework on the family. He told Grace everything, almost. He told her of the family and a little about Cole but he hadn't told her everything. The man was a certified war hero. He had a congressional medal of honor for his tour in Iraq. He was a lieutenant and he was a good man.

Tom had done his research on him and he couldn't have picked better for her himself. He had secretly thanked god that Cole had been the one to find her on the side of that road that day. He wondered if god didn't have a hand in it. They were made for each other. Sure Cole had issues. What man didn't? But he could also heal his sister, something that Tom had been trying to do for years now.

Grace had been made to endure a hard life. She had been trained by their father just like he was but unlike Tom she had been made to be a dancer. Grace had always wanted to go to the military like the rest of the family but Tom's step mother Janet had put her foot down. There was no way her daughter was going to be career military like her father.

He tried to see Janet's point and for a time he had. Grace was soft and feminine most times. Other times she could knock you on your ass literally. She had been made with a build of a dancer and she had been exceptional at it but it wasn't like she wasn't good at anything else either.

Grace was a unique person that didn't have one set of talents. She was good at anything. She would wow you in a tutu or with an AK-47 strapped to her side. She was both light and dark and never made for the life that she had to endure.

Tom understood dancing in her youth. After all dancing had given Grace the discipline that she had needed to improve her other skills. It made her more silent and deadly but she had never been made to lead that life. She needed both in order to function. That was Grace. She needed the light and the dark to give her balance.

She had been forced to be a ballerina and endure the social politeness that she had been born with. She had been taught to suppress the other half of herself in the process. When they had been children and were being trained by their father Grace had been exceptional. She enjoyed doing it. She like playing solider for the day and then going to put on the tutu and dance at night.

Over the years she had played less and less of the solider and had been made to wear that tutu more and more. Janet just didn't understand Grace at all. If she did she would have never subjected her to that life. She would have let Grace decide for herself and he knew what she would have picked for herself. She would have been that solider. She would have walked out right onto the front lines if they would have let her.

Now standing here backing slowly away from his sister did he see that light again. She may not want to admit it but she missed this. She missed the adrenaline rush that filled your senses. She missed the stalking of her prey that would be him. Hell she just missed having freedom and there was freedom here. And he was going to make damn sure that she got a little for herself for a change. Plus there was the added bonus that Baker would understand his sister better because

Cole watched Grace walk off hips swinging. He couldn't understand the change that had come over her. She no longer looked like the soft gentle Grace that had given his daughter back to him. She looked more like a warrior ready to do battle. He shook his head and tried to figure it out.

"Been a long time since I've seen you Cadet Baker," John started. "So you're the one that my Grace has found. Well you're a damn lucky man if I say so myself but let me warn you son. I won't see her beaten down again. I want you to pay attention to the woman that you're about to meet. I have the feeling that she will be sticking around for a while after this." John said as he stood beside Cole.

"I would love to understand just what in the hell is going on here." Bret said.

"Lieutenant Thomas Summers at your service," Tommy said shaking Bret's hand. "As you may have guessed I'm Gracie's brother. This is her father Sergeant John Summers, retired marine drill sergeant. In fact your brother's drill instructor if I read correctly. Nice to meet you but I need a moment to prepare for my sister. I have the feeling that I'm going to get my ass kicked today." He said as he walked off into the tree line.

"Ass kicked is putting it mildly." John said snorting. "My Grace is going to massacre him. Poor

by god if Tom was going to give her to Cole then he better damn well understand her mind.

"Now Grace come on, it's me the love of your life. You wouldn't hurt me would you?" He asked but he knew the answer. She would kill him in a moment if she could get close enough. He was wondering how much of this part of her life she would remember. After all it had been years since they had tried to best each other.

"Attention." John yelled.

Tom noticed that Grace stopped and sighed. He wanted to smile but instead he walked over to her side and gave her hand a brief squeeze. It would piss her off just enough and he knew it.

"All right there are rules to this. You remember don't you Grace?" John asked.

"Yeah dad I remember." Grace sighed but nodded.

"All right then, why not let them watch? If you're going head to head with your brother, why not let them see what you are capable of? Since we are on your turf you get the advantage. I will let you pick the place. Now before we start I want Grace to change. You can't possibly fight in those clothes pumpkin."

Grace just wanted to scream. It wasn't fair. Why did her family have to be so strange? She sighed. This was part of the being a Summers. They were competitive. They were cut throat and they had rules for everything but over the years she had begun to miss this.

She missed fighting with her brother in what her father called "the field of honor." It was a place that she could be herself. It was a place that she didn't have to hide what she was capable of. It was a place that she could just be Grace and she found that she was looking forward to it.

Since Bret's knee injury she found that she really wasn't mad at her brother any longer. She just didn't want to tell him that, so she let him think that she was pissed. The problem was the anger died a long time ago. It had been beaten out of her with polite smiles and fake laughs.

It had been suppressed for so long now she wasn't even sure if she could bring that part of herself back. It wasn't that she was angry all the time. Most times she was actually normal but there were times when all she wanted to do was scream and rave like a lunatic. The problem was Janet.

Janet had made her put away all of it. She had made Grace soft and she found that more than anything, that was what really pissed her off. Her mother had made her into someone else. Someone that was afraid to take what she wanted. Someone that was afraid to have people mad at her. Someone that was

afraid that people would think less of her. She had made her into a robot.

A damn machine that was perfect all the time. A machine that didn't have thoughts or feelings of her own. A thing that could be controlled and manipulated into Janet's perfect life and she was sick of it. She was sick of being grounded Grace. If today was the only day that she was going to get it all out then so be it. She would rather Cole see the real her now before things went anywhere, anyway.

Maybe that had been the problem with her relationship with Kurt. With Kurt she had been grounded Grace. She never lost her temper. She never gave away her emotions. She had just gone along with everything that he had said like a robot.

She smiled a bitter smile and turned to her brother. He was dead and he didn't even know it. The old Grace rose and she felt free again.

"You're a dead man" she said to Tommy and she walked off hips swinging into the house.

If she was going to unleash the old her then by god she would show them all. She would show them that she hadn't been beaten down by Janet Summers. She would show them that she still had the will to fight for her own freedom.

boy I just hope she doesn't break more of his bones." He said shaking his head.

"Would you mind telling me what's going on here?" Cole asked clearing his throat nervously.

"Sure," John smiled. "As you have guessed by now Grace has been running. While I'm all for my daughter having some freedom for herself I find that I can't contain her mother like I should be able to by now. A few months ago Grace was set to marry a patsy ass mama's boy. Hated the man from the moment I met him but my wife was all for the marriage. I knew what it was all about it but I never let anyone know, not even my Grace. I thought that I was protecting her by not telling her but I failed her you see. Mr. Patsy ass was marrying Grace for money. I knew it and when I told Grace to make him sign the pre-nup he came up with this excuse that he was married. I knew the real reason he backed out. First off the man is gay as the day is long. Could tell from the moment I met him but Grace has been blind. I'm sorry to say that it was my fault again. Her mother god love the woman had taken over Grace's life. She made her into the broken woman you have all known for the past few days. My Grace used to be full of life and passion but somewhere along the way she was beaten down by her life. I came here to fight for her and to push her. I haven't seen my Grace in years and I miss her. I miss her glares when she isn't getting her way. I miss the calls that I used to get all the time. Hell I just miss her but she wasn't ready. I came because now she is and it's all thanks to you." He said looking at Cole.

"I don't understand." Cole said shaking his head confused.

"And neither does she," John laughed slapping him on the back. "You need to understand my Grace son. Understand and she will be yours forever. I'm trusting you with my little girl Baker. Oh you may think that you don't want or need her but your wrong and I'm going to prove it. I'll give you until the end of the summer. Last night Grace called her brother and told him of the agreement that you two have. I know it all son but I also know by the end of the summer you will be coming to me to ask for her hand in marriage. I know this with everything in me. I'm a mean son of bitch as I'm sure you remember but I'm also smart. I know that you need her. I know of your past, all of it, everything that you think that you've been hiding. Everything that you didn't even know was hidden. Everything and I'm telling you mark my words, by the end of summer you will be begging for her and I'm going to give you her, if you can prove yourself."

"I know the darkness that you face. I know what you see and I know the pain that you feel. My Grace also has a world of pain going on inside of her. Heal her as she heals you and I will give her to you. If not I'll bury you permanently. Do we have an agreement?"

Cole shook his head. He couldn't figure out what the man was talking about. He also knew enough not to piss the man off. Oh he may not have a hold over Cole now but he would know which buttons to push if he didn't get his way.

This man had been like a father to him instead of a drill instructor. When he had lost his father during basic training he had snuck Cole off the base so he could attend the funeral. Leaves were not given during basic but he had done it. He had even stood beside him as they lowered his father's coffin into the ground.

He never let anyone know but Sergeant Summers had cared about Cole. Cole himself even felt as though the man was a second father. When all he wanted to was give up and quit, this man had been there. He had pushing him and screaming in his face but he had cared.

Years later after basic training when Cole had gotten into trouble. It was John Summers that had testified at his court martial hearing. The man had stood up for him and he would not fail him now.

He wondered how he knew that he would be proposing at the end of summer but he didn't question it. Getting a straight answer out of the man was like pulling teeth. John had always been mysterious and cryptic. It was one the reason Cole had liked and respected the man.

For his slender build he had been in great shape. He had run the O-course right alongside of him. Even during Hell week he had run beside him pushing him all the way. He was a tuff son of a bitch and Cole had liked him. Now it was his time to help John out, like he had done for him so long ago. He would help heal Grace even if she didn't want or need it.

"Ok Sarge, I'll do this for you but when or if I don't purpose you'll drop this. I have enough going on in my life."

"That's fair son but let me give you a piece of advice. Grace can and will help you whether you want her to or not. Already she is doing it for you and you just don't see it but you will. You won't even see her coming but before you know it she will have wormed her way into your heart. Just don't break hers or I'll break you."

"Would someone please tell me what is going here?" Bret asked loudly.

"Just a friendly agreement," Cole said smiling. "Bret you remember John Summers. He was my old drill instructor that got me off base for dad's funeral."

Bret's eyes widened, "My god sir. It's good to see you again. It's been a long time. I didn't know you were Grace's dad. It's an honor to have you here sir."

"You may not say that son when you meet Gracie's mother. Woman is the bane of my existence and my salvation. Just you wait, you'll be begging me in a week's time to take her home, to tie her to a chair or shoot her. Never met a woman like my Janet but I wouldn't trade her for the world. Come on boys and meet the real Grace Summers, it's a show that you aren't going to want to miss."

Grace walked out of the house and found her father, Cole and Bret where she had left them. When she had gone in to get changed she had told Ross to take Emma home to get the stuff for fishing. It wasn't fair to her that they were delaying her day but she needed this. She didn't tell Ross everything but she had given him a brief rundown and told him that she would explain everything later. Right now she was trying to locate her brother. She couldn't wait to take him on again. He deserved the ass kicking he was about to receive.

Grace walked over to the men and looked at her father feet braced apart and arms crossed over her chest.

"Well where's the coward hiding?"

"I'm not hiding anywhere brat. You're old and out of shape. I'll have you in three minutes tops." Tommy said walking slowly out of the woods.

"You think, well follow me and let's put that to the test shall we."

"Ok first off, hang on a minute. If they are going to truly understand I need something from the car first." John said as he walked over to the car and pulled out a bow shaped bag. He then slung the arrow holder over his shoulder and said. "Come on all of you. I can't wait to watch this myself. It's been too long for this."

Grace nodded and walked off into the woods. If she going to take on her brother, then she would need room and trees. The clearing for Bret's new home would provide everything that she needed in order to win.

Like her father had told her, she had the advantage and she would take it. Winning had always been in her blood and she would not lose today. When they reached the clearing Bret looked around.

"Why here?" Bret asked.

"Well there is enough open space so my brother won't hurt himself. It gives him more ground to run from me and it gives me an advantage as well." She said shrugging.

"Give me a moment to familiarize myself with the place. It's only fair Grace." Tom said looking around.

"Go ahead, look all you want but you have three minutes. Then I will find you."

"That's my pumpkin. Now then you boys will need these to see." John said handing them binoculars. "And this is for me," he said pulling out the bow.

"Ah dad, come on not the bow." Grace pleaded.

"Oh I miss my bow and you dancing for me. I told you they are going to know all Grace."

Grace sighed and nodded. It would be no use in trying to convince her father otherwise. He would push and pull until he got what he wanted anyway. She looked over to a very confused Cole and Bret. What would they think of her after this morning?

What she was about to demonstrate was not normal for anyone but she needed this. It didn't matter what they thought of her. She wanted to hunt and her brother was the perfect target. She turned away from them and closed her eyes. She unzipped the jacket and let herself get back into the mind frame that she would need.

It had been years since she had used her senses to hunt like this. Would it be the same? She sighed as she concentrated. She let the jacket fall to her feet and she let her senses roam. She blocked out the men behind her. They were not the target. The target was now walking through the woods. He was taking slow measured steps and her blood started to boil.

Her father came up beside her and whispered in her ear, "Do you feel him?" Grace didn't bother opening her eyes. She nodded once. "Then go and get him and happy hunting pumpkin."

Grace's eyes snapped open and she was off before she could even think to move. It was second nature tracking her brother. She looked for the signs of him and moved slowly. It had been years but she knew that he was watching from the trees. She could feel his eyes on her and she smiled.

The clearing left to much room for her to get caught off guard. She made a beeline for the trees and stood directly beneath the overgrown maple. These trees would give her the advantage that she would need. They had low branches that were perfect and the other maples were intercrossed into this one. This was the place that she would go in. She wished her brother happy hunting and pulled herself up into the trees.

Cole and Bret both watched as Grace set off across the field. They knew that she had not been watching which way her brother had headed because she had been looking straight at them. As soon as her eyes opened though, she was off in the same direction looking at the ground as though she was tracking deer.

Cole silently wondered what she was doing when she walked over to the maple trees and pulled herself up. Curious he walked over to John with Bret and asked, "What is she doing?"

John smiled and put his binoculars up to his eyes and answered. "She is hunting. Grace has a unique hunting style. She hunts in the trees like a big cat. She moves between the trees and when she's close she pounces. Tom doesn't stand a chance."

Cole held up his own binoculars more curious now. He wondered what Grace was really capable of. She had been so light and feminine that he couldn't imagine her hunting someone, assessing them for the threat that they were.

His gentle Grace was turning out to be more than he had originally thought. She was turning out to be complicated and fun. It was the first time he found himself excited about anything in a long time. He lowered the glasses and looked over at Bret that was now just as curious as he had been.

He wondered what they would talk about on their date tonight. Would he ask her about today? Would he want to know her better after this? Was he getting hard just thinking about what she was capable of like he was?

He groaned when he realized that he was rock hard again. Seeing Grace dressed in camo pants and a brown tee-shirt had been a damn turn on. He liked the soft Grace but he was intrigued by the hard Grace that he had seen only moments ago.

It was as though she was a different person. When she had walked out of the house dressed to hunt he had wanted to take her into his arms and ease the rage that he had seen in her eyes. That changed when he say her eyes flash open. There was rage there but there was light there as well.

It was as though he had never really seen her eyes before. They were large and wide with excitement. The emerald depths grew darker and made her look dangerous and damn sexy. Hell she was always sexy but seeing her pull herself up into that tree, with those breasts straining against her tee-shirt had turned him rock hard within a moment.

There had been no build up, no indication that he was turned on by this but it was there and it was damn uncomfortable. He momentarily readjusted himself to ease the ache but when he caught sight of her moving he realized it didn't help.

He could see her stretch those long sexy legs out for another branch and wrap around it silently as she moved into the neighboring tree. He spotted Tom on the ground crouched and looking up. He must have known that Grace was coming for him because he broke out into a run.

He made just outside of the tree line when Grace shot out of the trees from about a story or so up. His gut twisted as she fell but he soon realized that she wasn't falling. She crouched just in time to land on her brothers back and take him down. She hadn't even been jarred by her fall, while he was having a hard time not screaming at her. She could have broken her neck shooting out the tree like that.

John motioned for them to follow him as they set off across the field. Cole skidded to a halt as he saw Tom roll and take Grace with him. He looked at John who was smiling as though he was proud of the scene before him.

"You're getting soft." Tom said with Grace pinned underneath of him.

She folded her legs up to his stomach and ejected him with lightning speed. Before Tom could catch his breath she was sitting on his chest with a butterfly knife at his throat. "Do you give Tommy?"

He wrapped his legs around her and somersaulted her backward away from. He regained his feet and said, "Not a chance. We haven't even started. No fair that you brought a knife Gracie. Getting scared of your big bad brother in your old age?"

She smiled and threw the knife at the trees thirty yards away burying it half way in. "Not a chance. Come on Tommy don't hold back because I'm a girl."

"Won't dream of it," and he lunged forward.

Cole stood mesmerized as she lifted her foot and caught him right in the gut. A great rush of air left his lungs but she didn't stop. As he rolled she caught him again with her right foot. Tom ceased the moment and grabbed her ankle sending her backwards.

Cole thought that she must have anticipated that move because instead of falling, she placed her hands back fast enough to do a little flip landing on her feet upright. She smiled and wagged her finger at him, "Not fast enough brother."

She came at him fists flying so fast that he was having a hard time catching them. He noticed that Tom was blocking every blow though. He could tell that they had worked like this together before. It was as though they were anticipating each move and man could she move.

He was a trained solider himself and he didn't think that he would be able to keep up with her. Her fists and legs were moving at the same time. He didn't understand how she was able to stand but as he watched them the more it became like a dance.

One would lounge one would counter but their feet moved in perfect harmony with each other. Grace landed a great punch to the side of Tom's nose breaking it instantly. John tried to step in then but they ignored him and that's when he heard it.

He had heard Grace laugh before but never like this. When she laughed it was low and lusty but this laugh went straight to his groin. It was low and lusty but it was darker and more joyful then any that he had ever heard. She was enjoying herself and it was showing.

As blood poured from Tom's nose he too started to laugh before they both stopped and looked at each other laughing. She kicked him in the knee and he punched her in the gut. Before anyone could move they were hugging and Tom was on his knee's looking up at her.

"You win oh great Gracie. How can I humbly repay you for allowing me to walk out of here alive?"

She rolled her eyes at him and smiled. She held out her hand and pulled him up slapping him on the back.

"I missed this and you're welcome that I didn't break your knee cap again. I was surly temped but I'm just getting back. Here let me straighten your nose." She said as she took his nose between her slender fingers and snapped it back into place.

"Damn it Grace that hurt. I swear that's the third time you broke my nose."

"Then learn to protect it. Besides it's marked with a mark of valor now. Be happy that's all I did to you this time. You remember last time, don't you?"

"Oh god don't remind me. I had to wear that damn arm brace for a month. You broke my wrist and three fingers. I can't even type right anymore thanks to you."

"You know you love it." She laughed at his face.

"There's my Grace again. I wondered where you had been hiding her all this time. Now should we show them how you dance for me Gracie?" John asked.

She nodded and smiled. It was fun being carefree again. She missed this with her brother and father. It was the only thing that bonded them together. It also broke their bones together at times but she won't change it for the world. No they were conventional by any means but they were close and that was all that mattered.

"Yeah sure why not? I'm all warmed up now anyway. You boys having fun so far?"

Cole could only look at her with his mouth open. He had never seen this side of Grace before but he had to admit, it was damn sexy to see this new side of her. She was dark and dangerous and god he was not going to let any man touch her that was not him. He wanted the passion and fire for himself. She just didn't know it yet but she soon would. Very soon indeed.

Chapter 12

The next hour passed quickly as Cole sat in the clearing taking calming breaths. When John had asked Grace to dance for him, Cole took that to mean literally. Now sitting here watching Grace dance for her father he had a better idea of what they had been talking about.

Grace was dancing alright but now she was dancing for her life. Her father had gotten out the long re-curve bow and started shooting arrows right at Grace. Cole couldn't understand what in the hell the crazy man was doing but as he watched he became even more intrigued.

Grace had always been graceful when she danced. Cole noticed that the first night she and Emma had danced across the porch. Now Grace was just as graceful if not more so with arrows being launched at her head.

John would shot and she would move. It was time and it was precision. It was also art and damn entertaining to watch. He thought that he would never discount ballet again if this is what it had taken to teach her. Tommy sat beside him with his nose still swollen.

"Great isn't she?" He asked as he watched his sister.

Cole could see the admiration in his eyes. Hell Cole himself had admiration in his eyes for her. He had never known someone like Grace. He had thought that he had her pegged. Yeah right, he hadn't even scratched the true surface of her. She was caring and compassionate. She was loyal and strong. She was sexy and funny and most of all she was his. She may not know it yet but she would be his. He just wondered how he would back pedal with her now. He had made this agreement between them. He had worked it all out inside his mind and she had thrown him again.

Seeing her like this had changed something inside of him. When Grace had been compassionate it had been easy to make that agreement. It had worked out best for both of them. Now he knew the real Grace. She was fire and passion. She wild and carefree and she would never settle into the plans that he had made for her.

Already she had broken from that pattern. He thought that he could separate himself from her. He could have his cake and eat it too like Bret had said but he couldn't have been more wrong.

Grace would never conform to him and his rules because she had been made to conform to too many of them already. She had been beaten down and broken just like him but how to change all that?

The only person that could possibly answer him was her brother. Cole didn't know anything about the man but he knew that he loved Grace. Cole would need him if ever stood a chance of healing her again and catching her.

No man had ever caught her; the proof was in the fact that she was still a virgin. Her exact words had been she would not give herself to no man like that, even Cole himself. That was how she protected herself. She was smart enough to know that usually for women losing your virginity to a man meant feelings. Feelings would eventually turn into love and she was avoiding it. It was the reason that she had made the agreement but she would not let him take her.

He was starting to understand more and he needed Tommy to understand the rest. Tommy knew everything about Grace. He raked his brain looking for one question that would help him crack Grace. He ran over everything trying to remember when it hit him.

He remembered the night that the agreement had been made. She had been telling him that she didn't do one night stands because something that had happened to her friend. He would need to know that story in order to figure why she wouldn't do one. Maybe then he could get close enough to her. He just needed to open her up and find the right buttons to push to make her his. Cole cleared his throat.

"Listen I need a favor. I know that I have no right to ask for one but I'm going too anyway. I need to understand a few things about your sister and you're the only one with the answers."

"I think that I've fulfilled my obligations to you but for Grace, count me in. I would do almost anything for her." Tommy said looking at him with a raised brow.

"All right but not here. They are almost finished and I don't want her overhearing us. How about tonight? Grace is going out with Bret on a date. Why don't you come over to my house? We can talk after I put Emma to bed and no one will bother us."

"My sister is dating your brother? I think that I seemed to have missed something along the way here."

"When we first started this I thought that I could distance myself from her by telling her to date other people. I just didn't think that it would be my own brother doing the asking. He caught her off guard this morning at breakfast and asked her. I knew that she wanted me to tell her no. I could see it in her eyes but I had just got done telling her that there were no demands here and to go out and date. I couldn't tell her no in the next minute."

"Man you are slow," he said strangling on laughter. "Listen my sister is very rebellious. Well at least she used to be before him. Now I'm not so sure but with Grace no usually means yes. At least with Janet it does. The problem is Grace has never dated a man. I mean a real man. Yeah sure there was patsy ass but not an alpha male. She thinks that she's supposed to be doing what you're telling her because you are an alpha male. She knows that you wouldn't be bullied into anything like Kurt was and she's unsure of herself. She's loyal to fault. She will do what you're telling her to do because she doesn't want to challenge you. Grace is exceedingly smart, keep that in mind. She thinks around a person in a way. You tell her to date that is exactly what she'll do because she's pushing you to show her you can't handle it. She wants the reaction from you. She's getting a feeling for who you are and what you are capable of. With Janet she already knows how to piss her off and push her buttons. It's to do the exact opposite of what Janet tells her to do. For a while she was beaten down by her but she's rising up. The problem with Gracie rising up is, she will be shooting for the top. You're the top Cole. You're what she wants and needs in her life and she will push you to break. She will worm herself in there before you can even guess that she got close enough but take a lesson from my broken nose. With Grace, she doesn't grow on you gradually like most women do. She punches you right in the heart and takes it with her if she leaves. She does everything backwards. She will heal you first. She will make you feel things you never felt before. She will open you raw then she will pick it apart one issue at a time. Before you know it she's right in the middle having healed yourself all around her. You won't be able to get away from the love and caring that only she can bring."

"Ask me anything about her and I will tell you. She has been apart herself to long now. She needs to heal with someone holding her together in the middle. That someone is going to be you Baker. I know it so I'll help you anyway I know how." He finished getting up and walking away from Cole.

Cole sat there trying to clear his head. It seemed the whole family talked in cryptic phrases. As he ran over the conversation again he thought about it. Tommy had been right. In the few days that Grace had been here she had pulled him apart. She had also mended him with her right in the middle holding him together.

Damn it how could he have missed it? She had brought Emma back together just by showing her that she understood her feelings. By not making her uncomfortable with the no talking thing Grace had opened Emma up to talk.

She had shown Emma that it was alright to be silent because Grace would still understand her and her wants. She had also made it alright to talk again because although Grace understood that part of Emma the others had not. So in a way she had opened her up and made her talk so that Emma could voice her wants and needs to those that didn't get the silent messages.

It was damn confusing but it made sense. She made the person feel comfortable with her. Once you felt comfortable she would open you up and read what you needed to crack. She would crack you and then put you back together with her in the middle holding it all together for you.

She made him realize his faults and his fears. She had made him confront them by talking them out and crying for them. Then she had held him together as he broke and cried for all he was worth. Damn she was smart. The question was how to turn the tables right back on her. If she used those types of methods on other people then there was a good chance that it would work on her as well but first he needed her to crack.

So far she had only opened to him part of the way. She hadn't broken yet. She hadn't told him everything. She hadn't cried or showed much emotion either way. He would need to break Grace Summers and it would start with Tom Summers. Break the brother that held her heart. Then you broke the thing holding it together leaving him to pick up the pieces and put it all back together with him and Emma right in the middle.

He smiled and watched his opponent. She would now be considered his opponent because she was a damn formidable one. She was relentless and unforgiving and he would need to be just like her if he had a prayer of making her his. Bret walked over to him and sat. "What are you smiling about?"

"I'm assessing my threat and learning the ways to crack her. I just need that one piece to crack her and then she's mine."

Bret smiled looking away from Cole. He had finally figured it out and he was damned pleased with him but he was still going to push Cole. Cole had never come up against a woman like Grace. She wasn't one of those females that would cave to him. Bret figured that out this morning.

After watching her take her brother in what he could only describe as the art of war, he too had learned about Grace. She could lead you to believe that she was soft and willing but there was a shield there. One that he was sure hadn't been touched by any man. It was cold, set in stone and almost unbreakable.

After learning a little about her, Bret had come to the conclusion that Grace had built up that shield with life experiences. She had been taught not to let people in. She would take people in and heal them in a way but she didn't give much of herself away.

Yes she had told him of the fiancé but what she didn't tell him is what she had been feeling at the time. He knew the story but he didn't hear or feel the feelings behind it. Was she happy about the break up? Was she pissed off? Was she hurt or scared?

Hell she hadn't let him see anything but the tears of joy that she had laughed out. That was when he had realized he had a total conversation with her without her even saying anything.

She had told him the facts but she hadn't told him the answers or effects of it. She was damn smart that much was for sure. As he watched Cole watching her, he knew that his brother had also seen the same thing. Now it would be up to all of them to crack her. They would need to open her up so that his brother could put her back together the right way.

Bret had learned that Grace never showed anyone but them this side of her and that her fiancé had never seen this side of Grace but he understood that she needed both. Grace was light and dark. She was full of light and love but the darker side of her would inspire passion and fire.

The flames from her fire could ignite his brother back into the living again. They just needed to ignite her more and watch her break into a ball of flames that would cover them all. Bret smiled because he could wait for the fireworks to start. Clearing his throat he said, "so you are good now with Grace and I going out tonight?"

"Yeah I think that I am. You just remember that she is going to be mine and I am going to fight for her."

"Then you'll have a fight on your hands I fear. She is more than even I was hoping for. Happy hunting brother and may the best man win."

"I intend too." Cole said smiling bitterly.

Bret walked off smiling and flipping his brother off behind his back. He knew that he was going to push. He was going to push them both so hard that they would crack together. He was the man with a plan. He only hoped it didn't blow up in everyone's face at the end.

Grace stood winded and smiled. It had been such a long time since she had been able to open herself up like this. She couldn't believe that she had let Cole and Bret come and watch but she felt better about it. What did it matter what they thought of her anyway?

So far Cole was turning out to be a big jerk and Bret was leaving. The more Grace thought about it the more she thought about leaving herself. She sighed as she thought of Emma. She had just starting opening up and she didn't want to hurt the little one again by disappearing on her. Emma had enough loss in her life and Grace couldn't disappoint her.

Bret walked over to her smiling. He held out a water bottle and said, "That is the last time I take a ballet dancer for granted. What I really want to know is, did you learn ballet before or after your father shot arrows at you?"

"Well a little of both I'm afraid. I was just beginning to learn and dad thought that this would give me the inspiration I had been lacking. You get pretty inspired when arrows are being shot at your back."

"Did you ever get hit with any of them?"

"Yes I am afraid I did," she said smiling. "When we first started this dad thought to be soft on me. He used blunt tips but he soon found that it wasn't causing the motivation that I needed. He then turned to broad heads. He was always very careful but you find motivation real quick when you get skimmed with one in the backside. Six stitches later let's just say that I didn't need to be told twice. I got the message loud and clear the first time around. After that it was easier and I never got hit again. Strange method of teaching but efficient."

"I would say so. So where would you like to go tonight? I was thinking of driving to Wolfeboro. Sadly there are not a lot of good places here. I was thinking dinner and movie."

Grace looked at him confused. "You mean you still want to go out tonight. I thought…" She shook her head and smiled "you know what. That sounds great. Just so I know. What should I be wearing tonight?"

"While I find I like the camo I think that you should wear something more…"

"Just tell me," she laughed interrupting him. "Am I supposed to knock your socks off or tone it down a bit?"

"Knocking socks off but it won't be mine. It will be my brothers." He said looking over at Cole who was glaring at them again.

"While I'm all for getting him to open up I'm not sure about this. He said some really mean things this morning. I like Cole. I know that he's a good man but I won't stand by while another one tears me apart. I won't do it Bret even if I do like him. I'm done trying to figure out men's wants and needs. For now I'm going to concentrate on my own. This morning made me realize some things about myself. I have wants and needs too Bret. I will only take so much before I lash out like I did with Tommy. That is my warning."

"That is fair enough but answer just one more question for me. When you were dating Mr. Patsy Ass, did you ever be yourself, or did you try to be what you thought he wanted?"

"That's two and I'll only answer one. I was what he needed."

"Fair enough, then forget him and be yourself Grace. Let it show to the world who you really are and let them deal with it. This evening I don't want grounded Grace. I want the Grace you really are, hellion and all. Do that for me and I'll give you something in return. I won't tell you what it really is, just be prepared for it."

"Why do you feel the need to talk in cryptic phrases?" She asked raising an eyebrow. "Afraid I'll see right through you if you talk normally. I have your ticket as well muscle man and don't you forget it." She said walking off and winking at him.

Bret threw his head back and laughed. She had him alright and he would need to protect himself against her. She was his brothers and he would never cross that boundary no matter how much he was temped but she was temping him alright.

Bret would never admit how much he had been turned on by Grace this morning. She had seemed like a whole different person. She was silent and deadly and she was damned gorgeous. She was passion, fire and grit all rolled into a tight little package.

Her slender frame and slight build made a person want to protect her but she didn't need it, not even a little bit because she was more than able to take care of herself. Her skills and precision were unparalleled and wondered how she had managed to stay a virgin this long. If she was his he would have made her beg for it by now. He wondered how on earth his brother had managed to fall asleep last night when she was ready.

She may not have come right out and said the words but it was there on her face. Written like an unspoken bond all over her. It was in the way she moved. It was in her eyes and it was written all over those now swinging hips of hers. Oh she was ready alright and it would be Cole that got to take it. Lucky bastard.

Bret looked over to his brother that was now trying to talk to Grace. She smiled at him and flipped him the bird as she joined her brother and father walking back the path that would lead to her house. He shook his head as his brother's mouth fell open. Would he ever understand the treasure that he was about to give him because if he didn't Bret would never let him live it down.

Grace Summers was about to turn this family upside down and inside out but it was high time. High time indeed that it happened he thought to himself. His family was falling apart at the seams and she would be the glue that bonded them back together again. That is if she didn't kill them all first.

Later that day the family, Grace, her father and Tommy all decided to go fishing. After all they had all promised Emma that they would go, there was no getting out of it.

Grace had packed a picnic lunch and told her father and brother where they all were going for the day. She should have kept her big mouth shut because of course they had wanted to come.

They had made the hour and half hour drive to Wolfeboro National Park to do a little fishing and sightseeing. If Grace was going to live here for the summer she wanted to know the area more, to see the sights and things that it had to offer.

Jackson was a nice quiet town to live in but there really wasn't anything to do there. In Wolfeboro however there was plenty. It was a warm eighty five degrees and sunny. Grace always found that she loved the outdoors.

She loved the smell of the fresh grass and the pine trees. There was something freeing in the outdoors but as she breathed in the air she got a whiff of the high end perfume and she cringed.

She knew that perfume. It was her mothers and since it was getting stronger she could only assume that she was coming closer. Not wanting Emma to hear what was about to happen Grace decided to send Emma away.

"Emma why don't you go and show your daddy what you caught so far."

Emma nodded and picked up the bucket and skipped along happily away from her. She only wished that she could join her. This morning when she had invited her father and brother she would have thought that Janet would have stayed behind. After all the woman hated nature more than she hated bad manicures.

Grace snorted as she faced the woman from her nightmares. It shouldn't be that way between a mother and daughter she thought tragically. They should be able to be friends and voice their opinions to each other but not with Janet.

It was her way or the highway and Grace hadn't been doing a lot of Janet's way lately. She braced herself for the storm that was about to hit. She guessed her father and brother had anticipated this part because they came right behind her looking damned guilty. She wanted to make them pay but that would have to wait. Right now she would need to deal with momzilla.

"Hello Gracelyn. How have you been since you have ripped out my heart?"

"I still see that it's all about Janet Summers wants and needs." Grace sighed and rolled her eyes. "Don't you think that you should ask me something like, hey Grace are you alright? Did that bastard break your heart? How have you been feeling? Oh maybe, hey Grace are you happy right now?"

"Gracelyn Marie Summers, how could you say something like that to your own mother? I have been worried sick about you. You don't call. You don't tell your company that you're quitting. You don't even tell everyone why the wedding is off. You just up and disappear on everyone without an explanation for any of it."

Grace had a temper. She was well aware of it but she hadn't wanted to unleash it. At least not with Emma around but if her mother didn't quit she may just forget her good intentions and lose it thoroughly.

"Janet I want you to listen to me. I had my reasons but as usual you wouldn't be interested in hearing them. All you care about is the fact that I didn't do what you wanted me to do. Well guess what. I don't care. I don't care about any of it anymore and I will be damned if I will."

"Grace how could you be so irresponsible? You had a duty Grace. You had a duty to Kurt and to your company. How could you just turn your back on that?"

That was it the temper was up. Grace screamed the most loud and annoying scream she had ever screamed in her life. Everyone came running but she no longer cared. It was time to tell Janet Summers just what she thought of her duties and obligations starting with Kurt.

"You say that I had a duty. That is what you say to me." She started as she walked forward to her mother making her back up as she went. "You say that I had a duty to Kurt. You want to know why Kurt and I aren't getting married. Huh mom you really want to know?"

"Now Grace…" Her father started. She cut him a look "you can, can it dad. You and I are going to go rounds later but for now I am going to speak my peace and none of you are going to interrupt me. Is that understood?" They nodded watching her. She didn't care that they would think that she was crazy. Hell maybe she was but she was done not standing up to Janet Summers. That woman had burnt her bridges a long time ago and Grace owed her nothing, not even sugar coating the truth anymore. She looked at her mother again.

"The reason that Kurt and I aren't getting married is because he claims that he's married. He had his best friend come into our room while I was trying to seduce him and tell me that Kurt wasn't interested in me because he had a wife. He had a duty to me don't you think? He had a duty to tell me that he was either very gay or married but either way he didn't do his damned duty now did he? And as for my company, I did my duty there. I called them before curtain call and told them that I quit. That was plenty of time to replace my tiny little position in the back that you don't think is important because it's not the headliner position. What did you tell me? Oh yes that I was throwing the best years I had left in me to a talentless hack that didn't have half of my talent."

"But that was because she wasn't as good as you Grace. I just said that because you were the best."

"That's the point mother. I was the best, a long time ago, at a time when I loved dancing. At a time when that was the only thing that I wanted to do with my life but that ended at the age of sixteen mother. That was twelve damn years ago in case you forgot to count it right and I couldn't do it anymore. I told you then that I was done and that I wanted to go into the military. I told you that I didn't want dancing but did you listen? Hell no. You pushed me to do what you could never do. You pushed me into a life that I had come to hate. I thought about breaking my own leg just to be done with it. I begged you. I pleaded with you and what did you do? You patted me on the head and told me that if I didn't do it you would cut off my inheritance. See at that time I was young and dumb enough to believe you but I now realize you never had that authority. It was given to me by grandfather and you couldn't touch a dime of it. Were you that jealous of me mother? You were jealous because I could dance and you couldn't, or were you jealous that he loved me more and didn't leave you shit. I know all about the court hearings. You contested that will but he protected me as he has always done. He hired me lawyers because he knew the type of person you were. He knew that you would be so pissed off because his only granddaughter got everything not leaving you a penny. Did you ever wonder why he left me everything mother? Could it be because you would have blown all of it? Does dad even know the amount of gambling debts you are raking up and I am paying for? I went along with whatever you wanted from me believing that grandfather was wrong about you but I see just how right he really was. You are a vein selfish creature that doesn't listen to anything that I want.

You only see me for the money I can provide and the life that you never got to have. Did it hut you to see him give all of his love to me because he couldn't get close to you?"

"Grace that is enough," her father demanded.

She shook her head, "no father. You are just as much to blame as she is. You never listened either. Neither one of you asked me what I wanted. Just once would have been nice. It would have been nice not be forced to go to practices seven days a week for eight hours at a clip. It would have been nice to not have to be pushed into the social functions with all those stuck up people waiting to see me perform like a wind up monkey. It would have been nice to have a life of my own, one complete with friends and freedom. It would have been nice but that didn't happen for grounded Grace. Did it? Did it mother?" She finished as she turned on her heel and walked away.

She would never forgive her mother for this. She had driven her over the edge. Grace never lost her temper but she had blown it bad back there. Pacing inside of the trees to get rid of the anger she heard it. It was a tiny voice calling out to her and she called back to her.

"Emma stay where you are. I'm coming." She said angrily wiping the tears away.

Shit Emma had followed her and she couldn't even believe that she had let the little one see something like that. The child had been in enough pain as it was and she had just lashed out at her own mother in a big way. Emma's mother was gone and Grace was lashing out at hers. What would Emma think of her now?

She found the little one walking toward her. Grace wiped the tears away from her eyes and bent down.

"Oh Emma I'm so sorry that I did that to you. I didn't mean for you to overhear that. I'm sorry little one. Can you forgive me?"

Emma smiled and patted the ground next to her. Grace sat while Emma talked. "I never told anyone this ever. This has to be our secret ok?"

"I promise." Grace sniffed and wiped the tears again making a cross over her heart. "I won't tell a soul."

Emma nodded and looked at the ground as though she was ashamed by what she was about to admit. Grace couldn't understand why she would be shy now but decided to listen.

"Before my mommy died I said some pretty mean things to her. I was mad at her for not talking to my real daddy anymore. I thought that she wouldn't let me talk to him and I blamed her. I told her that she was a mean mommy and I would never forgive her for pushing my daddy away. She ended up getting into her car accident the next day. I never even got to say goodbye or that I was sorry about all the mean things that I said to her. That was the reason that I didn't talk. I didn't think that it was right that I had said so many hurtful mean things to her and she wouldn't get to talk anymore at all. That's when I decided that it wasn't fair that I got to stay and she had to go away, so I just stopped talking. I never said a word to anyone not even daddy, until you. You seemed know just what to say to make me laugh even when I didn't feel like laughing. You made me see that there was still beauty in the world even though my mommy was gone with your dancing. You gave me that Grace because your mommy made you the way that you are. If you wouldn't have come along who knows how long it would have taken me to feel this again. When you danced for me you gave me back the light. Maybe your mommy just wanted to see the light like I did."

Grace opened her mouth and closed it. The more Emma had been crying the more she had started to cry. Emma was such a smart child for one so small but Grace understood the lesson. Emma was trying to tell her to forgive her mother because even though she may not like her at the moment she would always be her mother whether she wanted it or not.

"Thank you Emma," Grace said hugging her close. "You gave me something that I have been searching for, for a long time now."

"What did I give you?"

"Understanding little one and that is more precious to me than anything in the world. Your mommy was a way lucky mommy and she knows just how much you loved her."

"How do you know for sure?"

"Because you turned out so great and you loved her. Every mommy knows that. Even mine because even though I just said some really mean things to her she will always love me, just like your mommy loved you. It's the code of things. You know written down in some manual somewhere. Mommy will love daughter even when she's being a brat."

"You really think that mommy knows Grace?" Emma asked still giggling.

"Well if you don't believe me why not tell her now?"

"But she's not here anymore," Emma said confused. Grace laughed and tapped her nose.

"Sure she is. She's right here" she said pointing at Emma's heart. "And she is all around us. Sometimes when people leave us they don't really leave us. A part of them stays behind in us. Like you, I have seen pictures of your mommy and you have her eyes. She is part of you. She gave you those pretty brown eyes that look just like hers did so you see you have part of her and she lives in your heart and memories. No one can take that away from you. She will always be a part of you as you were a part of her, so go on now. Tell her what you are feeling. There is no here but me to hear you and when you said your peace I'll go and tell my mother mine. Do we have a deal?"

"Ok here we go." Emma nodded and sucked in a breath. "Mommy if you're listening like Grace says you are I wanted you to know that I'm sorry. I'm sorry that I said all of those hateful mean things to you and I'm really sorry that I can't see you anymore to tell you. I wanted you to know that I don't blame you for what he did to us. It was him that left us mommy and I'm sorry that I didn't see it sooner. I'm sorry that I didn't get to tell you sorry and goodbye, so this is my goodbye mommy. I hope you are as happy as I am now mommy and you were right, Uncle Cole is really a better daddy anyway. At least he sticks around and loves me. I really hope you can hear me mommy and forgive me."

As Emma finished her teary heartfelt plea the wind picked up bring with it the scent of roses. Emma jumped up and down on Grace's lap.

"That's her Grace. My mommy loved roses. I would know that scent anywhere. She really is here and she really did hear me."

"See munchkin I told you. Mommy's always know when their daughter's seem to need them." Just like her mother did.

She may not have gone about it the right way but anytime that Grace had been having a bad day or was the least bit lonely her mother had always called. Yes she had been lecturing her to try harder but she had cared in some small way. Seeing Emma plead with her mother to forgive her while she was no longer here changed something inside of her.

Janet Summers didn't understand Grace but then again Grace didn't understand her mother either. Maybe with a little time and understanding they could become closer. It was at least worth a shot. The love Emma had for her mother touched Grace and she would not leave it like this between her and her mother. Even if they never came to an understanding they couldn't leave it like this. If they didn't speak their peace to each other they would end up having to do it like Emma had done and Grace didn't want that. Grace wiped the tears from Emma's eyes and faced her.

"How about tomorrow for the family dinner, since we wanted a change anyway, why don't we plant a rose blush? That way you will always have a reminder of your mommy and when you get lonely you can smell the roses to remember the good times that you two shared?"

"I think mommy would have liked that and I think that she would have liked you too Grace." Emma whispered hugging Grace close.

"And I have no doubt that I would have loved her as well. After all little one she's just like you."

Emma nodded and grinned and they both sat in the middle of the woods smelling the roses. They didn't move from the spot that was now filled with the wonderful scent. Emma just sat on Grace's lap listening to her heart beat and smelling the roses. Just like Emma had done with her own mommy not so long ago.

Chapter 13

Cole had tried to follow Grace after her big break down. He had seen her lose that composed temper of hers and he couldn't have been more please. Sure, Grace may have gone about it the wrong way but at least she was starting to get it out.

Even Cole understood that Grace was bottled and controlled. She needed to let the poison out of her just like he had done. Since his big break down last night he was feeling much better today. Almost lighter somehow and he knew Grace was the same. The small glimpses that he had been getting of her life had been bad.

She had been made to be disciplined. She never dated, that was for sure and she had made to be on a special diet. He wondered if she even realized that she was still following it. Since she had been here he had never seen her pick up more than a muffin to eat.

Smiling as he thought about his complicated Grace he could hear two voices in the woods. Pausing to listen he realized that Emma must have followed Grace as well. He knew that he should turn around and give them some privacy but he wanted to hear. He needed to know more about the women in his life. Even Emma.

He walked a little closer not wanting them to hear him. He could hear Emma crying and he froze. He hated the sound of her crying and wanted to go and comfort her immediately but he stayed back. He knew that Grace would help if she could and if she couldn't then she would come and get him.

Listening he heard Emma's heartfelt plea to her mother and his heart broke. The little one had never gotten the chance to say goodbye and it seemed like she was trying it now with Grace.

Cole leaned up against the tree and listened as Emma and Grace both cried. Would he ever truly understand women? They seemed to cry about everything but as he listened to his daughter cry he noticed his own tears. There was just something in her voice. A plea of desperation and he now understood the depth of her pain.

Emma had lost her mother but he never knew the amount of guilt the little one had been feeling. He would need to talk to Emma about some things it seemed and the sooner the better. He could hear them talking about getting a rose bush to plant tomorrow. Well if she wanted one to remind her of her mother then he would plant them all the way around the house.

He let them finish up and then there was nothing. He wondered if they had walked out of the woods another way. As he walked forward he caught sight of them. Emma was settled in Grace's lap and Grace was holding her tight both in tears.

He didn't say anything as he walked over to his family and knelt beside them. Grace looked up at him tears still clinging to her own lashes and his skipped a beat. She was the most beautiful woman he had ever seen.

Her beauty wasn't all on the outside either. It was deeply rooted in the person that she was. She was caring and compassionate. She was strong and determined and she was feisty when she was riled about something.

Not saying a word he hugged them both in a big hug and let them both get it all out in his embrace. Instead of pushing him like he had thought they would do, they embraced him instead and for the first time in his life Cole felt complete. He was completely human in their arms. He wasn't a monster and at least here in this perfect circle would be the love that he had needed.

He let them get it all out and when they were finished he walked Emma back to the fishing. He knew that Grace would need a few moments to sort out her own mind. When she was ready she would come to him.

Grace watched as Cole came up to her and Emma and embraced them. She wanted to shove him away. It wasn't like she needed his caring but as his big strong arms came around her she couldn't help but snuggle down into them. She needed the acceptance that she had not been getting at home. She needed to be held and loved and for the first time she would not push it away.

Emma had been through so much and still had the courage to ask her mother's forgiveness. Why couldn't she do that with her own mother? As she held the little girl she knew that she would need too. It may mean her pride but what was pride without her mother.

As Cole held them she settled into the loving embrace and let herself feel it for the first time in her life. Sure she had people like Tom but Grace wanted a different type of love. Her brother would always love her but now it was time to fight for another type of love.

Grace knew that Cole was a proud man. She was a proud woman but one of them would have to bend and it looked like it was going to be her. As the arms hugged tighter she wondered what it would be like to be held in these arms anytime she pleased. She sighed at her thoughts. That meant opening herself up too him and she wasn't sure if that was what he wanted.

With Cole most times it was hard to tell what the man wanted. He acted like he liked her. He acted like he cared. Then he told her to go with his brother tonight. He was damn confusing that was for sure but as he held on, she also knew that he was one of the good ones. To keep a man like Cole Baker interested was going to take a hell of a lot of skill that she didn't posses. Maybe Bret could help her in a way after all.

As Cole and Emma walked away she knew that he was trying to give her time and she was damned happy about that. While she loved Emma already she wasn't sure how she was supposed to be feeling about anything else. In the space of days she had opened more to Cole Baker then she ever had with anyone. Even Tom sometimes had to pry stuff out of her. She couldn't figure out her own mind anymore.

As she paced she thought. She thought about her mother and Emma. She thought about Cole also but no too long. Right now she needed a game plan and fast. She needed to make Cole Baker break. She needed to break more than he already was so that she would be able to mend him back together.

How many times could she remember her father saying "know your enemy." Now Cole Baker would need to become the enemy. She would need a plan and fast but she would start with Bret. Crack the brother and crack the man.

Bret and Cole were like each other in so many ways. She only hoped what would wow Bret would wow Cole. She smiled as she made her way back. She would give Bret Baker an outfit that would, as he put it knock his socks off and she knew just the person to help her do it.

Later that day while Grace and her mother shopped for her date. She wondered how she was going to right the damage done. Grace had asked for her mother's help with something after she had totally lashed out at her. At first her mother had said that she was tired but Grace knew that was only an excuse, so she had begged and pleaded until she had said yes. Now standing in the high priced store did she start to question if she had lost her mind. She turned to her mother at a rack of dresses and cleared her throat.

"Mom can we talk for a moment?" Grace asked nervously.

"All right, what is it that you would like to talk about now? I think that you have said enough today don't you?" Grace sighed and pulled her down to a bench in the store. "Mom I just need you to listen to me. First I want to apologize for this afternoon. I didn't mean to say those hurtful things to you but you never listen to me. After all these years I would have thought that we would have been better at this. At being a mother and a daughter but we aren't. I realized today that I don't understand you and you don't understand me, so I thought maybe if we talked it out we could fix that. I want you in my life mom but I want you to understand something. This is my life and if I want to screw it up, I think that I should be allowed. If I make a mistake then it's me that has to deal with it. I would like your input but no more criticisms. I want your acceptance even if I'm doing something totally screwed up and in return I will try to see your side of things. I know that you only wanted the best for me but it would be nice if you would ask me what I want for a change. Can we please try this? I know that it won't be easy but being with Emma that only just lost her mother I saw what came of her regrets. I don't want to regret you not being in my life mom, so for now could you be my friend and help me pick something, "sexy" out for my date tonight. I don't have a clue what to choose. I just know that I need to knock socks off."

"You know, I watched you today with all of them. You seem so…carefree maybe. I remember when you were little. Before dancing mind you, how you were so carefree. I know I did some things wrong in my life

Grace. I know that I pushed you into dance. I know that I made judgments on your life that I had no right too. I know all of this and it's like I couldn't help myself. I saw myself in you Grace. I wanted to be the dancer and you were right. I pushed you into a life that I thought that I wanted. I pushed you and pushed you and I saw how talented you were but I also saw the drain that it had on you. I thought that if I just pushed a little harder, just a little more that you would snap out of it and you would become Grace again but that was my fault. I pushed you so hard that you started to hate it and I'm sorry. I'm sorry that I didn't listen. The reason that I really came here was to tell you that I'm sorry that I didn't see it sooner but when I saw you today…"

"Well it was like the old me took over and all I could do is criticize. From here on out what you do with your life is your business. I will try and accept every part of it regardless of how I feel about it. I want us to be close Grace. I want what we used to have. I also wanted to tell you that I quit gambling. I started in a gamblers anonymous group and have given it up. I don't want you to have to support me or my vices anymore. Believe it or not you were right. My father knew about my gambling habits before he passed. It got so bad at one point that he had to pay off a loan shark because I had borrowed so much. I'm not proud of that but he knew that I would gamble all that money away. That is the reason that he gave it you and I'm happy that he did. I could never have managed it the way that you have. By now if it would have been left to me I would have went through all of it and never gotten the help I needed. Your father god love him understood this. He is the one that encouraged me to go and get the help. I too would like to be your friend Grace and have your support. I would like us to be friends and not have all the hate between us. Do you ever think that you can forgive me?"

"Of course," Grace smiled. "I always wanted us to be close mom. I think that I just needed to get it all out but I'm sorry if I hurt you, which was never my intention."

"Yes it was and I deserved it. I haven't been fair to you Grace. I was bitter about the money. I was bitter about the dancing but I'm tired of being bitter. I want to be in your life. I want to see my grandchildren. I want to see them grow and spoil them. That is the other reason that I went and got help. You and Thomas are getting older. I wanted grandchildren to spoil and I was going through too much money. If I would have kept going I would have run through everything and I wouldn't have ever gotten to give it to them. I am getting grandchildren right Grace?"

"Well about that mom. I actually have to have sex in order to give you grandchildren but I'm sure that Tommy is all over that by now." Her mother sucked in a breath and Grace laughed. She shook her head, "You mean that you never?"

"When was there time?" Grace started, feeling awkward about this conversation. "I never had a life remember and you always told me, never to do one night stands. I think that lesson actually stuck because I never have and never will."

"So you and these Baker boys? Now I'm not saying that there is anything wrong with them. After all they are all very good looking men but you haven't…you know? Not with any of them?"

"Nope and to tell you the truth I want to. I'm attracted to Cole. He's the youngest one but I don't understand how to be sexy. I never really tried and to tell you the truth I don't have a clue where to start. That is why I invited you mom. Your taste in clothes is impressive. I need some of that now. What do you say? You want to help me catch Cole Baker?"

"Honey I don't know him but he is a little cutie. My grandbabies would be adorable."

"Mom we are not talking about children here. We are talking about me trying to have a relationship with the man."

"Can't blame a woman for hoping, can you? Come on I know just the thing," she said leading her off towards the dresses.

Grace walked along with her mother. Would she ever understand this woman? She smiled as her mother held up all the dresses for her. At least with her mother and her on the mend she would be able to get her input. It wasn't like she understood men at all. They seemed to change with the wind and Cole Baker was the worst.

She sighed as her mother pushed her into the dressing room with a pile of clothes. At least her mother was trying. She was still pushing. Just now it would be about grandchildren. She grinned as she thought about what it would be like to be a mother.

Grace always knew that she had wanted children. She knew that she loved them in fact but now she would actually have a sex life to accomplish that. She grinned in the mirror looking at herself in the little black dress. It was going to take more than this dress to knock Cole's socks off but she was more then up to accomplishing that goal.

Looking in the mirror for the tenth time in less than a minute did Grace realize just how nervous she really was. It had been such a long time since she had been on a real date that she wasn't sure how to act.

Her mother today after a long talk and a little crying had thrown herself into helping Grace. She knew that it was only because she wanted grandchildren but at this point she was happy to have the help.

As the doorbell rang she thought that she just may puke. What did she know about dating? With Kurt it really hadn't ever been about dating. They would meet up every once and a while to have a meal together. She could have done that with a friend.

In fact the more that she thought about it. The more she realized that Kurt had been more of a friend than an actual boyfriend. He never really kissed her. He held her hand but very rarely. Over the course of their relationship people didn't even realize that they had been dating. Looking back on it now did she realize the same and her stomach dropped.

That would mean that she never dated anyone, ever and now she was going to be thrown into it. She took deep calming breaths and she opened the door. Bret was a knock out cleaned up she thought as she opened the door wider and attempted to control her breathing.

He was always cut nice. It was hard not to notice that when the man's shoulders were thicker than she was but now. Well now it really showed. She studied the not so silent Baker brother for a moment.

With the brother's a person could always tell that they were brothers. They all had the same jet black hair color. The eyes were different but each of them was well made. This one more than the others. His massive arms could make a girl quake with longing. These grayish, blue eyes were twinkling and she was sure that she was having a harder time breathing now. Bret was experienced and she didn't have the first clue how to date.

She groaned as she closed the door and walked over to the couch to sit. She put her head between her legs so she wouldn't pass out and called herself ten types of stupid. Men like, Cole and Bret didn't go for the skinner, curve less dancers. Who was she trying to kid?

"Aren't you even going to say hello before you pass out on me?" Bret asked.

The baritone in his voice dropped and she was sure that if didn't quit she was going to lose her mind. What was it about the Baker's that could just make a good woman lose all common sense?

As she looked up into those eyes she knew. They were too damn appealing for their own good and what was worse was they knew it. They knew how they looked to woman. They knew that all the women talked behind their backs and if what she heard about them was true. Then all the Baker boys just loved the attention. Well she would be damned if she would be one of those females. Cole Baker had another thing coming if he thought that she would cave first. With her confidence back in place she stood.

"Sorry about that. Just needed a moment to take everything in. How are you tonight?"

"Better now that you have talked to me. You look damn good Grace."

"Why thank you," she said smiling. "This really nice man happened to ask me out tonight and since he told me to wear something to knock his socks off. I figured that this would fit the bill." She said turning in a slow circle.

"I would have to agree with you. Shall we?" He asked holding out his arm.

Grace carefully wrapped her arm around his and took a deep breath. She needed to get her head on straight. It wouldn't be all that bad right? It was only after all a fake date but she couldn't help but feel like maybe it wasn't. She pushed the thought out of her head. Tonight she would be Grace like he told her to be. Then she would let everything fall into place on its own and that was that.

Cole stalked outside of the house. He knew that he should just leave things alone but he couldn't. He wanted to see how his brother and Grace would act tonight, so here he sat in the woods praying that an animal didn't make dinner out of him with a pair of binoculars in his hands.

He had seen Bret pull up in the truck. He had even seen Grace pacing the house and damn did she look good tonight. Her fire red hair was pulled up on her head and curling around her face. Her makeup was done and that dress. That dress had nearly made him go storming into that house to tear it off of her.

The low scoop neckline showed just enough of her to entice him. It was as though her breasts were calling to him. Saying come and get me Cole. Now sitting in the woods rock hard yet again did he realize just how soon he would need to have her.

He knew that if he didn't take her soon he would lose his mind but he had told his damn brother to take her out tonight so that he would have the chance to talk with Tommy. Earlier he had set everything up. Tommy and his parents were staying at the local hotel nearby.

Cole wanted to have Emma in bed before he would talk to Tommy but he couldn't stop himself from coming here first and seeing Grace. He raised the binoculars as they made their way to the truck and watched as his brother smiled at her helping her up. He even kept his hand there for a moment longer than was needed.

As his boil started to boil he saw his brother turn and look right at him. He gave a little smile and wave and walked to the driver side. Son of bitch, Cole cursed silently; Bret had known that he was hiding here.

He watched as his brother leaned over to Grace and kissed her cheek. He could see her blushing in response and his common sense about went out the window. He knew that his brother was doing it on purpose just to torture him. He was just about to jump up from his spot when he heard a voice.

"You know spying is not so creative, especially when you're sitting where anyone can see you son."

Cole ground his teeth together. Couldn't Tommy just come alone? Why did he have to bring the old man with him? Figuring that he was caught anyway he got up and glared.

"You know Tommy, I just may forget my good intentions and beat the shit out of you myself."

"The old man wanted to come. Would you like to tell him no? When it comes to Grace there isn't anything that he or I would not do for her. Sorry to tell you pal when you want one of us you get us all."

Tommy laughed walking up to him with Sarge at his side.

"You mean…" Cole looked around for a moment. He didn't get to finish. Sarge cut him off, "Yep, even her mother is here boy. I hope you brought your big boy underwear because she is a woman on a mission and I for one wouldn't get in her way."

"Just what are you all talking about out there? Get in here now. I have some very important things to discuss with Mr. Baker and I won't be made to wait." She said slamming the door closed.

"You really are a dead man. You just remember that you have one coming from me." Cole said as he shoved Tommy out of the way with his shoulder.

"Don't worry boy. I won't let her hurt you too much. Although right now she has sometime else on her mind. I would listen if I were you son because she is worse than my Gracie when she is riled. She said something about wanting grandchildren."

Cole groaned and Tommy laughed. "I would hate to be you." Tommy said still laughing.

"She was talking about you Tommy." John said bursting out laughing.

"But I'm not dating anyone." Tommy said nervously.

"I know son and your mother thinks to change that. You wait until you hear what she has in store for you.

She thinks that this is a lovely town to meet your future wife. She was even talking about buying property here, so you best be prepared, all of you cause there ain't no stopping the woman when she has her mind made up. Come on boys before she comes after all of us."

Cole shook his head and followed. It wasn't like he had any choice anyway. He didn't know much about Grace's mom except she seemed to know how to get what she wanted. If she wanted grandchildren from Tommy then he felt sorry for Tommy because he knew that he would be giving them to her. He only hoped that she did not require anything from him.

As the evening wore on Cole found more and more reasons to kill the famous Tommy. Cole had thought that since Janet had her mind set for Tommy then Cole would be off the hook. How wrong he had been. Had his own mother even talked to him like this? He shook his head trying to remember.

The famous Janet was riled when she was angry. Sarge hadn't been lying about that part but as she paced in front of him giving him the world's biggest lecture did he started to wonder just what Grace had told her mother.

The woman was now lecturing him on how to treat Grace. He didn't mind her caring about her daughter but she was telling him how to seduce her. He didn't know who more embarrassed about the conversation now, him, Tommy or Sarge.

All the men were now lined up on the couch as she paced in front of him telling him about Grace. She was also on Tommy about the grandchildren thing and Sarge was grinning like a fool. Cole looked at Tommy who was just as stunned into silence as he was.

"Are you paying attention Cole Baker?" She barked.

"Yes ma'am. I got the gist of it. You want me to treat your Gracie nice. You want me to seduce her and you will cut off my balls with a paring knife if I hurt her. Do I have all it straight?"

"Don't get cute," she hissed. "I know what you are doing Cole and don't you try and fool me. You care about my Grace but you're going about it the wrong way. You think to manipulate her into doing what you want her to do but my Grace isn't that dumb. She probably already sees right through you. I know that I do. You must understand something about me Mr. Baker. I may be ruthless when it comes to my daughter but I had good reasons. Grace was like me in so many ways. She was always stuck in her life. She needs rules and boundaries. I understood that but I pushed those boundaries with her and now you are doing it as well. Oh I know all about you sir. The moment your name came up I had this pulled." She said throwing a folder at him. "Go ahead and take a look for yourself Mr. Baker. Tell me what you see."

Cole didn't have a clue about anything but he opened the folder he noticed is entire life's history was here. It even included everything about his court martial. There were even things in here that were deemed top secret. As he read he started to choke. How could they get all of this on him?

In the folder was the whole time that he had served. There were things after. There were even things that people had written on Facebook about him. How in the hell had she gotten all of this stuff on him?

"I don't understand." He looked up and shook his head.

"And neither does Grace," she said sighing. "We hide who we are Mr. Baker, some more than others. I happen to be one of those people. What I'm about to tell does not leave this room. Is that understood?"

"Yes ma'am."

"Good because I like you Cole. Don't make me unlike you," she smiled. "It started before Grace was born. I too was military trained. I know looking at me you would never know but I was trained for something different. I won't go into the details because I'm still not allowed but I will tell you that I was at one time a part of a special operations team. I was good at my job, so good in fact that I was recruited to be in the FBI right out of the military. I was young and jumped on my opportunity Mr. Baker. I loved what I did. I got to be in a sense a spy if you will."

"I know that it sounds strange but I was and for a time I did that for the FBI as well. I was recruited to be an uncover agent for them. I was asked to infiltrate a mob ring in Nevada. They owned a certain club there. I was told to go in and watch them as a customer and that is how my gambling problem started. I would go in do my job and report. I did it every day until I met Sarge. He too was in Las Vegas when we met. I was on a job and we fell in love. We were married after knowing each other one short weekend. I was married but I still had a job to do and so did John. For a time we were married but went our separate ways. I stayed in Las Vegas and we talked every day. I loved him you must understand but I loved my job as well. About several months into my case I got the break I had been waiting for, one of my targets took a special interest in me. This was the break that I had been waiting for. He invited me back to his hotel room. You must understand that sometimes you have to get to close to your targets in order to take them down. John understood this. I made my case and was getting promoted but I never forgot my John or my duties as his wife. Even though I loved my job I was willing to give it up to be with him. I gave it all up and went to him. I had Grace exactly one year after my retirement. The reason that I tell you all of this is because you are hiding Cole Baker. You think that you can run from it. You think that if you don't talk about it will make you a different person. You think that you can hide that part of your life and it will cease to exist but the point is it doesn't. You need to trust sometimes and let another person in. I know what you hide from. It's all right before you but do you know what I see when I read all of that Mr. Baker? I see someone that was just as lost as I was until I met my John. I too have had to do some things that I'm not proud of. I too have faced darkness but sometimes there comes a light at the end of the tunnel. Grace and Emma are your light Cole. Don't be stupid because of pride and let that slip through your fingers."

"I'm not sure what you want from me." Cole said as he continued to look in his files.

"Just like me," she snorted. "You hear but you don't listen. Grace has been letting you in since the moment she met you. Do you honestly believe that she would have agreed to stay here even for the summer if she didn't have feelings for you? You know that she is protecting herself and you know all the right moves from what I've read to do something about it. Stop letting her protect herself from you Cole. Crack her as she has cracked you."

"How do you know she cracked me?" Cole asked raising an eyebrow.

"Because she is my daughter," she smirked. "It's not hard to crack a man when you know just what buttons to push. I read your profile. You are a lady's man yet here you sit on a Saturday night with us. If you aren't in love with her yet, you soon will be. I suggest you work on her returning the feelings for you. I wish you good hunting Mr. Baker and we will see you tomorrow for dinner. Come on you two. I think that I have spoken my peace for tonight."

Cole sat back on Grace's couch and listened to the door close behind him. He couldn't figure out what had just happened to him. Grace's mother was not at all what he had been expecting but she had been right. Grace and Emma were his light and he would do anything to keep them. Even seducing Grace for her own good. She may not realize it yet but she would be his and it would start tonight. Now all he had to do was sit back and wait until she got home.

Chapter 14

As Grace and Bret got home she knew that something was off. She could almost taste it. Turning to Bret she tried to ignore the feeling like someone was watching her. It was the same feeling that she had been feeling all night.

"I had a really good time tonight. Thank you for this." Grace said facing Bret.

"I did too but you remember me telling you that I would be giving you something?"

"I remember but I would like to know what it is."

"This is it Grace, go and make your own way now." Bret said nodding towards the window. "Don't be afraid to let him in. Just give him something Grace. He broke for you now it's time to return that favor honey." He said as he kissed her softly on the lips. "Don't be afraid Grace. He will treat you right if you will let him" and he walked off leaving Grace very confused.

She pressed a hand to her mouth and turned running right into Cole. He pulled her toward him and hugged her close. He pulled them through the door and before she could even guess his intentions she was being lifted into his arms.

He didn't let her say anything as he kissed her walking her up the steps. He was done letting her run from him. He wouldn't force her but he was not going to let her think about it either. Too much thinking and she would talk herself out of it.

He walked into the room debating if this was a good idea. He knew just where to touch to make her respond. He knew that she was ready. He just didn't want to hurt her. He gave up when she bit his lower lip. He groaned and threaded his hands in hair turning her for the bed.

He pulled her dress free. He stood up and looked down at her. Her flame red hair was spread across the bed and she had her usual faint blush on her cheeks. Her eyes had turned a deep emerald and he was lost. She was the most beautiful amazing woman he had ever met and he wouldn't let her down again.

He undressed himself and stood before her. He watched as she sat up and ran her hands up the length of him. He shuttered. Her touch was as light as a butterfly's. She had her hands around him when she bent to him. Before she could touch him he stopped her.

"Grace honey no." He pleaded.

"No but Cole, I thought your body was mine, just as my body is yours. I should be able to touch you the way that you want to touch me. Right?"

Complete innocence was reflected in her pretty face, in the gleam of her eyes. Hunger and curiosity lit her expression. The combination was erotic. Sexier than anything he had ever known.

"Ah god Grace," he groaned. "Cup my sac gently. The sac is tight; roll them slowly and gently between your fingers. Let your fingers just play lightly." He could barely get the words out.

When she started he thought he would die from the exquisite torture. She put her soft lips to his tip and he was lost. Sweat broke out on his forehead. His stomach hardened and his legs got weak.

He was teaching his young lover each move that would destroy his self-control and he knew it. He would teach her all that she didn't know. Everything that she had protecting herself from and he cussed.

Her soft moan vibrated around his flesh making his teeth mash and his fist tighten. He tightened every muscle in his body to keep himself from spilling himself into her mouth.

Her inexperience only added to her enthusiasm making his hips drive deeper into her mouth. Lips that were now stretched around the throbbing head on his cock, a hot little tongue that caught the spurt of impending release that slipped his control.

He couldn't do this. His body was straining. Pushed to the limit as her nimble, gentle fingers played with his balls. The sweat from his head ran down his temples. He felt tortured on a rack of flames, of ecstasy and hell combined. It was hot and consuming, low and slow burning and he was going down in a ball of flame so fever pitched he thought that he would melt.

"Grace sweetheart," he groaned, his hips jerking forward yet again against her mouth. He wanted to be in her. He wanted to bury every hard inch of himself as deep as he could get inside her.

She moaned against him, sank her mouth deeper on him, and he hissed in extreme bliss. Have mercy on him, her virginal mouth was driving him nuts. His hips surged forward again. His balls tightened further as little electrical currents raced up his spine and straight to his head. He threaded his hands in her hair and tightened the hold. He knew that he should pull back. He was the experienced one and she was the virgin but she was robbing him of his sense.

Usually he could control his body but with her sweet mouth on him sucking him, taking him deeper than he could have even imagined control was lost. He gave himself over to the feeling of her and her wonderful mouth.

She was running her tongue up the opening in his head, pulling gently on his balls. Her expression became hungrier, drowsier as her eyes gleamed in excitement. The gentle Grace that he knew no longer existed. She was gone in a sexual hunger and he wondered how she had made it this long being a virgin.

Her mouth moved more firmly on his flesh, tightening her tongue and stroked him harder than he ever thought possible.

He couldn't do this, he told himself desperately. Coming in her mouth wasn't part of the deal. It was an intimacy she wasn't ready for yet. It was one that couldn't force on her. She had no idea-

"Fuck sweetheart!" His hands tightened in her hair bringing her head closer to him. His control was shattering. He could feel the pulse of release building in his balls. Surging into his dick. "Grace" he breathed out roughly. "Sweetheart. You're not ready for this."

He tried to pull her head back from the throbbing shaft. His fingers tightened and she moaned. Her tongue rubbed faster, harder and he was gone. Never had control shattered so easily under a woman's mouth. Usually Cole came when he was ready to come not when his cock would make the decision. But today Grace's sweet mouth was pushing him over the edge, making the decision for him.

"Grace," he breathed out roughly as her tongue swirled around the head. "Sweet, I am going to come. I can't hold back." His hips tightened and arched.

"Fuck Grace!"

Grace tightened her hold on him and pulled him as deep as she could. She would not let Cole pull back from her now. She needed this. She needed to own a piece of him.

The harsh gasp he gave her was a warning. She wouldn't give this up. God knew that she may never have the courage to do this again. She had never done this before but it was second nature to love on this man. Even if she wasn't prepared she wouldn't pull back from him now. She needed this even more than she was willing to admit to herself.

She could feel him tighten the hold on her hair. Another piece of pleasure that she delighted in. She could feel the cock head flex when the first spurt of semen entered her mouth.

The taste was dark, salty and very sexy. Grace moaned around the taste and took more. Her mouth worked over the pulsing head as the flavor of him filled her senses and sent flames rocking through her body. She took all he had to give, swallowing drawing more to her eager tongue. And loving the shudders that tore through his body, the grip of his hands in her hair.

He was lost in his release. She could feel it; she gloried in it. Her femininity rose with a victorious shout as she moaned in rising excitement as the last pulse shot onto her tongue. If only she would have figured all this out sooner.

He was strong, powerful, and in that moment Grace felt herself claiming him. In her heart and soul. Parts of her she hadn't known existed rose inside her. Feminine, filled with an inner strength that she had barely recognized or know she possessed. She lifted her head. Licked her lips, and watched as he lifted his dark lashes and stared back at her.

Her hands rose, flattened on her belly, and moved up until she was cupping her swollen breasts touching her hard nipples. She felt empowered. As though another woman now lived within her body.

"You're dangerous," he growled reaching for her.

"Only for you," she whispered feeling his hands cover hers. His fingers working hers against the sensitive flesh of her breasts.

"All mine," he agreed, rising, sitting up, his lips moving between her breasts. "Come to me; be mine, Grace. For today and every other day."

"Maybe," she chuckled.

He grinned as he tipped her back as he pulled her hand from a breast. His lips covered the tight peak, sucking her inside with a hungry groan as she tightened the hold on the back of his head, crying out his name.

She could feel that caress over her whole body. Her

one hand covered the back of his head. While the other caressed her own flesh, following the direction of his fingers as he taught her how to pinch her nipples, how to make the pleasure hotter, and wilder.

Sensations twisted over her, all around her and throughout her. Grace lost all sense of fear as the arousal became a conflagration of flames that left room for nothing but his touch. His warmth surrounded her and she felt as though she was burning alive.

"My turn," he growled.

His hands gripped her hips, lifting her, and then lowered her until her back touched the bed.

Grace shuddered as he spread her thighs wide and moved between them. His head lowered; there was no hesitancy in his actions, no caution. His sexuality, his command, blazed around her until she was arching, lifting her hips to his tongue and begging him for more.

She screamed his name out as his tongue plunged inside the silky wet confines of her body. It was an intimacy that she never had before.

The licking strokes were destroying her own senses. He lifted one leg, holding it high as he pumped harder into her. It rasped against sensitive nerve endings, and sent her senses spinning.

She withered beneath him. She felt the light

coming and she welcomed it. In the loss of control there was rapture she never could have imagined.

She needed to feel him stretching her, burning her with the heavy length and width of himself. She wanted to now. She didn't want to wait.

He groaned as he pushed his tongue inside her again. He licked as her as though the taste of her aroused him as much as the taste of him had aroused her.

She lifted closer, her fingers pulling at her nipples now, imagining his lips there his teeth tugging at her. She wondered how she could have not wanted to experience this type of pleasure before. In that moment she knew. It was because she had been waiting for him.

When his tongue moved from the clenching inner muscles to her straining clit, she swore she would lose her mind. When his mouth covered the tight little nub and sucked it into his mouth she exploded.

This had been harsher, hungrier and filled with more than love or lust. It was something that her body didn't seem ready for but she responded to him anyway. If all she would have was tonight then she wanted to experience all of it.

Her hips bucked up in his grip, and she couldn't keep them still. Her nails dug into his head, and she couldn't force herself to release him. She was locked in a cataclysm that she couldn't seem to escape.

She was twisting in the destruction of her senses. Holding to him, keeping him to her, demanding, desperate for every ounce of pleasure she could experience, every touch, every cry, every spark of release that shuddered though her until she collapsed on the bed panting and needing more. As the flames became a low dull ache that left her ready for more, she wondered how anyone could not want the man.

"Now," she moaned, staring up at him as he came to his knees between her thighs and leaned over her, reaching for the drawer in the nightstand.

"No." She caught his hand, staring back at him as he watched her in surprise, his gaze narrowing on her. "I want to feel all of it Cole. If all I have is tonight than I want to know all. Please?"

He froze staring back at her for a long endless moment before easing back.

She wanted everything that she had never had. She wanted to be the woman she craved to be in her lover's arms. In Cole's arms. In Cole's arms nothing was wrong and she was starting to realize that. He was the lover that she didn't want but would crave in the morning and he could destroy her if he had the mind too. She only prayed that he didn't.

"You're going to destroy me Grace" he groaned pushing into her. It was hot pulsing and iron-hard.

Her breath caught as he pushed all the way into her. She felt the full length of him, stretching her, working into her and the bit of pain that seemed to follow. Grace moaned pulling her legs back further, watching him.

"That's it," he groaned. "Watch me take you."

She did as he asked. By this point her body was not her own. It now belonged to Cole. To use the way he saw fit.

Her hands locked on his wrists as his palms pressed beneath her thighs holding up her legs as he worked deeper and deeper inside her.

And she watched. The room was light and she could see everything that he was providing for her. She could see her juices shimmering on his flesh as he pulled back. Then he pushed inside her again deeper and harder.

"Yes" she breathed out roughly. "I want all of you, Cole. All of you." His body straining against his control. She could feel it. Sense it.

His hips bucked deeper and harder against her. Lifting to him Grace cried out from the wash of pleasure consuming her. She bucked against him thrust against him, her cries tearing from her throat as the pace he set destroyed her own self-control.

He drove inside her deeper and to the hilt. The blinding flash of pleasure and heat had her arching, her nails biting into his wrists as the breath seemed to lock in her chest. The momentary bit of pain was all but forgotten.

He surged his hips forward while she whispered words to him. He surged into her until he could feel her tighten for him. The muscles through her body began to stiffen. They seemed to grip him in a death grip and he groaned at the feel. No one would ever feel as good as she did to him right this moment.

When it came she could swear that her spirit lifted from her body. She was flying, exploding into fragments as she heard her own wail echoing around her, joining Cole's harsh groan as he thrust into her buried to the hilt and gave into his own release.

The feel of him coming in her gave her another burst of pleasure, another sensation and triggered another release. She arched to the breaking point her muscles drawing her tighter as she flew higher, harder, and imploded with a violence that left her shaken to her core.

She felt Cole coming over her, his arms surrounding her, drawing her against him as she shook and shuddered through the echoes of ecstasy that flooded her body.

He held her close, an anchor in a storm she should have been frightened of. Her anchor, period. He protected her, held her, and for the first time in her life

Grace thought perhaps she had the courage simply to be herself because if she fell Cole would be there to catch her.

His arms would hold her. His strength would renew her until she could strengthen herself and stand on her own again.

For the first time in her life, she thought maybe she knew what love could truly do. She would have strength because he gave her strength that she didn't even know she had. She would always feel strong in his arms.

She would feel safety. Held by him unafraid for the first time in years because in this moment the fear of the unknown vanished.

Intimacy, because she finally knew intimacy. She felt his seed spilling inside of her. She felt his laughter and for the first time she felt complete and so free. Loving Cole had been a freeing experience. She knew that she had broken some of her rules but that was alright. It was time to break some of those rules.

She looked in his eyes. Already they were clouded again. She shivered. She leaned up and kissed him hard biting his lip. He pulled back from her already wanting her again. He shook his head, "you're too sore."

"Are you sure? I don't feel sore," she smiled raising an eyebrow at him.

He shook his head and kissed her softly, “I’m sure. Now why don’t we go and take a nice long shower.”

She didn’t want to let this drop. She wanted to know Cole. She wanted to know his heart and his mind but for now she had no choice. She let him lead her off to the bathroom. She only hoped that she would be able to keep up with him.

In the shower Cole didn’t know what had possessed him but he couldn’t fight the need for her anymore. She was like a drug that he couldn’t get enough of. He had watched as she gently washed herself.

She had even taken the time to wash him. The rational part of his brain knew that she would be sore but the other part of him wanted her again.

She turned to him and kissed him. She let her hands run up his body. That was all it had taken. He was on fire again. He couldn’t stop himself from grabbing her by the back of the head and pulling her up against him.

He treaded his hands through her hair with one hand. The other wrapped itself around her bottom and turned her. He pushed her up against the shower wall. He waited for her to push him away but she didn’t.

She wrapped her arms around his neck and clung

to him. He gave up. He was not going to fight it any longer. He lifted her and pushed into her once again. He was mindless to everything but her. He didn't care that the shower was now cold and pounding on his back. The only thing that he could feel was her soft warmness beckoning him. He pulled away from her mouth and watched her lustful gaze.

"Are you sure about this?"

"I want you again Cole. Don't make me wait." She said before biting his bottom lip.

He gave up. He pushed all the way into her. He stopped when he was buried deep inside of her. Wrapping her legs around his back she arched against him from the wall.

He braced himself with one arm on the wall and pulled out of her. He watched as her head fell back against the wall. She moaned her surrender.

He was lost. He didn't know if she would be able to handle this but he was at least going to try. He took her mouth again as he thrust into her. He thrust over and over again with quick measured strokes.

She knew that it was new for her but she had felt as though she was designed to love this man. She didn't care that he wasn't being careful with her. He was showing her the real him.

She could feel his abs muscles between her thighs. She could hear his panting in her ear. She could feel his strong arms holding her and she loved it. She loved every moment with Cole.

She let her head fall back and he continued to thrust into her. She could feel the nervous energy starting again. Her body responded to him. With every thrust, every stroke he was bringing her closer and closer to her climax.

She bit his neck and let her nails scrape his shoulders. She knew that she should be turned off by this because he was not being gentle at all but she found that she loved this too.

It was new and exciting. She opened her eyes when she heard him groan her name. She looked at him as he pounded into her. She never looked away from his intense gaze. Even when the lights came again.

She screamed his name as she came again. He didn't try to silence her this time. He came shouting her name as well.

When the last tremors faded he lowered her to the floor. He braced himself against the wall keeping her pinned. He took a calming breath.

"I think that you're going to kill me.

"I shouldn't have fallen in love with you." She whispered against his lips kissing him softly.

He pulled back from her. He didn't know what to say. She had just admitted that she loved him. In one hand his heart soared. In the other the fear came crashing down around him.

He didn't know what to think so he decided not to say anything. He shut the water off and toweled her off slowly. He knew that she was waiting for him to say something, anything but he couldn't. He didn't know what to say to her.

He led her back to the bed and pushed her in. He covered her up and kissed her brow.

"Listen I need to think for a moment. Alright? You didn't do anything wrong. I just…"

"It's alright, I get it. You're scared, now go and take your time Cole and I'll be here when you return."

She turned away from him because she didn't want him to see her crying. She knew that she had shocked him but she couldn't help but blurt that out. She listened as he turned and walked to the door.

She heard him close the door and then and only then did she let herself cry. She buried her face in the pillows and gave herself over to the pain.

Cole paced outside on the patio. What in the hell was wrong with him? He had just made love with an increditable woman and he had walked out. It was her last words that had scared him. "I shouldn't have fallen in love with you."

Those words swirled through his head making it hard to breathe. This was the plan. This is what he had wanted. Wasn't it? So why was he running from it? He didn't understand anymore. He couldn't understand how she had turned him upside down and inside out in a matter of days.

It was so confusing but he couldn't leave her now. She had told him that she didn't do one night stands and he had practically forced her. He looked up at the window that was now dark. If he didn't know any better he would have thought that she wanted him to leave.

He shook his head at his thoughts. Maybe that was the best idea right now. Once again his head was a mess and it was only getting worse thinking about what he had made her do. He hadn't forced her but then again he hadn't given her time to voice her opinions either.

Standing out in the darkness that surrounded him he wondered just how much damage he had done to her by leaving right after. Would she forgive him? He shook his head and walked back in the house.

There was only one way to find out and he would have to man enough to face the consequences. As he climbed the stairs he could swear that he felt a cold ball of energy hit him in his gut. He stopped on the steps and looked around. Shrugging he made his way back up the stairs to find Grace completely covered and sleeping.

Great she had thought that he had went home. As he watched her sleep he wondered why she would ever pick him. She was smart and beautiful. She could have any man that she wanted. Why would she want someone as broken as he was? He sighed and kissed her cheek.

He knew that he should get into bed with her but he couldn't. He needed time to figure out what was happening to him. He wanted the distance to figure out what he really wanted from Grace.

She seemed like such a strong person at times and then there times like tonight, when she told him that she was falling for him. That she seemed somehow lost. He stepped back and collected his clothes. Tomorrow at dinner he would talk to her. For now he just needed the escape.

Grace knew the moment Cole left because the house was cold and empty now. Why did she have to tell him that she was falling for him? She knew men like Cole. They were used to taking what they wanted and walking away. It was in their natures but she couldn't be totally mad at him either.

She had asked for this. She had been warned on what type of man Cole Baker was and she had taken him to bed anyway. She sniffed and wiped at the tears. She had made this decision and she would have to live with the consequences. She wondered if this was how Sara felt after her one night stand.

It felt as though she was reborn in Cole's loving embrace. She felt the world tip when she told him that she was falling for him and when he left. All she could feel is the loneliness sinking down into her soul.

Kurt walking away had been bad. Cole leaving after what they had just experienced had been heart wrenching. As the tears came more she just wanted to forget about it. For tonight she would cry it all out.

If Cole Baker could walk away untouched and unaffected then she would do no less. She didn't know if she could stop herself from liking him but she would damn sure try. She would never leave Emma but as far as Cole Baker was concerned. She owed him nothing now nor would she give him any other part of her. He had taken everything that she had given and walked away. Just like Kurt. With that final thought she gave herself over to her tears. Tomorrow would be a new day and she would get it all out tonight. Even if it killed her.

Chapter 15

The next morning Grace woke to a bright light in the room. Rolling over to get away from it she realized that she was not alone in her bed. She screamed as her brother grinned at her.

"God Tommy you scared the shit out of me." She groaned into the pillow.

"Morning to you too sunshine. Listen I thought that we were supposed to go over to the Baker's for Sunday dinner. The problem is you weren't there and people are starting to notice. Don't worry Janet is all over the meal but Emma has been asking about you. I just figured that something was up, so I volunteered to come and see." He said grinning.

"I forgot. I didn't sleep well last night." Grace groaned into the pillow. Tommy laughed cutting her off. "I can imagine why. Your sheets are a mess kid and you're half naked. You might want to get up and get moving. Everyone is asking and something about planting rose bushes today."

"Go away Tommy. I'm not ready to get up. Tell them all I'm sick. I don't care. I just can't deal with any of it right now. I'm a mess."

“Wait, what’s the matter? You’re never like this and you never make promises that you don’t keep. Want to tell me what is going on here, or do you just want me to kick ass then ask questions later?”

“This doesn’t concern you in the least.” She groaned.

Tommy pushed himself up. “He did this didn’t he? That son of a bitch is a dead man.” He roared getting out of the bed and walking toward the door.

“Tommy no wait. You don’t understand. Would you stop a moment?” But the door was already slammed shut behind him.

Son of a bitch she cussed to herself. Tommy would kill Cole and she knew it. Racing to get dressed as soon as possible, she didn’t bother with her hair or her clothes. Grabbing the first thing she saw she raced out the door after her brother.

She really didn’t need her brother being arrested for hitting the sheriff and she really wasn’t in the mood to explain why Tommy was doing it. As she hit the driveway she cussed again. Her brother was nowhere in sight. She knew that he must have run through the woods.

Grace wasted no time racing off after him. She couldn’t really let her brother beat the shit out of Cole. Because even though he deserved it she didn’t want to see that look on Emma’s face.

While racing across the trail did she realize that she had forgotten to grab shoes. Hitting her foot on a stone she ran even faster. She needed to get to Tommy first so she could explain. As she made the house she knew that she was too late. Tommy was already in Cole's face shoving him.

"No Tommy don't," she said as she ran for them. But as she ran the world turned dark and everything went black again.

Cole could hear Tommy yelling from the front yard. Already Janet and John had made themselves comfortable in his house. Janet was happily talking to Emma about the dinner and John was with Bret on the couch watching some type of sport. As usual Ross was out in the garage tinkering with something or other.

After last night Cole had spent the better part of the morning pacing. Was Grace alright? She had said that she would be over early to help with everything and when she hadn't showed he became worried. He had wanted to go and check on her but Tommy had insisted that he would go.

It wasn't like Cole was hiding. Well if he was being honest he was. He didn't know why he had left last night. He should have stayed in that bed holding her all night. It wasn't like he got any sleep anyway. The rest of the night he alternated between pacing the floors and tossing and turning.

Every time that he would close his eyes she was there. His thoughts were all now consumed by her. His every thought centered around her and he was drowning in it. He just couldn't understand what was wrong. He had never run from a woman and here was doing it again and right after she had given herself to him.

He knew that he would need to apologize. He would apologize and then try and explain. He had run because he found that he liked Grace way more than he was willing to admit. He never had these types of feelings before and he was scared.

He snorted as he opened the door. Of course he was scared. He didn't let women get close to him. He never let any of them see the real him and she had. She had seen through him from the first moment they met but how to explain to her.

As he walked out to a screaming Tommy he knew that he was pissed about something. Obviously Grace had talked with her brother. He grinned when he thought about kicking his ass. At least now he would have an excuse but as he walked down the porch steps he caught sight of Grace. Tommy shoved him but he wasn't paying attention to him now.

She was running out of the woods and straight at Tommy. No doubt to stop him from fighting but Cole was more than willing to accommodate him. He watched Grace with her hair every which way and her clothes not on and smiled. She was in a total state of disarray and he had done that. He smiled when he noticed that she was not even wearing shoes but as she ran his smile faltered.

He could only watch helplessly as her eyes rolled into the back of her head and she pitched forward at an alarming rate of speed. He watched in horror as she fell to the ground and hit her head on a rock that was sticking up out of the ground spraying blood in every direction.

The roar of fury he let out had everyone running as he ran for her. Her body was motionless as he gathered her into his arms and held her. There was blood covering her head and in that moment he died.

He screamed for Bret and told Janet to call 911. He put his ear to her mouth but there was nothing. Bret ran up to him.

"Give her to me Cole." Bret shouted.

Cole couldn't seem to move. He knew that Bret was medically trained but his mind wouldn't let go. Couldn't let go because he couldn't lose her too.

"Come on Cole. Let me have her. I can't help her if you won't let her go."

"This is my fault." Cole said looking up at him tortured. "This is all my fault. I can't let her die Bret. I don't know what I would do."

"I know but I need to help her Cole." Bret smacked him on the back. "Give her to me."

Cole held out his arms but his mind wasn't working. Every moment that she wasn't breathing was a moment that he didn't want to breathe either. Tommy was beside him in a minute.

"Give my sister to Bret asshole." Tommy roared.

Cole looked over to him as Bret grabbed Grace out of his arms. He couldn't comprehend that he had just been punched because honestly he couldn't feel it. He couldn't feel anything now but emptiness.

In that moment Cole Baker knew what true darkness was. He had thought that he had been living in it. Hell no that was a walk in the park. He would take that pain ten times over. The pain that he was feeling now was ripping him apart.

Sarge was beside him next pushing him out of the way. He sat on the lawn stunned. He couldn't figure out what had happened. She had been so alive last night. She had been so wild and carefree and now she was not breathing.

He could hear people around him but it was as though he couldn't move. He couldn't understand anything. He couldn't understand why she fainted. He couldn't understand why he had left her last night. And he couldn't understand why he just wanted to curl up with her and die.

It wasn't making any sense but he couldn't think straight. Then Emma was in his arms crying. His brain registered the fact that he should be doing something to comfort her but he couldn't. He couldn't get himself to move at all.

Janet came over and picked Emma up from his lap as he watched Bret give Grace mouth to mouth. The ambulance pulled up and he watched as they came and put her on the stretcher. He tried then to get up but Tommy kicked him back down.

"You don't deserve to come asshole. I'll deal with you later" and he was off. Running to get to the ambulance as Grace was loaded up and taken away from him. Bret hunched down in front of him.

"She is going to be fine. She was breathing Cole." He shook him. "Are you hearing me? She is going to be fine Cole. She was breathing when I gave her to the ambulance crew."

The words were right but he couldn't respond. Losing Vikki had been bad. Losing Emma for that short amount of time had been bad. Losing Grace and there was nothing. He didn't want a world without Grace and he felt like an ass for not seeing it before.

It didn't matter that they hadn't known each other long. Somehow she had wormed herself into his heart in just a few short days. Bret shook him again.

"God damn it Cole, talk to me. Tell me what in the hell is going on here."

"I lost her," Cole said shaking his head.

"What in the hell do you mean, you lost her? I told you that she is going to be fine. She's breathing Cole. Head wounds always bleed like that."

"You're not listening." Cole screamed grabbed his shirt. "I lost her. I had her and I threw it all away. I am such an asshole. I can't believe I lost her." He said breaking on a sob.

"What are you talking about Cole? Make sense damn it." Bret snapped out shaking him.

"I'm telling you that I lost her. Last night after you dropped her off, I had her. I had her Bret and she told me that she was falling in love with me. I needed air and when I went back she had shut off the lights and gone to bed. I had her and I lost her because I'm an asshole that couldn't tell her what I was really feeling. She is never going to forgive me for this and I wouldn't blame her. I did this to her. If I would have stayed she would have never been running after Tommy and she wouldn't have fallen. God I just want to hit something. How could I have been so stupid? She was falling in love with me and I blew it. I blew it big with this stunt and she will never forgive me for it."

"Listen she will forgive you. Come on I'll ride with you to the hospital. Me, you, Ross, Janet and Emma. We will ride together. Come on if we leave now we may be able to catch up with them."

Cole couldn't move. He knew that he needed to but his legs wouldn't support him. Bret smacked in the face.

"Come on damn it she needs you. Grace needs you Cole."

Cole nodded and stood. Grace needed him. She needed him and he wouldn't let her down again because god as his witness he would never let her out of sight again. He raced for the car calling for everyone as he went. If he didn't get to her soon he was going to lose it.

The cobwebs that were surrounding her brain seemed to fade but with it, it brought a piercing pain. Why wouldn't the pain just go away? Putting her hands to her ears to block out the pain she wondered where she was.

Slowly opening her eyes she looked at the man standing above her. Who was this strange man above her talking in a voice that was so much like a roar she wanted to sink back down into the darkness.

In the darkness there had been peace. Here, wherever here was there was nothing but pain. Her head hurt and she tried to raise her hand to feel it, or rub it. Whichever would relieve the ache but the man stopped her.

Trying to concentrate she looked around at everything. Where was she? She knew that she should have some clue where she was but there was nothing. It was as though it was a big void of never ending darkness and she couldn't figure anything out at all. The man spoke to her again.

"Grace. Grace are you able to hear me? My name is Dr. Porter. Do you know where you are?"

Grace shook her head and winched at the pain. The ringing in her ears intensified and she groaned. Taking a swallow to clear her now dry throat she tried again.

"Who are you? And who is this Grace person?" She managed to croak out.

"You're not remembering anything?" He prompted.

She tried to probe her mind for an answer. Who was she? Could she possibly be this Grace to whom he was referring to? She searched but there was nothing. Only a big empty space of nothing.

"I don't remember what happened but then again I don't remember anything. There is nothing there." She said as she cried.

The crying only seemed to make the pain worse. She tried to calm herself but there were so many questions and she didn't seem to remember a single answer.

"Grace I want you to listen to me. You had a fall and hit your head. I know that you are confused right now but I will help you Grace but for now just rest. We'll figure it all out later. All right?"

That sounded wonderful to her. The blackness seemed to be pulling at her again. She knew there was peace in the blackness. She slowly let herself sink back into it and thought that the doctor that she didn't know was right. They would deal with it later. Later definitely sounded better than right now. She sighed and settled back into the peace.

Cole was pacing the room for the one hundredth time when the doctor came to get them. Cole wanted to shake the man. Since being here they hadn't let anyone to see Grace and it was going on three hours.

As the doctor stood there looking down at the chart he knew that something was wrong. The doctor shook his head and sighed. "Grace Summers parents?" He asked walking to them.

Cole didn't mind that he wasn't part of the family. He walked right over to them and stood with them wanting to hear also. Every moment that he didn't know what was going on was a moment that he was dying inside. Tommy shoved him.

"You don't deserve to be here. This is your fault."

"This is no one's fault." Janet said laying an arm on Tommy. "This was an accident. Now be quiet you two before I knock you both." She looked at the doctor. "I am Janet Summers and this is John, Grace's father. You wanted to say something?"

"I'm sorry, there is no easy way to say this Mrs. Summers but Grace has had a complication. At the moment she is being sedated but she is fine. I don't want you to worry but it seems that she is not remembering anything at the moment, including her own name. We have found the cause of her fainting spells and we are working on that at the moment but we don't know how long it will take for her memory to come back. When she is stable enough we will let you see her but for now I can't let anyone in. I don't want to overwhelm her."

"Why is she fainting all the time at least? At least tell me something." Janet broke on a sob.

"It seems that she has what we refer to as protein poisoning. Her levels were dangerously low, so low in fact that it was causing her to black out from malnutrition. Tell me, was she always a vegetarian? Has she ever eaten meat of any kind? I need to understand the cause of it. We usually never see cases were it gets so slow that it causes people to faint."

"No this can't be" Janet said covering her mouth and shaking her head. "She wouldn't be still following that diet. Would she? Oh god this is my fault." She said crying on her husband.

"My sister is Grace Summers and she was a ballet dancer. She has been on a diet that consisted of no meat. Could that be the reason that she was fainting all the time?" Tommy asked.

"Did she ever eat things like peanut butter or something with protein in it? Looking at her levels I would assume that she hasn't. Her protein levels are critical. We are giving her an IV now but we will have to see how it goes. I'm so sorry. I know that she will get better with the IV but I do not know how long it will take for her body to recover." He said smacking Tommy on the back.

Cole just stood there stunned. He never knew a person could get something protein poisoning. He had never heard of such a thing but that wasn't the real issue here. Like the doctor had told them, she would recover from that. The real problem was Grace didn't remember anything. Not even her own name and his stomach dropped.

He had heard of people getting amnesia but he never had dealt with anything like it before. What was he supposed to do now? When she was up again she wouldn't remember any of them. He would be a stranger again.

"Daddy is Grace going to be alright?" Emma asked tugging on his arm.

He didn't want to worry Emma but he didn't understand how to explain either. Bret walked over to her and picked her up.

"Grace is feeling a little under the weather now but don't worry. The doctors are going to take really good care of her. She just won't remember us sweetie but that doesn't mean we can't help her to remember. Grace has what they call amnesia. It is when a person forgets for a moment in time who they are but we will help her remember."

"I'm taking her home. She needs to be around people who love her and familiar things. When she is stable enough I'll take her back to California. I won't leave her here again." Tommy stated.

Cole was walking toward him when Sarge stepped in the middle. "Now I want both of you to listen to me." He said shoving them apart. "This is going to be hard enough for Grace without fighting about it. We all need to be united now, not fighting amongst each other. We all have played our parts in this but the blame stops now. It doesn't matter who did what to whom. All that matters now is that she gets better." He looked at Tommy. "I know that you love your sister. I really do and I know you want what is best for Gracie but she needs all of us." He looked at Cole. "And I mean all of us. If you can't be here for her, then speak now and I'll personally have her taken back but she needs you. If you can't, then man up and tell me. I won't have Grace hurt any more than she already has been."

"I won't leave her. I swear it." Cole pledged.

"Yeah just like last night. You are a real pro at that aren't you?"

"Listen if I had known that something like this was going to happen I wouldn't have even touched her." Cole started as he grabbed Tommy and shook him. "The point is I didn't. I didn't have a damn clue but you will not take her from me. Do you understand me? I don't care how far away you take her because I'll follow you. I won't leave her again and I don't care if you don't like me but he is right. All this fighting is not good for Grace and right now she needs all of us."

"But if you hurt my sister again Baker. Just one more time then there won't be a place on this earth that you will be able to hide from me. Just so we're clear."

"I can respect that. As long as you remember the same goes for me. I will defend her even from you Tommy."

"It's not me that hurt her Baker. It's not me that got all scared and ran out on her and that is something you'll have to remember for the rest of your life." He said shoving past him and walking out the door.

Cole ran his hand through his hair. He knew that Tommy was right. He would never forgive himself for leaving her alone last night. This was his fault but he was going to fix it. He just wondered how he was going to do that with everyone stacked against him.

He felt the small hand again and smiled. Well everyone but Emma. She would always be on his side.

"We'll help Grace remember daddy and this time maybe she'll start to love us back."

"I think that she already did honey but you're right. We'll help remember and then we will keep her." He said looking down into the familiar eyes of his daughter.

"Forever daddy," Emma nodded holding his hand.

The promise had been made. Forever it would be unless she ordered him away. Needing to read up on this issue Cole left his daughter to go in search of anything that would help him understand. He just hoped that he could.

Waking yet again she tried to remember anything but it was a loss. There was nothing there for her to remember. Trying to shield her eyes from the lights she felt a hand on her shoulder and a voice say, "Do you want the lights out?"

She nodded noticing the there was no pain like there had been before. God she felt so weak. Why was she feeling so weak? The lights went out and the man that had been there earlier appeared again.

"Hello Grace. Do you remember me? My name is Dr. Porter?"

Grace, who was this Grace person? Since he was looking straight at her it only seemed fitting that she was Grace. She remembered the face of him and she nodded. He had a nice friendly smile she thought.

"That at least is a good thing. Do you remember anything else?"

She searched her mind for a moment. There was nothing. No memories of any kind and she started to cry. Why couldn't she remember anything?

"Now don't go worrying about it now. For the next few days you'll be here with me. It's alright that you aren't remembering anything now. It will all come back to you when your mind is no longer protecting itself." He said gently touching her arm.

The word protection got her attention. There was something there. Just out of reach but she could feel it. Like she was supposed to know something about protecting but protecting who, or protecting what? She couldn't seem to remember.

"I will tell you what has happened so far and we can work on the rest. You have a condition called protein poisoning. It's where the body starts to shut down on itself from lack of protein within the body. In lame man terms it means you haven't been eating the way that you should. I'm told that you were a famous dancer and were made to be on a strict diet. That is the reason that you kept fainting. You fainted while running and hit your head. There's no swelling which is a good thing but your mind is protecting itself now until you heal and then you'll start to remember. Sometimes you remember little things at a time. Sometimes it all comes back at once and sometimes it never returns. We are really not sure because amnesia is not an exact science but I am sure that you'll start to remember at least some things. There are a lot of people here to see you Grace. They are going to help you try and remember so I don't want you afraid of them. They all seem to love you a lot. I just wanted to warn you before they all come in. Do you want to see them?"

Grace racked her brain. Did she want to see these people that would be strangers to her? She knew that she wanted to remember. She knew that they must be as scared as she was but it was all so much at once.

The thought of these people asking her questions to which she had no answers overwhelmed her and her eyes filled with unwashed tears. She didn't want to hurt anyone but she didn't want to face them yet. "I understand. You don't have too if you're not ready Grace. This is your choice."

"I don't want to see anyone yet. I just feel so overwhelmed and lost."

"I understand Grace. While I'm here I'll be attending to you myself. I'll introduce you to the staff before I leave for the day. That way at least you will know all of them and feel comfortable. For now I just want you to rest up. I'll tell them about your decision but don't you worry. They are your family and I'm sure that they will understand. I will be back in a little while. Are you hurting now?"

"No but am I allowed something to drink. My throat is so dry."

"Of course. I'll send in your nurse. Her name is Betty just so you know and don't worry. It will get better." He said as he stood at the door.

"Thank you Dr. Porter."

"You're welcome Grace and you can always call me Ben. That's my first name."

"Well I would tell you mine but it seems that I have forgotten it."

He laughed and she noticed that he had a nice laugh. He even had a nice smile. There was something comforting about the doctor. She took in his appearance. He had been taller for a man. If she had to guess it would be somewhere around 6'4. His chestnut brown hair was cut short and his eyes were a vivid shade of green. As she looked at him she wondered what she looked like. She couldn't seem to remember.

"It looks like you haven't lost your sense of humor."

"Wait Ben before you leave. Would you mind showing me what I look like? It seems that I am not able to remember that either."

He closed the door and walked over to the bed. "Well now I don't have a mirror handy so how about I tell you instead." She nodded indicating that it was fine. He smiled, "Well now, you are 5'9 according to your chart and you weigh one hundred and ten pounds. You have a slender build because you are a dancer but your face. Now that is a work of art. You have very large wide set emerald eyes with a small pert nose. Your cheekbones are impeccable and you have an oval shaped face. The slight blush that you have on your face only enhances your beauty and your hair. Well now that hair of yours is quite a thing to behold. It's flame red and has very large curls that curl half way down your back."

"If I didn't know any better, I would think that you're flirting with me."

"Oh but I am. Get some rest Grace and I'll have that nurse come in. I'll be back to check on you in just a little bit."

Grace nodded and sat back into the covers. How was it that she knew how to talk and what flirting was but not anything else. As her eyes started to close again she figured that it something to do with the way a brain would work. She was no doctor and she was not about to give herself a headache trying to over think it. Maybe when Ben came back she would ask him. He was a doctor and he would know.

She let the darkness claim her again. It wasn't like she was going anywhere any time soon from what she had gathered. Maybe after resting a little while longer she would start to remember some things. At least she could hope because she had family waiting for her.

Dr. Porter walked back into the waiting room not wanting to do this. He hated having to tell the family that she had refused to see them but he knew that this was overwhelming for her. She had just had a terrible fall and her head was a mess.

After all these years as a doctor he couldn't understand why the brain let a person remember some things and not all. It was a puzzling question but he was pleased with Grace's progress.

In the few short hours that she had been here already she was recognizing at least him. He could see that in her eyes and her sense of humor was right where it should be for someone on the mend.

What he hadn't been prepared for was the attraction to his new patient. She was a looker all right and he knew it went against what some would call ethical behavior, but he was a man and she was a good looking woman. Even with her matted to her head with dried blood.

He hadn't been lying about her appearance. When she had first been brought to him he was shocked at just how beautiful she really was and when she opened those eyes. He was pretty sure that he couldn't breathe.

They were just so large and green. It was a contrast to her loud red hair but he found that he liked that. He could see the confusion on her face so he had distanced himself from her but he had to admit. Grace Summers was getting to him just a little.

Walking back into the waiting room for the second time he wondered who all these people were to the lovely woman. He had already met the brother, mother and father but who were the other men in the room with the small child.

He shook his head. It wasn't his business but he couldn't help but notice the sheriff. He knew Cole Baker for a while now. He had never met the family personally but from the look of them he would guess the others were his famous brothers.

Growing up in Wolfeboro outside of Jackson he had got to know the reputation of the Baker brothers. They seemed to come to Wolfeboro purposely for hunting of women. He snorted. It wasn't his business but he wondered if any of them were with Grace.

Cole himself looked like maybe he was the one. He had shoved everyone aside to get to him when he had been talking about Grace. Cussing himself for not having his head on straight he called out. "Mr. and Mrs. Summer's?"

Janet and John both stood. He would just have to say it and be done. Then he could go back and check on Grace.

"I came to tell you that Grace doesn't want to see anyone today. I'm sorry but you have to understand, right now she remembers nothing. As you can imagine it's a lot to take in all at once." He smiled "but it seems that she's getting back at least her sense of humor. She asked what she looked like and I told her. She made me laugh with her comments. I would suggest that just for today you all go home and get some sleep. Tomorrow she may feel up to having visitors. I want you to remember something. Grace is strong but right now she is scared. She doesn't remember anyone or anything including herself. When you see her next please keep that in mind and don't overwhelm her. Bring in pictures of her, anything to help her remember. Sometimes the memories can be triggered from photographs or stories that you may tell her. Just keep in mind that she is recovering and shouldn't be forced to remember everything at once. For tonight I am on call and will stay with her. I have arranged to be here for the next five days just so she has a familiar face. Go home and get some sleep. I will see you all tomorrow."

"Thanks doc," John said shaking his hand. "I can't tell you how much this means. That woman in there is my world. Protect her for me."

"I will." He said smiling. Janet thanked him next. Tommy was last. "How long before she starts to remember doctor?"

"I honestly don't know. She is actually the first amnesia case that I have ever had but don't worry I have called in every brain specialist that I know and they all told me the same thing. It seems to be different for everyone. We just have to hope that she remembers on her own soon." Tommy nodded and shook his hand. "Thanks for taking care of my sister doc."

He turned and was walking out of the door when Cole stopped him. "I think that I remember you. You are Benjamin Porter right?"

"Yes and you are Cole Baker. I think that you and I met when you stole my date from me for one evening."

"Yes that sounds like me. I'm sorry about that but I just wanted to make sure Grace is alright. I know that you said everything is good but I want you take care of her. Regardless of how you feel about me that woman is important to me. Please tell her that I'm sorry. I know that she won't remember what I'm talking about but I'm sorry and I won't leave her again. Can you just tell her that for me?"

"Of course and don't worry about the date. Any woman that would leave with someone else wasn't worth my time anyway."

"I am glad and I'm sorry because I usually don't do things like that. Normally I don't take what belongs to someone else but call it a lapse in judgment but just so we are clear. I know that you probably like Grace because everyone does. Just remember who she belongs too doctor."

"I wouldn't dream of taking something that is not mine. Now if you will excuse me, I need to make other rounds."

Cole nodded and stepped back. He knew that he shouldn't threaten the doctor but he did remember him. Ben Porter had been dating Shelly when Cole had decided that he had wanted her.

They had all been at a local bar where Shelly and Ben were out on a date. Cole had known Shelly a long time before hand. He knew that he wanted her, just not permanently, so when she got up to go the bathroom he had played the game.

He gave her a wink and a smiled. When she had come out she had walked over and talked to him. It wasn't his fault that she found him more interesting than her date who only talked of his patients.

He had given her a night to remember and for a while they had tried to date but like all the others he had gotten bored within the week. He dumped Shelly and moved on but not before she had accused him of seducing her and making her give up a good man like Ben Porter.

Cole had shrugged and told her that she had made the decision to leave the doctor for him. But now that doctor would be seeing Grace all the time. He knew that he was being a bully but Grace was his and no one. Not even the great Dr. Porter was going to take her from him.

Chapter 16

The next morning Grace woke remembering that her name was Grace Summers. She kept saying it over and over in her head but as for everything else, it was still a blank. Every time that she had tried to think about it, it just made her head hurt.

The pain that she had been feeling was at least at a dull ache. Reaching for the water she noticed the doctor again. She smiled as he stood and stretched.

"Did you ever go home?" She asked.

"As a matter of fact no, I spent the night here at the hospital. How are you this morning?"

"Well, I remember that I'm Grace Summers. I remember that you're Ben Porter doctor extraordinaire but nothing beyond that I'm afraid. Why didn't you go home last night Ben? Don't you have people waiting for you?"

"Nope just a cat and I usually spend most of my time here anyway. I find that I really didn't have a life so why leave. It was easier to sleep here anyway. My shift ended at ten last night but I was on call first thing this morning. I always found it easier to stay on nights like that. It beats going home to an empty house with a cat but enough about me. Are you feeling any better?" He asked flashing a light in her face.

"I find that I have a dull head ache and I'm sore and weak but better than I was yesterday. At least I think. I can't seem to remember." She said grinning.

"Well your parents brought you some clothes. I don't want you to freak out when you walk into the bathroom to shower but you have dried blood in your hair. I just wanted to warn you before you saw it. After you try and eat something I will allow you to shower but there will be a nurse with you just outside the door. I don't want you tripping again and please let her know if you are feeling at all dizzy. You are still recovering from your fall."

"That's the thing, if I was a dancer how could I have fallen? Wouldn't I have to be graceful? I don't understand what happened."

"I honestly don't know because I didn't ask and I wasn't there. I'm sure that it was an accident but let's not worry about that now. For now I want you to eat. When you are ready to shower page your nurse and then your family wants to know if they can see you. I leave the choice up to you but your brother Tommy seems like he's going to kick down the door soon if he doesn't get to see you soon."

"All right, I guess I have put it off long enough."

He nodded walking to the door. At the door he paused, "there is one more thing. I know that you won't remember him but Cole Baker. He is going to be the new sheriff here. He wanted me to tell you that he was sorry and that he's not going to leave you again. I'm not sure what he was talking about but he seemed pretty serious. I told him that I would tell you. Do you happen to remember him?"

"No, I'm sorry but there is nothing."

"Don't worry about it," he said grinning. "If you were meant to remember him then you will. For now I want you to eat up. I will be coming back to make sure that you are eating correctly."

Grace sighed as she looked at the food in front of her. There was bacon and sausage on the plate. She wondered how she could remember what bacon and sausage was just not anything else.

"Why can I remember what bacon and sausage are but not anything else?"

"We are still wondering the same thing. Everyone is different with amnesia. Some people forget how to even talk. We don't know all the specifics yet Grace but medicine seems to be a work in progress. We have ideas and theory's but nothing is concrete. Now eat up and I'll be back."

She nodded and bit into the bacon. It was a nice tasting and she found that she like the taste. She moved onto the sausage and ate everything. It was as though her body was craving all of it.

After eating her fill she paged the nurse. If she was going to face all these strangers today she at least wanted a shower. Maybe then she would be more human. Right now she didn't feel like herself but she wondered if she would even recognize the woman in the mirror.

As the nurse helped her up she stood at the bed side for just a moment to get her bearings. It seemed weird to be standing on her feet but she stretched trying to relax her muscles. As she stood there she started to stretch her legs and bend and flex everything.

She flexed her ankles and felt something familiar. She kept it up hoping to remember whatever was eluding her at the moment. As she stretched more she kept going up into tip toes. She wondered what type of dancer she had been.

She raised her hands above her head and it felt easy somehow. Had she been a ballet dancer? She would have to ask someone but right now she was more curious about herself. She didn't even remember her own face and she was looking forward to seeing it.

Reaching the bathroom she gave one loud scream looking at herself. The doctor came running. He stopped just inside the door. "Grace what's wrong?"

She pointed at the woman in the mirror and turned to him. "Are you high? How could you see anything on me yesterday? I look like…like a. Oh what's the word I'm looking for?"

"Swamp monster?" He filled in.

"I am so glad you find this humorous. I look like I was in a fight."

"You were," he chuckled. "With a rock if I was told correctly. I think that you lost."

"I would say so. I think that you are blind by the way. The woman that you described was beautiful. The woman that I'm seeing is gross looking."

"Right now you just need to shower. Once you see yourself all cleaned up it will give you a better picture. Just don't get your stitches wet."

"Then how am I going to wash my hair and don't you tell me that I can't. I won't see anyone like this. I would scare everyone. I scared myself."

"All right I will have the nurse apply a waterproof bandage so you can wash your hair. Anything else?"

"I would say that the rock won. When I get out of here the first thing I'm going to do is find that damned rock and congratulate it. It got me good." She shook her head looking at herself in the mirror.

"You're something else. All right the nurse will be in and go and get your shower. If you want, when this is all over I will personally help you find that rock and we can dig it up and throw it over a cliff. How does that sound?"

"I just may take you up on that offer. Sorry I screamed. I know that you tried to prepare me but I don't think anything that you said could have prepared me for this." She said pointing at her head.

"It will get better just you wait and see."

"I want to say I will believe you when I see it but right now I don't think that the shower is going to help this one bit."

"You will be pleasantly surprised. I know that I was. Go shower Grace and no more screaming. I know that you are confused but you scared a good ten years off my life."

"Ok I got it. No more screaming. Now go and let me become human again." She waved him out the door.

He nodded and walked out the door. Grace Summers was something alright. He would just have to remember that she was not here to stay. It would be a very boring place after she left, that much was for sure.

After her shower Grace was surprised by the transformation. When she had been finished she had stood looking in the mirror for a good fifteen minutes. She studied her hair and eye color. She wondered which of her parents she would look like.

She sighed. She wasn't even sure if she was ready to face anyone. Everything was new and a little freighting but these were people that she had known all of her life. Shouldn't she recognize some of them?

She shook her head and made herself as presentable as possible. Of course being in a hospital and only being allowed to wear pajamas and robes it left a lot to be desired.

Settling back into the bed she pushed the call button. Dr. Porter told her that when she was ready she would have to page the nurse to go and get her family. As she waited for them she started getting nervous. What type of person had she been? What type of people were they? And why oh why couldn't she remember a damn thing?

The door pushed open slowly and she held her breath. The first to walk through the door was a rather large man. He was maybe only a couple of years older than she was. His hair color was a dark rustic brown and his eyes were a moss color.

He was built like he had worked out a lot and he was smiling. She figured this had to be her brother Tommy. She studied him for a moment trying to remember anything about him. Where they close at one time? Where they close now? And what would she say to him?

"Hey Gracie, do you remember me? I'm your brother Tommy." He smiled gently.

"No, I'm sorry there is nothing there. I can't seem to remember anyone."

"Alright, then I'll tell you all about you and about me. Maybe if I tell you'll remember something."

She smiled and told him to sit. Tommy got comfortable.

"Your mom and dad will be in a little bit. They thought that it would be best if we come in one at a time so we don't overwhelm you but I insisted I go first. After all you and I are really close. I think that they thought if you saw me first you would be more prone to remember me more than the others."

"I am trying to remember but for now there is nothing. Trust me it frustrating for me but tell me things. Where you and I really close?"

"Close doesn't even describe it. You and I lived together in California. Since we both were traveling a lot it seemed to work better that way. You were the world's greatest dancer at one time. You seemed to have it all until a few months ago." He sighed. "You changed after that. I tried to talk to you about some of it but you weren't there anymore. It was like someone stole my sister from me and replaced her with a different version of yourself. You decided that you didn't like living in California anymore. You called me and left me a message telling me that you were moving. You didn't tell me where you were at. You didn't tell me where you going, nothing and that's not you. You used to tell me everything. Then about two weeks after you left you called me and I knew that it was my sister calling me again. You came here to Jackson, New Hampshire when your car broke down. You called me that night and you were you again. The same sister I had thought that I had lost. There was a light in your voice that I had missed. I knew the reason for the change in you but I couldn't leave you here by yourself. This is my fault Grace. I should have just stayed out of it. If I wouldn't have come for you than mom and dad wouldn't have come. If they wouldn't have come you could have dealt with your issues by yourself and who knows, maybe you could have avoided this accident. I won't lie to you Grace because we never lied to each other. In each other we have always found honesty and truth and I won't change that for anything. You're the only one that I can tell all of secrets too and you don't look at me like I'm a monster. In return you have always done the same for me, so I'll tell you everything that you want to know, even how the accident happened if you want. They told me that I shouldn't overwhelm you and I won't but I want you to ask me whatever you want to know. Ask me anything and I wouldn't lie to you

Grace because I never could." He said with tears in his eyes.

Grace knew that this man must have loved her very much and in some weird way she felt connected to him. It was as though he was her other half of herself. She didn't understand where the feeling was coming from but she was not going to let it go either.

At this very moment she was drifting in a sea of strange faces that she didn't know. Everyone around her wanted her to get better but that was their jobs. Here sat a man that was connected to her. Someone that she had shared a part of her life with.

"Ok I will tell you that I feel the connection to you. I don't know where it's coming from but it's like I recognize you even though I can't remember anything. Would you stay with me? I'm afraid that when I meet the others they will want something from me that I can't give them. Everyone is so nice but I don't feel anything. I recognize my doctor's face but I'm scared Tommy. I didn't even recognize myself in the mirror this morning. It was like I was looking at a stranger even though it was me. Tell me how this happened to me. Help me understand Tommy because I don't want strangers telling me. I want my brother to tell me." She said tears rolling down her cheeks.

Tommy walked over to the bed and got in. He snuggled down beside her and held her close.

"Don't worry Gracie. We'll figure it out just like we have always done. If you don't want me leaving, I won't leave this spot. You know it's kind of comfy in here." He said settling down even further to the covers. He wrapped and arm around her and kissed her forehead.

She placed her head on his chest and breathed in the smell of him. It was somehow familiar and comforting at the same time. She wiped the tears away and sniffed.

"Help me remember Tommy. Bring me out of the darkness."

"That's a tall order kid but we'll work on it. I'll stay with you here in this room for as long as you want me Gracie. No one will be able to get rid of me if that's what you want."

"That's what I want. It feels familiar to me. You being here I mean and I don't want to lose that. I feel so lost."

"I know sweetheart. We will fix it."

The word sweetheart triggered something. It was right there just out of reach again but familiar somehow. She shrugged and settled into her brothers arms. Maybe if she could just rest a moment it would come back.

"Don't leave me alright. I'm just so tired." She said yawning.

"Not going anywhere. I think you and I both need a nap." He said yawning as well.

They feel asleep moments later with images running through Grace's head. She knew that she didn't recognize anyone but there were little snippets of dancers. Almost like sugar plums faeries running through her head and she smiled. She would just need to remember than it would be easier.

Cole's first day on the job sucked. He was so consumed with thoughts of Grace that he couldn't think straight. He had thought about resigning his position but he couldn't do that. Jeff had been a real friend. After Cole told him what was going on he had stepped up. He had handled every call like a pro and even kept Jacobs off his back. The man was constantly on him all day about one thing or another and it was wearing on his nerves.

He was supposed to be on call tonight but while Grace was in the hospital Jeff had taken over that as well. He was going to owe the man big time. Driving home he wondered if Grace was starting to remember anything at all.

He had tried to call several times to the hospital to get information but since he wasn't family he was getting nowhere fast. Now with his day over he drove to the house to pick up the rest of the family.

They had all insisted that they were going with him. Even Bret who was supposed to fly out this morning had decided to take some personal time off. He had called his commander last night to tell him that there had been an accident in the family and he was going to be taking the rest of the summer off.

During the course of his years in the military Bret had never really taken anytime for himself. This was a first and it shocked Cole. Even during the funeral for their parents and sister he had never taken so much time for himself.

When asked he simply said that he was maybe looking into to retiring soon and needed to know if he could handle not being there so much. Cole knew the truth. His brother had come to love Grace as well and he was not about to leave her either. None of them could leave her. Within days she had become part of this family and each one of them was worried about her.

Pulling up in front of the house the entire clan was waiting for him on the front porch. They must have known that he was coming for them. They all piled in the car not saying a word. Mainly because he was unreachable lately. He wasn't talking too much because his nerves were a mess. He only hoped that

Grace was ready to deal with him today because he was going to see her and there wasn't a person that could stop him. Not even Grace herself.

Reaching the hospital Cole's nerves started to get worse. He was stopped at the door by a nurse and told to go into the waiting room first. When he entered Tommy was waiting for him.

"We need to talk." He simply stated.

Cole nodded and walked with him away from everyone else. Tommy faced him looking as ragged as he felt.

"Listen Grace has asked if I'll stay with her. I told her everything. She doesn't remember anything Cole, not even me but she is starting to find familiar things. You are the last person I want anywhere near Grace right now but I think that she needs you and Emma. I will be in the room because she's scared and confused. I have never seen my sister so weak, so this is me telling you that you and I are going to be a team. I don't care if you don't like me because right now I can't stand you but Sarge was right. Grace needs all of us. She told me today that she's seeing images of dancers, which is a blessing but she needs you. You and Emma are the only thing that kept her from coming back home to me and you and Emma are the only things keeping her here. I asked her if she wanted to come home to California with me. She told me that she needed to stay here but she can't remember why. I'm asking you Cole, man to man if you can be here for her. Don't lie to me and don't tell me you're scared because right now my sister doesn't even recognize herself in the mirror. If you can't do this I'll take her back kicking and screaming if I have too but neither one of us are going to hurt her again. Have I made myself clear Baker?"

"I get it Tommy I really do. I hurt Grace and you have no right to trust me. I know that now but I'm not going anywhere. You couldn't order me away and I meant what I said. If you take her from me I will find you and you won't be happy when I do."

"All right then, let's go bring my sister back." Tommy grinned and smacked him on the back.

"Wait what did you tell her about the accident?" Cole grabbed his arm for a moment.

"I told her everything. I have never been able to lie to Gracie but I softened it a bit. I told her that she was coming over to your house when she caught you and I fighting. I told her that she tried to intervene but tripped and fell on a rock but beyond that nothing. I didn't tell her why we were fighting and she didn't ask. That is as much of a break that I'm willing to give to you Cole. You can do the rest from here. Now come on. Grace just got done eating and will probably need a nap soon. If you want to see her now is the time."

Cole and Emma followed behind Tommy. He didn't know what he was going to say to her but he knew that he just needed to see. If he could just see that she was alright than he would be fine.

They all walked into the room where Dr. Porter was sitting with Grace. He looked up when they all entered and smiled. "She seems to be doing just fine today."

"He means Grace remembered who she was today." Grace rolled her eyes. "Yay Grace." She said sarcastically.

"That is an improvement believe it or not. I will let you see your visitors now and I will be back to check on you soon."

"You know Ben I'm really starting to hate your cheery nature."

"She is getting back some of that temper you told me she was famous for." He smiled and clapped Tommy on the back.

"And I'm right here you two. I swear between the two of you I don't get a moment's peace. Go away Ben and I'll see you later."

"Charming isn't she?" He asked Cole.

Cole just glared at him. What right did he have to flirt with Grace? Didn't he even realize that Cole would bury him for that woman? He must have taken the hint because he smiled and said, "Alright I will leave you all to it. I will be back" and he walked out the door.

Cole walked over to the bed and looked down at his Grace. She had been so strong only two nights ago and now here she lay with tubes coming out of her arms looking so weak to him. He didn't understand how no one had known that she was sick. Right now it was written all over her beautiful face. He cleared his throat trying not to weep.

"Hey Grace I'm Cole Baker. This is my daughter Emma. You know us already but I'm afraid I don't really know what to say right now other than, you look great."

"You and Ben are really blind, or just really nice. I can't figure out which but hello just the same. I'm sorry but I'm not remembering anyone at this time. It's nice to meet you again though." She said holding out her hand.

Cole took that gentle hand that had only been holding onto him days ago and shook it. Even her hand shake was now weak. He pulled away and let Emma try. Emma walked over to the bed.

"I know that you don't remember me Grace but I remember you fondly. I brought you something. Here" she said shoving a DVD at her. "I brought this because this is you. I thought that maybe if you see it you would remember something."

"Thank you Emma. Here why don't you come up here and sit and we can watch it together. Maybe I'll remember something that way."

Emma didn't need to be told twice. She climbed up on the bed and settled in beside Grace. Grace grinned at her and gave Tommy the DVD. He put it in and they all sat back to watch the movie.

As the movie lit up the screen Grace couldn't believe what she was seeing. It was her alright and she was beautiful. She wasn't the same woman on the tape but she was mesmerized by the beauty of the woman dancing across the stage.

As she watched she realized that this is what she was having images from. She was starting to remember some things just not all. They all sat quietly as she watched herself. She was so graceful and elegant. The rhythm of the music and movements were slow and measured but they were art.

Grace watched herself dancing and little things started coming back. The roar of the crowd after a performance. The feeling of the energy in the place she was dancing in. The light that she used to feel afterwards. The happy feeling like she had just brought someone joy in their lives, even if it was just for a moment in time. It was all there and she started to cry. She wanted to remember more but it was just blackness. She couldn't even remember the people in the performance but she remembered the stage.

She remembered the feeling of the hardwood beneath her feet. She remembered the pressure in her legs and toes. She remembered the endless sea of faces watching from the audience but most of all. Most of all she remembered the pure joy she would feel while on stage.

Tommy thought that it was upsetting her and went to turn it off. She grabbed his hand saying, "no please don't. I'm remembering some things. Just don't shut it off yet. Please?"

Tommy nodded and wiped her face. He took his seat next to her and held her hand as she looked at the screen and tried to remember more. They sat that way for two hours before the tape ended.

She wanted to watch it again just to remember but she could feel Emma next to her. She looked at the little girl that had tears in her own eyes and smiled.

"Thank you Emma. Thank you for bringing this for me. Would you mind if I keep it?"

"This one is yours. Daddy helped me make you a copy for yourself that way you could watch it anytime that you liked."

Grace looked over at the man named Cole. There was something in his eyes as well but she couldn't put her finger on it. Love maybe but she couldn't be sure.

"Tommy, would you mind taking Emma here to get a soda for a moment? I would like to talk to Cole alone."

"Sure, come on kiddo. How about a really big candy bar? Might as well sugar you up for your dad tonight," Tommy said giving Cole a pointed look.

Emma hugged Grace and then got out of the bed. She turned and whispered to Grace. "Remember the light." Then she was off before Grace could even ask her what she was talking about.

As the door close she found the room getting warmer. This Cole person certainly was good looking. His tall frame and muscular build made her very aware of herself as a woman. There was something in his eyes that was pulling at her, something there trying to break free from the memories that were now contained. She cleared her throat and tried to speak.

"Tommy told me that the morning of my accident that you two were fighting. I wanted to ask him but I thought that instead I would ask you. Would you tell me what it was all about?"

Cole looked into her eyes. He could lie but he would never feel right about it. He had vowed that if she would live then he would never lie to her again, or not tell her what he was thinking or feeling because she deserved that much from him. She had given him so much in such a short amount of time and it was only fair to return the favor to her.

The problem was he didn't want to hurt her again either. Sighing he said, "It's not a pretty story Grace and I look really bad in it but I'll tell you everything because I don't want to hurt you again."

She braced herself for the truth and patted the bed next to her where Emma had been sitting. "Come here and tell me."

Cole debated if he wanted to get that close to her. He was pretty sure that if he started touching her again that he wouldn't stop and he couldn't do that to her again. He walked over to the bed and sat.

"All right here it goes. I found you broke down on the side of the road bawling your eyes out about a week and a half ago. Since that time you and I became close. I mean really close. My daughter Emma wasn't talking at the time that you came into our lives but that didn't stop you. By that next morning you had her up and talking again. You became our miracle Grace. My miracle. We got to know each other more the following couple of days. You told me about your life and I told you about my time in the military. A few days ago you gave yourself to me. You gave me a gift that so precious to me that I didn't understand what to do with it, so I ran. I ran and you were running after Tommy to stop him from hurting me for being an ass. You ran after Tommy and fell. This is my fault Grace. I left you because I couldn't tell you that I was starting to fall in love with you too." He said with tears in his eyes.

"What is this gift I gave to you?" She asked with a lump in her throat.

He couldn't even look at her when he mumbled out. "Your virginity."

She leaned closer, "What did you say?"

"Your virginity sweetheart," he said tortured. "You gave it to me and told that me that you were falling in love with me. I couldn't come to terms with everything. I needed a moment of air and stepped outside. I think that you thought that I had left you and you shut out your light and went to bed. I never got to tell you that I was sorry for leaving you. I never got to tell you that I'm not like that Professor you had in Julliard that had a one night stand with your friend and left her after. I never got to tell you that I'm an ass and I didn't see it earlier. I love you too Grace and I hope that when you remember that I'm an asshole that you will still give me a chance because my life sucks without you in it. You have only been here for two days Grace and already it's like I can't see the light anymore. It's like you took it all with you when you came here. I don't want my life without you in it. I want us to be together Grace but I understand that you need time. You time to remember because it's not fair for you to make that choice now. Once you remember you will probably hate me Grace and I can't stand the thought of you hating me. You turned my world upside down and inside out in a few short days but you gave me so much more in return. You gave me your love and loyalty. You gave me your caring and understanding. You gave me my daughter back and me and made me and my brothers close again. You have given and given and I like the asshole that I was I took and took. I took it all Grace but I never gave it back to you. All you have gotten out of me was my issues, my jealously and my anger. I am sorrier than you could ever know Grace and I only hope that one day that you will forgive me and give me a second chance. I know that I'm the last man on the planet that deserves it but I'm hoping that you will give it to me anyway Grace because I miss you. I miss your laughter and your smiles. I miss your glares when you think that I'm not looking and I miss the love that I have only been able to find with you sweetheart." He said hugging her close.

Grace tensed for a moment. Cole was a stranger but as he held her and begged her, she found that she like the smell and touch of him. She didn't understand what all happened between them but he had been honest. He had told her the whole truth even though he could have lied. It wasn't like she would know the difference anyway but he hadn't.

He had told her the whole truth of it, even his feelings for her. She didn't understand but she knew that she liked Cole Baker. She would need time but she knew that he was a good man. She could see it in his eyes.

It was in the way that he held her close. It was in the way that he had told her the truth even though she wasn't sure if she had wanted quite that much of it. It was in the way that he begged for a second chance and it was in embrace.

In Cole's arms she felt strong again. It didn't matter that they had problems. Maybe they could work on them together.

She pulled back from him and wiped the tears away from her eyes. She pushed his feathered hair out of his face and let her hand rest on the side of his face. She looked into his eyes and said, "Thank you Cole. Thank you for being so honest with me. I find that I like honesty with people. Even though I don't remember my brother he is much like you. He was very honest with me as well. I think that is the main reason that I wanted him here. Like him you are familiar to me somehow. You and your Emma.

Tomorrow if it's not too much trouble would you mind coming back to visit me? The doctor told me that if I kept eating the way that I was I would be able to leave in a few short days. Maybe we could spend some time together Cole. Is that alright with you? You and Emma. I find that I like her as well."

Cole nodded putting his forehead to hers. "I wouldn't be anywhere else. I promise, every day after work Emma and I will come for you Grace. You might as well know you have some other people here as well. They are my brothers. They love you just as much and insisted on coming here but I also promise to make it up to you. When you get out of here I'm going to take you home. Emma and I are going to be staying with you at the house. If you're not comfortable with that tell me and I won't. I just don't want to leave you again Grace. The thought scares me half to death."

"The only request I have is that Tommy gets to come too. I love my brother and I like having him around. I don't remember how many bedrooms are in this house that I'm staying at but I want him there. Is that alright Cole?"

"Whatever you want sweetheart. You want the whole family there and I'll arrange it. Emma is going to be sleeping in her old room. I'll sleep on the couch and Tommy can have the guest bedroom. I'll get everything set up for you."

"Thank you Cole. I know that I don't remember you but you are really sweet."

"No sweetheart I'm an ass," he laughed shaking his head. "A really big ass but somehow you never seemed to mind before."

"And maybe I won't again. Who knows?"

They heard the knock at the door and both looked up to Cole's brothers coming in. "Tommy told us that it would be alright to visit. If you want we could always come back?" Ross asked.

Grace shook her head gesturing them inside. "No, it's alright. I will tell you the same thing I told Cole. I'm not remembering anyone at the moment but feel free to come on in. The more faces I see the better. Maybe one of you will trigger other memories."

"You are starting to remember honey?"

"No, not really it's more like feelings. I remember feeling close to someone, or in the case of the movie of me, I felt that I was remembering feeling what it was like to dance. There is nothing definitive there but it's something. Hello I am Grace which I know that all of you know but I don't know who you are I'm afraid." She said holding out her hand. Bret took it and shook it. "I'm Bret the oldest Baker. You and I had ourselves a date the other day but all that will come back I'm sure."

"And I'm Ross, the funny, charming one that the ladies can't resist."

Grace shook her head and laughing, "And tell me Ross did I date you as well? It seems that I couldn't make up my mind with you boys. I can see why looking at all of you but I'm curious about all of this."

Ross shook his head and blushed. "No ma'am. We never dated. You just made me breakfast all the time and argued with me about money. Which by the way I won."

Grace looked at him confused but started to laugh. "Well I'm glad that you won. As you can see I lost with that stupid rock. I'm told that it was in your yard and I should warn all of you now. I don't remember how big it was but when I get out of here the first thing I'm going to do, is go to your house and dig it up. Then I am going to take it and throw it over the biggest cliff I can find."

"And I'll be more than willing to help you honey. In fact consider it done. I'll dig it up for you tomorrow and we will all chuck it over a cliff when you get out of here. By the way, when are you coming home Grace?"

"I'm not sure actually. I was told by the doctor that I had a problem with dieting. Something about me not eating right but since I've been in here he likes the progress. In fact he told me that if I keep it up that I can be out of here in maybe two days tops. Already I'm feeling much better. I find that I'm not resting as often as I normally would. I took that to be a good sign. I know that I look freighting because believe me I frightened myself looking in the mirror but I'm told that will change as well."

Cole brushed her hair out of her face. "You look as beautiful to me as you always have Grace."

She smiled and winked, "liar. Tell me something Cole. Do you normally lie to me like this, or is this the first time?"

"All right you got me. To everyone else I'm sure you look a little ruff but to me you still look beautiful even if you are sick. You just need more rest and then you will be my Grace that I remember."

"All right, I will take a complement where I can get it. Hey boys?" She asked looking at Bret and Ross. "Would you mind going to get me a chocolate bar? I've been craving one but I can't find anyone to get one for me. Would you two be dears and go and get me one?"

Bret shoved Ross out of his way trying to get to the door. "Get out of my way Grace wants chocolate."

Ross shoved him back. "She asked me to go and get it you big jerk."

Bret stopped and faced him. “Did you really just call me a jerk?”

“Yeah I did. What are you going to do about it?”

Bret shook his head. “Come on you idiot. We’re on a mission.” He said pulling him out of the room.

“You would swear that I’m the oldest even though I’m the baby of the family. I swear those two don’t know how to grow up.”

“The real question is, do you Cole Baker?” She asked as she gently kissed him on the lips.

Cole’s brain seemed to stop working the moment her mouth touched his. He remembered the silky lips and he wanted to grab her but she needed time, so instead he kissed her quick and pulled back from her. He pushed a hand through her hair and looked in her eyes.

“Grace we have all the time in the world for you to remember but I want you to remember before we start this again. I was really mean to you and I don’t want you to one day remember that you hate me and leave. For now I will be here for you. I won’t leave you but I can’t let us get back to where we were for me to hurt you again. I just can’t do it.”

“And tell me this Cole,” Grace started as she sat back. “What if I never remember? Huh what happens then? Do we just act like there is nothing between us just in case someday I do remember? Do we act like it never happened? You know what Cole I'm tired. Why don't you go think about these types of things while I rest? I think that I'm done for today." She said turning from him.

She wouldn't let him see the tears in her eyes. It wasn't like she willing to rushing into anything with the man for god's sake. After all she didn't remember him or know a thing about him. There was just something there though. Something that she couldn't pull away from.

When Cole had been telling his story she could hear the caring in his voice. When he had told her that he was in love with her, her heart had skipped a beat. Now he was sitting here saying that if she didn't remember that there could be nothing between them. She didn't remember why she felt so heartbroken she just knew that she was.

Cole Baker would get to her again if she allowed it. Like he had said he had done it once before and left her. Now she would just have to not allow him that close again. She only hoped that she could be that strong. After hearing the story she knew that he had gotten to her once. Maybe this memory thing wasn't such a bad thing after all. It was like a clean slate and maybe that is what she needed. A clean slate from everyone.

Chapter 17

Cole got up from the bed feeling like the worlds big asshole yet again. He had thought that he was doing this for Grace. That he was protecting her from himself but maybe he had been wrong. It wouldn't be the first time.

He wanted Grace's love again. He wanted the second chance and here he was screwing it up again. He ran a hand through his hair. Why couldn't he ever just say the right things to her? Why did he always have to screw it up and hurt her?

She had been willing to give him a second chance. He could see it in her eyes even though he had been an ass. He had told her the whole truth and still she had clung to him. Instead of accepting it he had told her that they couldn't get close again. What was it with him and commitment?

Hell he knew that he was in love with her. He had just told her as much and here he was throwing it all away again. He wanted to kick something but he needed air more. He turned and walked for the door. As he was at the door it hit him. He had done this very same thing with her before. Not wanting to make it worse. He said, "I'm sorry Grace and I love you sweetheart. I'll see you tomorrow," and he pulled up the door to his brothers.

He motioned for them to back up. When Tommy approached him he gave him the candy bar and told him that they were leaving. All of them were looking at him for answers but he didn't have them. Instead he walked out of the hospital looking for an escape again.

He paced the length of the walkway like a wild man. It was John that found him moments later.

"Son I need to talk to you."

"Not now Sarge I'm thinking." He said as he continued to pace.

"I think now is the time. Come on boy. What's a moment of your time?"

"All right if it will get you off of my back," Cole barked.

Cole followed John to his car. When they were both in Sarge offered him a cigar. Cole shook his head and John grinned. "The old woman hates it when I smoke. I needed a cigar. Tell me what's on your mind son?"

"I don't know where to start." Cole said sighing.

John chuckled blowing out the smoke. "Let me guess. You love my Gracie and are having a hard time with the commitment thing."

"How did you know?" Cole asked looking at him stunned.

"Are you stupid boy? Of course you're scared. Hell I was scared. Why do you think me and the misses were married only after one weekend together? I'll tell you, it was because I thought that if I didn't marry her then I never would. I get it Cole even if you haven't figured it out yet and I'm going to help you with it boy because she is my daughter and needs a man like you in her life. You are scared because you are a military man."

Cole looked at him confused. "I'm still am not following here. I haven't been in the military in months."

"That's true but it is in your blood. As military men we understand what it's like to attend your best friend's funerals. We stand by their sides when they are shot right before our eyes, helpless to a damn thing about it. We see it day in and day out and yet we can't change it because that's who we are. We are trained soldiers, taught never to feel emotions or pain. We are trained to bury it deep inside of ourselves, never letting anyone see behind the mask that we are made to wear but it's there alright. The pain that we carry and fear that we are next. The blame that we carry because we think that if we would have done something different, that it might have changed the outcome and we wouldn't be sending our friends home in the body bags."

"It's there and we deal with it. We protect ourselves from people never letting them get close to us because we know that the person standing next to us gets shot down sometimes. And we know that if we let them close that someday we'll have to stand beside their graves and watch another person we care about getting buried. We know this and we push everyone away. It's our nature. It's what we're taught. You remember the motto; rely on no one but ourselves. We see all those loved ones of the people we bury crying their very hearts out while we have to remain dignified and maintain. We are made to stand by like statues and watch someone we love get put into the ground and we can't show what we feel. That's why we push everyone away Cole. It's because we don't want to have to cause someone that amount of pain without showing it. We know they would cry at our funerals but we aren't sure if we are capable of giving them the same because of we were taught. I know that you are running Cole because you don't want to cause Grace pain but I want you to do something for me. Think about what it would really be like for her to love you with everything in her and you don't show her the same. Think about having Grace see you as that statue because you are cold and unfeeling. Think of her at your funeral Cole because if you don't wake up soon son that's how it's going to be. Grace is going to be that loved one at your funeral but you won't be dead son. You'll be just so closed off emotionally that she'll feel as though you were dead to her. Right now you are a statue Cole, even from your own daughter. You're not letting anyone in and they are feeling like they are burying you son. You have to let them in or you really are going to be dead to everyone with them left picking up the pieces of you."

Cole was stunned by the words. In some weird way they all made sense. He had been trained to show no emotion. He had been taught to lock that part of himself away and he had been hurting everyone around him because it.

Even Emma had not been able to reach him lately and he could see the changes in her again. Right now she was pulling away from him trying to protect herself from the pain of losing him too. John was right. He needed to let people in because if he didn't then he would be lost to all of them. Just like burying him and he would be damned if he would cause any of them pain while he was still here to do something about it.

The question was how to fix it? He didn't know how to open up to people. It was in his nature like John had said.

"How do I fix it?" Cole asked.

"Now that boy is a question that you should be asking. Come on I will re-teach you to be a part of your own family. It may take me some time but I am sure we can figure it all out. It will have to start with your brothers but by then you should be a pro and you can move onto something like my daughter. I got to tell you boy if you're not careful this time around you're going to lose her to that doctor in there. I have been watching them. I don't like the way that he looks at Grace. He's just like that patsy ass I hated. She needs someone strong, someone like you, so you better man up and pack a lunch son because it's going to be a push to get you to where you need to be again."

"Just like basic training again?"

"That was a walk in the park compared to this boy. Basic training is basically only physical. Physical we can handle, it's the emotional stuff that kills us." He said laughing.

Cole swallowed hard. What did he know about emotional things? It had been years since he had opened up to anyone. What if they looked at him with that pity look in their eyes? He wasn't sure if he could handle that again.

Pity was the one emotion he couldn't handle. He didn't pity himself. Why would he want other people to pity him? He just wanted understanding.

Understanding like Grace had shown him. He had told her his darkest secrets and she had only understood.

As he thought about everything he smiled bitterly. Ben Porter better watch his ass because if he was going to do all of this for Grace then there was no way he was letting her go to some patsy ass doctor. He walked back into the hospital with John at his side.

If this man could go through all that he had gone through and still talk about his feelings than he would do no less. He had always liked John. Always thought of him as a second father and he was about to make him proud. He just hoped he didn't kill everyone around him this time.

After their talk earlier Cole decided that John was right. He would need to start in his own home, with his brothers. Bret would at least understand what he was feeling and talking about. Ross would be there for him like he had always been. It was only fair to let them in first. If he could get them on his side then he had a better chance of making Grace understand.

He got Emma all tucked into bed and called a meeting with his brothers. When they were all seated he started. "This is not easy for me, so I am just going to say it and get it done. Tonight I hurt Grace again because I have been pushing her away. John helped me understand why I am doing it and I wanted to start with you guys first. When Vikki was alive it was her that I talked too. I think it was because she was always so open about herself that it was easy to open up to her but I want to open up to you two also. You are my brothers. The only family I have left in this world and I have come to realize that you are watching me bury myself. I buried myself a long time ago and you both have been picking up my pieces. I am not going to sit by and watch that happen again. I have been cold and closed off for so long now because it is all I have ever known but I miss my brothers. I miss the trouble that we used to get into. I miss the late night talks out on the porch. I just miss us and I am working on it. Now before I begin I don't want any of you to interrupt. I am sure that you will have questions but just let me get it all said before you quiz me. This is hard enough for me as it is but I am doing this for Grace and Emma. I can't let them watch me bury myself in my feelings. I'm counting on you two, so don't fuck it up for me here. All right?"

"We have always been here Cole. Anything that you need to say just say it. It won't change how we feel about you. We're brothers. We always have your back just like you have ours." Bret said whacking him on the back.

"He's right Cole, I have always been here. I may not understand all of it because I'm not military like you two are but we are family. We aren't going to bail on you man so just say it. Open up and become part of the family again man. I for one missed your sorry ass."

"Me too," Bret started. "It's been to long since we all have done this. How about we grab a few beers and go out to the porch for old time's sake. Maybe if you open up then I might be willing to do the same. There are some things that I need to get off my chest as well. Might as well make a night out of it. It's not like any of us are going to be sleeping anyway."

Cole knew what his brother was talking about. None of them had been sleeping well since Grace had been taken to the hospital. It was like a part of them was in there suffering with her.

Since she had been taken from them they all seemed closed off and mopey. Grace had been the light in their lives and with her gone it wasn't the same. Now it just seemed like they were all going through the motions of their day.

Grabbing a few beers for the porch Cole thought about what he was going to tell them. He knew that he needed to get it all out but he was a little nervous. These were his brothers. How would they look at him in the morning?

He shook his head. He needed to stop worrying about it and just get it said. That way at least it would be out there and he could learn to deal with the way they would look at him.

He stepped out onto the porch and like the old days they all took their seats. Cole handed them their beers and took a seat himself. He could remember being on leave at one time when they were all together. They had stayed out on the porch all night just talking and getting roaring drunk.

They had drunk so much that night that their mother had found them all out in the yard passed out. She had been so mad at all of them that she had made all of them drink her nasty concoction of fish oil and milk.

It was nasty but it did the trick. Within minutes all of them were hanging over the railing puking their guts out. It hadn't been fun by any means but they had all learned not to get drunk like that again with their mother around.

He laughed at the memory. Ross looked at him and asked, "What are you laughing at?"

Cole smiled and shook his head. "I was remembering the last time that we all got drunk together. Do you remember that night?"

"How could I forget?" Bret snorted. "That was one of the worst nights of my life. That stuff mom made us drink was nasty. I still have a problem with milk."

"And I can't stand the smell of fish anymore. That woman was something all right and she is certainly missed." Ross said grinning at the memories.

Cole held up his beer, "to mom, may she rest in peace and not haunt my nightmares when I get drunk again." The others joined him, "to mom." They said taking a drink.

Cole sat back against the house and sighed. It was time to get it all out. He started with the night that he had lost Brian. He told them all about the man and all the fun they had while on their tour. He told him of his death and the burden he still carried because it should have been him.

Brian Johnson had been Cole's best friend. He had been his combat partner and closer to him than anyone. He was also set to be his brother in law. Vikki and Brian had started to write each other after he had learned that Emma's father had walked away.

For months Vikki and Brian wrote each other. Cole had never asked and Brian hadn't talked about it but one time he had slipped. He had told Cole that he had planned on coming home with him to visit Vikki on their next leave.

Cole had been thrilled. There was no better for his sister than Brian. He was a stand-up guy and a great friend. With his personality he knew that Brian would be a welcomed addition to the family but he had lost Brian before any of it could happen.

They had been out on a routine patrol when disaster had struck. They had been in a bad part of town when a man had come out of nowhere with a grenade. They were checking out an old abandoned building for outcasts when the man had entered.

Cole could still here the clink of the pin dropping to the ground when he closed his eyes. Brian was there and shot the man but not before he had pulled that pin. Cole watched in horror as the grenade came right for them. He knew there were only seconds before they were both dead but before he could move Brian was there.

He had thrown himself right on top of the moving grenade letting himself take the impact. Cole watched in horror as his best friends body was lifted from the ground dying instantly. He never understood why Brian had sacrificed himself. Sometimes he could swear he could still hear him screaming but he knew it wasn't Brian that had screamed. It had been him screaming and the ringing in his ears still came back sometimes.

It wasn't until two weeks later that he had found the letter. It had been addressed to Vikki but Cole couldn't help but read it. The letter explained that he would be coming to get her and marry her. He had fully planned on making Emma his even though he was not the father.

He explained that it was his job to take care of Cole whether he wanted it or not and he would gladly give his life to see Cole live. Brian explained that he never had family and Cole was all he had left besides Vikki. He explained that if there ever came the choice where he would have to choose between his life or Cole's. He was going to choose Cole's every time because Cole had people waiting for him. He would have done anything to ensure his safety. Even throwing himself on that damned grenade.

While reading that letter Cole had cried. He hadn't cried at the funeral because John was right. He was trained not to show emotion but as he sat on that cot without Brian by his side reading that letter written by him he cried. He cried for the loss of a brother and friend. He cried because Brian was gone while he had been forced to stay behind with the shame and guilt and he cried because now it was his fault that Vikki was going to suffer as well.

After that day Cole had learned to bury the pain just like John had said. He was taught to bury it and move on. There were always other orders. Other missions to do and no amount of crying would ever bring his friend back.

Now sitting on the porch he let himself cry again. It wouldn't bring Brian back but maybe if he cried he could get rid of the pain and anger that he was feeling. And maybe just maybe the shame and guilt as well.

Bret walked over to him and hunched down smacking him on the back. "It wasn't your fault Cole. I too have lost people like that and it all happens so fast that there isn't time to think. He was a good man but you need to let him go. It was his choice and he wouldn't want you to deal with that amount of guilt. If the shoe had been on the other foot he knows that you would have done the same for him. He was the only one close enough. We all know how it had to end. It was either going to be you and him or just him. He knew that he made his choice. Either way he knew that he was going to be one of them, so he did what we all would have done. He protected you Cole because he knew that you had a life away from there. You had a family that loved you and wanted you to come home. He knew that and gave his life for you. Don't piss it away thinking about the what if's. Mourn him and move on. It's what he would have wanted because it's what I would have wanted."

Cole looked at his brother and nodded. Bret understood. He was a military man himself. He would have done the same thing Brian had done because like he said. It was either going to be both of them or just him. Cole would have done the same for him in a minute. He wouldn't have hesitated either.

"Thanks, I think that I just needed to get it all out."

Bret nodded and downed his beer. "I understand that. Hand me another beer and I'll tell you about Jim Barns. He was my Brian."

Cole handed him a beer and listened as his brother opened up to him. They all sat out on the porch remembering the good times. Sharing with the bad and for the first time in a long time he felt at home.

The sun rose in the sky and with it came the realization that he was in the yard. He could hear the crunch of the gravel. Someone was walking toward him but he couldn't see through the fog that surrounded his mind. His first thought migrated to Emma. Was she up and about? Just how long had he been laying here? And why couldn't he remember lying down in the yard?

Last night the brothers had all stayed up late talking on the porch. With their talks, like the old days, came the drinking. Cole's stomach rolled as he thought about how much he had drank last night.

The shoes came into view and he groaned. He knew those shoes and it was not going to be a good morning. "Having fun son?" John asked.

Cole shook his head and tried to not let it make him dizzy again. Pushing up from the ground he tried to gain his footing. He had been a fool to drink that much last night. He should have known better, been more responsible. He had Emma to think of now and he had a job that he had started only days ago. Right now he was probably due to be at work and there was no way he could go in like this. Stumbling he finally made it to his feet.

"You're a real mess son. Come on we'll get you all cleaned up and right again."

"I need to call into work. I was supposed to be there early."

"Like this? I don't think so. I already took care of everything for you. You don't need to worry about a thing for the time being. You're lucky I got friends in high places."

Cole shook his head trying to understand. "Will you please not speak in riddles this morning old man? I'm not in the mood to try and figure them out." He croaked.

John smacked him on the back. "Well it seems that I have known your sheriff for quite some time now. Me and Burns served together. Nice man if I say so. Anyway I may have lied just a little but who cares about that now."

"Would you please just spit it out?" He spat.

"All right, I told your boss that you are engaged to my Grace. I told him all about her accident and he decided that he couldn't have you take over right now. He gave you a leave of absence, paid of course, just until Grace is feeling better and then he'll train you properly and you will resume your duties."

"And he just let me have off paid?" Cole asked.

"To tell you the truth I just think that the old man wasn't ready to retire. He knows that he needs to because of his health but he loves what he does. This gives him the excuse to stay on for a while longer and it gives you time to put your head on straight."

Cole shook his head "you are something else."

"Yeah well I figured that your head is a mess right now and you need some time to figure it all out. I get that when you came home from the war that you needed a job and money to support Emma but in doing so you have never taken the time to get your own head on straight. You time to recoup, to deal with everything that went on over there and come to terms with all of that. Burns also understood that. We served in Vietnam together. He understands and I sure once your head is clear that you will too."

"I haven't drank like that in a long time." Cole groaned trying not to gag.

"Well now don't you worry about a thing, my wife is taking care of Emma. Tommy is with Grace and I guess I'm the lucky one that gets to clean you three up. You and your brothers are all in the same boat this morning son. Drunk as all get out and sick from last night. Do you mind if I ask what went on here?"

"Male bonding, I just think that it got a little out of hand."

"That is the understatement of the year. The misses is going to make all of you pay son. I just hope that you are ready for it."

Cole was confused by that statement but he soon found out. He walked into the house with the smell of freshly made bacon and sausage. The aroma of it hit him in the face hard. His stomach turned rebelling and he ran for the door. He made it outside just in time to lose the contents of his stomach.

"Man they told me that you were in a bad way but I didn't think that it was this bad."

Cole groaned to himself spitting out the rest. What else could go wrong today? Why couldn't they all just let him get it out of his system before they came to him with a thousand different things?

"What are you doing here?" Cole asked finally being able to lift his head.

"I came to check on you. Sarge told us about your fiancé. I have to say that I'm a little ticked that I didn't get a call. Why haven't I been told of you marrying the lovely Miss. Summers? I think as your partner I should have been the first to know."

"You think your funny don't you?"

"I can be on occasion. Come on and you tell me all about it. I think air would be the best thing for you."

Cole nodded and walked with him. Surprisingly the air did seem to clear his mind and help with his stomach.

"So you going to tell me what's going on here Cole?" Jeff asked.

"I would if I could figure it out myself. I swear that woman has turned my whole world upside down in a matter of days." He proceeded to tell him the circumstances surrounding him and Grace. He finished saying, "and now her father thinks that by the end of the summer I'm going to be marrying her. The man is delusional."

"No he isn't," Jeff laughed. "He's right because if I were a betting man myself I would be betting against you. Listen to yourself Cole this is the most that you have opened up to me since us meeting. You never have giving me specifics before. I remember when I first met your sorry ass. I knew that you were different. I knew that you carried a lot of shit on your shoulders and you wouldn't let anyone help, not even me. I tried to pull you away from your responsibilities and duties. I tried to loosen you up but you have always been so closed off. Then you met Grace and it's like something changed. I think the longest conversation you and I have ever had was about her. I should have seen it earlier, you do love her but its scaring the shit out of you. Hell man I would be scared too. She is a beautiful woman that takes your shit and begs for more. You're a dumbass man. You deny it, yet it's there written on your face. When you talk about her you should see yourself, I have never seen you light up so much before. Sarge was right, although I would only give you a few more weeks before you are asking her. Don't know why she would want you but you're in deep. The only way you're going to be comfortable with admitting it is when she feels the same for you. When that happens I would hate to see you then. You won't be denying it anymore, you'll just be kicking everyone's ass that looks at her the wrong way and I'll be there to help. You deserve some happiness Cole and if she's it, then by damn you hang onto it because there will always be someone else there trying to take it away."

Cole looked at his friend. He had never known Jeff to talk like this before. Sure he had always been more open than Cole himself was but never like this. Usually Jeff told you what you needed to hear and no more. He was starting to wonder if he actually knew the people in his life like he thought he had.

"I don't know what to think anymore but you're right. I want to deny it but I can't anymore because somehow that damned woman has worked herself into my heart in just a short week. I don't know what the hell to do about it. I'm trying here but I'm lost. Just when I think that I have her all figured out she throws me through a loop."

"When I was younger my mother, god love her, used to tell me that the passion is in the risk. I never knew what in the hell she was talking about until I was older and had my first serious girlfriend. You know the ones, they screw you up for all other women in your life. I had this one, her name was Sara. Man I loved her with everything in me. I was sixteen at the time and head over heels in love. She was a dancer and I was all set to be here. I asked her to stay with me at the age of eighteen but she had been accepted to Julliard. I asked her to stay and she was destined to go. We wrote each other but you know how those things go. She met someone else and so did I. We went our separate ways but there isn't a day that goes by that I don’t think about her. Even after all these years I still think about her from time to time but last I heard she got knocked up by her professor and dropped out of school. Her parents sent her away to have the baby and I haven’t seen or heard from her ever since but for her I would have risked everything, even if it meant my pride. The passion is in the risk. You need to risk yourself in order to receive the passion and she was mine. I lived for that woman, breathed for that woman and not a day goes by that I don’t regret not going after her. Don’t be like me Cole. Fight for what you want and don’t let anyone tell you that you are worthy to have it.”

Cole stopped and racked his brain for a moment. There was something here that he was missing. His mind would not let him pick up the pieces right now but there was something. He racked his brain trying to think when it hit him like a fist to his gut.

“Was her name Sara Long?” Cole shouted grabbing Jeff’s arm to hold himself steady.

“Yeah how did you know that?”

Cole stepped back. Jeff’s Sara was the same Sara that Grace had known. According to Tommy the two had been really close at one time and Grace had always agonized over her decisions regarding her friend. It was the same reason that Grace had chosen not to do one night stands.

Right now Grace was lost but she needed to remember and learn to forgive herself and him. Maybe there was something here but how to find the woman. Maybe if he could get her to come here she could help Grace remember.

His head snapped up, “I need to find her.”

“What are you talking about? Why do you need to find her?”

“Because don’t you see Grace and Sara were friends. Right now Grace can’t remember anything but she has a past with Sara. The two were close friends and Grace thought that she made some stupid choices with Sara. I would explain all of it but it’s too long. Right now I’m going to need help finding her. Do you have an idea where to start?”

“You could try her parents. I doubt they will help though. They are the ones that sent her away. Maybe they would know but I doubt it.”

“You are amazing and I owe you a round on me.” Cole said hugging him quickly.

“Yeah on a night that you’re not so far off. Tell me this, what is Sara coming here going to help Grace?”

“Sara is going to help Grace remember and then she’s going to forgive her. I’ll make damned sure of that myself.”

“Good luck with that Sara Long is not someone that’s a push over. It’s the reason that I fell in love with her back then. That woman has more fighting spirit in her than I have ever seen in anyone. She is one tough woman. She had to be with her parents and all."

Cole stopped and faced him asking, "What about her parents?"

"Well it's complicated. They are rich and snooty. Everything that Sara did was wrong, until she went to Julliard. Then they were only too happy that she was their daughter. I can remember when I asked her to stay here with me. Her mother laughed and told her that she was not going to throw everything that they had been working on to stay and marry some low life. I was crushed but she was right. Back then I was going nowhere fast. I decided that if Sara could change her ways and straighten up then I should too. They made me so angry that I decided to better myself. I went to school for criminal justice and became this. They are the reason that I pushed myself so hard. I thought that if I ever got my chance with her again I wouldn't be a nobody anymore. I would be someone that she could be proud of."

Cole slapped him on the back. "You're a good man Jeff. No one has ever watched my back the way that you do. Don't let them get to you man. Trust me I would rather have you watching out for me than anyone."

"Yeah well, don't let that get out. Don't want people expecting too much of me. Now enough of the mushy stuff. If you are going to find Sara then you are going to need help and I know just how to help with that. Let's go find my ex-girlfriend so we can bring yours back to you."

Cole laughed but it felt good. It had been so long since he had asked anyone for help. If he was being truthful he never really had to ask for help before. He had always seemed to know how to help himself but he didn't have the first clue when it came to Grace. With her everything was different. More complicated and he only hoped that he could figure it all out before it was too late.

He would need more help he realized as he walked back towards the house. He would need help from John and Janet on understanding Grace more. He would need Jeff to help him with Sara and he would need his brother's to look after Emma.

He only hoped that Emma would understand. Before they could leave to find Sara he would need to talk with her. He needed her to understand why he would be gone for a while. He only hoped that she would take it all because right now he needed Emma too. He always had.

Emma was one of the rare ones. She was blessed with such light and love and he couldn't disappoint her again. He needed to understand her as well. Emma like him kept everything contained.

Cole had never wanted to subject her to an endless parade of women in his life. He needed to get the ok from her to pursue Grace. He didn't want to lose Grace but Emma had to come first and if she wasn't ready for this he didn't know what he was going to do. He only hoped that she was because there was no way that he could live without either of them in his life. Both had given his life purpose and understanding. Two of the main things that he had been searching for.

He hadn't really known what he had been looking for. At first he had thought that he had gone into the military to be like his father. Thinking on it now did he start to realize that he had been wrong again.

He had gone into the military because that is what he had needed at the time. Cole had needed the structure that only the military could give him. He knew that he was a bad teenager. Well more than most and his mother was constantly on him to be better. To set goals for himself and try to reach for them.

Over the years Cole had come to rely on that piece of advice. Setting goals for himself had given him drive because someone had expected something from him. His mother expected him to be a stand up man and have a purpose in his life. His sister had expected him to be a father to his niece and show her the way.

Now Grace was expecting him to help her. She may not have come right out and said it but it was there. Like a silent request and he would not fail her now.

He would bring back Sara Long kicking and screaming if need be because he knew that this is what Grace needed. She needed to understand what happened to her friend all those years ago. She needed to talk with Sara and learn to forgive herself for things that she had no control over and it would start as soon as he could find Sara.

That was his goal now. Find Sara Long and bring her here. With that goal in mind he went to find his family. They would all have to be on the same page in order for this to work. They would all need to understand his thinking and he only hoped that they would be willing to help because he was as lost as Grace was right now. Helping her find herself would help him to find himself. Through each other they would learn to heal and love and then she would be his forever.

Chapter 18

After getting permission from Emma to pursue Grace, Cole felt much better about his decisions. The hardest was going to be getting Grace to cooperate. The woman was stubborn to her core and standing in her room watching her argue with her doctor did he finally start to see it.

She still was not remembering anything but she was insisting that she was leaving. The doctor's told her that her protein levels were normal and Grace thought that was her all clear to leave the hospital. They were trying to convince her to stay one more day but she was not having any of it.

"Look what's one more day when we all know that tomorrow will be no different?" She asked. "We all have established that I'm not going to remember any time soon, so why can't I go home where I can be in peace? In here I have people in and out of this room all the time and it's not like I'm getting any rest. If I have to learn how to deal with all of this, I would rather learn to deal with it without the hospital."

"I understand you wanting to leave Grace because so far your progress is fine but I would insist that you stay at least one more day for observation." Dr. Porter insisted.

"You can't make me stay Ben and there is no point in it. It has been almost a week and nothing has changed. Right now I feel safe going home with my brother and Cole and there's nothing that you can say to change my mind."

Ben sighed aloud. He knew that he was beat at this. He really couldn't make Grace stay. Yes, he was concerned about her safety but if he was being truthful it was more than that. Grace Summers had made him laugh. She kept him on his toes and he was going to miss her when she left. He knew he had no choice. "Alright Grace but if anything else happens you come right back here. I'll stop by the house in a few days to see how you are but if you insist, I'll have your discharge papers signed. Go ahead and get ready and I'll be back in a few minutes to sign you out of here."

"Thanks Ben. I really am going to be just fine. I just have to learn everything all over again." She said squeezing his hand gently.

"I understand, if you'll excuse me."

Cole watched the exchange between Grace and Ben Porter and he wanted to scream. He knew why the doctor wanted to keep her here. It wasn't for her health, which was obvious. He liked her and he understood the reason. It just was not making him happy with the good doctor right now.

"All right you two, if you are going to take me home I want to have everything packed up." Grace said getting out of the bed and stretching.

"Grace do you really think that this is the best idea?" Tommy stopped her by grabbing her arm.

"I know that you are nervous for me." She said cupping his cheek. "Believe me I'm feeling the same way but we both know that one day isn't going to change anything Tommy. I have been here for five days and nothing has changed. I'm not going to remember anything any time soon and I would rather be home where people know me and can help me to remember. Right now you guys are driving one and half hours to get here and back to see me. I want to be somewhere familiar. I want to be watching a television show without a nurse coming to take more blood out of me. I want to start living again even if I never remember a thing about my old life. Can you understand that Tommy?" She asked with tears in her eyes.

"More than you could ever know Gracie. More than you could ever know. All right, no tears. I can't take your tears. Come on let's get you all packed up."

"Tommy, do you mind if I have a moment alone with Cole?" She nodded and wiped her tears.

"Not at all, I'll be just outside if you need me."

Cole swallowed hard. It had been a few days since he had seen Grace. He had made a promise to come and see her and like a chicken he had backed out. Right now his head was a mess. He had been trying to find the elusive Sara Long with no results. He was starting to wonder if the woman didn't disappear.

After his talk with Jeff, Cole had started with her parents. They had immediately shut the door in his face. He then turned to the internet but there was nothing, no trace of the woman and he knew that he would need to ask for help again with this one.

Now standing here facing Grace did he start to feel nervous. What was it about the woman that made him feel like a school boy again?

"Cole before we leave I wanted to say something to you." She patted the bed next to her and he sat. She sighed, "There is no easy way for me to do this but I need to be fair to you. The last time that we talked I know that we kind of argued, well not really argued but we both said some things that made me think. I don't want to hurt you Cole but I can't be who you want me to be. I may have been that graceful elegant creature on the tapes at one time but I'm not her anymore because that person no longer exists. She may never exist again. I know that I put you on the spot with my questions last time we talked but I wanted you to know that there can't be anything here. You were right Cole. I don't remember what happened between us and maybe I never will but at this moment in time I don't want us hurting each other either. You fell in love with Grace Summers ballet dancer and she's no longer here. The fact that you remember me from my old life just proves that we are not going to work. You fell for her and I'm no longer her. I may never be, so I must ask you to stay away from me. I don't want you living in the house and I understand if you want me to move out of your sister's house. I know that I want to stay in this area for a while but after that I'm moving on. I have come to the conclusion that if my memory hasn't returned by now that it may never return and I need to deal with that first. I need to find myself again and I don't want to be tied to anyone while I'm doing this, so please Cole if you love me you will let me go. You'll let me alone and let me remember without the added pressure. I still would like to see Emma and you from time to time but I have to be fair to both you and her. When she told me the other day that she remembered me fondly it made me think that I don't want to hurt her either. Tommy has been filling in the blanks for me and I don't want Emma losing another person that she cares about Cole but that's the point, she already has without even realizing it. If I let you and her get close to me again there is no guarantee that I will stay. I may remember everything and leave or remember nothing and leave anyway. I just don't want to hurt anyone and I feel like I'm hurting everyone. My parents, Tommy, you and your family and I'm starting to get bogged down by those feelings, so for now can we just be friends."

Cole shook his head. His proud, strong, beautiful Grace was back in full swing trying to protect herself again. He should have been prepared for the possibility that she would do this but it honestly never crossed his mind.

He knew what was at stake but he wouldn't let her push him away again, or let her protect herself from him because if he was going to be hopelessly in love, then by god so was she.

He knew her game. She was pushing him away to protect herself but that was the beauty of Grace. She would protect anyone with everything in her, including him but she was not going to get her way. It was his turn to tear her apart and heal her with him and Emma standing right in the middle.

"Grace sweetheart, listen to me. I know that you're protecting everyone again. If I have learned nothing else about you it's this. For years you have protected yourself and those around you. You pushed them away and cut them out of your life never letting yourself enjoy anything other than dancing. I know that you think that you're doing what's right but sweetheart this isn't right and I'll prove it to you. I ask that you give me until the end of the summer. I won't go against your wishes and stay with you at the house but I want a fair trial Grace. I want to date you all over again the right way. I was an ass the other day when I said that I can't get close to you again to hurt you. I don't want to hurt you but I was not thinking straight. A common aliment when I am with you, I assure you, but I let you protect yourself from me. I know that sounds confusing but what we had was special and if you never remember so be it. I fell in love with the impossible Grace, the Grace that glares at my back when she's not getting her way and thinks that I'm not looking. I fell in love with the Grace that was moody and conferential and sexy as hell. I fell in love with the caring and compassionate Grace and most of all, I feel in love with the Grace that held me close and gave me the understanding that I needed when I told you of my time in Iraq. Sweetheart I didn't fall in love with the graceful creature from the stage because I never knew that woman. I only knew the real Grace, the one that hunted her brother from the trees. The one that gave me my daughter back and brought me closer to my own family. You did that Grace not the person from the tapes. The woman from the tapes was beat down by her life. She never stood up for what she wanted. She didn't fight or argue, she was the perfect robot and I for one loved the other side of you. The one that could be both light and dark. The person who said what was on her mind, like you just did, without caring if it hurt anyone or not but most of all. Most of all I want to know the new you. It doesn't matter who you were Grace. It doesn't matter what happened in the past. All I'm asking for is the chance to get to know the new you and fall in love with her too. I'm asking the new Grace to give this rusted, broke down sheriff a fair trial. We can take things slow if that's what you want. Hell I don't care if you just let me take you out on a real date, just the two of us, as long as you say that I have a fighting chance. Just please give me that. I know that I'm the last person that deserves it and if you do remember one day than we can deal with that as well. Maybe by then you'll remember that you loved me too, even when I was being an asshole. Just don't close the book on us Grace. Give me a chance to get to know the new you."

Grace sat on the bed trying desperately not to cry. This man had been moody the last time that she had seen him. She knew that they had problems but there was something about him from the first time that she laid eyes on him.

He could come across arrogant and overbearing but then there were times like this. When he knew just what to say to make her want to reach out to him and embrace him. It didn't matter what had happened in the past. It didn't matter that she didn't remember him because the connection was still there and she would not let it pass.

She hugged him close while she cried on him. It didn't matter that she used to a graceful dancer, that life was gone for now. All she could do know was go on with the new life and try again. If she didn't remember today maybe she would tomorrow but one thing she knew for sure. Cole Baker had loved her deeply. She knew it all the down to her soul. She wasn't sure how she would feel about him but she was not going to let this go either.

There was something easy about being with Cole. He didn't demand anything from her. He didn't talk about the past hoping that she would remember. It was the opposite in fact. He wanted to know the new her, even though she had yet to learn about herself.

She didn't want to hurt him or Emma. He had been right when he said that she was pushing him away to protect him and herself. It seemed like the natural thing to do but she didn't want to fight this.

From the first night there had been a connection between them. Even between herself and Emma and she wouldn't push them away. If she was going to start a new life, she may as well start it with someone who really cared about her.

"All right Cole I'll give you until the end of summer. I just hope that you know what you are doing here."

"Of course I know what I'm doing. I'm trying to convince the woman I love to love me back. What's wrong with that?" He smiled and hugged her tight.

"And what about Emma, have you considered what this will do to her?" She said getting up from the bed and swatting him playfully against the arm.

"Emma loves you just as much as I do Grace." Cole grabbed her hand. "She was the one that told me that I needed to fight for you. She wants you here just as much as I do. In a matter of a few short days you have become our miracle, our own saving grace and I'll do everything in my power to fight for you Grace. I will even fight with you and your protecting nature if that's what it takes. Now come on, let's get you home and settled in. Emma has a surprise for you waiting at the house."

Grace looked at him confused, "but how did she know that I would be coming home today?"

"Because it's you sweetheart. We all know how you are and we all knew that you wouldn't stay if there wasn't a need. Emma figured that if you wouldn't come home today then you could always see it tomorrow. Either way she knew that you would come home to us."

"You think that you are that charming Cole Baker?" She asked raising her brow. He kissed her softly. "Of course I am. How else do you think that I got you to fall in love with me once? It wasn't just my good looks sweetheart."

She rolled her eyes and snorted. Cole Baker and his macho attitude were back in full swing but she found that she liked that flaw as well. His domineering personality and strength attracted her to him rather than push her away. He was just so sure of himself that it made her sure as well.

She sighed and shook her head. She would need to learn more about Cole Baker if she were to stand a chance against him. She gave one last look at him smiling at her and turned to pack her things.

She swallowed hard. She didn't stand a chance against him with her heart and she knew it. She only hoped that this time around he would treat it kindly.

Arriving at the house Grace took the time to re-familiarize herself with the house. It was large and it was beautiful and she was instantly drawn to it.

Getting out the car everyone that had visited her at the hospital was there to greet her.

Her mother and father, Cole's brothers and standing up front was Emma. She broke away from everyone and ran at Grace. She didn't think twice as she knelt down to the little girl that launched herself at her.

"Well it seems as though someone has missed me." She said setting Emma back on her feet.

"I have a surprise for you Grace. Come and see. My uncles helped me but I picked it out for you all by myself." Emma giggled, pulling on her hand.

Grace had no choice but to follow the tiny child. She smiled as Emma made her cover her eyes for her surprise.

"You can open your eyes now Grace." Emma said.

Grace pulled her hands away from her face and looked at the beautiful rose bushes planted along the house. There was every color and the smell of them was incredible. Tears came to her eyes as Emma pulled her along talking about the roses and what they were called. They made it all the way around the house and Emma pointed.

"That used to be my swing Grace and now it can be ours. See I planted a rose bush next to it so we can sit up there and smell the roses."

Grace looked up at the balcony porch and smiled. There was a wooden swing complete with small potted rose bush next to it. “Do you like it Grace?” Emma asked.

“I love it. Did you think of this yourself?”

Emma shook her head “no, I know that you probably don’t remember but this was your idea. My mommy’s favorite flowers were roses. I had some things to say to her while we sat in the woods one afternoon. You told me that mommy’s always know when their daughters need them and told me to talk to my mommy, to tell her everything that I didn’t get to say to her before she died and I did and do you know what happened?”

Grace shook her head and Emma smiled, “The wind picked up after I was done and there was the smell of roses and that’s how I knew that she was there. You and I were going to plant rose bushes all around the house on the day of your accident but we didn’t get the chance, so I did it for us. Well me and my uncles. They helped some but I picked them out. Do you really like them Grace?”

Grace didn’t know what to say. This little one had lost her mother and she had taken time to do this for her. To plant the flowers that would remind herself of her mother to make Grace feel better. She picked

Emma up and looked into those brown eyes. “I love them.” She said nodding.

Emma giggled and hugged her close. “I just knew that you would. Would you mind if we go around smelling the roses for a bit Grace? I like to remember my mother. Opps sorry.”

Grace laughed, “Don’t worry about it munchkin I’ll remember someday.”

“That’s what you used to call me all the time.”

“What munchkin?” Grace shook her head trying to remember.

“Yep, from the day that I met you actually, see you do remember some things already.”

Grace knew that was not the case but something was nagging at her again. Like there was a memory there that was just out of reach. Normally it would have frustrated her to no end but right now she wanted to smell the roses with Emma. She could worry about the rest later.

She held Emma’s hand as they walked along and smelled the roses. There was something familiar and comforting about the floral blends but it eluded her. For the moment she took the time to appreciate the sun and the flowers, and the sound of a little girl’s happiness and laughter. After a few minutes Cole came looking for them.

"I thought that you two were lost back here." He said leaning against the house.

Emma laughed, "No daddy, we are just taking the time to smell the roses."

Grace looked at Cole there was something on his face. It was right there when he looked at Emma. Love maybe but she was having a hard time placing the look. It looked loving but there was pain there as well.

She wondered what he was thinking about but when she went to ask Emma pulled on her hand. "Grace we have one more surprise for you. This one isn't from me but I helped as well. Come and look."

Grace nodded and followed Emma with Cole following behind them. Grace wanted to ask what he had been thinking about but for now she needed to deal with more surprises.

Grace walked into the house with everyone standing there waiting for her again. She looked around the house as Emma pulled on her hand again.

"Here Grace, look at this." She said as she pointed to the couch.

It was familiar to her somehow but she looked at the photo book that was waiting for her. On the front cover were her and Tommy as children. She looked up at Tommy. He shook his head, "It wasn't me because believe me I don't want anyone seeing some of those pictures. Mom and dad figured that you would like to see the pictures. Since we were not able to have them at the hospital because we are away from home, they decided that they would fly back and have your stuff brought here. They also decided that they are staying as long as you're staying so we all moved our stuff here for now. Cole was nice enough to give up his rooms to all of us so we can stay with you."

Janet stepped forward saying, "Of course if you're not comfortable with all of us here your father and I will rent a place. We found something not far from here but we don't want to push you Grace. We don't want you to feel like you have to take us in while you are working on you. We just would like to be around while you try and remember."

Grace thought that was very nice of her mother to do something like that for her. She smiled, "Of course not I want you all here. It's nice to be surrounded by people that know me well. Please I want all of you to stay, that way if I have any questions you all won't be that far away."

"We have made some mistakes with you Grace." John said shaking his head sadly. "Your mother and I both did and as you start to learn about your old life we want you to keep in mind that we didn't mean to hurt you in any way. We only thought that we were doing what was best for you at that time."

Grace didn't have a clue what he was talking about but then again he looked really sorry. She decided that the past was exactly that. The past and no amount of wishing was going to change anything. Like her relationship with Cole everything would just have to be taken day by day.

"Thank you although I have no clue what you are talking about. I have decided that I'm going to leave the past in the past where it belongs. For now I'm only going to move forward but thank you for the apology just the same. I would like it if you and mom stay here. I want us to be close again."

"All right pumpkin we will stay but if you learn something and want us to go. We will understand." John said.

Grace smiled and nodded. What had these people done to her that they would think that she wouldn't want them around? Had her relationship with her parents been a bad one? Sometimes this memory thing was a curse and sometimes it could be a miracle, she thought looking at Cole.

She sat on the couch with Emma and Tommy beside her and opened the book. The first picture was her as a baby with Tommy holding her. She looked at her brother, "You were a cute kid."

"Yeah but not as cute as you. Just look at that mop of flame red hair." He said pointing at picture of Grace with a mop of loose curls.

Grace looked at the picture of her and Tommy together. They looked a little like each other. The eyes were the same but Tommy's hair was a darker colored red. It was so dark in fact that you could barely tell that it had red in it.

The next pictures were of her on her first steps and things like that. As she looked through the book she tried to remember something but it was not there. She sighed as she flipped through the pictures. One stopped her for a moment.

It was a picture of her and her mother in front of a private ballet school. There was pride and sheer joy in her mother's eyes but as she looked at hers she could see something else. In the pictures she was smiling but it seemed forced and she wondered why.

"When was this taken?" She asked holding up a picture.

Her mother stepped forward, "That was taken when you were ten years old. You had been accepted to the dance academy for girls. You were at the top of your class."

Grace held the picture and studied her own face. There was something there, a feeling as though she was losing something important. She studied it but it would not come. She just knew that this picture was telling her that she had lost something important but she wouldn't ask questions. Grace knew that it would only upset everyone but later when her and Tommy where alone she would ask him.

She glanced at the other pictures but there wasn't much there. It was as though a big chunk of her life was missing. She couldn't help but question that.

"Why are there no pictures from this one…?" She asked holding up the picture that she had been studying. "To this one…" She said holding up one of her at Julliard.

"I'm afraid that is my fault. You were away at ballet school for so long that we didn't take pictures then. You stayed as a full time student and we didn't get to see you much during that time."

"Cut the shit Janet and at least tell her the truth. I think that she deserves that much from you." Tommy spat.

"You're right Tommy, Grace the reason that there are no pictures of you is because we didn't come to see you. For the first couple of years you came home on summer break until we had a fight. You were fourteen at the time that you first told me that you didn't want to dance anymore. I thought that you were home sick so I pushed you to go back. After that summer you didn't come home at all. You chose to stay at the school. When you were sixteen you came home for a week before it started all over again. You told me that you were done and wanted to train to go to the military but like the selfish woman I was I wouldn't let you. I demanded that you go back to school. Three days later your grandfather died leaving you everything. You tried to come home again and I drove you right back. I can't tell you how sorry I am that I didn't listen to you. I pushed you and pushed you for my own selfish reasons and I can't take it back. After that something in you broke. You never came home again and when we did see you, you wouldn't talk to me. This is all my fault. I pushed you to do all these diets because I wanted you to be the best because I never got the chance. I wanted to be a dancer my whole life but my father thought that it was a stupid profession. Instead of letting me pursue my own choices he forced me into the military and I didn't want that for you. When you first told me that you wanted to go, I thought that it was because of your father and Tommy. Even I had been in the military and I thought that you were just trying to fit in with all of us. I didn't realize that you would be so good at it or that you really wanted it. I just knew that I had to throw away my dreams of becoming a dancer because my father wouldn't let me, but I see now that I am exactly like him. I made you go into dancing. I pushed you until you were left with no choice but to dance but that was all that you had known and all I had known for you. I didn't think that you would get sick after all of these years. I didn't think that you would still be forced to follow that diet that landed you in the hospital. God Grace I didn't know and I only hope that one day you will find it in your heart to forgive me. I have put you through hell. I have forced you to have a life that you didn't want. I made you give up your dreams so that you could follow mine and I have sued you in the process for a man's money that didn't even love me. I don't know how to make it right again but I swear from now on I will not push you to do one more thing, ever. Whatever you chose is your choice. I will support you no matter what. Just please forgive me. I haven't been able to sleep right since you have been in that hospital knowing that it was all my fault. I'm so sorry Grace." She broke on a sob.

Grace sat back on the couch and tried to remember. She tried to remember her mother forcing her into that life. She tried to remember but there was nothing. Not even the hate that should fill her for the woman.

Janet had told her all of the pain that she had caused but Grace couldn't feel the anger for it. All she could feel is the sympathy for a woman that had been made to endure hardship from a parent as well.

Getting up from the couch she hugged her mother close. “Don’t cry. I forgive you, it’s not like I can remember it anyway. We can start fresh. What do you say?”

“Do you mean it? We can really start over?” Janet pulled back from her laughing and crying at the same time.

“Why not? I am after all, all about second chances.” She said winking at Cole.

“I think that we all get a second chance Grace. Each and every single one of us.” He said looking at his daughter and brothers.

For all of them Grace’s accident had been a second chance. A second chance to get new parents for Emma. A second chance for him and his brothers to become close again, a second chance for Grace to live her own life as she saw fit. Each one of them was getting a second chance and what a chance it was.

The chance to learn to love and open up. The chance to let new people in and grow together. The chance to reconnect and become even better and in the middle was his Grace. With her same caring and understanding. She had unknowingly given all of them a second chance. Maybe this time around they would get it right.

The rest of the evening passed with Grace looking at all the pictures the family had brought. Even the brothers and Emma had joined in the fun. They all sat in the middle of the living surrounded by pictures of everyone.

After Grace had gone through hers Cole felt it only right that he and his brothers go through theirs. Bret had gone home to get the books of pictures they had and Cole collected the ones from his sister's house.

They all were now pilled in the living room looking at the pictures remembering the old days and good times in their lives. Even Emma had smiled as they showed her pictures of her mother when she was younger.

It was late when they called a halt to the pictures. Bret and Ross took Emma home with them knowing that Cole would need time with Grace. She was looking at a picture of him and Brian in Iraq together.

She smiled at the two friend's making bunny ears behind each other's backs strapped with semi-automatic weapons to their sides.

"You two must have given your leaders fits. Look at you two. Grown men making bunny ears behind each other."

"Yeah that was us, two idiots with weapons making bunny ears behind each other's backs. This picture was taken just a few days before I lost him."

Cole said taking the picture from her and smiling fondly.

"Would you tell me about him?" Grace asked.

Cole smiled and pulled on her hands. He helped her up from the floor and grabbed a blanket from the back of the couch and led her outside to the swing. When they sat together he wrapped the blanket around their legs and wrapped an arm around her.

He retold the story of Brian to Grace. He told her about Vikki and Brian plans of getting together after he got out. He even told her about their time together in the military and how he had never known someone like Brian. He told her the whole scary truth and true to Grace's form she listened.

She never once interrupted him. She just leaned on his chest as he retold the tale. At the end of it he could hear her crying. He pulled her face toward him.

"Why are you crying Grace?" He asked staring into her eyes.

"I'm sorry about your friend Cole but honest to god I'll thank that man every day of my life that he had the courage to do what he did. He let you come home Cole and he was a brave man that deserves my tears even though I didn't know him because he gave me you." She said as she kissed him.

Her mind was screaming that this was a bad idea but she couldn't seem to help it. Cole was opening up to her and sharing things that were hard for him. He trusted her to understand the pain that he felt. He trusted her not to tell him that he had made a mistake by letting his friend die. He trusted her with his feelings and she could only show him how she was feeling.

She was feeling blessed to have someone as strong as Cole love her the way that he did. She was feeling welcome and safe in his arms and maybe even a little loved. It was a familiar feeling, feeling Cole's lips on hers. It was as though he was made for her and she let herself feel the flames that were now raking her body. She wanted to touch him but he pulled away panting.

"Grace sweetheart. I don't think that this is a good idea."

"I know. I'm sorry I just couldn't help myself." She blushed.

"It's alright Grace. I'll wait as long as you need Grace. This time you get to decide but for now I have to go. You have had a long day and need rest but I'll be back tomorrow if you want."

"I want that very much Cole. You, Emma and the rest of the monkeys. I like your brothers Cole. They seem so close to me and I find I like the closeness." She said snuggling closer to him.

"You're going to be the death of me." He said as he helped her up from the swing. He walked her back in the house and told her good night. As usual Tommy was waiting for her.

"Come on Gracie it's bedtime honey. You can see the dumb shit tomorrow."

Grace smacked Tommy's arm saying, "Be so sweet."

"I owe him one honey. Now come on." He said pulling on her arm.

Grace waved at Cole and followed her brother up the stairs. By the time that she got to the top Cole was already gone.

She smiled as her brother helped her into bed. She didn't know why she felt like she had accomplished something today but she did. She smiled as she snuggled down into the sheets and fell head long into a nightmare.

Chapter 19

The nightmares continued to plague her all month long. It was as though she was trying to remember something that she had forgotten. During the nights she was tortured with a life that she had lived and couldn't remember but during the days, it was a different story.

Dating Cole had been the best decision Grace had ever made. He took her everywhere and showed her off to his friends. He made her feel special and very much loved. He never pushed for something more that she was willing to give and she appreciated that.

It was as though she was trying to pick up the pieces of her life, all while trying to start a new one. Her parents had even bought property close to Grace so that they could give her the space that she needed while remaining close.

Tommy had decided that he was just going to move in with her but Grace didn't mind having her brother around. There was something familiar about having Tommy around all the time. It was easy and natural. As natural as her dancing had been.

A few short weeks after her accident Emma had insisted that Grace come with her to ballet class to meet Ms. Honey. Grace had found that she like Ms. Honey. At first she told her that she could no longer dance because of her accident but the stubborn woman refused to believe her.

They agreed that they would meet up every evening to practice so that Grace could remember. At first the classes had been hard. It was demanding dancing ballet but Grace found that she liked the peace that it brought to her. Now standing inside the class room she wondered if she would ever be at peace again.

It was frustrating remembering nothing while everyone seemed to know everything about her. They would all tell funny stories of Grace growing up but she never could remember any of them. It was a blank and that blank was starting to get to her.

Dr. Porter had been true to his word. He had come to Grace a week after she left the hospital to see how she was holding up. She reported that she was still remembering nothing but there were familiar things. He couldn't have been more pleased but it was starting to get to Grace.

The nightmares that plagued her were making her frustrated because she knew that she was supposed to be remembering something important but no matter how much she concentrated she couldn't remember. She pushed the thoughts aside and faced Ms. Honey.

"Are you sure about this?" Grace asked nervously.

"Yes of course. It's called interruptive dance Grace. All you have to do is listen and dance what you are feeling."

It sounded easy enough but she was feeling a little nervous. It had been kind of fun learning ballet with Emma. They had been pretty much on the same level.

Over the weeks though Grace had improved much and Miss. Honey had approached her about teaching an evening class a few nights a week. It wasn't ballet but an interruptive dance class. She had promised Grace that she would help her but standing here she started to wonder what she had signed up for.

"All right Grace let's begin. I'm going to play the music and you are going to move. It doesn't matter how you much you move. Just let yourself feel the music."

Grace nodded. What other choice did she have? She peeked over at Emma who just smiled and waved at her. Grace gave a shaky wave back and took a deep breath. If she was going to embarrass herself at least it would only be Emma and Miss. Honey watching.

The music started and Grace closed her eyes and listened. The song was an upbeat rhythm but the singer was singing at a much slower tempo. As she listened she could feel her shoulders moving to the music. Before she could even thinking about what she was doing her feet were moving as well.

As the song continued she had found a rhythm that she had liked. As the singer belted out the lyrics to the music she moved slowly with her voice. When she wasn't singing she moved quicker and in no time at all she opened her eyes and watched herself in the mirrors as she danced all around the studio.

She could hear people clapping but she drowned them out. She watched herself as she moved with grace and purpose. It was freeing and thoroughly entertaining to watch. As the music cycled back through Grace found that she didn't want to stop.

She told Miss. Honey to play the music again and again she moved with a purpose. It was almost a routine but not quite there, yet. She smiled as she moved even faster mesmerizing the steps as she went through the motions again. It was a mix between ballet and free style and for Grace it fit. Her body didn't need to think of moving it did that all on its own.

As the music faded she took a breath and smiled. She had done it. She could hear the clapping of more than just Miss. Honey and Emma. It was as though there were a crowd of people clapping and Grace found herself blushing. She knew that she didn't want to open her eyes but she peeked anyway.

Standing on the opposite side of the studio by the doors were a whole group of girls ranging from eight to about fifteen if she had to guess and right beside them was Cole. She shook her head and smiled at him.

He was smiling at her clapping and she found herself getting warm from his stare. It was the same every time that she looked at the man. When he would smile so would she. When he had that irresistible grin on his face Grace blushed and when he would stare like he was doing now her insides would turn molten. She shifted uncomfortably and looked at Miss. Honey.

"Did I do that right?"

"How could you not? Did you see yourself in the mirrors? You haven't lost a thing since the accident. I personally think that your mind is blocking something else and you can't remember but the dancing. The dancing is one thing you can never block when you have raw natural talent as you do. It is in your blood and nothing, not even your accident can take that away from you Grace. Now then, that being said how about you taking on my night time classes. These girls here," she said gesturing at the girls at the doors, "are a little more advanced. They need a teacher like you Grace. They need someone that can listen to the music and interrupt it into steps. I'm a good teacher but I don't have half the talent that you do. You're one of the rare ones that can both teach and do. I'm afraid that all I have ever been able to do was teach. My body wasn't made to be a dancer. I have big feet you see but not you. You were made for dancing all the way down to your toes. You can teach these girls something that I can't do myself. I have interviewed qualified people but they don't have half the talent that you do dear. I know that this is kind of last moment but would you do it for me because I don't have anyone else."

The girls at the door surged forward and grabbed her arms begging and pleading with her. She couldn't say no to them.

"All right. All right I'll do it but I don't want to hear anyone complaining when I screwed this all up."

Ms. Honey smiled, "You could never Grace. That is the beauty of teaching something like interruptive dance, who's going to tell you that you messed up when it's up to you to decide how you are moving?"

"You have a point there. All right I'll do it as long as Emma can join me." She said looking at the little girl sitting on the floor.

"I can't. I don't know how." Emma said shaking looking around for an escape.

"But see that's the beauty of it, like Ms. Honey said who's going to tell you what's right? All you have to do is move with the music like I did. Come here and I'll help you." Grace said holding out her hand.

Emma slowly got up from the floor and moved past the other girls that were now staring at her. She hated when people stared but she couldn't disappoint Grace. She was a loner by nature. Others her own age didn't seem to understand her, the way that the grownups did but this was Grace. Grace would never embarrass her and she knew that.

"Now then I would like to see what you are capable of." Grace said looking at Emma.

"But what if everyone laughs?" Emma asked swallowing hard.

Grace smiled and knelt down and whispered, "They are not going to laugh. You know how I know that?" Emma shook her head and Grace chuckled, "Because munchkin none of us know what we are doing. Here I'll show you." Grace stood up and faced the whole group of girls. "Girls I want you to do what you just saw me do. I don't want you to take the same steps but I want you to listen to the music and move. I want to get an idea of how all of you move to get a better idea of how I want this to go. Miss. Honey will play the music and everyone will take a turn moving. We'll all learn together. When I'm satisfied with the routine I'll put it all together and we'll all learn together. How does that sound?"

All the girls jumped up and down cheering. Each of them wanted to go first and Grace smiled at Emma. “See no one knows how anyone else is going to interrupt this. For now we are all on the same level. Trust me honey, you need this as much as I do.”

Emma was confused but she didn’t want to disappoint Grace. Emma found that she really loved Grace. She was always funny and caring. She even insisted that Emma herself got to come on some of Grace’s and daddy’s dates.

Sometimes they would all go out to a dinner and a movie and Emma never felt as though she was being left out of anything. Grace made her comfortable and accepted her and her advice even though she was a little girl.

Grace made Emma feel as though she was her equal and no one, not even daddy had made her feel that way before. She looked at Grace and smiled. “Ok I’ll try, for you Grace.”

“That’s the spirit munchkin. Now then I’ll have Miss. Honey play the music and you’re going to move. Don’t be afraid honey because I know that you are going to be great.”

Emma nodded and stepped into the middle of the floor. She took a breath and nodded that she was ready. When the music first started she was a little nervous and didn’t know what to do with her body.

She thought that she was going to hear laughing from the other girls but instead they cheered her on. Emma closed her eyes as she had seen Grace do and started to move before she could even think of moving.

As she swayed and moved, she never once opened her eyes. She didn't want to see the other people. She just wanted to feel the music for herself. It was easy moving with the music with a strange beat. It was as though her body understood which way to go and as she moved, she smiled.

It had been such a long time since she had felt so free. The song fit her perfectly. Emma listened to the lyrics of the song as she moved. The woman was singing. "So serious all the time. I feel restrained. I feel confined. I cannot take your whispering. You're whispering. I want dance without you. Won't you just let me lose myself. I want to dance" and then the beat would pick up.

It was the most freeing song and feeling that she had ever experienced in her life. The song fit her. She felt restrained and confined. She wanted to dance without everyone. Without the whispering and the way that they made her feel different all the time. When the song ended she stood in middle of the floor breathing heavily.

She didn't want to open her eyes. She didn't want to see their faces. She didn't want to hear their whispers. She only wanted to dance again but when the clapping started she had no choice.

Emma peeked open an eye thinking that it would be Grace or her father clapping for her but to her surprise it was neither. It was the girls from the class. Each one faced her clapping and walking toward her.

The first instinct was to back up but she didn't. She wanted understanding and acceptance from people her own age. It was the one thing missing from her life, so when they came to ask her questions she didn't back away. She let them ask whatever they wanted and she answered each one.

She looked over to Grace and her father that were now standing with each other smiling at her. Grace even winked and Emma knew then that Grace had done it to her on purpose. She was making her feel accepted again. Emma waved back as the other girls shouted that they wanted to be next.

For the first time since her mother's passing she felt free. She felt free to live her life with happiness and joy instead of suppressing that because her mother could no longer enjoy it. Emma figured out that her mother wouldn't want to see her sad. Her mother would want to see her happy and dancing. It was the only thing that she had ever wanted for her.

Emma nodded at Grace and then sat with the rest of girls on the floor. She didn't feel like an outsider anymore. She felt included and free and Grace had given that to her. Now all Emma would need to do was convince Grace that she was in love with her father so she could stay.

Cole stood watching the girls in the class take their turns. He had come here today to talk to Grace about Emma but watching her now he knew that there was no need. His primary concern was that Emma was distancing herself from the other children.

He couldn't remember a time when Emma went to a friend's house, or when she would want a friend over. Now watching her he knew that Grace had taken care of that as well.

He leaned against the door watching her move. God she was a hell of a woman and he was damned uncomfortable watching her dance. There was something sexual about Grace. That feeling would never go away but her dancing. Well there was something that he would fantasize about later when he was at home in bed alone.

He sighed. Since Grace and he had started seeing each other again she hadn't brought up the topic of sex and if he was being truthful he was starting to hurt. Watching her day in and day out knowing what she was capable of in the bedroom drove him mad but he wouldn't push. He had pushed her once and that was when she had her accident. There was no way he was going to push her now but watching her move like that just may be the death of him.

The way that her body moved could be called art. The gentle sway of her hips and ass were intoxicating but it was her legs that drove him over the edge. Those long graceful legs would come off the floor and bend and he couldn't breathe thinking of the last time he felt them tighten around his hips.

He shifted uncomfortably and watched as Grace called Emma over to her. He knew that they were supposed to take Emma out tonight with them but he wanted her alone. Maybe if he could just touch her a little he would be better but with Emma that wasn't possible.

He sighed at his lustful thoughts. It wasn't Emma's fault that he was having a hard time controlling himself. He was just sick of Grace's brother Tommy rubbing it in his face how much fun he was having here while Cole wasn't having any fun in the bedroom at all.

He shook his head. That wasn't fair to Grace. This wasn't her fault and he needed to remember that. This was all his fault. If he had just stayed like he was supposed to none of this would have happened and he could easily be at home curled around Grace.

Emma walked over to him and smiled. “Daddy do you think that it would be alright if I go to Becky’s house with her and Amy? I know that we were supposed to go to the movies tonight but I really want to go. They want to work on our dancing. Can I please?”

“Where are Becky’s parents? I would like to make sure that it’s alright for you to go over there first. You know be responsible and all.” Cole looked at Grace who was smiling.

Emma rolled her eyes, “Dad come on. Grace knows Becky’s mom and dad already. Don’t you Grace? I’ll be fine and I’ll call you when I want to come home. Please dad?”

“You know them?” Cole looked at Grace.

“I do but Emma I can’t fault your father for wanting to meet them. I know that I would want to if you were my daughter, so go on and take your father to meet them. Then I’m sure that it would be no problem.”

“Ok, come on dad and come and meet them.” Emma said looking away from them.

Grace chuckled, “Afraid that your dad is going to embarrass you in front of them?”

Emma nodded looking at the ground. Grace smiled, "Then I'll come over with him. Is that alright? That way we all can talk to them and I'll restrain your father from embarrassing you."

Emma looked up at her and smiled. Cole frowned, "Hey I'm not that bad."

"Dad do you remember two days ago when you and Grace took me to the pool, that poor kid is still frightened of you." Emma said snorting.

Cole smiled remembering the little boy that he had scared away from Emma two days ago. They had decided that they would spend the day at the community pool. It gave him a view of Grace in a bath suit. He shook his head remembering.

Emma had been sitting beside Grace on a chair when a young boy about ten had gone over to Emma to talk to her. Cole had been in the restroom when he had come out and spotted him talking to Emma.

He could see her blushing and Grace trying not to smile. He walked over to the kid and told him to beat it. Emma had looked at him and said, "But dad he was only asking where to get ice cream around here. Do you have to be so embarrassing?"

He felt low but he had asked Grace about it later. She had smiled and told him that the little boy was asking Emma to come and get ice cream with him when Cole had interrupted. He didn't feel bad about making the boy leave but he did feel bad about embarrassing Emma. It wasn't like she had many friends here and he would need to remember to behave himself.

"Ok Em I understand. I was a kid at one time too. If Grace says she knows the parents and trusts them I'll only say hello and you are free to go but I want you to call me when you get there. I won't bend on that young lady." Cole said smiling at the memories of the scared little boy.

"Thanks daddy. I promise that I'll call as soon as I get there. I'll take you over now and introduce you to them." She said pulling him along.

"I guess it's just going to be us tonight." Cole said smiling at Grace.

"It seems it is. Whatever will we do with our free time?" She said winking at him.

Cole almost fell over right then and there. Did that mean what he thought that it meant? He stole another look at Grace that was now smiling and blushing and he thought that it just might. He wanted to run to the girl's parents but restrained himself. He would ask her in a matter of moments and if he was correct than he would carry her over his shoulder to the house to get her there.

He swallowed hard and tried to control his breathing as he met Becky's parents. True to his word he only said hello but that was because he honestly couldn't think straight. He let Grace talk to the girl's parents while he worked to get a hold of himself. Air was what he needed. With that goal in mind he turned for the door. Just a few moments of air wouldn't hurt would it?

As he reached outside he felt much better but he could feel someone watching him. It was a strange feeling and he didn't understand where it was coming from. He looked around the parking lot but there was no one there.

The doors opened and all of the girls came rushing out with their own parent's right behind them. He caught a glimpse of Emma and Becky and waved. She waved back and got into the car with Becky and her parents.

As the parking lot cleared it didn't take away the feeling of someone watching him. He scanned the area again but there was nothing. His back was turned when Grace touched making him jump.

"Are you alright?" She asked.

"Sneaking up on me is not a good thing. Now then sweetheart, since it's just us tonight what would you like to do?" Cole chuckled and grabbed her around the middle.

"I was thinking of a little something but you'll have to guess." She said as she licked his ear.

He was pretty sure that if she didn't stop soon he would take her here. He pulled away from her and asked. "Sweetheart are you sure?"

"It's been a month Cole. I haven't remembered anything and I don't think that I'm going too. I think that it's time we take our relationship to the next level, don't you? I want to know what it feels like Cole. I want to see you. All of you," she said as she ran her hands down the front of him. "I want to remember the feeling of you and me together. I want to build new memories and experiences Cole including this one. Now take me home and make it real for me before I get myself into any more trouble here. I'm having a hard time controlling myself. I want to touch you and be touched and right now I'm not caring where it is."

Cole didn't argue with her. If she wanted to be touched then by God that is what she was going to get. He lifted her up over his shoulder and ran for the house. If he didn't get to her soon he was as in as much danger of taking her here as she was.

Running through the woods Cole could feel Grace's soft chucking and soft breasts on his back. He moved even quicker to get her to the house. A moment spent not touching her was a moment spent in hell and he had been living in hell for a damned month.

Since Grace's accident Cole hadn't been seeing anyone but her. His every thought every action centered around Grace and damn John Summers for being right. Just days ago Cole had went to the Sarge to ask for his daughters hand in marriage.

The conversation had been long and awkward but Cole didn't mind as long as he would say yes. The only thing that he cared about was making Grace his. The new Grace that had emerged was soft and sweet just like the old Grace but she also had a grit side of her too. She would argue with him when he was being unreasonable and tell him that he was being an ass. She would make him open up and talk with her about everything and anything.

Two weeks ago he had returned to his job reluctantly but she had made him go. She told him that he would not sit around waiting for her to remember when it wasn't going to happen. She had pushed and pulled him into getting her way. She glared and him and stomped her foot but in the end, true to form Grace got her way.

Cole smiled while running. His Grace didn't get lost in the least. She was still the same as she was before the only difference was she didn't remember it. He had told her that one day and she had just shrugged at him telling him that she didn't care. This was her now and she would stay this way.

That was part of loving Grace. She was giving and caring but tough as nails and no one, not even Cole himself could change a thing about her. He fell deeper and deeper for her each day and now she was starting to feel the same way for him.

He could tell by the way that she would look at him, or the way she would always want him around. Now he was going to marry her and not even she could stand in the way. He was going to tie her to him if he had to drag her there.

When he had the talk with John the man had just smiled and told him. "I told you so." Cole wanted to scream but he kept himself contained. When John made him wait for the answer he thought that he just may have to fight the old man himself but he had finally agreed.

The ring that he had bought for her was now in his pocket and he had been waiting for just the right moment. He had been planning on doing it tonight at dinner after the movies but with Emma gone plans changed.

He reached the house and set her on her feet to open the door. He scooped her up and carried her in the door kissing her as he went. If he didn't touch her soon he was going to go up in flames.

"Hello Gracelyn it's been a long time." Cole heard the voice say. His head snapped up and he looked into the eyes of a stranger. He felt Grace tense and her scream as she fainted in his arms.

Chapter 20

Cole stood in the middle of the room holding a limp Grace in his arms staring at a man he didn't know. Instinct told him to protect Grace and run but for a moment he was paralyzed. His brain wouldn't seem to function because he somehow knew the face staring back at him. He had seen the man before but it was eluding him. Grace stirred in his arms and grabbed her head.

"What happened?" She groaned.

"Come on sweetheart we have to go." He said still watching the man. Cole set her on her feet and grabbed her hand.

Cole didn't have his gun on him and he cussed. The only thing that mattered right now was Grace's safety. He would need to get her out of the house before he could back for the intruder. Grace faced the man and gasped. "Kurt what are you doing here?" She asked shaking her head. She looked at Cole "I remember him but I don't know how."

"This is Kurt. Sweetheart are you sure about that?" Cole looked at the man and then at Grace.

"Yes I'm sure. I still remember the heartless bastard. What do you want Kurt?" Grace looked at the man answering him.

"I came for what is mine Grace and no one is leaving here until this is all settled. I brought you a little gift as well. Come and see." Kurt smiled holding up a gun.

Grace wanted to run. She remembered everything. She remembered Kurt and all the time they had spent together. She remembered her whole life when she had been out cold. It seemed that it had all come rushing back, flashing before her eyes and as the gun rose she knew that her life did flash before her eyes.

Everything was there again as though she had never lost it. She could remember the pain from his betrayal. She could remember Cole leaving after their night together. She could remember the pain and the embarrassment but she could also remember the loving way he had touched her.

She remembered everything and she just thanked god that Emma had decided to go with Becky tonight because Kurt would never touch her now. He may kill everyone else if she didn't play this right but he couldn't touch Emma.

She followed him into the study where David waited for them with Sara and a little boy tied to a chair. Her hand flew to her throat and she thought that she was going to lose it. She couldn't stand to see her friends hurt like this.

"What is all of this about Kurt?" Grace asked watching her long time missing friend.

"You hurt her Grace. You turned your back on your best friend and I thought that it was only right that I hurt you for her now. That is unless you want to give me what I want. If you are willing to give it to me then I may reconsider but if not…" and with that said he raised the gun to Sara's head.

She was openly crying while the boy cried as well. Grace's heart stopped and Cole stepped forward. "You will never get out of here alive. There are people here all the time."

"David and I are very well aware of that fact Sheriff. We know all about Grace forgetting who everyone was. I was very surprised that she remembers so well but it just makes this so much easier. We will let all of you go and Grace comes with us. She gives us what we want and she is free to go. If not I kill her and come back for everyone." Kurt laughed.

"Why are you doing this?" Cole asked hoping to keep them talking for a moment so he could decide what to do.

"Don't you get it yet Sheriff? Your Grace is the sole heiress to the Price fortune. I'm surprised that her mother didn't tell you, she certainly was happy enough to tell me. I knew then that I would have to go through the pretenses of marrying her until her father put a stop to all of it. He wanted her to get me to sign a prenuptial agreement, something that I wasn't willing to do, so I had David here come and tell her that I was married to make her leave. I just needed a moment to think of another plan when this one hit me. I would take the one thing that Grace held in her heart and threaten it. I knew that I couldn't go after her brother. He is after all a trained solider but I could take her." He said pointing at Sara and her son. "You see it took me some time to find her since she was hiding from mommy and daddy. They don't know that she kept her son yet. Do they Sara?"

Sara cried harder and pulled against the ropes. Kurt sighed, "As I was saying. It took some to trace her and then I had to trace Grace. When I found her she was in the hospital with the injury. It set me back but I got it all straightened out and now we're all together again. Doesn't that just make you so happy Grace? You can tell Sara how sorry you are for not standing up for her later. Right now we are running behind. You are coming with us and we are going to tie up your boyfriend. I commend you on your choice Grace he is a fine specimen of male."

David growled low and deep and Kurt laughed. “Don’t take offense honey. I still love you but he is nice looking. Can’t blame the gay man for looking, can you?” He looked at Cole. “Didn’t think that the gay man had it in him did you stud? You think that I just up and left and was never coming back but I have no choice here sheriff. David and I are sinking and without her money we will lose everything that we have worked so hard for. I’m sorry that it has to be this way but have a seat sheriff. You can fight and get everyone shot or you can do as you’re asked and be the hero. It’s your choice but let me be clear. I have every intention of getting everything that I want and right now I want that money.” He said as he cocked the gun pointing it at the little boys head.

“All right I’ll sit but let me warn you now. If you touch one hair on her head I will kill you. I will hunt you until you are so scared of your own shadow that you wish that you would have killed me just to save you the trouble. Are we clear on this?” Cole held up his hands.

“Yes of course sheriff. Hunting and all of that, yes, yes. I heard you but sit now or I start shooting, take your pick.” Kurt waved his hand.

Grace was rooted to the floor. With the memories of Kurt coming back there were other memories as well. Her and Sara together at school. The pain that she had been made to suffer from losing her only friend. The regret that she was made to feel because she had never been able to stick up for Sara and the fear of never knowing where she went.

"I will fix this Sara. I may have not done the right thing years ago but I will now. I promise nothing will happen to any of you. I swear it." Grace pleaded to Sara.

Sara nodded crying. Kurt snorted, "Isn't that sweet. Come on we have wasted enough time here, too much more and your father is bound to come and check on you. Tell your man goodbye Gracelyn."

Grace hugged Cole and kissed his now taped lips. She whispered in his ear. "I remember everything."

She pulled back from him and winked. He nodded once indicating that he knew exactly what she was talking about. She smiled and told him, "Baba, Iraq all over again honey. I will see you soon."

Cole chuckled knowing what she was doing. Grace was doing exactly what he had done and true to her form she turned and pleaded with them to let her go as he had done in Iraq. He knew as they dragged her out the door that they didn't stand a chance against Grace but he still couldn't help but feel the terror going through his whole body.

When they left he scooted the chair over to the edge of the desk and worked on the bindings behind his back. When he heard the door open five minutes after they left Cole felt relief. He kicked the desk as hard as he could and he could hear his brother coming back the hallway saying, "I swear when I find you Tommy I'm going to beat the ever loving shit out of you. Where are you hiding you chicken shit?"

Cole kicked the desk again and Bret came charging into the room. "There you are you little…" but he stopped. "Christ Cole what the hell?" He asked as he ran for him.

He pulled out a knife and undid his bindings. He next moved to Sara as Cole removed the tape from his mouth. "They took Grace, Bret. I have to find them."

Bret looked up as he worked on the child's bindings. "Find who Cole and who are these people?" He asked nodding at Sara and her boy.

"This is Sara Long and her son. Grace's ex-boyfriend and his lover took her."

Bret shook his head, "The gay guy? Jesus Cole where would they take her?"

"I don't know but they couldn't have gotten far. I'm calling Jeff now to have him track them for me and I'm calling the Sarge in because if anyone could find them it's going to be him. Now stay here with Sara and her boy while I run."

He didn't waste time explaining the rest. All he could think about now was getting to Grace because the two men that had taken her were dead men and they didn't even know it, yet. Cole pulled out his cell phone and called Jeff first. He told him the situation and told him to put up road blocks now.

He next called John and gave him a brief run down. John said that he would be over in minutes. He called Ross and told him everything so that he could go and get Emma to keep her safe. Bret walked out into the living room holding the small child rubbing his back.

"Do you need me Cole?" Bret asked.

"No, I got John coming any moment. In fact here he is." Cole said opening the door.

John came rushing into the house with the wife right on his heels. "Where's Grace? What have they done with her?"

Janet walked over to Sara and her son and took them into the living room to get them comfortable while they all talked about a game plan. The next one to knock on the door was Jeff. He told Cole that they had to have been driving something other than a car because no one had come through the road blocks.

"I thought that I heard ATV's but I couldn't be sure. They probably rode them in here and have a car stashed somewhere else." Cole said running his hands through his hair.

Jeff nodded, "That would make more sense because it's already been ten minutes and no one has come through. We will keep them in place until we know for sure but I just wanted to tell you in person Cole."

Cole slapped him on the back. "Don't worry they didn't get that far I guarantee it. Grace would never let them get out of town for that I'm sure. It's just a matter of tracing her here but right now, someone else needs you Jeff. Go on now," he said nodding at Sara.

"Why are they here?" Jeff's breath caught in his throat.

"They needed to make Grace go with them. We're all military trained and they knew they could never get to us. They went for someone that Grace was close with that was easy to get too. She and her son need you Jeff. Go to them I'll handle it from here."

Jeff nodded at him but he was not looking at him. Right now his attention was centered on the woman that he had loved and lost. She looked good he thought to himself and her son looked just like her. He didn't know what he was going to say to her but he wouldn't leave her either.

Right now she lost and scared and very much alone even though Janet was sitting right next to her. He also noticed that her son was clinging to his mother crying. He couldn't leave them so he sucked it up and walked forward saying, “hello Sara it’s been a long time.”

The pain in her eyes cut him to the bone. There was no light there anymore and he wanted to find the person responsible and beat him to a pulp. He shook his head. Sara Long was no longer his problem. He needed to remind himself that she had made her choices and left. It wasn’t his fault but as he watched her eyes filling with fresh tears he knew he couldn’t be that low.

Instead he walked forward and hugged her back as she clung to his neck with her son between them. He didn’t know if he could ever let her go again but for now this would have to be enough. Just until everything was over and settled with Grace, then he would cross that bridge.

With remembering came peace. Grace knew that these men were not making it out of here without her having a say in it. She let them take her because that is what she needed to do. She needed to be like Cole and let them take her willing so they wouldn’t know something was up.

She knew that Cole would be mad but she had to think of Sara and her son. She hadn’t protected them all those years ago and she would not fail her again, so she had climbed on the quad and prayed that it would all be there again waiting for her to embrace.

The training her father had taught her was kicking in and Kurt didn't stand a chance. That much was determined when he stole her from her sanctuary. He would be a dead man and he didn't even understand the danger that he was clinging to.

As they passed the clearing Grace took her opportunity. She threw herself and Kurt right off the side of the ATV and rolled. Kurt landed harder than she did and she ceased her opportunity quickly kicking him in the head. She heard the snap of his neck but she couldn't register the death of Kurt now. David was still on the other ATV and circling back for her.

She could hear the bullets but she paid them no mind now. Her mind raced ahead making her move side to side so that she would not get hit. She would need the trees for protection.

She raced forward jumping for the lowest branch pulling herself up just in time to hear David stop the quad beneath her. She moved quickly up the trees and jumped into the neighboring tree. She needed to disappear but he was right there and there was no time before he was firing bullets up at her.

She swung herself around the back side of the tree clinging to the big base trying not to get hit by flying bullets. As soon as he stopped firing she would move again. She waited and waited for her opportunity but she could hear someone coming. She closed her eyes and prayed letting her mind roam.

The people coming for her were being really quiet but she could sense them. She knew that someone was coming for her and she held on and waited for them.

John didn't waste any time lingering. He got his shot gun out of the car and handed it to Cole. He also handed one to Bret and quickly found the trail. There was no way that he was losing his daughter to some patsy ass momma's boy.

Finding the trail wasn't hard considering they didn't even try and hide them. John ran as he followed the trail coming to a stop when he was not far from the clearing. He stood still for a moment sensing what was around him. He could hear one ATV off in the distance but the other one had stopped and he smiled. His Gracie had taken her opportunity alright just like he knew that she would. He walked forward more cautious of his steps now that all the noise had stopped.

He had heard a few shots ring out but as the others started he could breathe again. If the person was still shooting then Grace was still alive. He motioned for the boys to be quiet and walked forward again.

He peeked around a tree and saw his target. There was no way that the man was going to live if he had anything to say about it. He motioned for Cole and Bret to take other positions as he called out. "I would put your gun down and come on out son. You are not getting anywhere."

The man yelled back, "she'll die first" and more shots came. John could never take a shot not knowing where Grace was.

"I mean it son you're going to die just like your partner if you don't come on out. You're surrounded by a lot of people here son. Just put the gun down and we won't shoot you." John said trying to calm his shaking voice.

He almost laughed at his own lie. The man was a dead man for taking his Gracie but he would never tell him that. Let him think that he was calling the shots. That is what he had always been taught and he wouldn't waver from it now.

The man laughed, "Go away old man you're getting in my way."

Cole looked at John as though he was losing his mind. Why wouldn't he just take the shot? It was going to be up to him to do it. He wouldn't negotiate with the man. Right now all he wanted to was find

Grace and hold her close for scaring the shit out of him.

Cole crept forward to get into a better position but as he did he could feel her. He looked up into the trees and smiled at his Grace standing above him on a limb. He could still hear the man firing at the other tree and he smiled at her.

She had climbed her way through all of the trees to get to him and was now standing above him. She waved as she climbed down to him grinning the whole time. He grabbed her around the middle and kissed her quick motioning for her to go to her father.

When she moved away from him he called out. “This is Sheriff Cole Baker. Come out with your hands up. If you take one more shot I will have no choice but to shoot you.”

The man laughed and fired a round off in his direction. Cole stepped forward and raised the gun. He took aim and fired as the man fell in front the tree he was standing below.

He and Bret came out of the trees guns at the ready just in case. They walked over to him but he was dead. Cole didn’t spare him another moment. He ran over to a dead Kurt and noticed his neck was broken.

God he would thank John Summers every day of his life that he had trained Grace so well. He ran for Grace next as Tommy broke through the trees guns raised. Cole smiled and waved at him as he ran for Grace.

When he was close enough she launched herself at him and he dropped everything catching her. Before he could think he was kissing her and hugging her tight. He would never let the woman out of his sight again.

She clung to him crying and kissing him. He knew that it was poor timing but a moment away from her was his hell. He didn't ever want to go through this again. He pulled her away from the clearing and over to a rock sitting her down to catch his breath.

"I know the timing sucks but with me it usually does," he started as he knelt down next to her. "Gracelyn Marie Summers I have never met a woman like you before. Your stubborn and opinionated. You drive me crazy with your stuns and glares. You make my heart sore with understanding and caring and you are the only woman I could ever picture sharing my life with. I don't care if you say no to me now that you remember the truth. I don't care if you say no because I'm asking at a really bad time. Just know that I love you like I have loved no other and say that you will marry me. Make me whole again Grace. You and Emma both. Make a life with me, Emma and our future children. Tell me that you love me a little and I will give you this ring even if you say no. I will give it to you as a promise that you'll be mine forever because the thought of losing you drives me insane. Tell me that I have a chance Grace. That I have a chance to love you forever the way that I know that you love me. Just give me one chance Grace. Just one and I'll make you happy forever. I swear it."

"I think that this is your second chance if I remember correctly Cole Baker." She smiled laying a hand against his cheek.

He looked up at her and nodded, "you're right about that. Maybe even my third or fourth but what do you say Grace. I can't deal with any of that back there until I have your answer sweetheart. For now the only thing that I care about is you."

Grace nodded and smiled. She knew why Cole was purposing this way. She knew that most women would be appalled with this proposal but not Grace. She understood this man even if he couldn't figure it out himself.

Cole was a person that protected what was his. He protected the weak and pulled them close to him binding them together. It was the same with Brian and Emma. Cole perceived them as weaker than him so he pulled them close to him.

Cole viewed Grace tonight weak and he was trying to tie her to him the only way he knew how. Cole may not understand that but Grace did. She knew that he wasn't conventional but then again she had never been conventional a day in her life. Her whole life had been like this.

She had been trained to fight and kill people. She had been forced to wear a ballerina suit. She had lived her life for someone else by their rules but right now the only thing she cared about was this man.

This man that had been her rock during the hard times. This man that had let her be herself and accepted her for it. This man that had been a constant companion these past few months. This man that had so much strength and character. This man, which she loved above all others, would be hers.

No her marriage proposal wasn't conventional but neither would her answer be. Most people knew the person that they were marrying for years on end but for what purpose. When you know someone is right for you, you don't need time. You only need the feeling that Cole made her feel when he would look at her a certain way.

Even when she couldn't remember him clearly she still could feel the connection with him down to her soul. If that wasn't a soul mate she didn't know what was, so she did what she felt was right. She sucked in a breath and said, "Yes Cole I will marry you."

Cole jumped up and grabbed her around the middle swinging her around. He didn't care about anything right now but getting this woman home and soon. As soon as he yelled Bret, Sarge and Tommy came running.

"What are you yelling about boy?" John asked.

"She said yes. I asked her to marry me and she said yes." Cole answered.

Bret shook his head, "You asked her now? Talk about stupid little brother."

Grace smiled, "It's actually quite perfect thank you. I couldn't have picked somewhere more fitting. We're not conventional by any means Bret so why would I want my marriage proposal to be conventional?"

Tommy chuckled, "She got you there Bret. Congratulations both of you, I guess this means I need to move out. I guess I'll need to find another roomie. What do you say big guy, would you like to live with me?" He asked as he slung an arm around Bret's shoulders.

Bret shoved him and said, "Not if you were the last man on earth. You and I have some unfinished business you little shit but for now we other things to do. Come on we'll clean up the mess while Cole takes his woman home. I'm sure that they would like some alone time." He said dragging Tommy along with him.

"Well pumpkin you picked better this time around. I have to say that I'm very happy with this one. Your mother and I both. Now that you are living here though I think that we'll stay in the property we bought. It's a little colder here but we will adjust. That is if you want us around." John asked nervously.

"Where else would I want you guys?" Grace asked hugging her father. "This whole experience has been about second chances. Why would I want you to leave when we just found each other again? Stay daddy, please?"

"For you pumpkin anything but you two go on now we'll get everything here. Why don't you guys take our house for the evening since everyone is at your house and Cole's? Just don't break anything please." John pulled back from her and smiled.

"Thanks for this John." Cole said holding out his hand. "I never told you sir but I think of you as a father to me and I would be glad to have a grandfather around for Emma."

"I'll be here as long as you want us boy but by god you better treat her good or I will haunt you." John nodded and shook his hand. He slapped him on the back.

Cole snorted, "Didn't doubt it for a minute sir."

"Good. Now go on and go have your second chance and have fun."

"Dad-dddy," Grace groaned.

"Sorry pumpkin couldn't help hitting below the belt." John said laughing.

It took Cole a moment to catch onto what he was saying but when he saw Grace blush he understood. This would be the second time that he would make love with her but it would be his second chance and he was not going to waste it.

He grabbed her and pulled her along. He didn't understand why this woman loved him. He knew that he didn't deserve her but he would kill any man that dared to touch her. She made him whole again. She made him breathe easier and made his heart soar. Even Emma felt the same as he did and for that he would always be grateful that she had been sent to him.

This was a second chance for him. It was a second chance at loving Grace. It was a second chance to love Emma and it was a second chance for him to have a happy life with all of them.

Second chances were all around him and he wouldn't waste another moment thinking of what if's anymore. Finally he was at peace with everything in his life and it was all thanks to Grace with her loving nature.

Cole Baker was not a man that thanked god for miracles. He was not a man that wept like a baby but the rest of his life he promised to thank god every day for her and weep with the joy that she made him feel.

Chapter 21

October was a magical month for the family. The leaves were changing on the trees. The smell of winter was mixing with the fresh leaves and it brought peace and happiness to almost everyone, except Bret.

The day after Grace had been taken was the day that Bret decided that he was going to go ahead and build the house in the clearing. He had even recruited the whole family for help. The new house hadn't even taken two months to build from the ground up with all the volunteers they had.

It seemed as though the whole community had turned up at one time or another to help with the project. Bret true to his form thanked everyone but shifted uncomfortably the whole time.

Tommy decided that he was going to move in with Bret, without his permission of course. The two of them were constantly bickering and arguing about one thing or another like they were an old married couple.

Bret always complained about Tommy but Cole knew that his brother liked having him around. They were due to start their new security company any day now.

Sara and Jeff were now officially dating and living together. The night Grace had been taken Sara and her had a long talk about their past together.

Sara had told Grace that she never blamed her for what happened and she actually thanked Grace for not sticking up for her. She knew what the consequences of defending her would be for Grace and she would not ask anyone to do that for her. Not even her best friend.

Sara's son Tyler was now calling Jeff daddy and Cole knew that his friend was going down again soon. If he wasn't in love with Sara now he soon would be.

Janet and Sarge had moved into the neighborhood and were the best grandparents for Emma Cole could ever ask for. They were constantly spoiling her and while it did sometimes grate on Cole's nerves he knew that he would never say a word to them.

Now standing up at his own wedding waiting for his bride to come to him did he start to get nervous again. It was like he couldn't breathe again and he pulled at his collar.

"Stop pulling on that son. You're going to break your buttons and I won't have the misses yelling at me anymore today." Sarge told him.

"I can't breathe." Cole looked at him with a panicked expression.

"Here boy drink this. It will cure those gitters right as rain." John laughed and handed him a mini bottle of whiskey.

Cole grabbed the bottle off his father in law and took in one swig. The fiery mix ran down his throat making him feel marginally better. Maybe if he just had another five or six of them.

"I need more dad." Cole pleaded.

"Come on now. I thought that we have been over this son. You love my daughter and couldn't wait to marry her three months ago. Why are you so nervous now?" John laughed smacking him on the back.

Cole grabbed his jacket, "because Grace wasn't pregnant then. God what if she trips and falls again? What if walking down the aisle she trips over her dress? What if I hurt the baby? I don't know what I would do without her dad. She's our world and Emma and I would be lost without her."

John laughed at his son. Since the day that Grace had announced that she was pregnant Cole Baker had become a nervous twit. He was constantly on Grace to rest and put her feet up. He followed her around all the time insisting that she was doing too much.

Cole was even starting to drive the misses insane with his demands. He would constantly have someone at home with Grace all the time. Helping her to walk up the stairs. Helping her with anything and everything. The man wouldn't give her or anyone else a moment's peace, even though the doctor assured him everything was fine.

He was driving everyone insane including Grace. She had begged John to take Cole away for one evening just so she could relax without him there. She had been trying to get the baby's room ready since the moment she had found out and he wasn't letting her do anything.

"Snap out of it son." John said slapping Cole in the face hard. "You're the one that knocked her up and now you are going to drive her and everyone including her insane. Come sit down for a moment and breathe." When Cole sat John sat beside him. "You're going to be fine Cole. Grace is going to be fine and you're making her a nervous wreck son. Hell even your brothers are avoiding you now because you are so crazy. Just take a deep breath and remember that everything is going to be fine. You are marrying my daughter today. She is the love of your life and mother of your children so ease up a bit boy and let the poor woman breathe and have a moment. My Grace is strong. I think that she's capable of walking down an isle without tripping. After all she is one hell of a dancer. Just remember all of you are going to be fine."

"Thanks dad I think that I needed that." Cole nodded taking a deep breath.

John snorted, "No son what you need is a fist straight to that crazy brain of yours but the women would get mad at me for giving you a black eye before the wedding. Come on now it's time for you to go and take your place. I can hear the music starting."

"Thanks again dad." Cole stood on shaky legs and hugged John close.

"You're welcome." John smiled.

Cole walked toward the door and stopped. He looked at John and said, "And thanks for having faith in me when I didn't even have it in myself."

"Everyone deserves a second chance Cole, even you. You go on now before you're late. I'll see you in a few moments and breathe son. Everything will work out for the best. This is my Gracie that we are talking about here."

"She's amazing isn't she?" Cole smiled thinking of his Grace.

"She is my daughter, how could she not be?"

Cole nodded and smiled and walked out the door. John smiled and took out his own bottle and downed the contents of it. It was time to walk his little girl down the aisle and he couldn't be happier.

The man waiting for her was a perfect fit. Sure he was rough around the edges but what man wasn't. He smiled and went in search for his red headed little girl.

Grace stood in her room crying. Being pregnant sucked she thought. Her dress wouldn't fit even though she had it altered two times already and here she was on her wedding day and couldn't zipper the damned thing.

She sat on the floor in a mound of lace and dress crying her eyes out when she heard a knock at the door. Tommy peeked his head in.

"Hey we are getting ready to start. Grace what's the matter?" He asked running toward her. He hunched down in front of her and pulled on her face. "Come on honey what's the matter here?"

"It won't fit Tommy. What am I going to do? I'm getting married in minutes and I can't zipper my damned dress." Grace wailed louder.

Tommy wanted to laugh but he knew that he would get his ass kicked if he did. His sister, god love her was an emotional wreck anymore and the problem was he couldn't even blame all of it on the baby. Grace's soon to be husband was driving everyone insane including Grace herself.

The man just didn't understand that women had babies all the time and Grace was going to be just fine. Cole was making everyone nervous all the time with his constant demands and it seemed as though he was the one that was pregnant.

"We can fix this." Tommy said sucking in a breath.

"How are we going to fix this?" She looked at him and glared. "It's not like I'm going to lose five pounds off my fat ass in two minutes Tommy."

Tommy chuckled, "No but I have an idea. Hang on a moment and I'll be right back."

Grace nodded as Tommy raced for the door. Emma entered next looking nervous.

"Mommy, are you alright?" She asked looking at Grace.

"Mommy is just having a fit because my dress doesn't fit right. I can't seem to zipper it up in the back." Grace smiled at her daughter and hugged her close.

Emma looked at the back of the dress. It was only an inch or so off from zippering. Emma looked around when inspiration hit her.

"Here take off the dress for a moment. I can fix it." Emma said holding out her hands.

Grace got up from the floor and took the dress off handing it to Emma. Emma took off her sash around her middle and asked for a pair of scissors. Grace found a pair quickly and handed them to her.

Emma cut tiny holes into the back of the dress and Grace cringed. Emma smiled, “Don’t worry mom. My mommy taught me how to do this before she passed. She taught me how to sew by the age of five.”

“I didn’t know that you could sew honey. I would like it if you could teach me before the baby is born. Maybe you and I could make some cute outfits for your brother or sister.” Grace sat down next to her daughter.

Emma nodded while working. She looped the material through all the holes and had Grace step back into the dress. She then pulled all of the material together and tied it in a big bow at the bottom. It exposed some of her back but it worked.

“There it is done now.” Emma said.

Grace walked over to the mirror and looked at her back. It was beautiful and the colorful sash improved the dress. Tears filled her eyes as she turned to her daughter. “Now it’s a perfect fit just like you munchkin.”

“I came to ask you a question mom. Well it is a favor really.” Emma giggled and held her mother hands.

“Sure honey ask me anything.”

Emma took a deep breath and asked, "Would you mind if we all wear roses today to remember my mommy. I know that she would have liked to be here and I thought that it would be a nice way to remember her."

"I think that it's a wonderful idea honey but where are we going to get a whole bunch of roses." Grace said wiping a tear away from her eye.

Emma smiled, "I brought them all with me. Would you mind if I go and hand them out to everyone?"

Grace motioned for her to wait a moment and peeked out the door. She called for Ross and Bret who were pacing in the hallway. They came into the room as Tommy came rushing back in with a white robe in his hand. "Here Grace I found this. I know that it's a robe but it will work…"

Grace laughed and shook her head. "My daughter fixed my dress thank you and she needs help with something. All of you are going to help her do it before we start and I'm not leaving this room until it's done. Do you understand me?"

"It's time pumpkin." John knocked on the door and peeked in his head.

"I'm not leaving until Emma and the boys have completed their task. Emma would everyone to wear a rose pinned on their shirts in remembrance of her mother and I won't walk down that aisle until everyone's wearing one. Hurry and help her pass them all out then we will begin."

"Come on munchkin before your dad comes back here looking for us. He's pacing as it is." Tommy sighed and held out his hand.

"Thank you for this mom and thanks for being a great mother to me." Emma hugged Grace.

"Thank you for being such a great daughter. You go on now with your uncles before your father comes back here. I don't want him to see me until it's time but we keep him waiting more he's is bound to come and check." Grace said kissing her daughters head.

Emma nodded and walked off with her uncle's. Grace paced the room when she heard the knock at the door. She walked over and opened it to her mother and Sara.

"Gracelyn Marie the ceremony is about to start. Can't you hear the music girl?" Her mother asked.

"Yes of course I do but Emma wanted everyone to wear a rose on their shirt to remember her mother. Here before I forget. Put this on" she said handing both of them a pin and a rose.

Sara smiled, "You look beautiful Grace."

"Thanks Sara and you'll look just as beautiful on your own wedding day."

"I don't ever think that I'm getting married. Jeff is great but I don't think marriage is on his mind."

Grace snorted, “Yeah right the man is positively head over heels about you and Tyler. I suspect that he’ll be purposing any day now.”

“You really think so?” Sara asked getting more excited by the possibility.

Grace winked, “I know so.”

“You need to tell me what you know.” Sara opened her mouth and closed it.

“Not on your life. You’ll just have to let it happen like it did for me.” Grace smiled a knowing smile.

“Well let’s hope that Jeff’s proposal isn’t as bad as Cole’s was.”

Grace laughed, “I thought that it was perfect but then again I think everything about the man is perfect.”

Cole knocked on the door and said, “Grace we were supposed to start already. Christ woman what’s taking you so long? Everyone is starting to whisper.”

Grace sighed, “Ah the man of my dreams now. Cole Baker you just better hold your horses. Our daughter wants everyone wearing roses and she is still handing them out. She’s doing it to remember Vikki. Now go and wait and when I’m ready I’ll come to you. Now go on and I’ll be out in a moment.”

“Ah Grace can’t I just have a little peek sweetheart. One little peek isn’t going to hurt is it?”

"I'm going to hurt you badly later if you don't get out of here now. You know that you can't see the bride you big jerk. Go on now I'll be out in a few moments."

Cole laughed "I love you too sweetheart."

"Yeah, yeah I know. You're driving me nuts Cole Baker. Just give me a moment and stop worrying about me. Go on now and I love you too."

Grace could hear Cole sigh through the door and stomp off. Sara smiled, "Is he getting any better?"

"No he's getting worse. The damned man won't give a moments peace." Grace sighed in frustration.

Janet grabbed her hand saying, "But that's just because he loves you so much Grace. He's a first time father and new to the experience. Your father drove me so bonkers when I was pregnant with you that I thought that I would have to kill him. Just give time and he'll get better."

"I sure hope so because I'm running out of patients with him. He won't let me lift a finger. I swear the man things that I'm invalid."

"Come on girls this show is starting now. Everyone has their flowers and we are going to start." John said knocking on the door.

Janet yelled out, "We'll be out in one minute. I just need to give Grace something then we'll be out."

Sara hugged Grace and left. Janet faced her beautiful daughter and pulled out a box. "This was mine when I got married. It contains this," she said pulling out a blue bobby pin, an old piece of jewelry and a new piece of jewelry. "This should cover the something old, something new, something borrowed and something blue."

She helped Grace get everything on and helped her fasten her rose on her dress. Janet wiped the tears from her eyes.

"Look at you my Grace, so lovely and beautiful. You make a beautiful bride honey and I'm so glad that I can be here today to share it with you. I wanted to say thank you for my second chance Grace. These last few months have been some of the happiest in my life. I can't tell you how very grateful I am to you. You have made me a better person and mother watching you with Emma. You are a wonderful mother Grace and I couldn't have asked for a better daughter and granddaughter then you two."

"And you mom. I have to say now that you've opened up and started listening you have been a great mother yourself. I didn't learn how to be a mother for Emma from just anywhere. I learned it from you."

The two women embraced and cried together. They cried for the years lost. For the pain that they had caused each other and for the loved they now shared. Still crying Grace heard another knock on the door.

"Damn it Grace if you don't get your ass out here I'm going to have to kill your soon to be husband. He's driving me nuts again. Let's get this thing started." Tommy yelled through the door.

Grace opened the door and looked at her frustrated brother. It would be his turn next she thought to herself. Oh Tommy never admitted that he was ready but she could tell. He was starting to settle down already. Now it would be his turn to find his love like she had.

She smiled at her brother, "All right. I'm ready now."

"Well thank god because Cole is driving everyone insane." Tommy threw up his hands. "Come on mom and let's go because I can't stand to hear him bitching one more moment."

Grace laughed and took her brothers arm. She met her father at the doors and took him on the other arm. She had decided that she had wanted both of them to walk her down the aisle.

Of course it was not conventional but what in her life was. She did everything backwards. Nothing in her life was straight forward except her love for Cole. In his arms everything was perfect and just how it should be.

As the doors opened she watched her soon to be husband stop pacing and freeze. His face transformed and he smiled that lop sided grin that she adored. Giving Cole Baker a second chance was the best decision she had ever made in her life.

She felt reborn in his loving embrace and as she walked toward him she wondered if life could get any better than this and she decided no. Her family was whole and complete now. Everyone was right where they were supposed to be with her in the middle holding all of them together.

Second chances were everywhere. They were all around her and she walked to the best second chance she ever got in her life. Today would mark the start of her new life with Cole and she knew that she would remember this day as one of the happiest in her life because from today and every day for the rest of their lives they had each other.

The people stood and the smell of roses filled her senses. Grace sent a silent to prayer to Vikki and Brian both. Wherever they were she hoped they were happy together and watching over all of them.

As she walked she could feel a gentle brush of a hand on her face and she knew that Vikki was here watching over them. Love filled her and she knew that everything would be just fine. She would have happy ending with the prince charming after all.

Lightning Source UK Ltd.
Milton Keynes UK
UKOW07f1452141214

243121UK00012B/134/P